Hands of Greed

THE WORLD OF VOIDPET
BOOK I

Linda Shad

VOIDPET INC.

Voidpet Inc.

voidpet.com

Copyright 2024 © by Linda Shad Chen

ISBN: 979-8-218-51871-4 (paperback)

Printed in the United States of America

Rules of the Void

Rule #1: Monsters are emotions.

Rule #2: People are ideas.

Rule #3: Money is power.

VOIDPET
SPECIES GUIDE

voidpet.com

#0. Envy

#1. Anxious

#2. Sad

#3. Anger

#4. Pain

#5. Spite

#6. Lonely

#7. Paranoia

#8. Sonder

#9. Sanctimony

#10. Abandonment

#11. Jealous

#12. Gluttony

#13. Pride

#14. Lust

#15. Sloth

#16. Wrath

#17. Greed

#18. Estrangement

#19. Nostalgia

#20. Judgement

#21. Salty

#22. Sadge

#23. Down Bad

#24. Cringe

#25. Grumpy

#26. Curious

#27: Glee

#28: Rejection

#29: Desperate

#30: Defiance

#31: Merry

#32: Apathy

#33: Disdain

#34: Panic

#35: Resistance

#36: Determination

#37: Wonder

#38: Mischief

#39: Persistence

#40: Ambition

Contents

Part I:
The Institute

Chapter 1: House of Mirrors

Char was going to be popular, no matter what. As he surveyed the dining hall, he saw a group glancing his way:

A frizzy-haired girl with an Anxious.

A scowling redhead in a wheelchair.

A melancholy individual with a sketchbook.

Nerd alert. He thought. *No thanks.*

It was Char's first day at the Void's prestigious Institute, and he didn't come all this way to sit next to the trash cans. He'd worked his whole life to get in on full financial aid, and there was no stopping him now.

As he continued to scan the breakfast crowd, Envy hovered by his side. His little Voidpet companion purred in the air like a carnivorous tadpole, its triangular eyes narrowed in solidarity. The picture-perfect Institute was not only the most elite school, but also the *only* school in the entire city—so his choices today would determine the rest of his future.

Beneath the windows overlooking the gardens, he spotted his sister Dyna. He remembered her kind words on their train ride to school: *'If you come near me, I'll kill you,'* and decided not to venture towards her or her upperclassman friends.

In another corner, beneath an open window flooded with sunshine, another group caught his eye. A boy tossed an orb of blue matter like a baseball. A tall girl sat in yoga pants, her midnight skin sprouting wings that looked like blades. An athlete lounged on a dragon, her head thrown back in laughter, all while their hoodie-wearing friend cracked jokes with his penguin.

That's it, Char thought.

Cool clothes. Cool powers. Cool Voidpets.

Those were the cool kids he needed to befriend.

Unfortunately, his knees began to wobble, and his legs refused to budge another step in their direction. As Envy nudged him forward, he looked down at his own stained yellow t-shirt. The color was an eyesore against his blue basketball shorts—a pair of cheap hand-me-downs from a family friend. He felt his face flush, suddenly conscious of everything. His height. His boring black hair. His small almond eyes. His baby Stage 1 Voidpet.

Char was in no state to introduce himself, and decided his entrance would have to come another day. He picked up a bowl of mac and cheese for breakfast, rummaging for two pieces of void matter from his pocket to pay at the counter. With his head down, he searched for a quiet booth to sit by himself.

The Institute's design was forgiving to introverts, but still, there was no denying the social stigma around sitting alone. The dining hall was lined with booths, each illuminated with sparkling lamps of void matter for those who wanted to study during mealtime. Even so, they were so rarely occupied that he could feel the whole school's eyes on him as he shuffled to take his seat alone.

He sat Envy on the table and pulled a small wooden chessboard out of his book bag. Between his hectic home life and the bustle of his parents' food stall, chess had become his refuge to regain a sense of control. He set up the pieces by hand, starting a friendly match with his Voidpet as he started on his macaroni.

As Envy accepted the King's Gambit, he noticed the contrast of his black pet with their sterile surroundings. They belonged here. Char was certain of that. But the Institute was so perfect, it was almost uncanny. The spotless interiors were all white, as if the academy was some sort of marble laboratory.

As the only modern building in the Void, the Institute stood out from the rest of the city like a swan in a rat's nest. The rest of town was a ruin of an ancient metropolis, but the school's castle floated in the sky, its pristine spires reaching into the clouds. Meanwhile, the dining hall was far too grand for the student body, resembling a cathedral more than a cafeteria. There couldn't have been more than 30 students in the room.

Suddenly, a shadow fell across the chessboard.

"Mind if I join you?" a playful voice chirped.

Char spun to see an otherworldly figure looming over him. The boy wore a patchwork outfit of shadows that seemed to shift in the light. Half of his face was covered with a theatrical mask, topped with feathers that adorned it like a crown. His eyes, both the exposed one and the one on the mask, glowed white, and the smile on his face mirrored the cartoonish one on his mask.

The jester-like figure extended a gloved hand. "I'm Bool," he warbled, his white eyes studying Char. There was a hollow quality to Bool's voice, as if he were speaking from the bottom of a well.

Char hesitated, then shook the offered hand. "Char," he said.

Bool's eyes flashed. "May I get the next game?"

Char scoffed, a little smile forming on his lips. "Sure," he answered, happy to make a friend over an activity he excelled at. He wasn't sure if this guy was popular or not, but he looked intimidating enough that he didn't want to refuse.

As Char made quick work of Envy with a swift checkmate to the back rank, Bool took a seat on the other side of the booth. "Winner goes first," he prompted with his glove.

Char opened with the same move he always did, pushing forth his white pawn to take the center of the board.

"E4?" Bool remarked.

Char nodded, his confidence growing. "Best by test," he quipped.

Bool's painted lips curled into a smile as he responded with the Sicilian Defense. Neither of them spoke after that, as they each poured their focus into the rapidly unfolding game. Char played with fierce aggression, each move aimed at creating tactical imbalances on the board. He'd honed his style in reverence to an ancient young prodigy, full of daring sacrifices and combinations. As they played, Envy's head bobbed from side to side, following each move.

Bool's moves, on the other hand, seemed almost nonsensical—amateurish. Char pressed on with his strategy, developing his pieces with textbook precision. As the game progressed, Bool's moves continued to baffle Char. The jester would advance pawns seemingly at random, move his king often, and make exchanges that appeared to weaken his position.

As they entered the endgame, Char realized that his textbook play had been countered at every turn. Bool's 'haphazard' moves had set up deep advantages, far in advance. Victory was nowhere in sight.

After a long pause, Bool walked his king into the heart of Char's attack. A baffling blunder that seemed to throw the game.

"Checkmate," said Char, trapping the black king with his pawn.

"Good game," the jester replied, "and just in time." Breakfast was over, and the dining hall was starting to empty out. He pulled out an envelope from his coat pocket and handed it to Char.

"Char, I cordially invite you to join the House of Mirrors." Bool's eyes gleamed as he flashed a white envelope, it's silver seal catching in the light. The creature in the motif bore the face of a jackal, the legs of a gazelle, and the winding tail of a dragon. It was the Mischief Voidpet—the mascot of wit and wiles.

Char's eyes widened in surprise. "What—What are you talking about? Is this a prank? Who are you?"

Bool cocked his head. "Your professor."

"But I... I haven't even taken any of my placement tests yet!"

The instructor's face broke out into an eerie smile. "Well, what did you think that was?" He stood up and disappeared, his grin the last thing to fade as the rest of his form disappeared into smoke. Char sat dumbfounded in his booth, clutching the white envelope in his hands.

Chapter 2: Low Profile

Promise Windfall revved his red convertible as he checked his reflection in the rearview mirror. He adjusted his shades to make sure his eyes were still blue beneath them and smoothed the collar of his leather jacket. His lips curved into a well-rehearsed smirk, one corner hitching slightly higher than the other in a performance of effortless charisma.

"Does my outfit look okay for school?" He asked over the rumble of the engine.

"It matches the private education attire we observed in our Ancient American studies," his elder sister Pandora responded from the passenger seat. She adjusted the peacoat she'd layered on top of her blouse, before running a hand through her gingerbread locks.

"At least, in the eastern coastal metropolitan areas," she added, stretching a seatbelt across her full figure. "But I really wouldn't know for sure. The Institute paperwork never specified a formal dress code, so I'm hoping everything will be fine."

"I think we all look fabulous," their younger sister Pecunia assured from the middle seat of the back. She examined her own reflection as she pouted to apply lip gloss in a pocket mirror, poised with both the flair and figure of a model. "I dressed you all, so I would know."

Pecunia Windfall wore a little black dress with cutout designs, her hair now a glossy platinum blonde. A pair of oversized sunglasses sat perched on her head, framing her face against a string of diamonds.

Volo, their youngest brother, nodded in agreement as he stared wordlessly into the Void. With jet black hair and eyes to match, his lean, muscular build sat masked beneath a soft cashmere sweater.

Meanwhile, Luden occupied the seat behind Promise, clad in a buttoned tee that allowed his bandaged arms to air out. With Promise's seat pushed his seat all the way back to accommodate his proportions, Luden sat with his knees tucked to fit the narrow space.

The sports car was based on luxury designs from ancient times, which meant that it wasn't supposed to have a backseat. But since the Windfalls had built it themselves, Pandora had redesigned the structure to accommodate their whole group.

She turned around to face Luden and the younger siblings, her gray eyes now masked by a pair of cat-eyed frames.

"Just remember, we don't know what these Institute people are capable of. We need to keep a low profile and make sure we don't overplay our hands."

She turned to each of them in the eye in a motherly fashion, "We don't know the difference between what Mom taught in our homeschool curriculum and what they've been learning in there. We're better off being underestimated than drawing attention to ourselves."

Promise ran a hand through his ash brown hair, his eyes still glued to his own reflection. "Yeah, yeah, yeah, don't flex on anyone. I get it," he smiled wider to spotlight a pointed canine against his golden complexion. "You've only told me a million times now."

Pecunia scoffed as she examined her Sloth ring in the light. "Heh. You know I have *no difficulty* playing dumb."

Volo's face was pensive. "Ok," he said.

Luden considered suggesting different outfits, or a different mode of transportation to suit their objective—but he held his tongue. He knew when to pick his battles with the Windfalls, and a dispute over style was not one he could win.

Instead, he decided to focus on laying low himself. "What's the plan if we slip up?"

Pandora gave him a reassuring smile. "Then we stick together. If one of us gets in trouble, the others cover."

"Makes sense," Luden responded with a little shrug. He realized he had subconsciously learned to mirror some of the Windfalls' mannerisms over the years.

"So... am I the only one worried about just fitting in?" Luden asked with a chuckle. He didn't expect the others to feel the same but had gotten comfortable accepting he was the simply the nervous one of the group.

"I mean, it's not just you," Promise answered to Luden's surprise. He took off his sunglasses and looked down to wipe them with the fabric of his designer tee. "It's weird being 17 and a total rookie at something other kids have been doing their whole lives." He slipped his shades back on and placed his hands on the wheel. "But there's gotta be a first time for everything, right?" he looked back at Luden and sported a grin, before turning up the speakers and slamming the gas pedal.

As they zoomed towards the Institute at a speed that would have been illegal long ago, the ancient metropolis loomed into view, the ruins of once-tall skyscrapers sparkling beneath a sky of colorful clouds and ethereal creatures.

Pandora clutched the admission paperwork in the passenger seat, her hair whipping in the wind. Her eyes darted across the documents one final time, lips moving in silent rehearsal. For the Windfalls, this wasn't mere enrollment—it was reconnaissance against an unknown enemy. The Institute stood as their gateway to the Void's hidden rules. It was a world their parents had distrusted, that they couldn't enter unprepared.

Luden peeked the documents from the middle seat. The price of tuition had gone up in the last five years, and it now cost 70k VM per student. The old Luden would have lost his mind trying to imagine a sum of 350,000 void matter, but the new Luden was more accustomed to thinking like a millionaire. He'd watched the Windfalls set up numerous ventures in the Void and was now a hardened accomplice in their endeavors.

Next to him, Volo slipped on a pair of wayfarers to shield his eyes from the wind. "Want?" Volo gestured to Luden with an extra pair of aviators. Volo's voice was hardly audible in the roar of the wind, but Luden nodded and put them on.

Volo and Pecunia began bobbing their heads to the music. Naturally, Luden joined in. As they crossed the river to the west side of town, Luden held his breath at the sight of the view. The water sparkled in the morning sunrise. Ancient towers emerged from the side of the western island, the remains of a glittering concrete jungle. Overhead, a vast sky smiled down on them, threaded with ethereal wisps of color.

Suddenly, Luden felt his heart plummet as the sound of sirens grew louder behind them. A white and blue car began to draw closer behind them, flashing its lights at them. A Voidpet in a navy uniform sat behind the steering wheel, its stern gaze fixed upon their vehicle.

"Promise, I think we need to pull over," Pandora yelled over the wind and music. Her voice was shrill with concern.

With a sigh, Promise eased off the gas and guided the convertible to the side of the road. The sports car's engine purred to a stop, leaving silence in its wake.

From the flashing car labeled with the strange acronym 'NYPD', a Grumpy Voidpet emerged in a navy uniform, its face set in a permanent scowl as it lumbered towards their convertible. Shiny badges clinked with each step.

"License and registration," the Grumpy growled. As Promise procured some strange papers out of void matter, the officer continued, "Do you have any idea how fast you were going?"

The Windfall siblings exchanged puzzled glances. Luden's brow furrowed in confusion.

"Heh. Pretty fast?" Promise beamed like a kid with a new bike. "This baby can really *zoom*."

"Well. The fine is 500 VM," the Grumpy announced, producing a ticket from thin air. As he held it out, the burly Voidpet obstructed their view, glowering over them like a giant gorilla.

Volo's eyebrows raised slightly, meeting Pandora's shades in the rearview mirror. She gave an almost imperceptible shake of her head, cautioning against any unnecessary violence. Pecunia's fingers twitched, ready to conjure a crystal bullet if needed, but Volo's hand gently brushed against hers, dismissing the threat. Luden observed this silent conversation, marveling at how seamlessly they communicated without words.

All the while, Promise lounged in his seat, unperturbed.

"Oh, okay. Thanks, Officer G.," he glanced the Voidpet's badge as he effortlessly spun up a basketball-sized orb. He chucked it into the Grumpy's paws with one hand, his other still resting on the steering wheel. "Appreciate the heads up," his tongue poked playfully into his cheek. "Didn't realize it cost extra to go faster."

As the Voidpet's paws clasped around the ball, his scowl deepened with confusion. "Drive... safer," the Grumpy muttered, before trudging back to its vehicle with the payout.

Volo looked skeptical as they pulled away. "We pay more to go fast?"

"I guess so," Promise made a bewildered face, already accelerating. "Strange, don't you think, since there's no one else on the road?"

Pandora frowned, surveying the empty highway and half-formed skyscrapers. "Well, it's nice that we can contribute to some infrastructure funding here and there. But that was odd. It's like the Voidpets are maintaining these emotional vestiges of the old city... even if they don't quite make sense anymore," She wondered aloud.

But her comment was lost in the rush of wind as they sped towards the Institute, the vacant roads stretching into the horizon ahead.

Chapter 3: The Freshmen

After five years at the Institute, Tilde had finally qualified for Level 1.

"WAHOO!" She shouted before her instructor, her voice filling the grand examination hall. The clump of void matter in her palm erupted into a pink ball of energy that danced like a flame.

Achieving Level 1 lucidity meant that she was officially able to manipulate 10 void matter—just in time for her freshman year of high school.

Professor Invidere's mask-like visage spread into a smile. "Congratulations Tilde. You've made excellent progress," her robotic voice resonated like an intercom speaker.

Tilde beamed at her instructor, whose transcendent form floated above the ground. Invidere wore a hooded dress with a geometric silhouette, and her whole presence was the color of smoke and shadows. Where most humans had legs, her torso balanced atop nothing but a pointed prism.

"You've also earned your invitation to the House of Blood," Invidere enthused, stirring a zoo of Voidpet spectators to cheer with applause.

"Whaaaat?" Tilde gasped, her hands flying to her cheeks as her warm void matter enveloped them.

The professor's hands were abstract shapes, attached to her body only by streams of a mysterious plasma. She handed Tilde a red letter, stamped with the scarlet seal of a red Defiance—an ornate dragon breathing patterns of flame.

Tilde was both unsurprised and baffled. She knew Invidere was the one professor who always commended her spirit, who'd recruited her to begin with—but at the same time, she was so doubtful of her own track record, she feared she might never receive a house assignment at all.

"Thank you, oh my goodness, thank you Professor Invidere!" Tilde gushed, holding the letter to her heart.

She noticed her teacher's energy surge, little particles of plasma bubbling up from her arms—was she glowing with pride? "You should go have lunch now," Invidere nudged. Her voice was warm as she conjured a pumpkin to feed one of her giant Voidpets.

Tilde loosened her focus on the pink flame in her hands, and let it return to a crystalline solid. She stuffed the ball in her pocket, lifted her pet Anger onto her lap, and rolled her wheelchair to the dining hall with a look of elation.

She noticed her friend group, already seated at the table in the near corner. Her friends were easy to pick out—Hyphen's curly hair atop a bright pink dress, and Alt's usual black shirt with sleeves that extended past his hands. And besides, they always sat in the same place, so she never had any trouble spotting them.

Tilde swiped her ID to waive the fee on her lunch. She headed to her table with a slice of pepperoni pizza.

"Hellooo friends!" She sang, sliding to the edge of the table and setting down her meal. She looked at her peers with happy hazel eyes.

"Soooo…," Hyphen's amber complexion glowed, "Which one did you get?" Her Anxious was parked on the table, a wiggling baby dino with circular eyes.

Tilde lifted the red letter to her face and beamed. "Guess!" She squealed, unable to contain her joy.

"House of Blood?" Hyphen gasped, her jaw dropping, "No way!"

Tilde giggled. Perhaps the name didn't suit her pale face and strawberry hair—but it was known to be full of the toughest Voidpet trainers, which was what she aspired to become.

Alt looked up from his sketchbook with a warm smile, still drawing with his pencil hidden beneath long dark sleeves. "That makes sense since you like to yell and punch."

Tilde snorted, and Anger agreed with a puff of flame.

He wasn't wrong.

Tilde beamed. "What about you two?" She asked, taking a big bite out of her pizza.

Alt glanced at Hyphen before looking at Tilde sympathetically. "We both got House of Bones," Alt said, taking out a charcoal envelope with an ink-black seal. The insignia featured a skull and a black cat, sporting three hypnotic tails adorned with peacock feathers. A Curious, representing the pursuit of exploration.

Tilde felt a pang of dismay that her two best friends would be in the same house without her, but she smiled with encouragement.

"Well, that's amazing for you both, especially 'cause *you* love crazy science experiments... and *you* make the coolest stuff in art studio!" She looked at Hyphen and Alt respectively. "I think I'm more of a fighter, anyways," she chuckled.

Hyphen looked down. "Actually, I haven't quite decided yet," she mumbled.

"What?" Tilde asked.

"I... also got an offer for the House of Reason." she grimaced as she produced two envelopes from beneath the table—one charcoal, like Alt's, and the other a sapphire blue, featuring a Judgement with a pen in its talon. Even in the low light of their table, the two insignias gleamed.

"Hyphen, that's amazing!" Tilde gushed.

"Yeah, you should be proud of yourself," Alt added. "That says a lot about how smart you are."

Hyphen blushed. House of Reason was known for its rigorous intellectualism, with focus on philosophy, logic, and theoretical math. Emphasizing first principles over hands-on observation, it traded whimsical laboratories for towering libraries and stately tomes.

"But we'll all be rooming next to each other, anyways!" Hyphen chirped, placing her hand on Tilde's to make sure she felt included.

"Yeah, we can still study in my room together, even if we're in different courses," Alt offered.

Tilde felt relief at her friends' support. Alt's dormitory was an oasis of paintings, plants, and candles, which she much preferred over the barren mess in her own. Though there were some differences between houses, the core curriculum remained the same for everyone.

"You two are the best," Tilde responded, before pushing the spotlight away from herself. "So what new classes are you most excited for? And are they gonna be with that skeleton teacher? String?"

Hyphen nodded with excitement. The House of Bones leader, String, quite literally looked like a skeleton from the head down. As a skilled craftsperson, String helped students conjure supplies out of void matter and was well-liked by many.

"I've got *Intro to Small Objects* in the morning and *Void Matter Metamorphosis I* in the afternoon," Hyphen said, grinning ear to ear, "both with String—"

"I'll be in *VMM* with Hyphen," said Alt. "There might still be spots if you want to try and sign up."

"And... I've also got *Principles* of *Lucidity* with Cogito after," Hyphen added with a shy smile.

Alt's Sad lifted its head, peering out with eyes that looked like crescent shaped teardrops. From its whimper, Tilde could read her friend's mind: Alt was doing his best to be happy for Hyphen but still disheartened that she might choose a different house.

"You know, all of this is just sort of like, a school spirit thing anyway," Tilde offered. "It's not like our houses will define our futures or anything."

"Yeah, you're absolutely right," Alt agreed, "It's definitely good to keep the bigger picture in mind."

From the corner of her eye, Tilde noticed a dot of yellow enter the dining hall. A boy stood looking lost, tray in hand.

"Hey, is that one of the new freshmen?" she whispered.

"Yeah, I think so," Alt said,

"Should—should we invite him to eat lunch with us?" Hyphen stammered, her cheeks blushing at the thought of reaching out to a stranger.

Alt looked at Tilde, counting on her bravery to make the first move.

In that moment, Tilde found herself unsure if she wanted to approach the new kid. She'd been a part of the same friend group for years and was only just getting comfortable with life at the Institute. As she glanced the boy's narrow-eyed Envy, she thought suddenly of her horoscope, which had warned that she might make an unexpected enemy today. Tilde hesitated, her usual boldness faltering.

She lowered her voice to a whisper. "You know what? Maybe we should let him find his own group," Tilde said, surprising herself with her reluctance. "I mean, the three of us... our situation is a little weird, you know? We're... not exactly... regular Institute students." She glanced at her friends, a shared look of sorrow passing between them. "It might be better if he just hangs out with the other day students."

Alt began to fiddle with his sleeves, his eyes downcast. The way he hunched his shoulders to hide his disfigured hands betrayed his embarrassment.

Hyphen seemed crestfallen at first, but then nodded, relief flickering across her face.

"Yeah, you're probably right," Hyphen agreed, her shoulders relaxing. "Besides, I don't think he'd want to sit with us anyway."

The new boy dithered for some time before shuffling to a corner.

Chapter 4: Void Matter Metamorphosis I

A harp melody blossomed from Alt's 12:45 pm alarm, bathing the dormitory in an ambient pink. The glow caught the edges of the paintbrushes and houseplants on his desk, drawing a forest of shadows across the walls.

Alt struggled to wake up from naps, but today was different because he had something to look forward to. Void Matter Metamorphosis was rumored to be one of the most interesting classes at the Institute, and he couldn't wait to attend with his two best friends. Apparently, you could customize your appearance with all the colors you could dream of.

He opened his eyes, stopped the alarm, and caressed the head of Sad, who lay curled up on his stomach. The little Voidpet yawned and wiggled awake, extending two tiny wings from the back of its shell.

"Hey, it's time for class," Alt said to his pet, who didn't want to get up. His phone buzzed with a text.

Tilde: *Don't be late!*

He smiled. Tilde was one to talk since she was always late too.

Alt lifted his pet and carefully deposited her, still half asleep, into his handmade messenger bag. He swung his legs over the side of the bed, then stretched, releasing a yawn. He was already dressed, wearing the same long-sleeve and cargo shorts from the day before. As he grabbed his bag and headed towards the door, he looked at the incomplete painting that sat in the middle of his room—a soft landscape of deep blues, brushed with silhouettes of jungle ferns. It'd been sitting unfinished for a while. Alt had been putting off the project for far too long now, but he swallowed the guilt and headed out. He made his way down to the common area where Hyphen was waiting, Anxious fidgeting in her arms.

"Ready for class?" Alt held back another yawn.

Hyphen nodded, her dark curls bobbing as she tapped her foot in haste. "I hope we don't have to present anything today. I didn't prepare…"

"It'll be fine. It's only the first day," Alt reassured as they stepped out into the afternoon sun. The Institute's grounds were alive with activity. Students hurrying to and from classes, and wild Voidpets scurried about. They made their way across the quad, passing under shadows of the school's graceful spires and towering library. As they approached the Sciences building, they spotted Tilde waiting by the entrance, her wheelchair decorated with new dragon stickers.

"About time!" Tilde called out with a grin. "I thought I'd have to start without you two."

Alt smiled back. It was great to see Tilde on time as well.

The trio entered the building, the halls thrumming with the energy of contained void matter. They found their classroom—a circular laboratory filled with whimsical equipment. Glass tanks swelled with colors that moved like lava lamp liquid. Rows of glass jars glowed with exotic reagents. Microscopes, scalpels, and syringes lined the shelves, along with bizarre contraptions none of them had seen before.

The three friends found a lab table in the back. Alt pulled Sad out of his bag, placing her on the table next to Anger and Anxious. There was a fourth seat next to Alt, and he crossed his fingers hoping no one would sit there.

At the front of the room, Professor String's skeletal form floated in front of the whiteboard. Two bony arms guarded a cooler overflowing with white smoke.

Alt noted that the professor wasn't just a regular skeleton. They had a wild head of ash-purple hair that swirled in the air and wore a mask—or face—that looked like the shadow of a cartoon jack-o-lantern. Beneath a skeletal ribcage, String's legs—if you could call them that—swam freely like two detached eels of dark matter. Like all other professors, String had eyes that glowed a blank white, devoid of pupils or irises.

The Institute professors hardly looked human, but String took metamorphosis to the next level. Alt found himself transfixed by the sight of his instructor, who seemed to have created themselves in the image of an entirely abstract entity.

As the rest of the class settled in, String's hollow eyes swept over the students, a smile spreading across what Alt still didn't know was their mask or face.

"WELCOME," String's voice crackled with age, "to Void Matter METAMORPHOSIS! In this class, we will begin to unlock the true potential of the substance that shapes our world—and our bodies."

"I made ice cream for us today." With a skeletal hand, String flung open the cooler at the front of the room to reveal an assortment of frozen treats. Alt was wary, but after a table full of second years cheered their way to the front, he decided it was okay to get up and grab a snack.

As Alt returned to his seat with a chocolate-covered cone, he noticed a new figure hesitating at the doorway. It was the boy from earlier—the new freshman they'd left alone in the cafeteria. His eyes darted around the room, searching for an open spot. String's hollow eyes turned to the newcomer. "Ah, you must be Char. Welcome. Please, find a seat so we can begin."

Alt squirmed, realizing the only available seat was the one next to him. As Char made his way toward their table, he caught Tilde and Hyphen exchanging guilty looks. Alt felt cold in his seat, suddenly ashamed of his previous reluctance. He managed to eke out a grimace as Char approached, his sleeved hands hidden as they sat tucked beneath his rear.

Char responded with a little wave—though his Envy plopped on the table with a *thud* and glowered at the other Voidpets. As he sat down, Alt noticed the faint scent of vegetable oil and stir-fry.

"Hmm..." Tilde whispered, "Something smells like ...cooked veggies?" She sniffed the air as she held her raspberry popsicle in hand.

Char's face reddened. He turned away to mutter under his breath, "Maybe it's you."

Tilde's eyebrows shot up, her popsicle frozen halfway to her mouth. "Um, excuse me?" she said, her brows knotting as she gripped her wheelchair armrest. "What's that supposed to mean?"

Char's eyes widened as he regretted his words. "Wait, I didn't mean—"

"Then what *did* you mean?" Tilde hissed, clearly offended.

"Nothing," Char shrugged, not meeting her eyes. "Just like, whoever smelt it dealt it."

Tilde's pet Anger puffed up on the table, its red scarf flaring. Envy responded with a growl, its triangular eyes narrowing. Alt winced. He wanted to intervene, to smooth things over, but didn't know how to explain without making matters worse.

As the enmity threatened to boil over, a sudden hush fell over the classroom. Alt looked up to see String's hollow eyes fixed directly on their group, the teacher's skeletal form now hovering uncomfortably close. "While I appreciate a lively discussion," String's voice crackled, "I think it's time for us to begin our lesson now. Shall we?" The jack-o'-lantern face tilted, somehow managing to look both stern and bemused.

The Voidpets on the table immediately settled. Tilde's face flushed, matching her popsicle, while Char seemed to shrink in his seat.

"Good," the professor nodded, floating back to the front of the lab. "Now, let's begin our exploration of Void Matter Metamorphosis. Who can name one of my Three Principles of Void Matter?"

Hyphen's hand weaseled up.

"Void matter is neither created nor destroyed, but it can be transferred from one form to another."

"BEAUTIFUL," String exclaimed. A floating feather transcribed her answer to the whiteboard.

Char raised his hand, a determined look in his eye.

"Void matter can change form when acted upon by the lucidity of a sentient being."

"FANTASTIC!" String shouted again, as Alt noticed the hint of grin flicker on Char's face.

From across the room, a boy in a white quarter-zip raised his hand.

"All things are made of void matter."

Char suppressed a snicker.

"ALMOST!" String's mask twisted into a clever *gotcha* expression. "So, tell me, what's void matter made of?"

"More void matter?" Tilde blurted out loud.

"Atoms?" a voice murmured.

String's face looked thoughtful. "Let me clarify the third principle."

The floating marker scribbled on the board as String spoke:

"Void matter is the *PRIMARY CONSTITUENT* of our reality.

"This means that while most things we interact with are composed of or influenced by void matter, void matter *itself* is fundamental. It cannot be broken down any further—as far as we know today," String added with a chuckle.

"Void matter is the most basic building block of our reality, from which nearly all physical things, *including our currency*, are formed."

String paused, allowing this to sink in. "Of course, there are exceptions—And understanding these exceptions is key to mastering metamorphosis."

String extended their bony arms against the whiteboard. "Allow me to demonstrate."

From the heart of String's ribcage, a black liquid began to seep outwards like blood racing through invisible veins. It fully encased each bone, then faded to reveal two living human arms suspended in mid-air. They were complete with not only muscle and flesh, but also tattoos and a watch.

"TADA!" String sang, spinning around and busting a dance move with the new appendages.

The whole class leaned forward in their seats, bug-eyed at their teacher's uncanny transformation.

"As you can see, this was a rather complex action, because I had to focus all my lucidity into finalizing the details."

Suddenly, the human arms dissolved back to liquid. They morphed into a mess of jellyfish tentacles. Then a ruffled pair of wings. Then two misshapen chicken heads that clucked. Then, back to bone.

String unleashed an exuberant cackle. "Notice how that time was *much easier*, because the forms were abstract."

"A successful metamorphosis depends on three core factors:"

String raised a skeletal finger in the air to count.

"One: how much void matter you have to spare.

"Two: how well your lucidity can hold your new form.

"Three," String's voice turned spooky, "How well your body can handle the *rejection* of its original form.

"Any questions?" The professor perked up and smiled.

Alt's mind raced with questions, but he, like many others, was too stunned to speak.

"Alrighty then," String continued, "Today, we'll take it easy. Lab #1: Changing our hair color!"

Alt grinned and breathed a sigh of relief, seeing his friends relax around him. This was the part everyone was waiting for.

"The human body works in mysterious ways," String mused. "Some find it easier to transform the matter within their own bodies..." the teacher flexed a hand in demonstration, "...while others find it easier to work with matter that's outside," the professor conjured a shimmering orb for comparison.

"In this course, we'll only be transforming the void matter within ourselves. And we'll be starting with our hair, because that's one of the safest things to alter."

With the flick of a hand, String sent a cloud of particles to a drawer in the back of the classroom, releasing a fleet of mirrors into the air.

Each mirror floated to a different student, carried by a propeller of twirling feathers.

Alt gasped as he picked a mirror out of the air, his hands still hidden beneath his sleeves. He gazed into it, studying the short sandy bangs that brushed across his olive skin. Alt wasn't a fan of his own reflection, but today, he was excited about the possibilities ahead.

"Remember, everyone is different," said String. "Depending on your lucidity, your hair composition, and your unique strengths, you may be able to do more, or less, with the amount of VM in the assignment. The objective here is simply to change your hair color, even if it's only one strand."

As String spoke, a thread of liquid void matter swirled out from a large beaker, depositing a crystal of 10 VM at the hands of every student. Alt picked it up and rolled the material between his sleeves like a stress ball.

He looked up to see that Tilde was already attempting the assignment before the professor was finished explaining. A stream of smoke began to waft from her direction, accompanied by the sulfuric smell of burning hair.

As Char picked up his 10 VM, passing it back and forth between his hands, Alt noticed that he was trying to not laugh.

"Don't forget that void matter metamorphosis is one of the most *dangerous* applications of lucidity," String warned, the skeleton teacher's voice suddenly ominous. Alt wondered if that was in subtle response to Tilde's hair burning.

"There's always the risk of serious, permanent injury—which is why we start slow and take it step by step."

String's voice changed to a meditative lull.

"Step one is awareness. You must understand the current reality of your body and ACCEPT it without judgement. Only then shall it respond to your will."

Alt stared uncomfortably into the mirror.

"Step two is the vision. You must IMAGINE your new reality; your new form taking shape. Embrace who you are now, AND who you want to become. Accept that they are all a part of you—your past, your present, and your future."

Alt closed his eyes and imagined a new hairdo. He wasn't quite sure what he wanted yet, but he knew it had to be something fresh. Something iconic. His mind drifted to album covers, pop stars, and notable artworks as he searched for inspiration.

"Step three is the process. To see through the metamorphosis, you must EMBRACE every step along the way as a part of your journey. Every color in the gradient, every frame in the animation. "

Alt opened one eye and saw Char and Tilde exchanging glances, racing each other to see who could complete their transformation first. While Char had already coaxed a few strands into deep royal blue, Tilde was fuming, her red hair splotched with messy patches of coral.

Hyphen's hands trembled as she held her crystal. Her curls seemed to resist change, paling to a bright turquoise before snapping back to black. Her tiny Anxious quivered on the table, its hair bow jiggling as it rooted for her to succeed.

"You see, Voidpets are the original masters of metamorphosis." String explained. "They naturally change form as they get stronger, and freely transform throughout the day. Emotions are ephemeral by nature. They are mutable and abstract."

"As with all applications of lucidity, you should trust your companions to guide you." As if on cue, a Stage Five Curious spawned on top of String's head. It perched like a cat, with three monstrous tails that spilled onto the floor. Each tail tapered into a feather with a giant eye in the middle.

"I have Curious to thank for each and every one of my powers," Professor String said with a cryptic smile.

Alt tried to apply the vague instructions and placed his sleeves onto Sad's back. As he felt her warmth on his fingers, he thought of all the ways the little Voidpet had been there for him. Sad kept him company when he couldn't get out of bed. She so dearly enjoyed his art, candles, and music whenever he was feeling down, which always inspired him to keep creating. As Alt recounted how much progress he'd made over the years, he felt a rush of energy.

A tingling sensation spread across his head, like a thousand tiny pinpricks. When he opened his eyes and looked in the mirror, he gasped. The crystal in his hands had disappeared, and his sandy hair had transformed into a pastel lilac.

Chapter 5: Master of Reality

Professor Cogito's chalk glowed as it scribbled itself on the blackboard. Afternoon sun lit up the gilded tooling on the books that lined the walls.

Hyphen opened her blue notebook, labeled *Principles of Lucidity I* in bouncy calligraphy, and flipped open to the first page. From the fuzzy pencil case beside her, she extracted a matching gel pen and transcribed the quote in sparkly blue ink.

Hyphen rarely saw Professor Cogito on his feet, but as he stood before the chalkboard, she could see that he was easily 7 feet tall. He wore pointed pieces of armor that gleamed like obsidian, with two rows of scales running down his abdomen to create the illusion—or perhaps reality—of a sculpted physique. His eyes were completely hidden by a protruding mask that looked like a dragon's skull. Hyphen felt hypnotized by the mask's two eye sockets, each moving with him as if they were alive.

"As we delve into the nature of lucidity and void matter manipulation, consider this," Cogito began, stroking the beak of his mask with a metal talon. "What makes our power over reality legitimate? And what happens when we doubt that legitimacy?"

Commanding and clear, his voice locked Hyphen into a trance.

Even back in elementary school, rumors about Professor Cogito circulated like wildfire. Some said he could read minds, while others swore he'd once turned a student into a book. According to the upperclassmen, he was also rumored to be quite handsome underneath his mask—though no one could confirm for sure. With all the mystery, there was an undeniable air of excitement in the room. Everyone at the Institute knew that Cogito's classes were the most academically challenging, and Hyphen felt honored to have qualified for his course.

"Let's begin by discussing the nature of void matter," the Professor announced. His chalk scribbled the subject header and drew a big circle around the words:

THE NATURE OF VOID MATTER.

"Void matter is a fickle substance. Like humans, it doesn't blindly obey; it follows what it perceives to be true. It's a rule-breaker by nature, yet paradoxically, it must be guided by principle."

He held up a crystal between two of his clawed fingertips.

"You see," he brooded, "void matter doesn't just respond to raw power or desire. It responds to authority—to a command so legitimate it becomes indistinguishable from truth."

He snapped his fingers. The crystal erupted into an indigo plasma, then disappeared into the air.

Hyphen switched to a thinner pen as she realized this was going to be an intense lecture. She looked around out of habit, intending to offer her pens to Tilde and Alt, but neither of them had qualified to take this class with her. To her surprise, she turned around and saw Char sitting behind her instead. He was taking notes with an old pencil, almost worn down to its stub.

Do you need a pen? She mouthed to him, and he accepted. He must have scored high on his entrance exam to have gotten into this class as a new student.

Cogito's chalk drew an arrow extending from the first bubble, and then circled the new text:

RULE OF LEGITIMACY.

The professor held his talons behind his back as he began to pace in front of the chalkboard.

"As the ancient sages used to say, 'Reality bends to the will of those who dare to redefine it.' Void matter, in its quest to break rules, ironically seeks out the strongest 'rule' to follow—the most unwavering belief, the most unshakable conviction." He paused, turning his mask to face the class. "The most legitimate ruler."

"...In essence, void matter is drawn to those who can create their own legitimacy. We don't just control void matter—we work to become beings whose reality void matter *chooses* to obey."

Hyphen glanced up from her notes to see Cogito casually levitate a fountain pen from his desk. He twirled it between his metal talons, then planted it back onto the table as if it were a tiny sword.

LIKE THE MIND.

The chalk scratched three underlines beneath.

"You see, void matter, like the human mind, has the power to reason nearly anything to be true.

"Our minds are constantly racing to piece together a model of reality. A model of the world that makes sense to us, given the limited information that we know. We find patterns. Rules. Contradictions. And then we adjust our model of truth to account for the new information we digest.

"But the world is filled with infinite facts and opinions. So how do we decide which to consider? Which to act on?"

Cogito paused again for effect, posing his rhetorical question to the class.

Hyphen nibbled the tip of her pen, wondering how she'd answer. Would she equally consider all the information she'd learned? Prioritize the opinions of her trusted sources?

"As humans, we like to follow new sources of truth." Cogito explained, "But more importantly, we have preferences for the knowledge we digest."

He lifted his hand and extended a claw for each point:

"Knowledge that's easy to understand.

"Knowledge that affirms what we already know.

"Knowledge that validates our own sense of self.

"Knowledge that comes from a place of authority."

A murmur rippled through the classroom. Some students seemed to find this explanation controversial.

Cogito paused. "Any questions so far?" His voice echoed into silence as the students avoided eye contact, no one wanting to challenge him. The only sound Hyphen could hear was her own pen scribbling, and the faint scratches of others taking notes.

"Well then I'm glad that this lecture is easy to digest." Cogito deadpanned, to which no one laughed.

The professor seemed to sigh as he noticed the faces of the class. "I'll give you 10 minutes to discuss amongst yourselves," he said, and the class breathed a collective murmur of relief. "Partner up and reflect on your current relationships with void matter. Demonstrations are welcome."

The class quickly animated into discussion, with students summoning colorful orbs of VM and Voidpets swirling through the air. Char tapped Hyphen on the shoulder.

"This is what I've got," he grinned, summoning a droplet of royal blue in his palm. "You?"

Hyphen grimaced. "To be honest, I can't really do stuff like that yet," she admitted. "I'm really into the theory and all, but VM doesn't respond to me well."

"Oh, how come?" Char asked.

"I don't know, I think maybe it has something to do with anxiety," she mumbled. "Like when I doubt myself, I'm telling the void matter to doubt me too..."

Char nodded, thoughtfully retracting his little demo.

"Well, I'm sure you'll get it soon," he offered. "Like, we're in this class, right? At some point, I feel like all our hard work has gotta do *something* to offset the doubts. At the end of the day, there's no reason anyone can't use void matter if they put in the effort."

Hyphen managed a small laugh. "I guess. Maybe someday."

Minutes of discussion passed, and Hyphen grew restless. She was the kind of student who preferred lecture over practical application.

Thankfully, the break was short.

"Back to business now," Professor Cogito declared, and a hush fell over the classroom. "So, who here can offer me a definition for lucidity?" he scanned the room as the chalk scrawled the on the board.

WHAT IS LUCIDITY?

"Don't be shy," Cogito prodded, "Your participation grade doesn't care if you're right or wrong."

A few timid hands raised.

"The power to use void matter?" Piped a small voice in the back.

"How focused you are?" Another kid guessed.

Hyphen's hand peeked halfway up, and Cogito called on her before she could put it down.

"It's what our grading system measures here at the Institute, I think," she ventured, "It's an exponential measure of how much void matter a person can wield at once, with each level corresponding to a power of ten."

Cogito held his luminous gaze on her. "That's certainly a correct answer. Thank you Hyphen. Though I'd now like to offer you an alternate, theoretical one."

Hyphen felt her face warm as she shrunk into her seat, clutching Anxious with her left hand. It was unclear if he'd found her answer insightful, or simply juvenile.

"I like to define Lucidity as the power to *present a new truth* to void matter."

Cogito's dragon eyes swept the room once again, and he took a deep breath before elaborating. "Lucidity is one's ability to extend a formal invitation to accept a new paradigm. It's the ability to consider an exception, and boldly define it."

"It's not the *absence* of logic—in fact, it is *inseparable* from logic itself. It is the application of known logic onto a special occasion that invites you to dance between the pillars of what you currently know.

"As you are already aware: one's lucidity determines one's proficiency in void matter manipulation.

"Which makes the difference between this—" he explained, conjuring a little blue flame.

"—And this." With a whoosh, it sparkled to life in an aurora of electric blue, eliciting a chorus of gasps as the light filled the room. As the matter danced through the classroom, the light touched on his mask, drawing shadows across the book-lined walls. His voice shifted from academic to conspiratorial, drawing the students deeper into his theory.

The chalk drew a little arrow to create a side note.

(THINK: DREAMS.)

"Why is it that you can go through an entire dream without realizing that you are in a dream?"

He paused for effect, observing the class. "Because your subconscious understanding of the known universe *overrules* all. And you are not made privy to the existence of any exceptions."

"But then, there are lucid dreams. Has anyone here ever experienced a lucid dream?"

The class murmured, and students turned around to look at their friends.

"The kind of dream where you realize you are in control?" He clarified.

A few hands tentatively raised, and Cogito's dragon mask appeared to betray the hint of a smile. "Excellent."

"With the newfound awareness that you are in a dream," he continued, "there comes an invitation to write the next step of your experience."

He extended his talons in a grandiose gesture, before snapping them back to lift his fingers portentously. The aurora faded into a nebula of shimmering particles for effect.

"But you are limited. You can only create permutations of the systems and memories that already exist in your mind. And you must remain in control, in a state of power, of *presence*, or else the dream will fade."

As the professor let the class ponder this line, Hyphen found the puzzle pieces starting to make sense in her head. The dream metaphor struck a chord with her, invoking her experiences with nightmares and panic attacks. In both, there was sometimes a 'way out'—a sudden moment of clarity that transcended the intensity of her current experience. It was sometimes attainable, but often out of reach.

Cogito picked up a book from his desk and let it fall open in the palm of his claw.

DREAMS ARE CREATED FROM EXPERIENCES.

"Propositional logic. Probability theory. The laws of math and physics.

"We study them to understand truth.

"It is only from knowing truth that you are then able to use it to color the canvas of your imagination."

He snapped the book shut.

"The closer you align your will with the existing rules of physics and nature—the closer you align your rule with the existing values of a population—the more likely your authority is to be accepted."

"We study. We act. We think. We feel. We create. And that richer understanding of the world allows us to exert more legitimacy in our desires."

Hyphen jotted down the professor's words verbatim, before stopping to massage her cramped hands.

"Lucidity is not wishful thinking, but in fact, dare I say, the opposite of it. Wishful thinking is only called such due to the knowledge that it is fiction. But to manipulate void matter, you must do more than wish. You must convince it."

"And now for a little demonstration." A circle of six books began to float in the air behind Cogito, each emitting a soft blue glow.

"These books aren't in the air because I *believe* books can fly—or simply because I imagined them to.

"They are because I've had a lifelong relationship with void matter. Because I've studied how leaves float underwater. I've studied how balloons float in the air.

"I understand that paper and leather won't float in the air on their own... But these materials are ultimately derivations of void matter—and void matter... will consider.

"Since void matter likes to change its properties, I can temporarily invite it to adopt the density of air—or lighter." As he said this, the books began to float higher, adopting a quality of aimless balloons.

He gently prodded one of the books with a claw.

"The mass of void matter *accepts* my invitation because it trusts my authority. It responds to the lifetime of energy I have cultivated in my mind. It accepts my request as reasonable. It senses my agency and happily executes."

Hyphen's pen flew across her notebook, capturing every word in precise penmanship before drawing diagrams of the floating books. Behind her, Char alternated between scribbling notes and stealing glances at her meticulous work. Hyphen glanced backward and their eyes met briefly, sharing a moment of amazement as Cogito held the books suspended in midair.

"Yo," Char whispered, "can he make our homework vanish next?"

Hyphen did not have the nerve to banter in Cogito's class, but she managed to squeeze back a smile.

Meanwhile, the chalk produced another header.

CHALLENGES & LIMITATIONS.

"Now keep in mind," Cogito placed a talon between two books to keep them from colliding into each other, "this is achievable because there is no equal and opposite force acting against me to insist against my will.

"If another human, or creature, or force of your environment is countering your invitation..." Cogito lowered his voice and gestured with his talons, "The void matter will have to decide whose will to obey. If you have not earned its respect," his claw curled into a fist, "it will not obey you."

"If your command is filled with contradictions, filled with doubt," he loosened his grip, waving his hand through the air, "it will not listen." He lifted his hand to the snout of his mask in thought, "In that sense, the fundamental building blocks of our world behave much like a group of people. Or perhaps, in some ways, like the primal reaches of our own psyche."

Hyphen found herself self-conscious as she processed this section of the lecture. She turned her attention to Anxious shivering in her lap. Was she shouldering doubt her mind? Were her goals filled with contradictions? There wasn't much she could do about it though, at least, not overnight.

IN SUMMARY:

Cogito maneuvered the books back into a stack on his desk as he prepared to wrap up his lecture.

"Lucidity comes with confidence, which comes with practice. It develops as you slowly build your relationship with void matter and realize that you have agency in the world. We can have fun talking about all the theory behind the concept—but practically speaking, you must simply keep using your lucidity to improve it."

The towering professor tilted his head, and his armor clinked in a playful shrug. "That's all for today." Professor Cogito finished, letting the chalk nub come to rest on his desk beside the books. "Any questions?"

A silence settled across the room once more, as the class digested the lecture. As others slowly began to raise their hands, asking Cogito to repeat some information they had missed, Hyphen turned around to

Char and showed him her notebook. She pointed at quote from the beginning of the lesson, scribbled in sparkly blue at the top:

Men are not corrupted by power, or by obedience; but by the exercise of a power which they believe to be illegitimate.

"Did he mention anything about this?" She whispered, tapping on the word 'corrupted'.

"No, I don't think so, you should ask," Char whispered back.

Hyphen shook her head and turned away, still doubtful of her previous answer.

"It's a good question, you should really ask it," Char urged.

When she finally gathered the courage to speak, the room fell silent. All eyes turned to her, then to Cogito.

"Ah, so, Professor—regarding what you said at the beginning— what happens if... the void matter deems your power to be illegitimate? How does it... become corrupted? Does it just ignore you?"

"Good question." Cogito looked at her. "Where do you think Nightmares come from?"

As Cogito's message lingered in the air, it was clear that no one else had anything left to ask. Following a curt nod of acknowledgement, the glowing chalk began to scrawl a list of fantastical titles that sounded like works of fiction:

REQUIRED READING:

1. *"The Republic"*
2. *"The Prince"*
3. *"Leviathan"*
4. *"The Social Contract"*
5. *"Beyond Good and Evil"*
6. *"Discipline and Punish"*

Cogito's metal talons clacked against the board as he tapped the list. "You all have access to my library in the east wing of the Institute. There, you will find these seminal works on power, legitimacy, and the nature of reality."

He turned to face the class, his mask's eye sockets gleaming. "Your assignment is to read one of these texts and write a 10-page paper addressing the following questions: 'One: How is the concept of legitimacy presented in the context of human governance? Two: What are the potential consequences of wielding 'illegitimate' power? Three: What is your response to this author's perspective, and how does it contradict or inform your practice with void matter?'"

Some students murmured at the thought of a 10-page paper, but Hyphen secretly celebrated. She loved writing and couldn't wait to spend more time in Cogito's beautiful library. As she raced to write down the titles, she noticed that they were the same six books that were floating earlier.

"Your papers will be due in two weeks. Remember, I expect original thought and critical analysis. If you cut corners..." the mask's eyes narrowed as he surveyed the room, "it'll be your own powers that suffer for it."

"And a word of caution:" Cogito added, as the class jotted down the assignment, "My library has some protections in place. So please treat the books with respect."

Another silence hung in the air as the professor sat back into his armchair, burying himself in one of the many tomes on his desk as he poured himself a cup of hot tea.

"Class dismissed," Cogito murmured with a wave of his claws, giving his wide-eyed students permission to pack their things and file out, the buzz of chatter once again returning to the classroom.

Char turned to Hyphen, holding out her pen. "Hey, thanks for letting me borrow this."

Hyphen smiled. "Keep it. You might need it for the paper," she said with a small chuckle.

Char looked surprised but grateful, "Really? Thanks!"

"Yeah, maybe we can study together sometime!" Hyphen said, the words spilling off her tongue before her anxiety could stop them. There was something about her earlier act of kindness that had suddenly emboldened her to take the lead.

"Yeah, maybe," Char grinned, before hurrying out of the classroom, his Envy trailing in the air as his backpack bounced behind him.

Hyphen scurried to the door with Anxious in her arms, afraid to be the last student in the room with the professor.

"Thank you, Professor Cogito," she chirped on her way out, avoiding further eye contact with the dragon mask.

"You're welcome, Hyphen," he responded.

Professor Cogito had remembered her name, which set off a flurry of nerves. With his acknowledgement also came the pressure to meet, if not exceed his expectations.

Chapter 6: Classmates

Char had to move fast. Hyphen was nice, but she was clearly a bookworm, and he didn't want to become besties with her before he had a chance to make other friends. From what he'd seen so far, she seemed like the type to get clingy if he wasn't clever about keeping his distance. Unfortunately, she was walking right behind him on his way to the dining hall.

"Hey Char, are you going to grab a bite?' She chirped, catching up to him.

"Uh, yeah, are you?" He stammered, realizing it was too late to finesse an exit.

"Yeah!"

An awkward silence ensued. The only sounds that could be heard were their footsteps echoing on the marble floor. Char noticed that Hyphen's footsteps were uneven—hinting that her right foot had been injured somehow.

"Do you want to sit together?" He wasn't sure if it was social obligation or a sense of pity that compelled him to blurt that out, but he felt wrong saying nothing.

"Oh! Yes—of course!" Hyphen replied, her brown eyes sparkling as a radiant smile spread across her face. He noticed her cheeks turn a subtle shade of dark rose.

"I-I normally just read by myself in the afternoon," she said, fiddling with a curl of her hair and looking away.

"Oh, I mean, if you want to sit alone, I totally get it—"

"No!" She interrupted, before her hands shot to cover her mouth. "I mean—my other friends are busy this time of day," Hyphen explained, "so it'll be nice having a new pal to sit with in the afternoon!"

Char nodded. He didn't love the implication that he was going to be her snack buddy every afternoon in perpetuity, but he figured he might as well embrace the one new friend he had just made. It wasn't like he had the nerve to follow through on his popularity goals right now, anyway.

"Oatmeal?" Hyphen suggested, and Char followed her into the dining hall. As they stepped into the room, the space greeted them with magnificent arches, decorated pillars, and the warm aromas of baked goods. The far side was lined with windows, each looking out into the school's manicured courtyard. A floating buffet table stretched at the front, attended by Voidpet staff. Char marveled at the room, even though it wasn't his first time dining here. It somehow looked brighter and more cavernous than it did at lunch—perhaps since there were fewer students at this hour.

As the two freshmen perused along the buffet table, Hyphen chose a bowl of cinnamon apple oatmeal. She loaded it with an arrangement of colorful berries before scooping a little fruit bowl for her Anxious. While Char decided to get a plain boiled egg with rice, Envy nipped his shoulder, growling as it eyed the fruit bowl Hyphen had prepared for Anxious.

"What is it, Checkers?" Char asked his Voidpet, before noticing the fruits. He rolled his eyes at his pet affectionately before going back to get him some too.

Char followed Hyphen to the cash register, manned by a Judgement in a hat and apron. The winged Voidpet tallied up their items with its tail, then gestured at the total with its beak.

As Hyphen swiped her student ID at the register, Char noticed the machine flash, indicating that her meal had been paid for with a fee waiver.

"Thanks Derek," she chimed, before stepping aside to wait.

Char's student ID had nothing attached to it. He dug up 3 VM from his pocket, handing it over to Derek's claws.

"Uh... thanks Derek?" Char echoed, and the pterodactyl cashier tipped his hat.

The dining hall was relatively empty at this hour, since it was between meals. Hyphen walked towards an empty table near the window—which was normally occupied around dinner and lunch—and Char took a seat across from her.

As Char started on his egg rice, he felt restless. The hall's quietness amplified every scrape of spoon against bowl, every crunch of Hyphen's berries. He could hear some distant chatter from a handful of other students, mixed with the soft clinks of cutlery, and occasional chirps and growls from various Voidpets.

"So," Char began, desperate to break the silence, "how long have you been at the Institute?"

Hyphen's eyes lit up, grateful for the conversation starter. "Oh, I've been here ever since the start of elementary school!" She gushed, "My parents used to go here, and then they became researchers, and then they got a place nearby, and then..."

Her cheeks turned a deep red as she looked around frantically, "Oh gosh, I'm sorry, am I oversharing?"

Next to her, Anxious curled up into a ball and peeked from behind its own tail.

"No, no, go on, I'm the one who asked you," Char responded, shoveling a bite of plain rice into his mouth as he noticed her shoulders relax a little.

"My parents sent me here as soon as I could walk, but then they got sick from a Nightmare attack, and then..." Char assumed from her pause that they had passed away, so he gave her a sympathetic nod.

"And then, the Institute took me in as a boarding student," she finished.

"Wow, so you must really know your way around here then," Char responded with encouragement. "No wonder Professor Cogito knows your name!"

Hyphen looked down with embarrassment, an awkward smile squiggling across her lips.

"Yeah, I guess maybe that's from being elementary school valedictorian," she mumbled, her small demeanor belying her pride. "But I've only taken classes with Invidere, because she teaches the lower grades. We mostly learn about taking care of Voidpets—and just regular school stuff."

As Hyphen spoke, Char thought strategy. It seemed as if he'd stumbled into the most knowledgeable freshman at the Institute—which couldn't be bad, even though she was a bit of a geek. Envy seemed to flatten, unclear if purring or growling at the thought of her potential.

"What about you?" Hyphen asked, taking a big breath to recover from her introduction. As she said this, Envy meandered to Hyphen's side of the table and stole a lick of her oats.

Char gasped to apologize, scooping his pet back. "Well, I just got here. But I mainly came to have a fresh start. So... I don't need to go into all the boring details about where I'm from." He felt bad stonewalling after she'd just opened up, so he tried to offer something up, "Long story short, I've wanted to go to the Institute ever since I was a kid. But I live far away, and tuition was expensive. So, I studied and saved up until I could attend on scholarship."

"Oh," Hyphen nodded sympathetically, "that's really admirable of you."

She couldn't relate to his long work hours and grueling commute, —but since he couldn't relate to being orphaned, they were even. He locked eyes with Anxious before rushing to change the subject.

"What're you gonna do for Cogito's paper?" Char asked.

"Oh! I was planning to head to the library next for that!" Hyphen bubbled, her previous solemnity replaced by effervescence, "I think I'll start by reading the six books first, and then decide which one makes the most sense to write my paper on!"

Char nodded, taking a bite into his boiled egg. As Hyphen launched into an enthusiastic tangent on lucidity theory, his attention drifted to the large window beside them. The afternoon light glazed the Institute's courtyard, spotlighting the white road that spiraled up to the castle.

A strange dot of red caught his eye.

"Whoa, what's that?" Char interrupted, pointing towards the window. Envy spun around to watch, its triangular eyes narrowed into slits.

Hyphen turned, her words trailing off as she spotted what had captured Char's attention. A car—more specifically, they realized, a cherry-red convertible—was winding its way up the spiraling road beneath the Institute, leaving a trail of disturbed Voidpets in its wake.

Before Char could make sense of what he was seeing, Envy puffed up and hissed, knocking its empty fruit bowl to the floor.

"Is that...someone commuting to school in a *car*?" Hyphen wondered aloud, squinting to get a better look.

Anxious forgot its meal and began to tremble on the table. Char stood up and pressed his face against the glass. Despite all the magic and monsters he'd seen already, Char could deduce from Hyphen's reaction that this was no ordinary occurrence at the Institute.

"Yo Hyphen..." he trailed, his gaze locked on the spectacle outside the window, "let's check out what's going on."

Char grabbed his bag and made a beeline out of the dining hall. Hyphen scrambled to return their empty trays, sprinting after him with Anxious in her arms. Together, they scurried to the courtyard to observe.

Chapter 7: New Kids

Pandora scanned the ether ahead. As loud music bumped from the speakers, the others bounced to the beat.

"Drive slowly," she cautioned Promise through cat eyed shades, "I see wild Voidpets all over the place."

The convertible was driving through the sky, up along a ribbon-like path that snaked towards the Institute. As the ghostly road suspended the sports car in midair, Pandora observed the creatures in the surrounding atmosphere. Little Spites wiggled to and fro, some larger ones soaring overhead like prehistoric pterosaurs. She identified Paranoia, Anxious, even Sonder—looping, dancing, strutting to the beat, with a handful of colorful Vivids among their numbers.

Eager to greet their own kind, the group's Voidpets made an appearance. Promise's Greed scampered to his shoulder, its long foxtails flowing in the wind, and Luden's Cringe peeked over his head like an oversized gecko. Pecunia's Sloth spawned into her lap to look at the sky, and Pandora's Pride blossomed from her belt, the maned dragon taking into the open air. Even Volo's Lust emerged from his spine, its bulbed tentacles meandering out the back of the vehicle. In sync with the humans, the pets bounced to the music too.

"ARE WE THERE YET?" Pecunia hollered from the back of the car.

"NOPE," Promise yelled back, easing his hands off the wheel as the mysterious road began to carry them automatically.

"ALMOST!" Pandora trilled. The Institute grew closer overhead.

Before they knew it, the car had been ferried thousands of feet into the sky. A Spite soared above them, its long scythes tucked into its belly, and a Sad slipped beneath the road to make room for their automobile. The path deposited the car on ivory rock, right before the front courtyard of the castle.

The campus looked like a marble island. A river wove around the perimeter, a ribbon of turquoise around the castle. As Pandora's eyes followed the water, she saw it spill over the edges, plummeting into waterfalls that faded into mist. An array of floating trees lined a wide set of stairs, all leading to three towering arches. Grass areas patterned the courtyard, each full of small Voidpets playing.

"So, this is it," Pandora breathed, taking in the fairytale landscape over the sound of the bass, "the forbidden lair of our foes."

Suddenly, the music cut out, and the car's engine shuttered down. A towering figure in a dragon mask held an outstretched talon in their direction, staring at them with colorless eyes. His dark armor clinked against the pathway as he strode out of the courtyard to where they were parked. A cape spilled over his shoulders, billowing behind him.

The figure loomed before the teenage group. A hefty tome floated at his side, its pages rustling in the wind. The white eyes of the mask seemed to bore into each of them in turn.

"I presume," he said, his voice as dry as parchment, "that you have a reason for this... boisterous arrival?"

Promise readied a retort, but Pandora elbowed him sharply. She identified the individual before them as a potential professor, perhaps even a founder of the Institute itself—a being of unknown power who was not be trifled with. Luden's Cringe, sensing the social faux pas, tried to shrink back into his body. But the professor's gaze fixed on it, freezing the Voidpet mid-disappearance.

Pandora stepped out of the vehicle, her voice steady. "Professor," she began, pausing in case he needed to correct her, "we sincerely apologize for our disruptive arrival. We're new students, eager to begin our studies at the esteemed Institute."

Pandora bowed her head as she raced to string together words.

"Our enthusiasm got the better of us. We meant no disrespect," she continued, "We've traveled a long way and are unfamiliar with proper protocol. If you could guide us to the registration office, we'd be deeply grateful."

The professor's mask revealed no emotion as he regarded the group. "Very well," he said after a long pause. He tilted his head curiously. "I will inform you that it is already quite late in the afternoon."

Pandora swallowed. Despite her rigorous research, she hadn't had to show up on time for anything in years and overlooked this key detail.

"But we can still get you placed and registered for your classes," the man finished curtly.

As the five kids climbed out of the car, Promise whispered to Pandora, "What about my—"

Pandora shushed him, her eyes darting to the professor's back. She now doubted their decision to study ancient high school TV dramas as a primary reference for academic etiquette. "Just leave it, I'm sure this place is secure," she hissed back.

As they approached the arched entryway, Pandora's head whipped towards a rustle in the courtyard bushes. White void matter coated her fists as her survival instincts kicked into gear. But she remembered she was now on Institute grounds, which meant that it had to be nothing more than a small Voidpet playing.

Inside the white castle, they passed through arching hallways that seemed to defy gravity, a long pool filled with shimmering liquids, and rooms where objects floated freely. Finally, they arrived at a door marked "Admissions."

The masked professor turned to them, his black mask gleaming in the ethereal light. "You may address me as Professor Cogito," he said.

"Thank you, Professor Cogito. My name is Pandora, and these are my siblings—"

"I am aware," he said. "It is an honor to have you attend my school, Miss Pandora Windfall and company. I look forward to seeing you at your placement exams."

Professor Cogito bowed towards them before turning on a dime and walking away, his cape flaring behind him like a wave of dark water. His clawed feet clacked as he strode into the distance, leaving the five children confused in front of the admissions office.

"Well at least we know our reputation precedes us," Promise slipped his hands in his pockets, head tilted at a smug angle.

"I think it's because I sent in the admissions paperwork beforehand..." Pandora muttered, shaking her head.

"I mean, that dude looked like he could read minds," Luden gawked, his Cringe still stunned from earlier.

"Indeed," said Volo, to which Pecunia nodded.

Pandora figured it was best to get moving, so she pushed open the door and marched inside.

Chapter 8: Placement Test

Hyphen was not ready to get out of the bushes, but Char was.

As soon as Professor Cogito and the new students were well out of sight, he burst forth from the foliage, sprinting to the front of the courtyard where the red convertible was parked.

"Yo, you gotta come take a look at this!" He yelled, bonking the hood of the vehicle with zeal.

Envy spearheaded the investigation, immediately sniffing the wheels. It licked the red paint like candy.

Hyphen hesitated, unsure how she felt about snooping on someone else's unattended property—but her curiosity got the best of her, and she weaned herself from the shelter of the bushes. With Anxious in her arms, she tiptoed towards her new friend and the mysterious automobile.

Suddenly, the front wheels on the car blinked open to reveal a pair of googly eyes. The hood of the car yawned like a mouth, before the whole thing shrank into a little black Voidpet. It sneezed a cloud of black exhaust, then shook itself clean on the courtyard floor.

Char leapt away in surprise, as Envy cannonballed backwards into his arms. Char gawked in Hyphen's direction, his mouth agape as the only word he could say was, "Bruh."

As Envy recovered from the shock and went down to sniff at the new stranger, Char began to laugh. He gestured with hands at his temples, as if to mimic his brain exploding. "What kind of black magic was that?"

While a functional automobile was already a rare sight in the Void, seeing a Voidpet transform into one was even more unheard of. But the sight of a small Voidpet emboldened Hyphen far more than the convertible. She smiled upon realizing it was a harmless Lonely, in its baby Stage 1 form. Her legs moved before she could stop herself, and she soon found herself crouched in front of the creature. She extended a hand for its little snout to sniff.

Hyphen placed Anxious on the ground so she could rummage through her backpack for snacks. She found a granola bar and unwrapped it to split between Anxious and Lonely. While her pet gingerly nibbled its half, the Lonely clamped down on its portion with its whole mouth. It downed the whole piece in one gulp, then tilted its head, blinking its large googly eyes as if expecting more.

Hyphen giggled and pet the Lonely.

"You're a hungry buddy, aren't you?" Hyphen cooed, as the Lonely buried its snout into her bag, digging for more.

Hyphen hardly noticed Char standing behind her, his Envy snarling as she rubbed Lonely's head with affection. "That's one spoiled pet," he scoffed, his arms crossed as he observed.

As he spoke, they saw a tall boy in a leather jacket emerge from the entranceway. He was nearly as tall as Professor Cogito, although he appeared much sparer in stature. Unlike the professor, whose regal presence augmented his size, this boy almost looked like a shadow, his slight frame accentuated by his languid posture.

"Come 'ere, Lulu," he raised a willowy arm and snapped his fingers.

On command, the Lonely extracted its head from Hyphen's bag and levitated into the air. It paused to study Hyphen, then blasted off towards its keeper, disappearing into the halls of the Institute.

For some reason, Hyphen found it notable that this new boy was keeping a Lonely. Something about his voice, or perhaps his demeanor, stood in contrast to his wide-eyed Lonely, a species known to be common and gentle. She wondered if she would have been afraid of him had she not met his Lonely first.

"I already don't like that guy," Char shook his head.

Hyphen turned to see her friend's face contorted with contempt.

"Why?" Hyphen said, surprised. "Friendly humans tend to have friendly Voidpets, so it seems fair to think he's nice."

"His pet is a brat."

Hyphen frowned, feeling a need to defend the Lonely. "I don't think that's... necessarily true. It was just hungry."

"Oh, come on, you know *those* kinds of people...," said Char.

"What do you mean?"

Char's eyes hardened. "Trust me, I've seen this type before. They waltz in here thinking they own the place."

As Char's expression brewed with resentment, Hyphen wondered what had happened to make him to feel this way.

"There's people like *us*," Char began, "and then there's the kind of people who are used to getting whatever *they* want," he said with a bitter frown. "I already know that Voidpet is bad news, and so are the kids who came with it."

"I mean," Char paused, noticing Hyphen's doubt, "would your Anxious ever behave like that?"

Hyphen looked at her tiny Voidpet, still nibbling on its half of the granola bar. She shook her head no.

"It's important to keep your guard up so people don't take advantage of you," Char pressed on, looking Hyphen in the eyes, "Especially 'cause you're someone who works super hard. And treats everyone with kindness."

Hyphen bit her lip. She wanted to believe the best in people, but Char's words had made her feel seen. She found herself nodding along, her earlier defense of the Lonely fading. "Maybe you're right. We should probably be careful around people like that."

Char nodded with vindication.

"Now come on, let's go snoop on their placement test," he said, waving her towards the entryway.

The idea of snooping made Hyphen's stomach churn, but Char's enthusiasm was infectious. She swallowed her discomfort, assuring herself there was no harm in curiosity. She felt guilty for straying from her values but pushed it aside. After all, Char seemed like a clever person who understood things, and she didn't want to disagree with her new friend.

Char strode ahead with confidence, but Hyphen noticed the tight set of his shoulders. She looked at Anxious, wondering if there was more to his dislike than he was letting on.

As they entered the Institute's main building, the usually bustling hallways were quiet. Char led the way, his determined stride pushing the pace of Hyphen's hesitant steps.

"The new student placement tests are held in the Amphitheater—in the North Wing, right?" Char whispered with excitement. "I heard Professor Invidere mention it at orientation."

Hyphen nodded, her heart racing. "Are you sure we won't get caught?"

Char flashed a reassuring grin. "If we get caught, we just tell 'em I'm a new kid who got lost."

Hyphen was impressed by his courage, but still unconvinced. "What's my excuse, though?"

Char was undeterred. "You saw me go the wrong way and came to help. Duh."

As they climbed up a spiral staircase to the second floor of the auditorium hall, curiosity began to overrule anxiety. "Wait, Char," Hyphen whispered, "How do you know they're getting a formal placement test right away? They don't usually do those on the first day new students arrive..."

"You heard Professor Cogito from the bushes, right?" Char answered, surprising her with his astuteness, "He said he'd get them placed today."

Hyphen was confused. "That's weird. Usually, new students go through orientation first, then at least a few days of regular classes. Placement tests come later, once the professors have had a chance to observe everyone."

"Maybe there are some exceptions," Char replied with a smirk.

"Maybe you're right," Hyphen nodded, "But it still doesn't make sense for them to skip the usual process."

Char's eyes lit up at her words, his excitement glowing. "That's why we *need* to see this. Whatever's going on, it's not normal."

Their whispered conversation was cut short as they heard voices from the chamber ahead. Char pressed his finger to his mouth. They slipped through the back door of the Amphitheater, entering a large colosseum with a glass dome that opened into sky. Each clutching a Voidpet and bookbag, Hyphen and Char crouched down in the back row of seats, their earlier debate forgotten in the face of imminent discovery.

The enormous auditorium was occupied only by two small groups in the front. The five new students stood on stage, while the five professors occupied the five seats in the front row. Despite the lack of spectators, the glass surfaces of the dome broadcasted closeup shots like giant screens—making it convenient to snoop.

From the left-most seat in the audience, they could hear Professor Invidere's distinctive voice ringing out like a polished intercom speaker. "Now, let's begin with a simple demonstration of your abilities," she said, conjuring a large crystal of void matter and floating it towards the center of the stage. "We invite you each to manipulate this into any form you choose."

Char and Hyphen exchanged glances, their curiosity piqued. They leaned in, eager to witness what would unfold.

Just then, Anxious let out a tiny, involuntary squeak. Hyphen stiffened, her eyes round with panic. Char quickly placed a hand over the Voidpet's mouth.

While the other four professors sat facing the stage, undisturbed by the sound, it was only Professor Bool whose gaze rotated to the back of the auditorium. He raised a finger to his lips and winked, before fixing his attention back on the exam.

The younger girl on stage studied the crystal with childish innocence. "Wow! What's this shiny thing?" she poked it with her fingernail.

"That's void matter, dear," Professor Invidere explained, "Or VM, as some call it."

The girl gasped. "Void matter? VM? What's that?"

At this, Professor Bool began to cackle. "My, my, Miss Pecunia Windfall, now that's the best joke I've heard all year," he howled, his half mask grinning with unfiltered amusement. The jester walked right up on stage, handed her a white envelope, and disappeared into a cloud of smoke. His laughter echoed through the amphitheater as his form faded into thin air.

The girl held the white envelope, her platinum locks highlighting the red rushing into her tan. As the screen magnified her embarrassment, Char squinted to scrutinize her face.

"Who would like to demonstrate first?" Professor Invidere asked without missing a beat.

There was a moment of silence. Then, the bigger girl spoke up. "I'll go."

She stepped forward with confidence, her bold stance topped with a rosy smile. "I'm Pandora," she introduced herself, "and I'll do my best to demonstrate my abilities."

"Very well," Professor Invidere nodded. She gestured to the crystal in the middle of the stage.

Pandora walked up to it and placed her hands around it. As she took a deep breath and closed her eyes, the void matter slowly morphed into a metal spoon.

Pandora scanned the professors' faces, judging their reactions. Hyphen was blown away, but the professors didn't seem to be. The four kids on stage looked at each other as if silently conferring on how to proceed.

Cogito looked at her, his dragon mask tilted to the side. "Unless you want to join the clown house too, Pandora, I encourage you to continue," he advised.

Pandora gulped, her eyes darting to meet the others on stage.

From the tone of Professor Cogito's voice, Hyphen would have guessed that he was already familiar with this Pandora girl somehow—but then again, he often spoke like he was familiar with the unknown.

After a few more seconds of calculation, Pandora opened her palms, exploding the spoon into a shower of particles. They swirled around Pandora in a shimmering display before coalescing into a complex, three-dimensional graph.

"This," Pandora explained, clearing her throat and deepening her voice, "is a visual representation of the Mandelbrot set." The fractal pattern shifted, its intricacy becoming more apparent as it filled the air around her. Tendrils of void matter traced the edges of the set, creating a mesmerizing galaxy of nested swirls.

"*Nerd alert*," Char whispered to Hyphen, who was giddy with fascination. She'd never seen a student as impressive as Pandora and was already daydreaming about studying with her.

"As you can see," Pandora spread her fingers as if she were enlarging a screen, "the pattern repeats infinitely as we zoom in."

At Pandora's command, the void matter began to zoom into a specific part of the fractal. As it magnified, more intricate patterns unfolded, each one a perfect microcosm of the whole.

"This fractal," Pandora cleared her throat again, "represents…"

Her eyes darted as she paused, as if searching for an answer, "the boundary between chaos and order in complex dynamics. It's a visual demonstration of how simple rules can create infinite complexity."

Professor Cogito stood up, his admiration apparent through his dragon mask.

"The House of Reason awaits your acceptance," he declared. He bowed and floated a blue envelope into Pandora's hands.

Pandora nodded her head and compressed her fractal back into its crystal form. She picked the envelope out of the air. On the screen, the tall boy could be seen whispering something in Pandora's ear, to which she crossed her arms and huffed.

As Pandora stepped back, the air in the amphitheater sparkled with residual energy from her display. Hyphen held her breath, wondering how the next student could possibly follow such an act. The void matter crystal, reset to its original form, hung expectantly in the air, awaiting its next challenger.

"That was incredible!" she whispered. "I've never seen a high schooler use void matter like that!"

Char nodded, his earlier disdain warring with begrudging admiration. "I mean she was just moving dust around, but yeah the math thing was neat."

Hyphen frowned, torn between Char's skepticism and her own amazement. "But imagine being able to create something so intricate and complex..."

Their whispers were interrupted again as Professor Invidere's voice rang out. "An impressive display, Pandora. Now, who would like to go next?"

A pale boy with black hair stepped forward with the menacing grace of a wolf. "I'm Volo," he said, his voice calm and steady.

He walked up to the crystal and began to mold it with his hands, expanding pieces of it like malleable glass. Slowly, the void matter transformed into a model of the human skeleton, hovering in mid-air.

"BEAUTIFUL," Professor String exclaimed with glee, "That looks like ME!"

Next, Volo closed his eyes and put his hand inside the ribcage. In response, gossamer threads of red energy began to weave through the skeleton, forming an intricate nervous system. Layer by layer, he added musculature, each fiber carefully placed.

Professor Cogito leaned forward, intrigued. "Fascinating. A student of human anatomy."

Suddenly, the anatomical model sprang to life, attached to Volo by a thread connected to his hand. It lunged at him, throwing a punch with startling speed. Volo dodged, his movements a blur. The puppet and Volo engaged in a dance of attack and defense, showcasing not just anatomical knowledge but also martial prowess.

"Remarkable," Professor Invidere hummed.

"Okay, that's kind of cool," Char admitted, his eyes fixed on the fighting anatomy model. Hyphen nodded, too engrossed to speak. As Volo's demonstration progressed, transforming into a full-fledged sparring match with his own creation, her mind filled with awe. These new students were in a different league. She wondered what their lucidity levels were.

As the fight reached its climax, two red blades shot out of Volo's wrists. With surgical precision, he severed the model's arms, one at the shoulder, and one just below. The professors gasped, but Volo wasn't finished. The now-armless figure shifted, its head tilting to the side, a knee shifting forward, and its skin transforming into what looked like white marble. The severed arms dissipated, and the model's stance adjusted. When it settled, Hyphen recognized the pose of an iconic sculpture.

"Life imitates art," Volo deadpanned.

There was some soft laughter in the room from those who enjoyed the reference, and the professors exchanged impressed glances. Hyphen found herself grinning as she took in the sculpture of the ancient goddess. On the big screen, the tall boy's mouth was agape with mirth, and he shook his head at both Volo and Pandora.

Professor Cogito spoke first, "The House of Reason would be honored to have you, Volo."

"As would the House of Blood," mused Professor Invidere, absently feeding an apple to Pandora's Pride.

"And *especially* the House of Bones," Professor String chimed with delight.

"Don't forget the House of Mirrors," Professor Bool's voice echoed, though he was still invisible.

Professor Esse stood up from the middle of the row, extending him a golden envelope. "It seems you have your pick, young man. But I believe the House of Legends would be the best fit for your diverse talents."

As she stepped forward, Hyphen realized that she rarely saw this professor on campus. While she was short, her hair towered upwards in a majestic ponytail, meandering through the air like an eel underwater. She was clad in a regal robe, which gave her the appearance of an ancient empress, and had a long, draconic tail spilling out of its folds. Like Cogito's, her hands were talons—and she wondered if, perhaps, they were related somehow.

Esse paused, her eyes boring into Volo. "The House of Legends is *unique*," her voice rang, clipped and brusque. We only invite those who are recommended by all *four* of my esteemed colleagues. It's a rare honor, reserved for students who demonstrate *exceptional* potential across multiple disciplines."

Volo bowed respectfully. "Thank you."

As Volo took the golden envelope, adding it to the stack of five he now held, Char leaned in close to Hyphen. "So *that's* how you get into House of Legends?" he whispered, his eyes wide. "No wonder they're known for being hardcore."

The big screens were locked on the stack of five envelopes in Volo's hands, and Hyphen noticed the gold insignia in full detail on the top: a serpentine Estrangement, woven around a staff in a cursive loop. Some believed it was the school of history, and others insisted it was the school of leadership.

Hyphen nodded, equally impressed. "I've always wondered about that house. You hardly ever see any of their students around."

Their chatter was once again severed by the sound of Professor Invidere's voice. "Thank you, Volo. Now, who's next?"

There was a moment of hesitation on stage. Then, the tawny-haired boy with bandages inched forward, his Voidpet still clinging to his shoulder for dear life. "Um, hello everyone, I'm Luden," he mumbled, his voice barely audible.

Hyphen leaned forward, curious about this quieter member of the group. As Luden approached the remaining void matter crystal, there was a palpable shift in the atmosphere. The confidence that had permeated the previous demonstrations seemed to evaporate.

He attempted to manipulate the void matter, but as soon as he touched it, it turned into green goo that glopped onto the floor of the stage.

A silence settled across the Amphitheater.

"Um..." Luden grimaced, his voice echoing across the huge auditorium, "That's kind of all I can do." He shuffled his feet, inadvertently spreading the goo further.

Hyphen swallowed, feeling second-hand anxiety for the boy on stage. She saw his bandaged hands trembling and wondered what had caused such an unusual ability.

Char leaned in close. "Well, that's... different," he snickered.

Before the silence could stretch too long, Professor String's voice cleared the air.

"The House of Bones welcomes all, my friend," the skeleton professor said. "There's potential in everyone's unique abilities, and I'd be honored to have a hand in your journey of self-discovery."

"Oh, uh, thank you m-mister, or madam, or, uh, I mean, uh, Professor," Luden stammered, almost falling off the stage as he grasped for the black envelope that floated his way.

Hyphen felt a wave of empathy for Luden, especially considering that he had to perform right after Volo. "I'm always inspired by how kind Professor String is," she whispered to Char. "I hope Luden will be happy in the House of Bones."

Char nodded, his earlier disdain softening slightly. "Yeah, I guess everyone's got their own thing. Even if it's just making goo."

As Luden retreated to stand with his peers, the green substance on the stage slowly returned to void matter, leaving behind a faint, shimmering residue. The other students shot encouraging smiles at Luden, their earlier confidence replaced by a show of unity.

Finally, the lanky boy in the leather jacket stepped forward, slinking forth with the demeanor of a fox. "My name's Promise."

Hyphen's heart raced, while Char frowned. Up close on screen, his ice blue eyes were impossible to ignore, and she recognized him as the boy who owned the Lonely from earlier. From his air of confidence, she was sure his demonstration would be fascinating.

"And I'd like to opt out of being tested," Promise said, his unusually tall figure leaning back with his thumbs tucked in his pockets.

Hyphen felt goosebumps as he spoke, and Anxious began to squirm in her arms. The auditorium fell silent, the professors exchanging glances of surprise.

"What a jerk," Char whispered harshly. "He thinks he's too good for the placement exam?"

Professor Cogito's mask betrayed no emotion, but his voice carried a hint of intrigue. "That's an unusual request, Promise. May I ask why?"

Promise's gaze met the eyes of the dragon mask, punctuating his words with a forward head tilt. "I don't like being evaluated."

Char scoffed from the back of the room. "Tch. Who does this guy think he is?"

Hyphen hushed him, her eyes fixed on the unfolding scene.

The professors huddled together, speaking in inaudible tones. After a moment, Professor Invidere spoke up. "Very well, Promise. If you choose not to demonstrate your abilities, we'll simply place you based on our initial impressions."

"Fine by me," Promise replied, his voice crisp.

Before Promise could respond, Volo stepped forward. "Professors, if I may," he said, his voice steady. "I'd like to offer him my spot in the House of Legends."

A wave of murmurs echoed through the auditorium. Even Char looked shocked.

"*Why* would you want to do *that*?" Professor Esse asked, clearly taken aback.

Volo's face remained neutral. "I've always wanted to be a doctor. The House of Bones would be a better fit for my goals. And I believe my brother would excel in the House of Legends."

Promise's cool facade cracked, surprise flickering across his face.

"Volo, are you sure?" Pandora asked, her voice filled with concern.

Volo nodded. "I am."

As Volo confirmed his suggestion, Hyphen noticed Professor Esse's posture stiffen. Her hair, which had been flowing serenely, now bristled like an agitated sea creature.

"*Volo,*" Professor Esse's already curt voice was now terse with indignation, "the House of Legends is *not* a gift to be passed on at will. It's an honor earned through demonstrated *excellence.*"

Hyphen watched as the professor's gaze shifted to Promise, her eyes narrowing as if seeing him for the first time. Promise met her stare, evaluating her back.

"*However,*" Professor Esse continued, her tone shifting subtly, "perhaps there's honor to be found in this unprecedented situation." Her tail swished behind her as she studied the two brothers.

"Volo," she nearly barked to address the younger boy, "Tell me why you *sacrifice* your acceptance to nominate Promise for the House of Legends."

Volo's voice remained stoic. "Because he is a legend. My brother pushes the boundaries of what's possible, even when it means standing alone. History remembers those who dare to be different, and that's how legends are made."

A quiet settled across the room as the professors contemplated Volo's words.

"Plus," Volo added, "Promise cares about going down in history more than I do."

To Hyphen's surprise, the empress professor laughed, a strong, melodious sound that filled the amphitheater. "How very intriguing,"

Esse declared, turning to her colleagues. "The House of Legends *does* thrive on challenging the status quo, does it not?"

The other professors nodded, as if none of them dared disagree.

"Very well," Professor Esse announced, her hawkish voice carrying a note of excitement. "Volo, I accept your nomination. Promise, you may join the House of Legends—if you accept, of course."

Promise looked at Volo for a long moment, something unspoken passing between them. Then he nodded. "I accept."

Hyphen felt goosebumps, sensing that she'd witnessed something unusual. Char turned to Hyphen, his expression aghast. "I can't believe this. That guy does nothing and gets the best spot? What a scam!"

Hyphen nodded thoughtfully. "It is strange. But Volo... that was really kind of him."

"Yeah, I guess," Char grudgingly admitted. "Still, something about this whole group just rubs me the wrong way. Like maybe that was a stunt they planned all along."

"Or maybe 'cause his brother would bully him if he didn't give it up," Char murmured, still ruminating.

Hyphen studied Char's face, noting the tension in his jaw and eyes. She wondered what could have cemented his distrust of these newcomers when her own heart had been set alight with joy.

As the placement test concluded, Hyphen felt enraptured. Of all the years she had been at the Institute, this was the most excited she'd been to meet the new students.

Chapter 9: Seeds of Doubt

Char was having a no good, very bad day.

He slouched in his seat, picking at his lunch as Hyphen chatted animatedly. She'd dragged him to eat with her usual group, insisting it'd be fun. *Fun*, he thought bitterly, *if you enjoyed being surrounded by weirdos with crazy hair and dopey Voidpets.*

As the others yapped, Char noted each student's vulnerabilities. Tilde, the redhead who now sported peachy locks, was clearly desperate for attention. Alt, the emo artist with the pink bob, seemed to crave validation. Meanwhile, Hyphen's need to please was as obvious as the turquoise eyesore that now colored her curls.

"Did you see Volo in VMM?" Tilde gesticulated wildly, "The way he changed his eye color was crazy!"

Alt's sullen eyes perked up as even Sad seemed to smile. "I know, right? And he signed up for practically every professor's class. Like, how can someone be so cool *and* so smart?"

Char fought the urge to roll his eyes. All they could talk about was Volo this, Volo that. It was absolutely nauseating.

"Volo reminds me of the lead actor on *Seven Layers of the Soul*," Tilde sighed dreamily. "Tall, dark, and mysterious."

Char clenched his fork. Mysterious? More like *suspicious*, he thought. But navigating school was like chess. He realized he had to be strategic about attacking his opponents, or risk compromising his own position.

He leaned in, his voice furtive. "Yeah, you know, it's always funny when people seem *too* perfect on the outside."

"What do you mean?" Hyphen lit up with curiosity.

Char ran his hands through his head of now royal blue hair, feigning nonchalance. "Well, it's just... don't you think it's a bit odd? I mean, we all work so hard, and then this guy shows up and seems perfect at everything."

He paused, letting the seed of doubt take root. "Makes you wonder, doesn't it?"

Tilde's brow furrowed. "Wonder what?"

"Oh, nothing really," Char said, waving his hand dismissively. "I'm probably just being paranoid." But he could see the curiosity in their eyes. He had them hooked.

"Wait, tell us," Alt pressed, leaning forward.

Char sighed, as if reluctant to share. "Well, it's just... we saw their placement test. And let's just say, things didn't seem entirely... fair."

Hyphen shot him a nervous glance, but he pressed on, his voice dropping to a whisper. "Honestly, guys, Volo might not be as independent as he seems. His family... well, they have a lot of influence."

He held his tongue to observe the table's reactions. As he watched Tilde and Alt's bewildered faces darken with skepticism, he realized it was now acceptable to proceed.

"What do you mean?" Hyphen asked, her voice hesitant.

Char leaned in closer, his eyes darting around as if checking for eavesdroppers. "Promise, Volo's brother? He basically *scammed* the whole placement test. And Volo... he just went along with it."

"Wait, what do you mean?" Hyphen asked, "I thought that it was really honorable and kind—"

"Hold up, you guys watched their *placement test* together?" Alt asked, a frown of judgement passing on his face, "Isn't that kind of—"

Tilde cut him off, her voice giddy with excitement, "Wait, you HAVE to tell me about Volo's placement test!"

Char looked at Hyphen and smirked.

"Hyphen, maybe you should catch your friends up on what we saw."

Hyphen fiddled with her hands and looked away, "Well," she said, clearing her throat, "I know I shouldn't have been there, and I feel really bad for watching something I wasn't supposed to—"

"TELL ME!" Tilde mouthed aggressively over a whisper, shaking her fists with excitement as Anger puffed in union.

"Volo's test was honestly amazing," she said softly, "he built this whole skeleton model and did battle with it on stage," her words trailed, "And he got an offer from *all five* of the professors, which was incredible! I've never seen anything like it before. But then Promise refused to take the test for some reason, and then Volo offered him his spot in the House of Legends..."

As Hyphen's story petered out, Char seized the opening, "I don't want to spread rumors," he said, "but it just seemed... off. Like they had an unfair advantage, you know?"

He looked around, "Like, imagine if one of *us* had refused a placement test, or turned down an invite like that? Haven't you three been studying here for years, working hard to get your house invitations?"

Tilde's eyes narrowed and she started to nod along.

"Isn't that a little strange? Almost like—" Char began.

"Like they *cheated* the system..." Tilde gasped, finishing his sentence.

He watched as the information sank in, carefully gauging each person's reaction. Now that Tilde was coming to her own conclusions, he'd successfully controlled the narrative. Alt scowled, offended by the idea of cheating. Tilde's grip on her wheelchair intensified, her competitive nature riled.

"But maybe I'm wrong," Char added quickly, playing the role of the reluctant whistleblower. "I mean, they seem nice enough. It's probably nothing."

"Well now that you mention it," Alt murmured, "it is a little unfair that the rest of us didn't have the option to share our invites and skip our exams."

Char grimaced, nodding in agreement. "I feel bad even bringing it up," he said, injecting a note of guilt into his voice. "They're probably just super talented. I'm sure there's a perfectly reasonable explanation." But he could see the damage was done. The seed of doubt had been planted, and it was starting to grow.

"No, no," Tilde said, her voice low. "If people are cheating the placement tests, that's a serious problem."

Alt nodded in agreement. "It's not fair to the rest of us who work hard and follow the rules."

"Should we say something to the administration?" Alt asked, clutching his face between his sleeves.

"We could, but..." Char's voice was thick was drama, "What if the *Institute* is in on it too?"

"Think about it," he said. "Do you think any of *those kids* are..."

He paused, lowering his voice to a hiss:

"On financial aid?"

The group's gaze drifted to the far window of the dining hall, where the new students sat together, clearly enjoying themselves. Pecunia's platinum blonde hair glinted in the sun, and she sat with her legs crossed in her stylish black dress. Volo smiled beside her in a preppy black vest, eating steak. Luden was giggling in a trendy linen button down, while Promise leaned back on his chair, sprawled out in an expensive leather jacket. Next to him, Pandora sat draped a luxurious pink peacoat, savoring a decadent array of desserts.

An uneasy silence fell over the table, and Char knew it was checkmate. His last words had slammed the nail in the coffin, sealing the opinion of the friend group. They each looked down at their plain clothing and simple lunches, painfully aware of their table in the shadows, next to the trash cans. Now that the others were convinced they were victims of injustice, the gossip started to roll freely off their tongues.

"So, how old do you think Pandora is?" Alt asked, frowning.

"Well, she looks *way* too old for high school," Tilde scoffed, crossing her arms.

"Maybe she got held back or something?" Hyphen speculated, an attempt to show empathy that only added fuel to the flames.

Char piled on. "Why even start high school if you're already a senior? It's just bizarre. Unless..."

"Unless what?" Alt prompted, leaning in.

"Unless she's here for some *other* reason," Char said cryptically. "I mean, think about it. What if they're not here to learn at all?"

"And what about Promise?" Tilde asked, her voice tinged with newfound suspicion, "That guy just seems fishy to me."

"Promise can't even *do* anything. All he knows how to do is use other people," Char's voice grew sharp with contempt, "You should see the way he treats his own Lonely. He uses it as a car, doesn't feed it all day, and then orders it around. That can't possibly be humane, right?"

Alt shook his head, his frown deepening. "That's messed up. If that's true, someone should report him."

Anger growled in Tilde's lap. The implication of Voidpet abuse hit a nerve with them both. Tilde began to redden with rage as her mind fixated on the subject.

"Luden seems pretty sweet, though?" Hyphen suggested, trying to deescalate the animosity despite her own growing frustration.

It was then Char realized he had a gift for gossip. As soon as he saw how it easy it was to align his own frustration with the group's personal pain points, he could fuel the flames to his heart's content. Now that everyone was on his side, his no-good day was starting to look fantastic.

"Luden just oozes goo," said Char, "And I'll bet he's the group lackey. Seems like he's just tagging along to suck up." He looked Tilde in the eye, "he looks like someone who cares more about fitting in than standing up for what's right."

Then, for Tilde's pet, he added, "Seems like Luden would be complicit in abuse if it meant he got to ride in a sports car."

The little Voidpet puffed up, its red scarf expanding as it let out a guttural snarl.

Alt's face hardened. "You're right. They're all part of the same system. We can't trust any of them."

"And I HATE the idea of doing NOTHING about it!" Tilde's voice escalated in a sharp crescendo, her fists pounding the table as they glowed with pink void matter.

Char sat back, watching the seeds of doubt blossom into full-blown resentment. He had transformed their admiration into anger, and all it took was a few well-placed words.

Tilde's face was feral, her knuckles white as she gripped her wheelchair. "You know what? We can't just sit here and let them get away with this." She raised her voice so that she was practically yelling, "ESPECIALLY not the Voidpet abuse!"

"What are you thinking?" Alt asked, suddenly concerned.

Tilde's eyes blazed like wildfire. "I'm going to FIGHT Promise," she exclaimed with a pound of her fist, "TODAY. Someone needs to stand up for his poor Voidpet."

Char's eyes bugged out, not having anticipated this level of reaction. "Whoa, wait, are you sure that's a good idea?"

"He's got no powers, right? How hard can it be?" She snapped, already turning herself away from the table.

"Well not that I know of, but..." Char faltered.

Tilde was already wheeling herself away. "Meet me behind the school after class," she barked to her friend group, "I'm challenging this guy to a DUEL."

As Tilde left, the group exchanged nervous glances. Char wasn't sure if duels were normal at the Institute, so he held his tongue.

Hyphen bit her lip. "Maybe we should try to stop her?"

Alt shook his head, already defeated. "You know how Tilde gets when she's angry. Once she's made up her mind, there's no changing it."

Hyphen nodded. "We should at least be there to support her and make sure she's safe."

As they agreed to meet after class, Char felt a rush of adrenaline. He hadn't meant for things to go this far, but now that they had, he was eager for the drama to unfold. The others hurried off to class, leaving Char to linger behind, lost in thought. He felt a new sense of power in his hands—a newfound ability to position the board—and a strange power emanating beside him.

Char turned to look at his Voidpet and saw that Envy had changed dramatically. No longer the small, worm-like creature it once was, it now resembled a ghostly raptor, almost half his size. Its body was sleek and tapered, complete with a pointed snout. Most striking were its new claws—disproportionately large for its body, each adorned with a triangular eye, each ending in two points of polished obsidian.

"Well, would you look at that," Char mused, "Seems like we've both leveled up today, Checkers." Envy let out a small puff of smoke, its pointed eyes glinting with the same mischievous light Char felt inside. As he headed to his next class with his evolved Voidpet by his side, Char grinned.

It finally felt like he was gaining control over the game.

Chapter 10: Pandora's Ice Cream

Pandora was pumped about her week of school. The dining hall buzzed with energy, and she glowed with anticipation over her action-packed schedule. She'd already volunteered as teaching assistant for Professor Cogito, started tutoring underclassmen, and was brainstorming more ways to get involved on campus.

She sat by the window where her group had congregated for lunch. Unimpressed by the dining hall offerings, the team had crafted their own feast from void matter: Volo had produced some dry-aged ribeye steaks, while Pandora had conjured a box of colorful macarons.

As they enjoyed their meal, a commotion caught her attention. A pink-haired girl rolled up to their table in a wheelchair, her face flushed.

"I CHALLENGE YOU TO A DUEL," she shouted, pointing directly at Promise, her eyes blazing.

Promise raised an eyebrow, his mouth full of steak.

"Meet me in the back garden after school, you TRASHBAG!" the girl roared, before wheeling away dramatically.

"Mmkay?" Promise mumbled through his mouthful, only slightly bewildered.

Pandora blinked, confused by the sudden interruption. Was this a normal occurrence at the Institute? Perhaps it was customary to challenge other students to sparring matches? She couldn't tell if her insult was just some playful Institute slang.

"Well, that's exciting," said Pandora. "It'll be nice to have some self-defense practice now that we're in school."

"We'll be there to back you up if things get out of hand, right everyone?" Pandora looked at Luden and her younger siblings, "But make sure you hold back if she's weaker than you."

Promise nodded.

While her siblings were ruthless Nightmare slayers, they had never battled other humans before. The issue of holding back had never come up, and she was struck with the worry that this duel might take a dangerous turn.

"You know how to fight... not to... *kill*, right?" Pandora asked her brother, the words feeling awkward on her tongue. She'd never had to make this distinction before.

"Well, there's a first time for everything, right?" Promise grinned at her, his teeth flashing as he reached for a pastry.

Luden shifted awkwardly in his seat, his mouth full of steak, "Uh... do you think maybe we should just call off this whole duel thing then? I feel like there's a big chance of someone getting hurt."

"Does Promise even *have* defensive moves?" Pecunia wondered out loud between bites of her raspberry macaron, "Vo knows marital arts, Pan's got metal armor, but Prom—"

She counted her fingers: "He's got fire, razor wire, that black water thing..."

"He can also teleport and turn corpses into cash," Volo offered.

"Maybe you can do a black water *splash* instead of a blade?" Luden suggested.

"His black water is laced with petroleum," Pandora sighed, "it's flammable and toxic."

Luden looked bewildered, as if he hadn't known that all these years.

"Can you... make it regular water instead?" he offered.

"He can't," the others said in unison.

"Ooh, what if you just keep teleporting out of the way until you wear her out?"

"He'll die."

The four looked at each other, lost for options, as Promise munched on his pastry.

"Promise I think you need to pull out of this duel," Pandora concluded, "I'm not seeing a safe strategy for you to win."

"Naw, come on," he protested, making a face, "you can't make me look like a chicken on the first day of school,"

"We also can't let you murder someone on the first day of school," Pandora countered.

Promise pouted with puppy dog eyes, to which Pandora scoffed.

"Explain how you'll make sure your opponent doesn't get hurt."

"Oh, come on, I can't believe you guys think I would physically injure another student," Promise drawled, wiping his crumbs on a napkin, "At most, I would do some light psychological damage."

At this, Luden looked concerned, unsure if he was serious or joking.

"And your plan for that is...?" Pandora remained dubious.

"I mean it's kind of an in-the-moment thing, you can't really plan for it," Promise replied with a shrug, popping the last macaron into his mouth, "I was just gonna show up and wing it."

And with that, the conversation about the duel was over.

Pandora looked around to see that most of the dining hall had emptied out. Luden and Pecunia stood up to go to class, and Volo headed to the gym for a midday workout. Now that she was alone with Promise, she figured it was a good time to discuss her plans to improve the Institute.

She organized their trash into the now empty pastry box and conjured a pot of tea to split with her brother, the mood changing.

"So," Pandora began, pouring two cups of jasmine tea before continuing, "I was thinking about the limited options in the dining hall. I think there's a real opportunity here for a side business."

Promise nodded, used to Pandora's constant stream of plans. "Mmm," he hummed in agreement, sipping his tea, "Captive market, limited competition. I like where this is going."

"Exactly," Pandora grinned, her hand balling into a fist, "And I was going to talk to Professor Cogito about setting up a booth to sell snacks. There's quite a lack of diverse food options here, and I think the student body could really benefit from having a wider selection."

"What d'you wanna sell?" Promise asked her. He leaned to the side with his elbow propped on the table.

"I'm thinking we start small, ideally something delightful and cheap," she ventured, "potentially popsicles, or maybe ice cream?"

Promise leaned back, considering. "Ice cream could work. Low overhead, high margins. Plus, who doesn't love ice cream?"

"My thoughts exactly," Pandora said, her eyes lighting up. "And we could use void matter to create some really unique flavors, don't you think?"

As they continued to discuss flavor ideas and profit margins, the upcoming duel seemed like a distant event. Their conversation flowed seamlessly from ice cream flavors to distribution logistics, then to potential expansion plans, without a single mention of the challenge that had interrupted their lunch. "You know," Promise said, inhaling the steam of his tea, "if the ice cream booth takes off, we could look into automating it. Or paying other people to run it." He scrunched his nose in a speculative expression as he gestured with his hand.

"I do love the way you think," Pandora nodded, "We could revolutionize student life here with these little projects. Speaking of which, I have a meeting with Professor Cogito later about some independent study ideas. I'll float the ice cream concept by him then."

"Perfect," Promise said, "Let's get started this afternoon."

"Don't you have a duel with someone?"

"Oh, yeah, we'll get started right after that."

Chapter 11: Afternoon Duel

Tilde could hear her pulse pounding in her ears all afternoon as she readied herself to face her new enemy. She didn't care how scary he was, whether he was bigger than her, older than her, or anything at all—all she knew was that he was mistreating his Voidpet, and if she and Anger didn't stand up for the poor creature, then perhaps, nobody would.

She found herself gripping her Voidpet close as she fought to ground herself with its warmth. Anger mirrored her rage and breathed little licks of flame from its nostrils, its little red scarf swelling with each labored breath.

Tilde wheeled herself to the back garden, her heart racing with righteous fury. The sun drenched the manicured lawn in gold, and a breeze rustled through the leaves. All would have been peaceful if not for the storm brewing her heart.

As she positioned herself in the center of the garden, Tilde ran through her plan one last time. She'd challenge Promise to a fair fight, force him to admit his mistreatment of his Voidpet, and make him agree to do better. Simple, right?

Minutes ticked by. Tilde's knuckles paled as she gripped the arms of her wheelchair. "Where is he?" she muttered, scanning the garden entrance.

Anger, sensing her impatience, grew larger on her lap. Its red scarf billowed like a battle flag, tiny embers dancing in the air around it.

"It's okay, buddy," Tilde whispered, stroking Anger's head. "We're doing the right thing. Someone's gotta stand up for the little guys."

As time stretched on, doubt began to creep in.

What if Promise didn't show up?

What if he did, but brought his whole crew?

Well, she was doing that too, but, what if…

Tilde shook her head. No, she had to stay focused. This was about justice, about protecting those who couldn't protect themselves. She thought of Promise's Lonely, imagining it starving and neglected, and felt her resolve strengthen.

"If he doesn't show up," she said to Anger, her voice low and determined, "we'll just have to find another way to help. We won't let him get away with this."

Just then, she heard slow footsteps approaching in the gravel. Tilde straightened in her chair, chin lifted defiantly. Anger puffed to the size of a small dog, flames licking at its mouth.

"Ready or not," Tilde murmured, "here we go."

As Promise emerged from the arched gateway, Tilde felt a surge of adrenaline. This was it. No backing down now. Whatever happened next, she was going to make sure Promise understood that mistreating Voidpets—or anyone—wasn't going to fly at the Institute. Not on her watch.

"Hey there, sweetheart," Promise called out, a callous smirk playing on his lips. "Ready for our little playdate?"

Tilde felt her stomach churn. She hated people who tried to get in her head, and this guy was perhaps the worst of the sort.

His chilling stare consumed her, and a lopsided smile twisted across his face. "So how do you want it today?" He cracked his knuckles and positioning his fingers in a mocking battle stance. "Quick and easy, or slow and satisfying?"

He seemed to be enjoying himself, which Tilde found sickening.

Oh, it was on.

Before Tilde could charge forth, she froze, seeing Promise's whole entourage line up behind him. His two sisters, his brother Volo, and the Luden boy with the goo, followed by a zoo of exotic Voidpets she had never seen before. And a little Lonely. All four teenagers were physically formidable in different ways, taller and brawnier than everyone in her friend group. The kids and pets crossed their arms, sizing up Tilde and Anger with poker-faced intensity.

Ugh. Of course, his crew was on time, and hers was late. Where was her friend group? Alt, she understood was always late, but what about Hyphen and Char?

"WAIT until my friends get here," Tilde ordered, a bead of sweat forming at her brow, "Otherwise it's NOT FAIR."

"Sure," Promise shrugged. He tucked his hands into his pockets and started to tap his foot, "The more the merrier, right?"

Tilde nodded with a grunt. As they faced off in silence, the afternoon breeze tousled her hair. Her eyes followed the Institute's spires up into the pastel sky, the pleasant afternoon almost insulting her. She didn't expect her first duel to begin this way, but at the very least, she expected her friends to have her back.

"I just... hope they're not *too* late," Promise quipped, sliding his sleeve back to reveal an obnoxious gold watch, "I've kind of got places to be."

Clouds rolled overhead, cooling the garden in a lull of shade. Tilde's heart thumped as the sun hid behind a wash of gray, and Anger squirmed in her lap.

At last, a flurry of footsteps broke the silence.

"Oh my goodness Tilde, I'm so sorry, I'm a terrible friend!!" She heard Hyphen cry, as she sprinted out into the garden, "I lost track of time at the library, I hope I'm not too late for the duel!!"

Char strolled in behind her with a guilty look on his face. "Hey," he waved, not quite meeting her eyes.

Finally, Alt stumbled in with Sad on his head, looking as if he'd just woken up from a nap, "So sorry I'm late, Tilde!" he gushed, stifling a yawn.

"You're all right on time!" Tilde grinned at her friends and felt the sun shine brighter.

While Tilde's group looked like a ragtag team of schoolchildren in mismatched clothing, she felt strength upon seeing them line up at her back. She loved her friends. She knew they wouldn't have left her alone.

Tilde turned back to Promise and launched a finger towards him with newfound gusto. "Alright, now first things first, FEED your Lonely!" She demanded, her eyes burning.

Promise's eyes narrowed, but he seemed to oblige.

"Yes ma'am," he said, walking over to his Voidpet and conjuring a tin can from his hands. He opened it to reveal a bed of dark granules, placing it on the ground in front of the pet. To Tilde's horror, the poor Lonely began to chow on the black goo balls, licking its way through globs of what looked like some fishy excrement.

He looked down at the hapless creature with what could only be a sadistic smile, watching it gobble the muck in a starved frenzy.

Char was right. Promise was feeding his pet filth, and worse, he liked watching it.

Tilde gasped, indignant. "Stop RIGHT there!" she yelled, her face turning as pink as her hair.

Promise looked up, confused. "Huh?"

"That's DISGUSTING. How DARE you?" Tilde shouted, her voice cracking with indignation.

As her fury reached its peak, she lifted Anger and hurled it at Promise's feet. The fiery Voidpet barreled into Promise, who jumped back, bewildered.

"What the—?" Promise muttered, dodging Anger's snapping jaws as the Voidpet rolled around on its belly. It squirmed out of control in its quest to chomp down on his legs.

"This DUEL is to put an end to your rampant Voidpet abuse!" Tilde raged, her wheelchair scooting forward menacingly.

Before further discussion could take place, the duel was on.

"I'LL FIGHT YOU TO THE DEATH IF THAT'S WHAT IT TAKES!" Tilde bellowed. As the momentum of her chair carried her forth, she grabbed two handfuls of void matter from her dress pockets, summoning a pink ball of flame in each hand.

"RAHHHHH," Tilde roared, hurtling herself towards her rival.

"YO," Promise grabbed Lonely out of the way before blinking them both to the other side of the garden.

"Maybe watch where you're going then..." he snapped, his casual demeanor now bristling with annoyance. Black smoke trailed from the seams of his jacket.

With no one to collide with, Tilde rolled straight over a rock, depositing herself straight onto the grass. As she made contact with the lawn, a pouch of void matter slipped from her dress pocket, spilling a small pile of blue crystals.

While the dust settled from the first attack, the peanut gallery began to murmur. Tilde wondered how Promise managed to escape her steamroll technique, and it began to dawn on her that he must have teleported himself. That was a forbidden technique that only Professor Bool had mastered, and one that was rumored to be impossible. To even attempt to teleport for the first time, one not only had to be ready to face death, but...

"Wait, are you carrying void matter in a *bag*?" Promise asked, interrupting her train of thought.

"WHERE ELSE WOULD I PUT IT? HUH?" Tilde shouted back, "MAYBE I SHOULD PUT IT UP YOUR—"

Before she could finish, Pandora cut her off, suddenly standing in front of her. "If you keep your void matter in a bag, it can't interact with your body's natural energy field and accrue interest over time," she explained, attempting to help Tilde back to her chair.

Tilde had no idea what that meant and was not happy with Promise's sister interfering to patronize her. "I don't need your pity help in MY duel..." she snarled at Pandora, "Now BE QUIET and get out the way!"

Pandora stepped back respectfully, before Tilde, still fuming, summoned another ball of matter from the ground.

"I won't sit by while you use your pets like TOOLS, feed them TRASH, and think you're so cool and clever for mocking the helpless!"

She hurled the half-formed fireball at Promise, who somehow caught it in the gravitational field of his own hand. As he absorbed it into his palm in a crackle of black, his gaze fell on her with a look of exasperation. "Look, I get it. You care about Voidpets. That's admirable."

Tilde, breathing heavily, paused her attack. "What?"

Promise blinked, as if unsure where to begin. He looked at the can of food in front of Lonely, then back at Tilde.

"Have you never seen... *sturgeon caviar?*"

Tilde faltered for a moment, then narrowed her eyes. "Well, no, I've never heard of that..."

"Well." He looked at her like she had never heard of sliced bread, "It's Lulu's favorite."

Promise raised an eyebrow, now eyeing Anger with amusement. "What are *you* feeding your pet?" he asked.

Tilde puffed out her chest proudly. "I feed him fresh rice, three times a day!"

Promise choked, stifling a laugh. "You *only* feed your pet *carbs*?"

"They're full of energy!" Tilde protested.

"And your only move is throwing your pet at someone," Promise's voice dripped with sarcasm. "If that's not abusive... I don't know what is."

Tilde's jaw dropped. "I... but... you..."

Her friends exchanged uncomfortable glances. Char face palmed.

Alt, still half-asleep, mumbled, "Can someone explain what's happening?"

Promise's siblings were trying to contain their laughter, but Pecunia collapsed onto the grass, clearly unable to. The goo boy covered his face in second-hand embarrassment, and Pandora masked a chuckle with a sugar-coated smile, "I think there's simply been a misunderstanding here?"

Tilde, her face now matching her hair color for entirely different reasons, slumped in her wheelchair. "I... I just wanted to help," she mumbled.

Promise's expression softened. "Hey, look, your heart was in the right place, and that's what matters. How about we start over?"

"What's your name?" he asked, walking up to where she sat.

"Tilde," she mustered, her face still feeling flush.

"Tilde," he looked at her slowly and lowered his voice, "I think it's pretty *bad* that you were game to duel me to the death." As he spoke, it dawned on Tilde that 'bad' meant 'cool'.

"You're a real tough warrior. You've got a heart of gold, and I hope I'll never have to face you in battle again." He turned away, and Tilde wasn't sure if he winked at her or just had something in his eye. Either way, she felt warm as his compliment sank in.

As Promise scooped up his Lonely and headed back inside, his group followed, leaving Tilde alone with her friend group.

They rushed over to comfort her. Hyphen gave her a big hug applauding her bravery, and Alt came to ask how she was feeling. Char stood to the side, his eyes downcast.

It was then that Tilde wondered if her anger should have been directed at someone else.

Chapter 12: Time to Build

As the convertible departed from the Institute, Promise stared ahead with one hand on the wheel.

"Pandora, I can't," he said. "I can't go back there."

Pandora shot him a look from the passenger seat. "You can't *drop out* on the first week of school."

"Watch me," Promise retorted, his hand steadfast on the wheel.

"We paid full tuition for the entire year," Pandora's voice rose. "You at least have to give it a chance."

"Nope."

Pandora took a deep breath. "At least until you learn something."

Promise scoffed. "I've learned everything I need to know."

"Don't forget why we came here," Pandora said, her tone softening. "Just because one student was a little misguided doesn't mean there's nothing to learn at the Institute."

"How can the school be good if that's how *any* of its students turn out?" Promise continued to stare at the road with dead eyes. "And besides. I just don't care about the parents thing anymore. It's been five years already. Every time I try to think about them, my mind goes blank."

"It's boring to think about them. Like, they're literally dead."

"What if they're not?" said Pandora.

"Well, we have our *own* goals now that don't involve them," Promise drawled. "We're going to rebuild our old house and rebuild the Void."

From the back seat, Luden's eyes widened. "The whole... Void?"

Promise grinned, his eyes still dull. "Yeah, why not? This place is all we have, might as well make it nice. How hard can it be?"

As they drove off the floating road, the first street they touched down on was Something Park South, just five minutes from campus. The afternoon wind whipped their hair, heralding their entrance with a chorus of rustling leaves. They reminisced at the wide street they once lived on, one side lined by trees, and the other by neat rows of limestone.

Pecunia looked out the side of the car. "Funny to think if we still lived in our old apartment, we'd be home right now," she sighed, "Our new hideout is so far away."

Promise eased off the gas as he looked wistfully at his old neighborhood, "True."

Without warning, he braked and swerved up to the curb, swinging the vehicle to a stop in front of 212 Something Park South. The view was just as surreal as they had remembered: a majestic apartment building reduced to rubble, with cracks spreading throughout the surrounding city block. Without enough humans to care about the aftermath, the site looked just as it did since the incident years ago, their beautiful limestone home now resembling an ancient ruin.

"You know, they used to call this street Billionaire's Row, back in the old days," Promise stepped out of the car. "I've always found that quite enchanting."

"So, let's move back," he looked at the group. "Pandora, you're good with metal, right?"

Pandora stepped out, her pride getting the best of her. "Yeah, you could say so," she couldn't help but smirk.

"Alright then," Red void matter began to crackle around Promise's hands as Greed perched on his shoulder. "Volo, are there any humans inside these buildings?"

Volo sniffed the air. "No."

What followed was chaos. Promise summoned a ball of matter at his fingertips, and the others looked on, their eyes gleaming with red light.

"Everyone stand back for a sec, I'm gonna clean up this mess," he warned, before unleashing a screaming red beam right into the foundation of the old building.

The air seemed to warp around the beam as it lanced toward the ruins. It pulsed through the air like a freight train, emanating shockwaves from where they stood. Upon impact, there was a moment of silence before havoc erupted. The beam tore through concrete and steel like tissue paper. Windows shattered in a cascade of shards. Stone disintegrated. The roar of collapsing structures filled the air, punctuated by the screech of twisting metal.

Clouds of dust billowed outward, shrouding the street in haze. The ground trembled as the ruins pancaked down to rubble. As the teenagers shielded their faces from the blast, their hair lashing backwards in the hot hair full of debris, the dilapidated limestone crumbled into the epicenter.

A surreal scene emerged from the settling dust. Where a chunk of city block once stood, there was now a vast crater. Twisted remnants of steel beams jutted out like skeletal fingers. Piles of debris smoldered at the edges.

"Damn, wish I could have done THAT during the duel," Promise whooped over the demolition, his earlier boredom vanished as the last of the beam fizzled out. His left hand was poised like a pistol, and he shook the smoke from his fingers.

The crew watched, mesmerized by the residual mayhem. While no one was surprised by his behavior, this blast was the most devastating they'd seen to date. Volo noted that it had to have cost at least ten times more than the one from the Nightmare attack five years ago and was held with enough sustained control to vaporize millions of cubic feet of stone and steel.

"Bruh," Volo remarked matter-of-factly.

"That was *so* extra," said Pecunia, rubbing her eyes.

Luden was speechless, and Pandora let down the shield of void matter that she had reflexively conjured around the group.

"A bit more of a warning would have been nice," she grumbled, though she noted that her brother had indeed communicated his intentions.

As the dust settled and the last of the crumbling subsided, Promise turned to Pandora. He gestured towards the crater and yelled, his voice raised to compensate for the ringing in everyone's ears, "So you can make a metal structure here, right?"

Pandora blinked, still processing what she'd just witnessed. "What? Me? With my bare hands?"

"Yeah."

Pandora shook her head, disbelief written across her face.

"Two thousand twenty feet tall—that's a nice number, right? Full glass windows, big steel beams," Promise cried, "I gave you plenty of space!"

Pandora's jaw dropped. "I can't build a two-thousand-foot-tall skyscraper *by myself*!"

Promise waved dismissively. "We'll get a team to help you. Just do it one floor at a time. I mean, if people did it in the old days without VM, how bad can it be?"

Luden glanced around as he began to recognize this pattern of the older two bickering. It tended to be over things that should have been impossible, yet they'd mutually convince each other to do something ludicrous.

"Did you even pay attention in architectural design?" Pandora snapped. "You can't just slap in steel beams randomly as you go."

"Well, *you* paid attention, didn't you?" Promise rolled his eyes. "Or did you space out so much you can't even remember how to build a basic tower?"

"No, *of course not*, I aced that subject and remember everything!" Pandora insisted, taking the bait, "I just can't—"

"You can defy gravity and shoot laser beams from your eyes. What's the issue?"

"I don't have the time!" Pandora exploded, "I literally just enrolled in *school*. I'm not going to drop out to manage a construction site for you. We both have better things to do than move rocks!"

"What could be more important than rebuilding the world we live in?" Promise's eyes blazed. "Just come do it after school," he insisted. "I mean, if you're not going to do it, then *I* will."

Pandora pinched the bridge of her nose. "Oh, no, *no*, you're going to do it all wrong and it won't be structurally sound..."

"Oh, *goodness*, no!" he said, feigning despair, "Maybe you'll just have to *help me* with that then—"

"I'm down to help after school," said Volo.

Promise and Pandora paused, as Volo's engagement tended to mean that a plan had passed its ideation phase.

Pecunia shrugged. "I mean, I'm not going to play builder, but I can help recruit."

Luden shuffled his feet. "Um, I'd love to help too, but I don't know what I can do."

"Oh, don't worry," said Promise, "I have plenty of things in mind."

He then looked at each of them in turn, his tone syrup as his eyes sparkled with adoration, "You know I'd be totally screwed without you guys, right?"

"Tch, you sure got that right," Pandora scoffed. She squared her hands on her hips and rolled up her sleeves.

Chapter 13: Elderberry Tea

Hyphen's fingers twisted in her lap as she sat in the common room, the plush armchair doing little to ease her discomfort. The sound of thunder boomed outside, and Hyphen shuddered. To ground herself, she tried to focus on the soft glow of floating lamps, the faint scent of old books and brewing tea. Anxious quivered.

Across from her, Tilde's wheelchair was locked in place, her face set in a frown. Alt perched on the edge of his seat, his eyes darting between his two friends.

"Hyphen, I hate to say this, but I think Char's a toxic friend," Tilde broke the quiet. "You might want to stop hanging out with him."

Hyphen's stomach dropped. She'd known this conversation was coming, but hearing the words out loud made it all too real.

"He snooped, he gossiped, *and* he manipulated us into getting upset at people we don't even know," Tilde's voice rose with each accusation, "And I don't think we should invite him to our lunch table anymore."

"Yeah, I guess, I see your point..." Hyphen found herself shrinking back into her chair. "Just... also—it's pretty fair to be curious as a new student, right?" she ventured weakly, "He opened up to us about his feelings and what he saw. It was on us to think critically about what he shared."

Tilde frowned, her face reddening at the indirect accusation.

Hyphen began to wonder whose side she was on. She knew Tilde was quick to place blame when she got angry, and though her frustrations were always understandable, they were sometimes misdirected.

"Tilde, we haven't made any new friends in years..." Hyphen said, "And it feels wrong to judge someone we just met. You have to remember that Char's new here, he had to work really hard to get into the Institute, and he was just telling us how he felt."

"Yeah, but he tricked me," Tilde's face scrunched.

Hyphen took a deep breath and replayed the conversation in her mind. Sure, Char had a cynical take on what he observed, but he never lied.

"Tilde, it was..." Hyphen swallowed, unsure how she felt about the words that were about to come out of her mouth, "It was... your own decision to fight Promise."

Her words hung like a dead weight in the room, leaving Tilde and Alt both shifting in their seats.

"It's not your fault that the duel didn't go as planned, but..." Hyphen breathed to slow her racing heartbeat, "it wasn't Char who started the fight."

Tilde scowled, her voice rising as she tried to defend herself, "Hyphen, I know you want to be nice to everyone, but some people are just bad news. Sometimes you need to protect yourself so they don't get to your head."

Hyphen suddenly realized that Tilde's words sounded a lot like what Char said about the Windfalls. Unfortunately, she was even more skeptical of Tilde's reasoning, as it masked her refusal to take accountability for her own actions.

"Tilde, I really understand how frustrated you must be feeling about the mix up," Hyphen said, trying to empathize, "You're justified for feeling upset about a big misunderstanding—"

"Yeah, and it was Char who MADE me upset! So PLEASE, just stop talking to him, okay?" Tilde urged, her cheeks flush with what Hyphen wondered was embarrassment.

Hyphen felt a coldness settle in her shoulders. She'd really enjoyed studying with Char. He was ambitious, sharp, and the best study buddy she had ever had. Perhaps Tilde was jealous that she had made a new friend? Or maybe she resented him taking advanced classes she couldn't get into?

"I'm allowed to have other friends…" she said softly, as the conversation took on a darker mood.

Alt looked tormented in his chair, and finally intervened.

"Hey, can we take a step back? I don't think it makes sense to turn against each other over this," he moved Sad to the carpet as he stood up.

"I think we've just all been on edge since that new group showed up," Alt shuffled across the room to fetch the elderberry tea that had just finished brewing.

"Char had a real point about Promise. Sure, he wasn't outright abusing his pet, but he didn't seem like the nicest guy either. Honestly, he and his whole crew were laughing at us," he said, arranging three teacups for everyone in the group.

"And his comment about carbs kind of gaslit you," Alt offered, pouring tea into Tilde's cup.

Tilde's jaw dropped, enlightened.

"It's normal that we can only afford rice as students, I don't know anyone else who feeds their pet what he does," Alt continued, "He made you feel embarrassed for trying to stand up for what was right, and then left you doubtful of your own ability to care for your pet."

Tilde nodded, her composure returning with her dignity.

Alt sat down and frowned, taking a sip of tea, "And then he acted all chummy at the end, which ended up turning you against your friends."

The tension in the room began to lift as Hyphen and Tilde looked at each other, both apologetic. The soothing scent of elderberry relaxed them.

"I don't think we can blame Char for what happened. He's one of us, and I say we give him a second chance," Alt concluded. "All he did was express concern about something he thought was unfair. And I think we'll all start feeling better if we just stay away from that new group."

Hyphen felt a sense of relief as she realized the conflict was coming to an end. She was glad she wasn't the only one who saw the good in Char. She took a sip of her tea, letting its warmth calm her nerves.

"I'm sorry guys," Tilde said, lowering her head, "I overreacted again. It was wrong of me to blame Char," she took a long sip of tea and closed her eyes, exhausted as rage left her body.

"It's okay," Hyphen smiled, placing a hand on her Tilde's, "Your feelings are valid and I'm glad we could talk things out."

As the solemnity dissipated, Tilde straightened up in her wheelchair, a spark returning to her eyes. "I may have jumped the gun, but at least I'm not a CHICKEN, right?"

Alt nodded, a smile spreading across his face. "That's true. Not many people have the guts to duel a stranger on the first week of high school!"

"Especially a tall upperclassman guy like that," Hyphen added, giggling, "You really went all in!"

Tilde beamed, her earlier embarrassment fading. "Size doesn't matter when you've got a hot head and SICK MOVES," She did a little dance for emphasis. As she moved, sparks danced around her fingers, and Anger puffed up, its scarf glowing brighter than usual.

Alt noticed the sparks. "Hey Tilde, is it just me or are your powers getting stronger?"

Tilde looked at her hands in surprise, watching as the sparks danced between her fingers. "Huh, I guess they are. It's like... the more pumped up I get, the stronger they become."

Suddenly, Anger began to glow in her lap, its inky form morphing. The others watched in awe as it transformed into a Stage 2 Voidpet— now resembling a rotund crocodilian with one pair of grabby claws. Its red scarf remained bundled around its neck, and a new pair of eyes opened on its tail.

"Whoa, no way!" Alt exclaimed, leaning forward. "Tilde, your Anger just evolved!"

Tilde looked at her Voidpet in surprise, watching as it waved its new hands and snapped its powerful jaws. "That's... incredible! I guess all that excitement really fired us up, huh Angy?"

In response, Anger let out a small puff of flame, causing everyone to jump back slightly.

"Seriously though," Alt said, leaning forward, "you're mega brave. You saw something you thought was wrong and you didn't hesitate to act. No wonder you're leveling up!"

Hyphen nodded enthusiastically. "Yeah, you've got main character energy for sure!"

"Maaaybe I'll fact-check next time before charging into battle..." said Tilde, "But DON'T count on it!"

The three friends giggled together, enjoying their tea and the warmth of the common room.

Things felt normal again, and Hyphen was happy.

Chapter 14: Seven Layers

Pandora found Cogito's library to be a thing of beauty.

Morning light filtered through the stained-glass windows, bathing the pearlescent room in a gloss of little rainbows. Small Voidpets were everywhere—she recognized Curious, Wonder, Judgement, and Sanctimony. Pandora thought of the extinct animals each Voidpet resembled: cats, butterflies, birds, and lizards—and romanticized the scene to resemble a living garden from ancient times. Strings of ivy laced the white shelves and draped the staircases that spiraled up the corners of the tower. The library had seven floors, but an open space ran through the center, all the way up to a glass skylight.

Pandora wandered up the first flight of stairs, Pride prowling up the steps behind her. She wondered if this place held the answers to all her questions. She'd been living under a rock for the past 18 years, knowing nothing beyond the world of her mother's homeschooling and the vagabond adventure that followed.

Being the overachiever she was, Pandora expected to be the only student in the library this early in the morning—so her eyes perked with surprise when she saw another human on the third floor. It was a tiny girl in pink dress. Between her mane of curls and stack of books, her face was barely visible.

She recognized the girl from yesterday's duel. It was Tilde's friend—the one who held a teensy Anxious in a hair bow. At the sound of Pandora's footsteps, she looked up from her papers like a deer in headlights. Likely, she also expected to have the library to herself at this hour.

Pandora smiled and did a little wave. It was prudent to make friends whenever she had the chance.

"Hi," she said softly, not wanting to disturb the hush of the library, "I'm Pandora! I remember you from yesterday!"

The girl covered her paper with her hands and tried to soothe her shaking Anxious. "I-I-I'm Hyphen," she whispered, "I remember you too."

Pandora debated leaving Hyphen to study in peace or seizing the opportunity to befriend her. She chose the latter.

"Nice to meet you, Hyphen! What class are you studying for?" Pandora scanned the titles of the books on her desk, noting that they were all philosophy works she was already familiar with. "Is this one of Professor Cogito's assignments?"

"Yeah, how'd you know?" the small girl replied, a smile breaking out on her face. Her Anxious stopped shivering.

"He's my professor too, and I recognize the books you're reading," said Pandora, extending the warmest smile she could. "May I?" She asked, pulling out the chair across from Hyphen.

Hyphen's face froze, and Anxious began to shiver again. "Actually," she squeaked, "I was saving that seat for a friend..." her voice trailed.

"Oh!" Pandora gushed, "I shouldn't impose, I'll be on my way."

Before she could take another step, another human descended silently from the third floor. Both girls flinched. Pandora quickly recognized the boy as her youngest brother and rolled her eyes. Of course, Volo was already in the library too.

"I thought you were going for an early-morning workout," said Pandora.

"You don't know my schedule," said Volo, disappearing down the stairs with a stack of science books in his arms.

At that same moment, a short boy in a yellow shirt pranced into the lobby. "Hey Hyphen!" his holler echoed across the library, met with a collective shushing from the resident Voidpets.

Hyphen looked over the edge of the railing and waved silently.

"Woah, looks like we've got a whole nerd herd today!" the newcomer exclaimed, running up the stairs to meet his friend.

Suddenly, there was a loud thud from the spiral staircase, followed by a yell, and a crash.

In the next moment, the boy was lying on the table before her. He wore a pained grimace, disoriented from Volo's speedy rescue. Volo was crouched over him, his stack of books balanced in one hand. The kid must have had collided with her brother on the stairs before taking an unfortunate tumble.

"Char, are you okay?" Hyphen gasped, jumping to her feet to examine her friend.

"He's fine," said Volo, "This is all he needs." Volo stuck a Voidpet-patterned bandage on Char's forehead, followed by a bag of ice he had produced from void matter. Then, he resumed his exit.

"Urgh" Char groaned, moving his hand to stabilize the ice, "I'm good, I just need a moment."

"Char... I think you should visit Professor String for a checkup, just to be safe," Hyphen advised, biting her nails, "Whatever just happened sounded pretty bad."

"Here, let me take you—"

"No, you need to keep studying, you can't let me distract you" Char interrupted her, "I've got it under control."

"No wait, are you sure?" Hyphen asked, "You shouldn't go alone!"

He swung himself off the desk to his feet, still holding the ice to his head as he slowly made his way downstairs, "Yeah, don't make this into a big deal, I'll catch you next time."

Her study session having taken an unexpected turn, Hyphen was now flabbergasted. Pandora's eyes followed Char down the stairs, confirming he'd made it out of the library okay.

"Um, actually, Pandora, you can sit here with me if you want now," Hyphen suggested, pointing towards the chair that was apparently no longer reserved for its intended occupant.

"Oh!" said Pandora, accepting the seat with composure, "Well, thank you!"

Pandora didn't skip a beat. "Would you like some tea or cookies?" she summoned a ball of white void matter into her hands.

"Oh! Ah, I'd love—well actually..." Hyphen's big brown eyes glittered as the smells of cinnamon and spice began to waft from Pandora's hands.

Hyphen looked nervous as a small Judgement descended on the railing ledge to interrupt. "Please no food or drink in the library," the Voidpet cawed.

Pandora apologized.

"I'll save you some for later then," she whispered at Hyphen, retracting the matter back into her hands.

"So," Pandora began, glancing at the headline of Hyphen's assignment, "Did you need any help with your paper? I'm Professor Cogito's new teaching assistant for that class."

"Oh! Well, thank you, but I think I'm okay on my own!" Hyphen began to fidget with a curl of her hair, "I already did all the readings and finished my outline."

"That's wonderful," said Pandora, her thoughts racing behind her rosy smile. It was clear Hyphen was on top of her studies, so perhaps she'd make a good resource for gathering intelligence.

"Which book was your favorite?" Pandora asked.

Hyphen's eyes sparkled at the question. "That's a tough one! They're all so fascinating in their own ways. But if I had to choose, I think I'd say, 'The Social Contract' really stood out to me."

Pandora nodded with genuine interest. "What about it resonated with you?"

"Well," Hyphen began, her fears fading as she delved into the topic, "I really connected with the idea of collective will. I want to use my education to help others and learn how to use void matter for the greater good. What about you, Pandora?" she added with a chirp, clearly thrilled to swap notes with a new study buddy.

Pandora's eyes scanned the titles, wondering which would make a good impression on this freshman girl. Judging from Hyphen's response, *The Prince* was off the table, and so was *Beyond Good and Evil*.

"When I read 'The Republic'," Pandora began, "I found the idea of the philosopher-king intriguing. The notion that those who rule should be the wisest and most knowledgeable—it made me proud to be a bit of a bookworm."

Pandora chuckled, and Hyphen smiled back.

"Speaking of which," said Pandora, "where do you recommend I look if I want to research the Void's geography? This is only my first week at the Institute, so I haven't quite learned my way around yet."

"Oooh, which layer are you thinking of?" Hyphen asked.

"Layer?" Pandora asked, unsure if she heard correctly.

"Which of the Seven Layers of the Void are you most interested in?" Hyphen clarified, covering her mouth to contain her excitement.

Pandora blinked. In all her homeschooling, she'd never heard of the Void having any sort of Seven Layers and wasn't ready to reveal her naivety to Hyphen.

"Just the one that we're on," Pandora tilted her head coyly.

"Oh, just Layer One, that makes sense, so you're looking for practical knowledge!" Hyphen released a nervous laugh, "I guess the geography in the other layers is essentially theoretical fantasy since no one has really been there anyway... but the lore is amazing, right?"

Pandora's head was spinning. Why had she never heard of the Seven Layers before? Was this her first piece of breakthrough knowledge, or was it just a distraction? A myth?

"You're going to want to go to the top floor for that," Hyphen explained. "It's kind of confusing at first, but Professor Cogito designed each floor of the library to represent each of the layers, and Layer One is technically at the top. That's where you'll find all the stuff about ancient civilization and our local geography."

"We're currently on the third floor, which corresponds to Layer Five—the Realm of Logic! That's why all the philosophy and abstract math books are here!"

She opened one of her books with a decorative λ on the cover, revealing strange artwork of a princess. The artwork was annotated with lines of lambda calculus notation.

Hyphen, in her excitement, leaned forward to ask Pandora, "What do you think about the theory that Nightmares can travel between layers?"

Pandora froze as a core memory flashed in her mind. The night a Nightmare had attacked her home. "That theory... I've never quite thought about it before."

"And have you read the legends of people getting lost in the layers below?"

"No... I haven't."

Pandora felt goosebumps as her mind begin to connect the dots. The room looked surreal as she let Hyphen's words sink in, digesting the influx of knowledge that the freshman had casually shared with her. She'd gained more clues about her parents' disappearance in these five minutes than she ever had in the past five years, and was now itching to dig into the library's knowledge herself.

"Hyphen, it's been an absolute pleasure chatting with you today," said Pandora, suddenly standing up.

"Thank you for helping me find my way around. I best get on with my research now, though I'd love to catch up again sometime."

With that, Pandora marched up to the top floor as fast as her legs could carry her. She was in such a hurry, she almost forgot her Pride at the table.

Chapter 15: Game Design

Char sat across the lunch table with a bandage on his forehead. It was decorated with little doodles of Pain, which looked like squawking ducks with three heads.

Tilde leaned forward, her brow furrowed with concern, "Char, what happened to you?"

Char shrugged, trying to act casual, "Just... an incident with Volo."

Tilde's eyes narrowed, "What did he do?"

"It was really nothing," Char insisted, his voice dismissive.

Alt studied Char's face. He knew Char must have felt bad about the conflict he started earlier, and it seemed like he was trying to hide information that might upset people. "Are you sure?"

Char nodded, a bit too quickly, "I'm pretty sure it was just an accident."

 "I'm just glad you're okay," said Hyphen, "I was worried all morning."

Tilde's head snapped towards Hyphen. "Wait Hyphen you were there?"

"Yeah," Hyphen admitted, her eyes downcast.

"So tell us what happened!" Tilde exclaimed.

Hyphen fidgeted as she spoke. "Char was coming up the stairs to study with me, and Volo was going down them at the same time, and..."

"Then what??" Tilde urged, leaning closer.

Hyphen's voice wavered. "Honestly, I'm not sure, it all happened really fast..."

Char jumped in, clearly trying to downplay the situation. "I just fell backwards and hit my head is all."

Alt tried to piece things together. It sounded like Char was trying not to cause trouble, but was clearly minimizing what must have been a traumatic injury to his head. Also, if he had just fallen backwards, then why was his bandage on the front of his forehead?

"I mean I don't want to jump to conclusions, but it sounds like what happened was that Volo pushed you down the stairs...?" Alt began.

"Wait no—" Hyphen started to protest, but Tilde steamrolled in.

"Doesn't he have like, super strength and super speed?" Tilde squinted in deep thought.

Alt nodded, a dark thought crossing his mind, "So like, if he *did*, you wouldn't even have been able to *tell*..."

Hyphen tried to interject. "Wait but didn't Volo try to help... well I guess..."

Char held up his hands, "Look I don't want to blame anyone and cause trouble again, okay?"

Tilde wasn't ready to let it go. "Do you know what Voidpet he has?"

"I think Lust..." Alt mumbled, trying to remember which red-eyed pet had assisted Volo during Void Matter Metamorphosis.

Hyphen's voice rose, defending Volo, "But Volo wants to be a doctor. He likes helping people and saving lives!"

"Lust is a weird pet for that," said Tilde.

Hyphen's face fell. "Are we really going to judge someone off of what Voidpet they have?"

Char sighed, and Alt felt sorry for him. He too would be feeling terrible if he had accidentally instigated conflict two days in a row. "Guys just forget about it," said Char, "I was dumb for running in the library, it was just an accident."

Alt understood the situation yet couldn't stop thinking through the details. "Wait... but if you were running and he was walking, how were you the one who got knocked down?"

As Tilde and Alt started arguing about physics, Char's expression turned optimistic. He pitched forth an idea to resolve the conflict.

"Ok look, I have a better plan than trying to read into what happened," said Char, "I don't love that group of kids either, you guys know that. But I've got an idea to get them off our backs, and I think I have a way we can win. We can't beat them with brute strength, but maybe we can outsmart them and put them in their place with some teamwork!"

Alt shook his head. "Honestly, I think the best plan is to just disengage. We shouldn't rile ourselves up thinking about them."

Tilde, however, was excited at another chance to rumble. "Wait. Tell us more."

Hyphen's eyes lit up with hope, "Ooh, are you thinking maybe a friendly game to smooth things over?"

Char grinned, "Yeah, exactly! Well said."

Alt mulled it over. "Ok, I can maybe get behind the idea of that."

Char's eyes gleamed as he pulled out a sheet of paper. "Here are the rules I came up with. I wrote them down during class!"

He proceeded to explain his elaborate game plan, detailing the rules for 'hunting'. All you had to do was snap a picture with a foam weapon to someone's head, so it was more about strategy than brute force. Each team would get points for kills, and dead players were out of the game.

Alt was hoping for something more like musical chairs or tic-tac-toe, but he kept listening.

"We'll be able to win, as long as we work together and have a good plan," Char explained, as Tilde nodded in support.

The game would last multiple days until everyone was killed.

"The Institute is the safe zone—which gives us the advantage," said Char, "They all have to commute off campus, which is where we get the jump on them."

"Wait but how will they agree to that?" Hyphen asked, "That's too unfair. What if we just never leave campus?"

"That's why I also designed the scavenger hunt portion," Char said announced with glee. As he unveiled a second sheet of paper, full of city landmarks, wild Voidpet species, and silly challenges, everyone leaned in, impressed by the thought he'd put into it. Alt recognized city landmarks like Angel Station Clock, Atlas Statue Foot, and Neon Square Ball, each worth 10 points, along with rare Voidpet variants worth anywhere from 10 to 50.

"For each of these items," Char narrated, running his finger down the rows of his own neat penmanship, "You have to take a group picture with all your living team members to claim the points. And once your team claims the item, it's yours."

"And we have a secret advantage here too," he said with mischief, "There are more points to be gained from doing the scavenger hunt, but the others might get distracted focusing all their energy on trying to kill."

"The game can also end once the scavenger hunt is complete, so if they try to hide, we can still win by claiming all the tasks for ourselves."

Tilde raised a valid concern. "Wait, but they have five people, and we have four, isn't that unfair?"

Alt nodded, thinking about how Promise's group outnumbered their own.

Char smirked, confident in his strategy. "An extra team member is also a *liability*. One more person to be killed, and one more person that needs to be there to complete the scavenger hunt tasks. It shouldn't imbalance the game."

While the game sounded far more complicated than Alt expected, he found himself excited about all the new adventures they could have. Alt struggled for motivation to get out of bed, but the idea of this epic competition had gotten him fired up. Plus, he trusted that his friend group would be at an advantage when it came to teamwork.

As the group expressed their admiration for Char's game design, Alt wondered if this would turn out to be a wholesome bonding experience or a toxic recipe for disaster. But the excitement was hard to ignore, and he found himself nodding along. After all, it did sound like fun, so he figured it was worth a shot.

"Alright then, now how do we declare our challenge on them?" Tilde asked the group, gripping both arms of her chair with zeal, "Should I just pull up to Promise and yell at him again?" she said, giggling.

The group looked over to the Windfall's table, and noticed that Promise was not there.

"Maybe I can show Pandora at the library?" Hyphen suggested, her voice meek, "We're sort of friends now, I think?"

"You're *friends* with one of them now?" Tilde snapped, eyeing Hyphen with budding rage before reeling her emotions in. "Well, I mean that's totally fine, that's real nice of you, I just got a little thrown off is all," she blurted, slinking back into her chair.

"Oh, who am I kidding, I don't think I'll have the nerve to challenge her to a game, she's my TA," Hyphen gushed, covering her eyes with her hands, "I'd be too scared to bring up anything that isn't schoolwork."

The group giggled, and Tilde put her hand on Hyphen's.

"It's okay, that's why you have me," she said with a grin.

"EY, YO, PANDORA," Tilde yelled across the dining hall, before grabbing Char's papers and barreling forth in her chair, "LET'S PLAY A GAME."

Chapter 16: Ashes

Promise stood in the crater where his old home used to be.

212 Something Park South.

He put on his sunglasses to keep the dust out of his eyes. As an ashy wind battered his hair, it whipped his leather jacket and streaked his tee with stains of black. The scene around him looked like an apocalyptic wasteland, though the dust had long settled from the day before.

Ash was a workable substance to reverse-channel.

A soft, simple carbon resembling Nightmare fuel, it was easier to turn back into void matter than solid stone and steel. He wouldn't be able to recover the value of all that'd been destroyed, but such was expected in a demolition. The fact that he could extract anything at all was a privilege he didn't take for granted.

Greed raced to perch on his shoulder as he channeled their shared technique—*Singularity*. As he extended his left hand above his head, a little black hole formed in his palm, drawing in streams of dark ash from all reaches of the crater. Given the high volume and the low purity of the material, he wondered how many hours this haul would take.

Whatever it was, it was too long to do the entire process himself.

After he collected his initial sample, crushing the hole in his palm to see the total void matter yield, he passed the task to Greed. Swallowing the black hole, the little fox began to prance through the wreckage, collecting a trail of floating ash in its wake. He calculated that there was anywhere from 100k to a million void matter to be siphoned from the site, which, while nothing compared to the cost of constructing a new building, was a worthy sum nonetheless.

He'd have to wait and see whether the demolition turned a profit. Most likely, it wouldn't, but if it did, then the implications would be momentous. The freedom to raze down and rebuild anything he desired, with the privilege of keeping the change. Wishful thinking, perhaps, but why not wish?

As Promise stood in the middle of the site surveying the dust collection, his phone pinged. He withdrew his device from his pocket to look at the two images Pecunia had texted him.

Attached were two pictures of handwritten files, detailing the rules of some challenge his family had been confronted with.

Pecunia: *prom you comin back for this?*

Pecunia: *us vs anger girl and co*

Pecunia: *starts tmr*

He studied the attachments, lifting his sunglasses to read the fine print on the screen:

A scavenger hunt through the city...

...foam weapons to the head...

...taking selfies to kill your enemies...

A slow smile spread across his face as he read over the handwritten rulebook, apparently created by one of the freshman students. Whoever made this game knew how to have a good time, and he could get behind it. This little mastermind was a punk to be reckoned with. *Respect*.

As he surveyed the scorched earth before him, thinking of his old apartment, his parents, and all that he'd once known, a new thought crossed his mind. It was worth it to enjoy what few opportunities he had to be a kid, and this seemed like one of them. Maybe the Institute was good for something after all.

"*K im in,*" he replied to the group chat.

He had the rest of the day to pick up ashes.

Tomorrow, he'd look forward to returning to campus.

Chapter 17: The Hunter Game

Word got around about Char's game, and there were now four whole friend groups who wanted to participate. As the Game Master, he was suddenly the most popular student on campus and was loving every minute of it.

Char reviewed his notebook, where he recorded logistics and gossip.

The Freshman team was Tilde, Hyphen, Alt, and of course, Char himself. No notes needed there.

The Sophomore team, to his surprise, were the four cool kids he'd remembered from his first day:

1. Sine, the athletic girl with a split hairdo and deep voice. She had approached Char during lunchtime, wanting in.
2. Point, Sine's bestie who always wore yoga pants. She had striking indigo eyes, ethereal dark skin, and apparently, was a fitness model. She also seemed like a no-nonsense player who was in it to win.
3. Catch, the preppy boy in the white quarter zip. Everyone knew his family was rich, and he was running for student body president this semester. Despite his popularity, he was rumored to have an unrequited crush on his teammate, Point.
4. Loop, the sandy-haired dude in the hoodie. He always looked zoned out and smelled like grass, perhaps because he liked to explore outdoors.

Overall, the Sophomore team was a tight knit group of sporty friends who seemed like they could be a serious force to be reckoned with.

Next, there was the Junior team, which seemed like a hot mess:

1.   Verve, the queen bee brunette, was the leader. Verve's mom just died, which meant she got extra sympathy from everyone. He didn't need rumors to know that his own sister was viciously jealous of her.

5.   Malloc, the buff guy in the muscle tee, was allegedly in a 'situationship' with Verve. Most people knew him a nice dude who just liked to go to the gym. Apparently, he'd also survived cancer in kindergarten, which made him mega popular.

6.   Raster, the basic blonde guy, was possibly *also* in a situationship with Verve. The rumor mill said he was a closet pyromaniac with a bad temper—which seemed like a weakness to exploit.

7.   Dyna, his sister, didn't even want to participate until her friends did. She only caved into peer pressure when Verve insisted. Char already knew her problems all too well, and didn't need to write them down.

Char predicated that this team would make for easy pickings. Dyna and Verve would tear each other apart before anyone else had time to, and Malloc seemed like he cared more about keeping the peace than winning the game.

And then, finally, there was Team Windfall:

Pandora, Promise, Pecunia, Volo, and Luden. He didn't need notes to remember them.

As Char looked up from his notebook, he heard the dining hall abuzz with bets going around. Lots of people were putting money on Malloc, which was understandable, because he was buff and popular. Sine and Point had quite a few fans as well, and it sounded like their team was the favorite to win. Another popular whisper was Volo for most kills—at which Char scoffed.

There was even a rumor that the professors were placing bets, though it didn't seem like any of them outwardly wanted to get involved. Word got around that Professor Cogito had made a video game style tier-list of all the students, but that sounded like fake news. (If anyone did that, it had to have been Professor Bool.)

Char and his friends were animated with excitement. In preparation, they first made a group chat for all the players. Then, they pooled their void matter to craft an arsenal of foam weaponry, which Alt hand-painted to look extra fantastical.

That afternoon, they scrambled to prepare in all the ways they could think of. Tilde hit the gym to pump iron, Hyphen jogged laps around the garden, and Alt went to the park to sketch a detailed map of all the scavenger hunt locations.

As his final class was dismissed, Char shouldered his backpack and headed down to the subway station. Envy hovered close, shooting a backward glance towards campus where most of the other students were still hanging out. As they embarked down the airborne spiral of Ghost Road, Char's two-hour commute stretched before him, a daily reminder of the distance between his life and the Institute.

When he finally got on the ghost train, Char began his hour-long ride in an empty car. The subway rattled and swayed, ferrying him further from his newfound popularity and deeper into the outskirts of the Void.

He studied his notebook, reviewing his notes from earlier. Envy peered over his shoulder, eyeing all the rival players' names. But as the stations blurred past, doubt crept in. Everything he'd prepared was completely speculative. Though Char had architected the challenge, there was no way he could have been prepared for the chaos that was about to unfold.

Chapter 18: Midnight Mayhem

As midnight rolled around, Char sat clutching his phone from the comfort of his bed.

He was shocked to see that teams were already uploading their first pictures to the full group chat. The game had technically started that day, though Char hadn't expected any action until the next morning.

At 12:00 am, Team Windfall posted a midnight selfie, toasting cans of energy drinks into the air. They had already taken Something Park Pavilion, balancing wild Voidpets on their heads for extra points. *10 points, +5 bonus.*

Crap, Char thought, as his heart sank. Was their plan to pull an all-nighter and sweep the entire scavenger hunt on the first day? Or were they just trying to get into everyone's heads?

12:00 am came with another plot twist: Alt was already dead. He was tied to a tree with a slice of pizza on his head, and Verve was holding a foam knife to his neck.

That 30 points to the Juniors, plus 5 bonus for the pizza.

Char scrambled to text his team what was going on.

Alt, u ok????

I got abducted, Alt replied with a crying emoji.

Verve and Dyna kidnapped me in the park

They held me there until midnight

No way... Char thought. Were the Junior girls really taking the game that seriously?

At 12:05 am, The next message was a video from Pecunia. Promise had slapped Sine's phone into the lake and held a foam pistol to her head as she crawled in the water to retrieve it. Sine was dead too. 30 points, plus 5 bonus for drenching the target.

Rats! Was *everyone* out in the park playing except for his team?

12:10 AM: The Junior team posted a selfie in front of the Golden Sad statue in the park. They were all posed making peace signs in a sorority squat, with Verve in the middle holding the camera. That was 10 points, plus 5 more bonus because their pants were all down.

As Char sat in his bedroom, miles away from the park in his childhood home out east, he realized the game had taken on a life of its own. It wasn't just about battle strategy or skill. It was a lawless game about who could play the dirtiest, and who had the liberty to take it to the extreme.

Char's mind raced. His carefully crafted plan had devolved into chaos within minutes. He needed to act fast.

Guys, we need to move. Now. He messaged his remaining teammates.

Tilde responded instantly: *On my way. Meet at the garden?*

As Hyphen started typing, Char was relieved to know that she was still awake.

I'm not sure it's safe to go out this late, she texted. Char groaned.

He was distraught. With Alt already out, Hyphen hesitating, and himself miles away from the action, their team was at a severe disadvantage. Suddenly, he realized that all the opposing teams were clustered in the park. This was the perfect opportunity to let them kill each other off. Maybe Hyphen had a point after all.

Ok ur right, stand down, he replied, *stay in and watch this play out.*

Wait im already out, Tilde texted back, and Char held his breath.

Stay away from the park tho, he warned, but he was too late.

The group chat dinged with another notification.

12:20 am: Tilde was in the park. In her blurry picture, Anger could be seen clobbering Loop with a foam bat, his Salty penguin looking disappointed in the background. A second sophomore was dead, and the Freshmen had earned their first 30 points.

Char pumped his fist silently from his bed. Tilde was the real MVP when it came to action—though she was extremely lucky that Loop was alone. Char was surprised that the Sophomore team had decided to split up and wasn't sure why they thought that was a good strategy.

NOW HURRY BACK TO YOUR DORM, Char followed up frantically, realizing that Tilde had just exposed her location to all their opponents.

12:28 am: The Juniors had claimed Something Park Playground. This time, Malloc and Raster were doing handstands, while Dyna and Verve hung from their legs on the monkey bars. 10 points, plus 5 for everyone being upside-down.

12:30 am: Team Windfall had claimed the Atlas Statue Foot, which was quite far off campus. Promise held a red flame in the air, while Pecunia took the selfie. 10 points, plus 10 bonus for fire.

Char grit his teeth seeing Promise snipe the fireball bonus. That one was designed as a freebie for his own team, since it was supposed to be Tilde's signature ability. To make matters worse, it meant the Windfalls had left the park, and were no longer duking it out with the opposing teams.

This was not good. Why were the upperclassmen all focusing on the scavenger hunt instead of killing each other off? *Fudge nuts.* Char suddenly remembered that the Windfalls had a *car*, and could go anywhere they wanted. The Juniors had large, flying Voidpets, which gave them mobility by air. Char groaned at the strategic oversight. How could he have missed such a key detail?

12:55 am: Point and Catch posted a selfie with a wild Phantom Paranoia, puffing their cheeks next to the avian creature as it inflated like a puffer fish. Since they were the only two sophomores alive, that was a 20-point Voidpet sighting for their team. Even more clever was the fact that they had gone for a wildlife sighting instead of a landmark—which meant that they revealed nothing about their location to the other teams.

Char kept his eyes glued to the screen for updates.

By 2 am, the Juniors had conquered all of Something Park, and the Windfalls were making good headway into the city. Point and Catch were spotting Voidpets as a duo, careful to reveal nothing about their location. At this rate, Char was worried that the scavenger hunt could end the game before the hunting did.

Suddenly, the selfie stream came to a lull. Had everyone finally gone to sleep? Char closed his eyes and breathed a sigh of relief, hoping that the other teams had called it in for the night.

A message at 2:42 am suggested otherwise.

Char studied the new selfie, sent by his sister Dyna from the grand concourse of Angel Station. As the two girls posed duck-faced into the camera, he recognized the rope-bound hostage between them as none other than his main rival, Promise Windfall. He looked wryly into the camera, with duct tape over what Char knew had to be an insufferable smirk.

Dyna's Jealous had entangled him in vines, while Verve's Disdain had slithered its tail around him for extra security. Clearly, the Juniors had captured him somehow.

Char felt adrenaline surge through his veins as he reanimated from his bed, wide awake. *Finally.* This was the type of chaos he was waiting for. *Although...*

Char's eyes narrowed with suspicion. That sleazy dude could teleport. He'd seen it with his own eyes. So why was he just sitting there? Maybe he was trying to play fair? No that couldn't have been it—clearly it was some kind of trap. Had he gotten captured on purpose? Or maybe he was just the team's weak link...?

Char suddenly stood up from his bed. His parents were fast asleep, and it seemed like the perfect opportunity to regain control over his game. Besides, his sister was already out causing trouble, and his parents were too busy to keep track of when he was at home anyway.

"Meet me at Angel Station in one hour," Char texted his group, before grabbing his book bag, slathering on some deodorant, and tiptoeing out of his brick walkup in the dark of the night. With Envy emboldened by his side, Char jogged back to the subway station, foam sword in hand, racing to catch the 3:00 am train back to the city.

"On my way," Tilde replied, and Char felt his gait quicken.

In the quiet of the witching hour, Char could hear everything. His sneakers pounding on the pavement, his breath in the air, and the faint rustle of small creatures in the distance, both Voidpets and Nightmares alike. Thanks to the presence of his pet's larger, evolved form, he felt fearless in the dark. As soon as they caught sight of Envy's foreboding claws, the noises faded, and the creatures shied back into the shadows.

A small stand was lit up at the platform where Char was waiting for his train. For 2 VM, he picked up an energy drink from the Apathy attendant, and quickly downed the beverage with a clink of metal and a pop. Before he knew it, he was back on the train, speeding straight towards Angel Station.

Chapter 19: Angel Station Showdown

Tilde hurtled through the streets, powering her wheelchair with rockets of flame. Behind her, Alt and Hyphen rode in a borrowed garden wagon, attached to Tilde by a jump rope from the gym.

It was just past 3:00 am, and the empty roads were peaceful. Ancient buildings smiled quietly all around them, and the paved streets sprawled through the dark in a perfect grid. The only sounds were occasional yelps and thumps from the wagon, as Alt and Hyphen weathered the ride with their Voidpets beside them.

The plan was simple. Show up to the station and smack all the upperclassmen with her baseball bat.

A grin spread across her face as she felt the fresh strength of her leveled-up technique. Anger was perched in her lap gripping the foam bat in its new claws, its red scarf blazing through the night like a battle flag.

Tilde knew she was getting near when she saw large Voidpets circling overhead. The three-headed phoenix had to be Raster's Wrath, and the girthy serpent worming through the sky must have been Malloc's Sloth.

Tilde thought about the picture in the group chat. If Dyna and Verve had captured Promise without eliminating him from the game, then the Windfalls couldn't make progress with the scavenger hunt. Since they needed all their teammates in the picture to win points, they were forced to confront the Juniors and rescue him.

She realized then, that the Juniors might have planned some sort of ambush to eliminate the Windfalls. Therefore, they probably didn't expect the freshmen to show up.

"I THINK WE HAVE THE ADVANTAGE OF STEALTH," she yelled back to her friends, who nodded vigorously from the wagon.

By 3:30 am, the group had arrived at the station. Suddenly, Tilde saw the flicker of a white quarter zip in the night.

"ALT, GET READY TO TAKE A PICTURE," She bellowed at her friend, who quickly fumbled for his phone. Even though Alt was eliminated, there was no rule that said he couldn't assist as a photographer.

"RORORORORORORORO!" She barked, as an explosive charge of flame blasted her towards the boy in white.

He turned around like a deer in headlights, as Tilde, Anger, and the wheelchair-wagon hybrid rocketed towards him. The next thing everyone knew, he was on the ground, Anger was holding the baseball bat to his head, and the sound of Alt snapping a picture echoed through the night.

"Aw sheesh, you three really got me good," the boy said with a smile, after recovering from the shock.

Tilde was suddenly flustered. She'd never spoken to this boy before, and felt a little bad for charging him head-on. She realized he must have been Catch, the Sophomore, and therefore, one of the underdogs in the game at this point.

"I really just got lucky," Tilde blurted, guilt suddenly settling as she collected both Anger and the bat back into her lap, "We just caught you away from your friends."

"Naw, you were just clever!" Catch reassured her, placing a friendly hand on her shoulder, "You came out here at 3 am to sneak up on the action, right? That's a great strategy."

Tilde found herself smiling, happy to discover that this Catch kid seemed like a genuinely good sport.

"Wait, how come you're all alone?" Alt asked, as he hesitated to post the picture.

"The Juniors airlifted us with their Voidpets and split us up," Catch sighed with defeat, "We got wrecked right from the beginning."

"Oh bummer, that's really mean of them..." Alt said, his phone hand faltering.

"These upperclassmen are a menace, we honestly never stood a chance." Catch said with an embarrassed laugh, "Like, I can't believe Promise smacked Sine's phone into the lake... But at the end of the day, they're just going all out at the game, right?"

"Yeah, I guess we're all just doing our best to win, right?" said Hyphen, her kind words sparkling like a bell in the night.

"Yeah totally, it's all a friendly competition, nothing personal," Catch replied, grinning at Hyphen. He segued to his next phrase without skipping a beat, "Do you mind if I just take a quick look at this for a sec?" Catch asked Alt, his hazel eyes warm as he gestured towards Alt's phone.

"Yeah of course," Alt responded, handing his phone to Catch with his sleeve-covered hands.

Without warning, Catch swiped the phone out of Alt's grip and erupted into the night with a sprint.

"Sorry bud, nothing personal!" his words faded as he disappeared, "I'll give it back later!"

Tilde, Hyphen, and Alt stood dumbstruck on the street, still processing what had just happened.

"Did he just..." Alt stammered, "Did he just steal my phone?"

"I... I fear that might have been what occurred," Hyphen's voice fell, as she realized Catch had already rounded a corner and was long gone.

"DARN, that was..." Tilde fumed, rage inching into her voice, "Well actually, that was kind of clever." Tilde admitted, echoing Catch's words to her from earlier.

"At least he was trying to be nice about it," Alt offered, though he was clearly ashamed for getting tricked.

As Tilde processed the full situation, she began to realize that it was indeed a bit of a bummer. That picture was worth 30 points to her team, and now, it was gone for good. She wasn't quite angry at him, though. She was starting to embrace the spirit of the game, and was filled with newfound motivation to win.

It was now 3:45 am, and Char had just emerged from the station entrance beside them.

Hyphen jumped for joy upon seeing the whole team united, and Tilde smiled from ear to ear as she saw her new friend emerge. As skeptical as she'd been of Char, she had to admit that life had gotten more fun since he showed up at her table.

Char's eyes scanned the group, and he zeroed in on Alt's guilty look. "You okay?" Char asked, his eyes narrowed, "Did something happen?"

Hyphen bumbled to explain the mishap. "We almost scored a hunt on Catch, but then he grabbed Alt's phone and ran away."

Char frowned and nodded.

"That's okay. We'll figure out another way to get ahead," he said, his voice reassuring.

Tilde watched as Char began to pace, his yellow t-shirt bright in the night.

"Let's take it easy on the offense for now," he concluded, "We're in dangerous territory, so let's play it safe and lay low. We need to wait for the older kids to battle it out, and then pick of the ones we can get alone."

"Wait, what if we just go finish the scavenger hunt?" Tilde asked, suddenly remembering Char's strategy from lunchtime.

"We can't," Char responded, "Because there aren't enough locations left. If we finish the scavenger hunt, the game ends, and we're still in last place. Our only path to win is to score kills."

"Team Windfall is winning, with 140 points, and the Juniors are right behind with 120. Juniors can't end the game now, and Windfalls can't finish the scavenger hunt if they're missing a member. So they need to start hunting people to win. We also have to watch out for the Sophomores, they're coming in close with 80 points, and we've only got 30 so far..."

"So we *ambush* them all!" Tilde exclaimed with her fists clenched, and Char's eyes lit up with approval.

"Now *that's* what I'm talking about!" Char clasped his hands together with zeal. He pulled out his phone to study the picture of Promise held captive, and the team huddled around him.

"Dyna and Verve are holding him in the grand concourse of the train station," Char deduced, pointing at the gold clock in the background. "Right now, they've got a 360 view of everything around them, so we probably can't sneak up."

Char paused, tapping his chin, "But the Windfalls have to rescue him, so there's gonna be some sort of showdown to stir the pot..."

"So we hide out, and then we attack once everyone's distracted!" Tilde exclaimed, finishing his sentence.

"Bingo!" said Char.

And with that, the team commenced their stealth mission to stake out Angel Station.

Tilde led the mission, with Char, Hyphen, and Alt now packed into the garden wagon together. Envy floated behind the handlebars of the wheelchair, lending an extra push to help with the oversized load. They cruised through the night, circling the central building of the train station until they found a solid vantage point to camp out.

Tilde peered into the golden concourse and was surprised by the sight before her eyes.

The three upperclassmen sat in the middle of the floor, their backs against an information booth. Promise's mouth was no longer covered in duct tape. All three of them appeared to be joking around, laughing even.

Dyna held a bag, tossing something that had to be candy into the air. as Promise, still tied up in vines, was trying to catch it in his mouth. Meanwhile, Verve was sitting next to him, her head resting playfully on his shoulder as she giggled and scrolled her phone.

"Huh?" Tilde asked, as Char immediately leapt out of the wagon to glue his face to the window.

"Why are they acting all friendly?" Tilde asked, "And why is your sister feeding him candy?"

Alt poked his head out to join the watch. "I guess they had extra time on their hands? It's nice to see that people are bonding over the game despite playing on different teams—"

"NO THIS IS BAD" Char gasped, suddenly scrambling back into the wagon, "WE GOTTA GET OUTTA HERE."

"Huh?" Tilde asked, "But what about the ambush?"

"WE'RE THE ONES GETTING AMBUSHED," Char yelled, wildly gesturing for everyone to get back on the wagon.

Suddenly, Tilde saw the red convertible pull up to the sidewalk. It parked elegantly, and Pandora stepped out of the driver's seat with Volo striding behind her. Pecunia and Luden sat waiting in the car.

Across the street, Wrath descended from the sky, dropping Raster on the sidewalk with a foam axe in hand. Malloc stood on the other side of the block, his arms flexed, brandishing a pair of foam maces. Both boys loomed in the dark, their large weapons only adding to their intimidating silhouettes.

On a rooftop behind him, Tilde noticed a group of four lurking, which had to be the Sophomore team. Everyone was here, and the game was about to get wild.

"Rats, we're cooked!" Alt gasped, realizing that the Freshmen were completely exposed on the sidewalk. As he buried his face in Sad, bracing himself for foam death, Tilde heard a sudden smack in the middle of the street.

Volo and Malloc had collided in battle, with Volo's twin machetes locked against Malloc's maces. In the next second, Pandora was on Raster, her foam fists clashing against his foam axe.

She had no clue who was ambushing whom after all.

As Tilde's eyes darted, she saw Pecunia and Luden leaning over the doors of the convertible, phones poised to capture a kill. The Windfalls had two cameras and the Juniors had none—but their advantage was short lived.

Suddenly, Wrath airlifted Luden from the convertible. His startled wail faded into the distance as the winged Voidpet took to the sky, ferrying him away into the night.

"There goes your paparazzi, Windfall," Raster cocked his head at Pandora with his tongue in cheek, amber flames swirling around his axe as he swung at her with a series of turbo charged slices.

Next, Malloc's Sloth had wrapped itself around Pecunia, and she had to summon her own Sloth to fight it off.

He stuck his tongue out at her before parrying another slash from Volo with his maces.

"Good luck with that," he hollered, as his deep voice echoed across the streets.

"YO THIS IS OUR CHANCE," Char cried, seizing his carefully planned opportunity. Pecunia was entangled between a battle of two Sloths, Luden was out of the picture, the rest were locked in combat, and neither of them had any cameras to capture a kill.

"TILDE, CAM ME UP," Char yelled, charging forth into the fray with his foam sword outstretched.

The Sophomores seemed to have had the same idea. At the same time, Point swooped down from the rooftop opposite, gliding through the air on a pair of blade-like blue wings. She held a foam spear, diving head-on at Pandora, who had the shortest-range weapon to counter.

Char was also going for Pandora's back and picked up his pace. Unfortunately for them both, Pandora spun at the last minute, dodging and pivoting her stance as she leapt back from Raster's axe.

"Oof," Tilde said, as she accidentally took a picture of Char meeting the business end of Pandora's fist. Luckily, no one on Pandora's team was around to capture the kill, so Char was still in the game.

Tilde was quickly proved wrong, as her phone pinged with a notification at 4:05 am. The same picture had been uploaded, albeit from a different angle, coming from what was apparently Pandora's phone. Tilde was baffled, unsure how Pandora could have snapped the picture if she was in battle, but she quickly spotted the ace up Pandora's sleeve: Pride. Her silver Voidpet sat by the window, licking itself as it clutched her phone in its paws.

Darn. Another 30 points to team Windfall, and Char was now eliminated from the game.

Meanwhile, Point was gone as quickly as she'd come, circling back to the rooftop to join her team.

4:05 am came with another plot twist. With Pandora still recovering from the double dodge, Raster had summoned Wrath to blast smoke at her, disorienting her just enough to create an opening. Dyna had emerged from the station in time to snap a picture of his foam axe to her neck, which was now in the group chat, heralding the first death for Team Windfall.

"Get TOASTED!" Raster whooped, swinging his axe in a glowing arc of triumph, before throwing an arm around Pandora in a show of sportsmanship. That was 30 points to the Juniors.

Tilde's eyes turned to Volo and Malloc, who were still duking it out in the middle of the street. As time went by, Volo seemed to grow fiercer, but Malloc showed signs of fatigue. Her eyes widened as another underhanded tactic turned the tide of the battle.

"Volo, watch out!" Pandora yelled from across the street as she fought to catch her breath, but it was too late.

Dyna had snuck up behind Volo and leapt onto his back. She locked her legs around his waist and cast a burlap bag over his head, before pulling a foam knife to his neck. With Volo restrained and unable to see, Malloc had time to pause and snap a group selfie.

"Good fight, my dude!" Malloc declared, clapping a hand on the shoulder of Volo, who nodded from beneath the burlap bag.

Another 30 points to the Juniors. Volo and Pandora were both dead, and the whole Junior team was still standing. Verve pranced out of the station to join them, and the full group posted for a selfie in front of the Angel Station clock, grinning from ear to ear in the moonlight.

10 more points to the Juniors, and the scavenger hunt was almost over.

As Tilde turned around to glance at her teammates, she noticed that Hyphen was missing from the wagon.

Another picture had hit the group chat.

At 4:21 am, Hyphen held a pink foam water gun to Promise's head. The picture looked rather silly, with Promise's head lolled to the side and his tongue out in defeat. His torso was held in place by Verve's hissing Disdain, while his legs sprawled aimlessly across the floor. Meanwhile, Hyphen's expression remained sheepish, her posture small, and eyes averted as if embarrassed of her victory.

The Juniors were checking their phones too, and Verve's eyes immediately shot towards where Tilde and the freshmen were sitting. Her face tilted into a sneer, and she lashed out her foam knife out by her side.

"Did one of you brats... just steal *my* kill?" she snarled, cornering Tilde with a menacing stride.

Trash talk or not, Tilde wasn't one to stand for her best friend being called a brat.

"PREPARE TO DIE," she roared back, this time brandishing her baseball bat in her own hands. Char immediately whipped out his phone from his position in the wagon, and Tilde blast towards Verve with a rocket powered ram. Char uploaded a candid shot of Tilde's foam bat, frozen in time against Verve's cheek, and the Junior girl was out of the game.

Unfortunately, Tilde became an easy picking after the assault. Before she could even process what was going on, the tip of Dyna's blade was at her neck, and Dyna's head was duck-faced beside her. The selfie was snapped, and Tilde was out of the game.

"Sorry babe, you're dead," Dyna crooned, shooting Tilde a mocking pout.

The Juniors earned another 30 points, securing a tremendous lead.

A lull spread through the night as Tilde realized that the street skirmish had settled down. All the Freshmen were out except Hyphen, who was nowhere to be seen. The Sophomores had retreated after their surprise attack had failed, and Pecunia had fled, perhaps taking her defeated siblings with her.

The full Junior team stood victorious in the middle of the chaos, cheering at their lead.

Tilde wasn't keeping track of the score, but she knew she had a night full of fun. She started whooping with them, howling like a wolf and banging her chest like a gorilla. Tilde's hoots echoed through the night, a bold contradiction to the somber faces of her teammates. She spun her wheelchair in a victory circle, oblivious to the fact that it wasn't her team's triumph she was celebrating.

"We kicked some serious BOOTY today!" She said, grinning at Char and Alt. Her two friends in the wagon both looked a little disappointed, but she pressed on. "Did you see me take down Verve? That was EPIC!" she exclaimed, her eyes sparkling with excitement. Char cracked a small smile. "Yeah, Tilde. You're a juggernaut." As the Juniors continued their victory chants in the background, Tilde suddenly paused, a realization dawning on her face. "Wait a second... we're losing?"

Chapter 20: Good Game

Char's game had been a disaster. Since it ended last week, everything was going downhill, and Char was kicking himself for letting it happen.

Somehow, Pandora's stupid Voidpet had the bright idea to take a live video, and GIFs of Char were going viral—Pandora's fist TKO'ing him endlessly in slow-mo edits.

Meanwhile, *Luden* had skyrocketed to popularity for being the last man standing. Rumors spread of the goo boy's prolonged survival, and within days, nobody would shut up about his striking green eyes and mysterious bandages. He earned a reputation as the secret mastermind behind the Windfalls and was treated like a king on campus.

Promise had dropped out of school, which caused a domino effect of chaos in Char's life.

At home, Char wouldn't hear the end of Dyna's complaining. Drama ravaged her toxic friend group. The first problem was that the junior boys were now more interested in the Windfall sisters than they were in Verve. In retaliation, Verve had told everyone she had 'dibs' on Promise for the homecoming dance—but now that he was no longer enrolled, she had set her sights on Volo. This was a friendship violation because Dyna had *bonded* with Volo over the burlap bag attack, and they were starting to spend lots of time together. Verve's queen bee status was crumbling, and she and Dyna were once again at each other's throats—meaning Dyna was all the more unbearable at home.

Since the game, his sister's horrible friend group had expanded to include the Windfalls, and Char's headcount of rivals was only getting bigger.

"I honestly want nothing more than to wipe that smug grin off of Volo's face," he confided to his friends, to which Hyphen pointed out that she had never seen Volo smirk before.

"Are you sure you're not talking about Promise?" Hyphen asked, looking confused.

"You need to stop thinking about that guy," Alt urged with concern in his voice, "he doesn't even *GO* here anymore."

"No, I'm talking about Volo," Char sighed.

He held his tongue as he knew he'd have to be careful defaming someone so well liked.

In every way that Promise was too much, Volo was known to be 'just right'. Volo was a man of few words, who only spoke when he had something nice to say. Volo liked to volunteer. Volo shared his study guides before the exam. Volo shared his steak with the students who were short on lunch money. Volo worked hard and treated people with respect. Blah, blah, Volo this, Volo that.

"Look, the fact that the guy with a pet Lust is supposed to be the most wholesome person on campus simply does sit right with me," Char snarked, trying to conceal his distaste with an awkward grimace.

"I feel like Promise got on your nerves and you're taking it out on Volo," said Tilde, who scrunched her nose in confusion, "He only attended this school for one week and still lives rent free in your head."

"They're brothers. Both scumbags. And all scumbags look the same," Char scoffed.

Before Alt could point out that such a statement was potentially problematic, Hyphen jumped in. "Did they do something to you that we don't know about?" Hyphen asked, placing her small hand on his.

Char froze. He didn't expect this question, and suddenly found his mind lingering on a memory from long ago. Given that Hyphen had asked so earnestly, now seemed like most opportune time to confide.

"Actually kind of, yeah...

"A couple years ago... Promise came and bought my parents' store..." he trailed, not ready to disclose the full backstory of the dumpling shop. "He bought it for a lowball offer, taking advantage of the fact that we were desperate to pay my sister's tuition."

"Wait, *Promise* paid your sister's tuition?" Tilde asked, confused.

Char scowled, as that was not how he saw the situation, "*No*, not at all, he took away everything we had to our name and exploited the fact that we had no other options. And then... he shut it down."

"Oh..." Hyphen said, her face falling. "That's really unfair."

Char nodded. Life wasn't fair, and sometimes, it was better to get riled up about it than just sitting around being complacent. He breathed a sigh as he looked down, burying his gaze in the stains on his yellow shirt.

Suddenly, a Wonder in a news cap fluttered into the dining hall with a package hanging from its tiny claws. As the Voidpet plopped a black box onto the table in front of him, Char was surprised to see his own name on the gift wrapping in gold calligraphy.

"Woah, what's that?" Tilde exclaimed, leaning forward to watch him unwrap it. Hyphen and Alt leaned in as well.

"I dunno," Char said, as he tore open the inky wrap. He did a double take as he opened the box, checking the label again to confirm that the package was indeed for him. Inside was a blue varsity jacket with two embroidered Gs on its chest. The sleeves were a supple white leather, adorned with a trim of gold and navy.

A little card lay on top of it with a note:

For: The greatest GM.

Thanks for putting on the game of a lifetime.

"Whaaaat, who is it from?" Tilde asked, grabbing the packaging to look for any notion of a signature, but there was none.

Char stared at the jacket, his fingers tracing the embroidered Gs. The material was soft, thick, expensive—nothing like he'd ever owned before, and Alt noted that it reminded him of a luxury designer he'd studied in fashion history.

"Aren't you going to try it on?" Tilde asked, her eyes sparkling with excitement.

Char hesitated. The jacket represented everything he hated. It was the kind of thing someone obnoxious would wear, flaunting their privilege as they walked over everyone else. Yet, as he held it, another thought crept in. The other students had enjoyed his game. Despite the chaos, despite his plans falling apart, he'd created something memorable. And he couldn't lie—the jacket was sick.

"I don't know if I should keep it," he muttered, voicing his inner turmoil.

"Why not?" Hyphen's gentle voice cut through his brooding. "It's a thoughtful gift, Char. Your game brought people together."

Alt nodded. "Yeah, man. For a week, you had the whole school buzzing. That's real cool."

Char's grip on the jacket tightened. He thought about the thrill of planning, the excitement of seeing his ideas come to life. For a moment, he allowed himself to feel proud.

He slipped the jacket on. It fit perfectly.

"Well?" he asked, looking at his friends.

"You look like a serious Game Master now," Tilde grinned, clapping as she leaned back in her chair.

Hyphen nodded and did a little cheer, while Alt's eyes remained fixated on the garment's craftsmanship.

"Who do you think it's from?" Char asked, feeling a strange flutter as he admired the fitted sleeves.

"I doubt it's just from one person," said Hyphen.

From the look in her eye, Char couldn't tell if she had masterminded this whole thing or was just being nice. But as his mind began to process the possibilities, he realized the gift was something he could appreciate. Besides, it was about time he had a new look for school.

Chapter 21: Atlas Statue

Promise lay in a poorly constructed tent in the center of his crater. A single steel beam lay strewn outside—a testament to Pandora's competence, and his inability to follow through on top of it.

He'd been camping there since he dropped out of school, but hadn't made progress on construction at all. Meanwhile, his siblings were back in the safety of their hotel hideout, commuting to the Institute on Pandora's 'Pride Jet'.

That night, he lay awake wondering if he'd bitten off more than he could chew.

Promise had little competition when it came to blowing stuff up, killing, and making a scene. His talent for destruction was honed ruthlessly over the past five years, and he impressed even himself with the raw firepower that exploded from his fingertips. Unfortunately, building nice things required a different set of skills than tearing them down. Despite his extraordinary lucidity, which theoretically should be applicable to all forms of void matter manipulation, it was possible that he just didn't have the skillset to make a skyscraper.

Even making the tent was harder than he expected. Getting void matter to coalesce into a strong solid had always been something he struggled with, and it was particularly activities like these that brought such a weakness to light. It wasn't beyond him to make little things like tin cans and plastic cups, but even just making a set of tent poles that didn't snap was an ordeal that took almost an hour.

As he lay on his back, he toyed with a ribbon of blue void matter between his hands. It wasn't that he never liked to create or didn't have it in him. When he was a kid, he remembered crafting intricate little Voidpet figurines out of ice, playing battle with his siblings. But over time, he'd gravitated towards the role of a risk taker, trailblazer, and destroyer. He took it upon himself to clear the path for others to walk. He ran towards danger until it wasn't dangerous anymore.

Promise smiled to himself as he willed the blue matter into an ice figurine. The little Lonely spun slowly, glittering between his hands.

If any of his siblings were around, he wouldn't be thinking these sorts of thoughts. Pandora would have set up the steel beams already, Volo would've already built the first floor, and Pecunia would have made sure everyone had nice beds to sleep in. But tonight, he was by himself. Sleeping in the middle of a demolition site like the maniac he was.

He put down the ice Lonely, then turned over to wrap his arms around his real one, who was curled up under his head like a pillow. Lulu's round body filled him with warmth as she purred and nuzzled him back. He nodded off to sleep, surreal shapes drifting through his vision as reality started to blur into a dream.

Suddenly, his eyes opened again, and he found himself standing in front of the Atlas Statue from the game—one of the few ancient landmarks whose name had not been lost to time. Had he teleported in his sleep?

A white light illuminated the base of the statue, and the tower windows flickered to life in a skyward cascade.

The statue opened its eyes, and he recognized the red eyes of his pet Greed. Had his Voidpet decided to possess the statue as some sort of prank?

"You promise, but you don't deliver, isn't that right?" A thunderous chuckle rolled from the statue, shaking the giant rings it held over its shoulders.

Promise winced at the sound of his name being used in such an accusation. He looked around at the surreal world around him, unable to make out anything beyond the statue but shifting shadows. As he beheld the living sculpture that towered before him, he flexed his hands, instinctively reaching to summon fire.

Nothing happened—which meant that this was a dream, and not the good kind.

The statue stood in front of a building that reached up into the sky. It now stood at what had to be at least 70 stories tall, the half-formed ruin mysteriously restored to its former glory.

"What do you want?" Promise snarled, taking a step back from the red-eyed behemoth.

"I think you must be mistaken," Atlas boomed back at him, his steel face contorting with amusement, "You're here because you want something from *me*."

Promise looked around, still unsure how or why he got here. As his gaze ascended the tower soaring behind the statue, he began to connect the dots.

"You and your people built this city, right? You, or whoever you're supposed to represent," Promise took a step back, his head tilting upwards to take in the full spectacle before him, and the statue smiled.

"So how did you do it? How did *you* deliver? How did you do it all without even using void matter?" Promise asked, his voice raising as it surged with urgency.

The statue laughed and heaved a rumbling breath.

"I only gave my life," it replied, leaving silence in the air.

"What does that *mean*? What am I supposed to *do*?" Promise pressed, his raw confusion spilling forth unfiltered in this subconscious dream world.

"You give your life too," the statue said slowly, its gravelly voice booming, "And the rest will follow."

"Well how *do I* do that? How do I do what *you* did?" Promise begged, noticing himself devolve like a kid throwing a tantrum.

Atlas laughed again, jiggling the giant globe above him. "Are you asking to inherit my curse?"

"Of course I am," Promise snapped back, surprising himself with the desperate certainty in his own words. For some reason, this dream had him feeling more agitated than he'd ever been in real life. He found himself breathing heavily, tears forming in his eyes as a strong wind began to blow.

"I want it more than anything else in the world." His voice cracked, more shrill than he could have imagined, and echoed through the buildings with a sharp ring. Promise's knuckles where white as he gripped the pedestal of the statue, his eyes wild with childlike anguish.

"Do you understand the consequences?" The statue asked, curious.

"I do," Promise replied, as a cold silence ensued.

"Well then," the statue smiled, its red eyes alight with a wicked gleam, "If you insist."

Suddenly, the rings of the globe on its shoulders dissolved as the Greed-Titan fusion stood up straight and flexed its arms.

As this happened, Promise felt a searing pain unlike anything he'd felt before. Black rivulets began to snake around his palms, his own petroleum concoction eating his flesh away. It seeped down his wrists and forearms, casting the full surface of his hands in a black lacquer that trailed off in a series of dark veins. A tortured scream escaped his throat as he collapsed to his knees. His legs were shaking, his eyes blurry as they flooded with tears.

"Enjoy your turn, brother."

The statue stretched with freedom as the black metal from its own body began to crumble away to reveal a layer of human skin. It stepped down from its pedestal, shrinking down to the size of a regular person, and walked away into the darkness. The metal melted into a dark liquid, which dripped onto the floor and rose at a surreal pace.

Promise watched the young man walk away as he crumbled to the stone floor, clutching his hands in agony. Pain was screaming through his bones, and he felt his vision slowly fade as the liquid submerge him.

Then, he woke up.

A living Nightmare was sitting on his chest. It peered down at him with a head full of red eyes, warbling a strange cry that was ringing in his ears. *No wonder.*

He reacted instantly. His fingers pierced its chest like a dagger, and the monster immediately dissolved to dust, its haunting cry petering out into silence. As he watched the dust spill over his hand, he saw that his hands remained an obsidian black, as they had been in the dream. They felt heavy, as if they were made of steel, and tapered into a set of pointed claws.

In some ways, they resembled Pandora's iron fist technique, but instead of glowing white, they were an absolute black—so dark they appeared to consume the light around them. As he instinctively began to collect the Nightmare fuel that fell to the ground, he felt a new power activate. At his fingertips, a tiny black hole gobbled the dust in seconds, crackling with electricity as it grew unusually large and violent. He absorbed the fresh void matter into his body, feeling a bolt of adrenaline shoot up his spine.

It wasn't a feeling that begot a villainous cackle. Instead, the new power was sobering. For a gift so unholy, the cost had to have been heartbreaking.

In Promise's mind, the statue's words rang clear—the price of power was a fractional lifespan. The Hands of Greed would multiply his abilities at the expense of his longevity. But he was too young to understand the true meaning of what he'd signed up for.

Part II:
The Windfalls

Chapter 22: Nightmares

Madison Windfall was the mother of four children:

First, Pandora, the eldest daughter and most astute.

Second, Promise, who was brilliant but troublesome.

Third, Pecunia, the younger sister, adored by all.

Fourth, Volo, the youngest son and golden child.

As Madison shepherded her children into the abandoned brick building, the dilapidated structure loomed around them, its empty windows like hungry mouths in the moonlight. A musty scent hung in the air, mingling with the acrid tang of Nightmares. Shadows danced along the walls, cast by the flickering light of Madison's void matter. She had brought all four of her children here to train, far out east from the city center.

She flipped her leather-bound journal open to November 22nd, scanning her rubric for tonight's test. As the children stood behind her in earnest, Madison felt a familiar weight settle in her chest.

This was the life she'd chosen for them—far from the gleaming white walls of the Institute, where children their age were supposed to go. Her rigorous homeschooling was exhausting, but necessary—for any advantage was necessary against the treacherous forces that ruled the Void.

"Pandora, you're up first," Madison called.

Her eldest daughter, 14 at the time, stepped forward. With her trusty companion Pride—a shimmer of silver at her side—she marched into the middle of the floor. As usual, Pandora knew she was ahead of expectations. As a hissing, ghoul-like Nightmare leapt at her back, she spun around to reply, her fist making contact with a resounding smack.

The creature sailed out the window, leaving Pandora standing with her victory pose held strong. Her fist swirled with silver void matter, fortified with the strength of Pride's metal energy, while her full figure cut a powerful silhouette in the moonlight. Pandora's gray eyes glinted with satisfaction, but she held her expression neutral. Such was Pandora's style: to the point, measured, and with restraint.

Madison jotted down a few observations in her journal, her pen hesitating over the phrase "room for improvement in agility and tactical approach." Pandora's methods, while different from what Madison envisioned, were undeniably effective. Madison pursed her lips into a smile, offering Pandora measured praise. "Well done," she said, her tone warm but not effusive. "Your strength is commendable. A-grade work. Perhaps going forward, we can work on incorporating more varied techniques."

Pecunia, her 12-year-old daughter, beamed at Pandora from the sidelines. She was a sweetheart, shy to fight, but eager to follow in the footsteps of her big sister. Meanwhile, 11-year-old Volo looked on in earnest, restless to take part in the action himself.

As Pandora stepped back into the shadows and allowed a smile to spread across her face, Promise whispered something to her. In response, she made a face and snorted.

Madison shot them a stern look, her eyeliner as sharp as her Judgement's switchblade wings, and reminded them to take their training seriously. Pandora's turn was regular practice, but Promise's trial was his annual exam. Tonight was his 13th birthday, and his test would determine his eligibility for more advanced training.

Madison let out a tired exhale. She took a sip of black coffee from her canteen and touched up her concealer to hide the bags under her eyes. Standing tall at 5'11", the former actress performed a polished example for her children and expected them to follow suit.

"Promise. I'm ready when you are."

Promise cast a wry grin at his sister, still smiling at whatever inside joke they had shared. He cracked his knuckles and sauntered to the center with his hands in his pockets. If her daughter's gait was like steel, her son's was like water—he moved with long, fluid strides, slipping across the moonlit hall like a shadow. He was the spitting image of Madison at that age—the same olive skin, ash brown hair, slight frame, and piercing eyes—which she found oddly unsettling to watch.

As Promise turned to face Madison, he pulled both hands out of his pockets and raised them to his sides. Void matter swirled above his open palms like floating rivulets of black water, beckoning a chorus of Nightmares to growl from his surroundings.

Promise had a gift for showing off with void matter. While Pandora was a pragmatist, channeling it efficiently and close to her body, Promise preferred for his to fill the room, snaking through the air like psychic strokes of ink. As murky figures rushed forth to attack, he sliced his hand through the air, commanding the matter to slash them away in a ripple of destruction. Madison winced as the arc of liquid rushed forth, leaving scars on the walls, and a mess of dark splatters on the floor.

As the first wave subsided, Promise flexed his fingers and assumed a ready stance, tucking his hands in towards his chin. While the fallen Nightmares wailed and dissolved to dust, the liquid ribbons of void matter followed his pace, recollecting themselves like a serpent that had just struck. All the while, his little Lonely pet sat in the corner, tucked away from danger as though the emotion had no place on the battlefield.

Promise grinned at Madison for approval, but she gazed back solemnly.

"Don't smile when you kill things, honey, that's disrespectful."

Promise's grin faltered, replaced by a look of exasperation.

Madison's eyes narrowed. "I'm teaching you to defend yourself, not to be a prize fighter."

She explained that he'd met expectations with his typical use of the water style and should continue.

Promise nodded and kept going. He carved through Nightmares with fluid grace, his matter taking on ever more volatile forms; first cleaving through the air like a wild blade, then radiating like liquid shockwaves. Madison watched, her unease growing with each wave of noises that followed.

As the mood intensified, the building creaked with the sound of larger Nightmares making their way up to the open floor. The sound of insect legs clattered through the walls, while humanoid screeches echoed from below. Promise glared up through his brows. With a sneer, he thrust one hand forward, fingers splayed as the black matter began to collect as a rich, red plasma in his palm. The air around shimmered as the red swelled, crackling with latent power.

Madison was surprised. Her son had switched to channeling void matter with fire energy, which was indeed out of character for him. She didn't know where he'd learned this but continued to observe quietly.

Before the next wave of Nightmares could emerge from the shadows, he directed a viscous slash of blood red matter into the walls. The strike combusted, continuing to sear across the length of the building opposite from the spectators.

Madison observed the new technique. The remaining Nightmares couldn't penetrate the wall of fire, and Promise's talents had undeniably exceeded her expectations. Still, she hesitated to voice her admiration.

"Your control over void matter is proficient," Madison stated, her tone measured. "You've passed." She closed her journal with a soft snap, her face a carefully constructed mask of neutrality. Promise's eyes narrowed at her tone.

"Oh? Just... passed?" He echoed, his voice cold.

Madison weighed her words carefully. His technique was exceptional, stunning, even, but she couldn't bring herself to applaud his attitude—let alone encourage it in front of the other children. Wasted void matter and tactless destruction were not traits she wanted to encourage, yet criticism seemed equally misplaced for such an advanced display.

"Correct. You've met all the requirements," she affirmed with a weary smile.

"You've earned a solid A-minus."

Promise's fingers twitched involuntarily, void matter swirling around his hands. A bitter smirk played at the corners of his mouth, at odds with the smell of smoke and crumbling walls surrounding them.

"...Extra credit, then?" he ventured with derision.

Without waiting for a response, Promise flexed his blistered hands. He lashed them out, commanding the void matter to shred the burning walls in waves of black and red. The flames danced in his eyes as they swelled, hastening to devour the abandoned structure. The fire roared, feeding off his energy. Promise hesitated briefly, alarm flashing in his eyes as he saw a wall collapse a few feet away from his Lonely— but he continued to push harder, drawing fresh streams of void matter to pool at his singed fingertips.

His new style took the shape of neither water nor fire. It was a mesmerizing concoction of liquid power like blood, lava, and crude oil, thrashing like a living beast as the building groaned ominously around them. A fierce exhilaration blazed in Promise's eyes as he admired his handiwork, his siblings transfixed by his creation.

From the corner of her eye, Madison noticed Pecunia's wide-eyed fascination, her small hands clutching at her sides as if to contain her excitement. Volo, usually restless, stood still, his eyes tracking every movement of Promise's technique. Even Pandora, who typically reserved pride as an emotion for herself, seemed to take delight in her brother's cinematic performance.

Suddenly, blades of white sliced through the firestorm, Judgement's four, magnificent wings dissipating it instantly. Madison stood with her arm outstretched, her eyes blazing as she summoned her Voidpet to end the exam. "Enough!" Her voice cracked like a whip, cutting through the settling debris. "I said you've passed."

Judgement boarded Lonely and the other children onto the safety of its back, as Madison's gaze bore into Promise in a silent command that brooked no argument.

"We're going home. All of us. Now."

"We don't need to waste any more void matter tonight."

Promise looked crestfallen, and Madison's jaw clenched. The word "waste" felt harsh on her tongue, though she was at a loss for what else to say. She hurried her family home, acutely aware of the demolished site crumbling into ashes behind them.

The train ride home was quiet. Madison's gaze flicked between her children, noting their furtive glances and half-hidden smiles. Promise sat slumped with his arms crossed, his reflection in the train window stubbornly avoiding her eyes. Yet, beneath his sullen exterior, an unmistakable satisfaction was there—a ghost of a smile suppressed as he idly admired his hands.

In her son's posture, she saw a troublesome reflection of her past self. Having traded one master for another until she'd finally broken free, Madison herself was no stranger to the allure of power. Unfortunately, she'd learned humility the hard way, and now shouldered the responsibility of imparting it to her children.

As the ghost train whisked them through the haunting vacancy of the underground, Madison closed her eyes. She took a deep breath and resolved to get to the bottom of whatever dark forces were leading her children astray.

Chapter 23: Broadway

Broadway Windfall was at work when he received a text message from his wife.

Madison: *When you get home, we need to talk about our son.*

"*Which one?*" Broadway typed, before revising his message to "*OK honey*".

He took a second to admire Madison's picture in the little bubble on his phone—the serene smile of her thumbnail a stark contrast to the tone of her message. She was, without a doubt, the most brilliant woman he'd ever met, and the most beautiful too.

Broadway settled into his dressing room chair, exhaling slowly as he transitioned from the chaos of the set to his private sanctuary. He was the lead actor for *Seven Layers of the Soul*— a superhero comedy where each episode took place in a different dimension, and, of course, the Void's most popular show.

As he adjusted his costume, his Sanctimony shimmered around his wrist in the form of a gold watch. His back straightened reflexively as he was filled with the virtue of his companion, emboldened to become the hero he portrayed on set. Sanctimony was not a popular Voidpet, but for Broadway, it had helped him change his life. *Fake it 'til you make it*, they say, and so he did.

Broadway checked his reflection in the mirror one last time. His cheekbones glowed under the fluorescent bulbs, and a thin scar running down his left one added to his rugged charm—a souvenir from his previous employer. He ran a hand through his jet-black hair, and flashed a wide, warm smile at his reflection.

He enjoyed being a celebrity, for it was, in many ways, better than being a gangster. It was nice knowing that the mobs gathering outside his door were just the paparazzi. And that his new boss was just the director.

A commotion outside interrupted his trance. Shouts and screams erupted from outside the dressing room.

"Nightmare!" yelled the Paranoia cameraman. "It's breached the gate!"

Broadway was on his feet in an instant, still fully clad in his superhero costume. As he burst out of the studio, he saw it—a gangly mass of spidery appendages, lashing out at the crew. Fear rippled through the air, feeding the creature. This Nightmare was a medium-sized Spiral: one of those that looked like insects and feasted on fright.

Instinctively, Broadway's hand flew to his watch. Sanctimony responded, unfurling from his wrist in a blaze of golden light. His wyvern Voidpet circled above him like a helicopter, its three detached wings rotating around its reptilian body like a spinning torpedo.

"Everyone, stay calm!" Broadway's voice boomed across the set, infused with the power of Sanctimony. The Spiral faltered, sensing the shift in the landscape.

For someone who only dressed up as a superhero, Broadway knew how to deal with monsters. He stepped forward, radiating golden void matter through his fists and eyes, swaggering up towards the Spiral with a performer's poise. Sanctimony lurched at the monster with its talons outstretched, and Broadway flared his golden energy in display of his prowess.

Ever since he left the streets of his hometown, he resolved not to use violence unless absolutely necessary, and at this low level of threat, there was no need to engage in battle.

With each step, the Nightmare retreated, burrowing back into the earth as its form diminished. His Voidpet coworkers applauded his prompt damage control, and show business resumed as usual. As the last of the creature disappeared, Broadway felt a familiar rush—not from relief, but of concern. These small attacks were becoming more frequent, especially during the daytime.

The rest of the day unfolded in a series of scenes and takes, each one blurring into the next. Yet, even as he poured his presence into the fictional absurdity of his role, Madison's text gnawed at him.

Broadway's character, Bob Wong, was an ordinary dad from Ancient America who gained superpowers from a radioactive dumpling. In each episode, Bob would blunder through various dimensions, leaving a trail of inadvertent chaos as he fought absurd villains.

In today's scenes, Bob laser-beamed down an army of blue tentacle bears, only for viewers to learn they were key to curing cancer. Next, he thwarted a mind-control plot, unintentionally plunging Ancient Texas into anarchy as citizens faced withdrawal from a peace-causing poison. Each adventure ended with a 'womp womp' sound effect. His Sanctimony screamed like an eagle as it soared across the ancient star-spangled banner, and triumphant music immediately followed.

The show's recurring theme was Bob never facing consequences for his actions, remaining a beloved hero despite the mayhem he unknowingly caused. Broadway didn't fully grasp the appeal, but figured the nihilism resonated with the Void's melancholy populace.

"That's a wrap," a portly dragon called. The Nostalgia director's voice snapped Broadway back to reality.

As he returned to a world where he did, in fact, have to face the consequences of his actions, worry crept back into his mind.

He hoped it was something innocuous. Maybe Promise was gay. Or, perhaps, fed up with being homeschooled—which would also be valid.

As he returned home late that evening, the elevator ride seemed longer than usual, Sanctimony's weight on his wrist heavier somehow. He stepped into his apartment, relieved to see Pandora and Promise studying in the living room. Still feeling a sense of dread brewing in his gut, he rushed to greet them with a hurried hug, before heading straight to his bedroom where Madison stood waiting.

Broadway could feel Madison's turmoil as soon as the door closed behind him. He leapt to speak, deciding it was better than saying nothing at all.

"Honey, I want you to know that I love our children no matter what," he blurted, hoping to resolve the issue before it started.

"Oh—well that's good—but I'm not sure—"

In her arms, Madison held a squirming, ink-black creature that seemed to devour the light around it. "Broadway," Madison's voice was tight. "I found *this* in Promise's room."

His eyes fixed on the Voidpet, whose body wriggled like a giant maggot. Despite its short, plump form, it had the face of a large snake, bearing deep, red eyes, filled with desire. He'd seen its like before, in his less savory past. *A Greed.* How had Promise captured and befriended such a thing? And more importantly, what would it mean for their family?

As the gravity of the situation sank in, Broadway realized that his earlier intuition had been correct.

Mr. and Mrs. Windfall were both distraught. As they had laid awake discussing the night before, Broadway had hoped it was a Determination, Defiance, or even an Anger; all of which were noble, fiery, dragon-like Voidpets known to bring blessings to their keepers. If his son was having an episode of teen angst paired with the sudden onset of novel fire techniques, then the most likely culprit was simply a new pet.

But Broadway's worst fears were confirmed when he saw the Greed: a harbinger of darkness that foretold a future of corruption. From the fact that it was purring in Madison's arms, clearly comfortable being held, he deduced that his son must have been hiding it in his closet for an untold amount of time. It was significantly larger than most Voidpets in their nascent first forms, and they suspected that Promise was feeding it scraps of void matter from his allowance.

"We already had our concerns about Pandora keeping a Pride, but a *Greed* is a step further," Madison said, her voice delicate as she began to spell out her woes.

"Pride... Pride is sometimes celebrated as a positive trait, but... no one *ever* talks about *greed* like it's a good thing."

Broadway nodded with understanding, wordlessly placing a hand on her shoulder in support.

"And the legends of Greed keepers..." Madison pressed, "They're *all* ridden with tragedy. Untimely deaths. Horrific punishments. Legacies of destruction. Such is always the fate of people who claim to have mastered Greed..."

"Are we cursed?" Madison looked up, her voice cracking, "this must be our karma..."

Broadway's heart sank at the despair in his wife's tone. He saw the weight of their past etched in the lines of her face. His partner in crime, both figuratively and literally—the incredible woman he'd fallen in love with, the woman who'd fought so hard to leave that life behind— now stood before him looking more vulnerable than he'd ever seen her. Broadway's mind raced, searching for the right words, the perfect script to make everything better.

"No, we can't be cursed," he said softly, reaching out to take her hand. "We've worked too hard, come too far for that to be true." Madison's eyes, usually sharp and certain, now swam with unshed tears. "But our son... a *Greed*, Broadway. How could we have missed this?"

"Listen," he began, his voice firm, "we've both done things in our past that we're not proud of. But we *changed*. We chose a different path. We made so many sacrifices to get where we are today." He squeezed her hand, willing her to believe him. "Promise is young. He's got a lot to figure out, and a lot to learn. But he has us to guide him."

Madison nodded slowly, but doubt still clouded her features. "And if we can't?"

The question hung in the air between them, heavy with unspoken fears. Broadway felt the cool pressure of Sanctimony on his wrist, a reminder of his own journey from villain to hero. "Then we'll face it together," Broadway declared, pulling Madison into a tight embrace. "Whatever comes, we'll handle it as a family."

"Everything is going to be a-okay."

He embraced his wife firmly, feeling reassured by the sound of his own voice.

As usual, he decided to fake it until he figured something out.

Chapter 24: Sandwiches

Promise paced.

With his hands in the pockets of his black jacket, his lanky silhouette stalked the living room like a caged tiger. In response, Pandora munched over a plate of peanut butter sandwiches, seated on the couch with her books. Her Pride was curled at her side, licking itself, and Promise's Lonely sat snug in a nest of couch pillows. The rest of the family was fast asleep, and the two eldest siblings were up late studying.

"Pandora," Promise wondered out loud, "What do you think Mom and Dad are always so *scared of*?"

"Like, if you look at their faces *90%* of the time..." he pulled a random figure for emphasis, "it's like they don't know anything other than being afraid."

Pandora shrugged. "I wouldn't know," she mused as she took another bite, "but I assume the Void must be a dangerous place."

"But like... *is it* though?" Promise asked, his eyes narrowing with sass. "Aren't we *way* overqualified against all the Nightmares we fight? Like, are you sure they don't just have *anxiety* or something?"

Pandora thought about it. "I mean, I think it makes sense that Mom is training us one step at a time," she said slowly. "We're still so young, and there's a lot we haven't seen yet."

Promise rolled his eyes. "Come on, Pandora, use your brain. Either they're paranoid, or they've got big tea they're not telling us. Which do you think it is?"

Pandora huffed.

"Look, we weren't born into this world to live by fear," Promise began, his voice taking on a dramatic lilt, "to be trapped inside cowering minds, afraid to feel things to their fullest. Isn't the whole point of work, of learning, of knowledge, of all we do, to expand humanity's capacity for joy?"

He absently produced a stream of void matter from his hands, and started swirling the energy into a dark liquid between his fingers.

"If they were as strong as you and me... they'd act like we do."

Pandora chuckled, unsure what he meant by that. "So like, they'd start dropping five bucks to add flair to their yaps?" She teased, noting her brother's habit for channeling valuable void matter while he spoke.

"Chill, I'm not going to like, use it up," Promise replied with an eye roll.

"But you get it, right? They're afraid. Everyone's afraid. Everyone's *afraid* of the *world*. They'll work and wear themselves to death because that's all they know how to do."

Pandora enjoyed listening to Promise rant. He possessed a smoldering conviction that made him a captivating speaker, and a theatrical intensity that, as his big sister who was quite familiar with it, she found comical. She wondered if others would call it charisma, or perhaps manipulative rhetoric—although to her, it was simply refreshing.

"Our parents don't realize they *hate themselves*." He continued. "They recoil from joy because they're convinced they don't deserve it. They're terrified of seeing us happy... because they don't know how to feel anything other than their convoluted layers of repressed anxiety. They're so, deeply... viscerally... afraid of their own mistakes, they're addicted to the piety—the *safety*—of regret, and will drink from that poisoned well until the day they die."

He paused, and lowered his tone.

"And of course, they'd rather die than go to therapy." He added, raising his eyebrows.

Pandora chortled at the hyperbole while taking another bite. Her brother's descriptions were entertaining. In moments like these, she saw how they were clearly the children of actors—not to mention, homeschooled weirdos who read too many books.

"Most people are ruled by fear because it's the easiest instinct to obey. They like the certainty of being told what to do. And you know who lives by fear?"

He slowed his swirling void matter for dramatic effect, holding up his blue light to reflect in his eyes: "Creatures who don't know how to do anything besides survive."

"If they saw the world how I see it, if they felt what I felt, if they truly understood that they could be the greatest in the world—they'd be smiling every day, they'd be running in the sunshine, they wouldn't just be surviving, they'd be living free."

He spoke with slow pauses between phrases as he searched for his words, mid-monologue.

"If they had any idea what I—what *we*—were fully capable of... they'd never worry about a single stupid thing again. They would realize that *we* are the ones who are destined to protect *them*."

Pandora interjected. "Do you think your worldview might be limited at age thirteen?" She asked.

"No."

Pandora scoffed, but decided not to interrupt further.

He paced up to the window and continued with his back to her, speaking to his own reflection with his hand against the glass, overlooking the night.

"I am the greatest in the world... I already know it." He declared, as his void matter rippled from his pressed palm, dancing across the window in shades of electric blue. Blue was his color when he was pensive, for it was when his water type energy ran dominant.

"Nobody else knows it yet, but they don't have to for it to be true. I don't have to prove anything to anyone, because I know who I am. Just you watch. Give me 10 years... Maybe 20. And I'll go further than anything they've ever imagined. The future already exists, and I know what lies ahead in my timeline."

"Is that so?" Pandora mused, as her Pride placed its head in her lap and purred.

"Hey, I'm just manifesting," Promise swiveled around to face her with a breezy smile, shrugging with his hands raised in modest defense as his void matter thinned like steam, "I mean like, we all have the potential to be great and whatever."

Promise glanced down with a hint of embarrassment before noticing that Pandora was still at ease, and carried on.

"Of course, they're going to hate us for it. The stronger we get, the more they're going to hate us, because no matter how much they care about us, people can't help but hate whatever breaks their world view. They'll care about you and all, but it won't change the fact that when they look at you, their minds won't have room for anything beyond fear and worry. It's already becoming like that now, you can see it right?"

He continued, his tone curling into a snarl.

"The saddest thing is, people fear out of fondness. They're so scared they're going to lose everything they love, and that's why they can't bring themselves to act right. But the irony is... their feelings are suffocating when they come from fear."

"And I get it. It's poetic, almost, but it's a shame." He hung his head slightly, and his Lonely shifted in its pillow nest.

"People who lose their minds over saving void matter are the same people who know they don't have the capacity to wield any more. They know they can't handle it, so they clutch onto every last drop in their hands like they'll never see it again. They're scared. They're limited. They're afraid of themselves."

"I *believe* I deserve more," Promise continued as fire energy crept into his aura, "I deserve the most because I *do* the most, as I always have." He admired his own power as his void matter fluctuated between ice blue flames and blood red liquid.

"You're not afraid either, because you know you deserve it too."

"I'm not afraid of anything because there is no one above me."

He looked at Pandora and added darkly. "There is no one above us."

She burst into laughter and rolled her eyes.

"Ok, now cool it before anyone hears you acting *bananas*."

Promise's eyes were alight with zeal, his void matter blooming in a now steady plume of blue fire. She didn't disagree with his sentiment, but she chortled and shook her head.

"You at least need to *pretend* to be normal if you want to make it out of here. If you get locked up somewhere, I won't have anyone to talk to."

His act evaporated instantly, and he started laughing along with her, plopping down onto the couch with his arms spread around the backrest. The undirected void matter dissolved into transparent energy that siphoned back into his hands.

"Okay, okay, you know I'm just kidding right?" He said, his face breaking out in a devilish grin.

"You're literally not!" Pandora giggled, her mouth agape, "You're literally *unhinged*!"

"I'm literally just like, saying affirmations." He stared at her with a sheepish look, a caricature of innocence with his hands in the air.

"No but like, when we take over the world it's gonna be non-violent, ok?" He prodded, holding his mouth open in an expectant grin.

"I mean how hard can it be, there's like, nobody here!"

"Okay Mr. Peaceful Supreme Leader of the future," Pandora joked, "Since you're so fearless and almighty, how about you do my calculus problems for me then?"

"Alright I take it back, forget everything I said, I was just hungry." He grabbed Pandora's sandwich and took a bite, before she laughed at him and snatched it back.

"Eat your own, doofus!" She reached from the plate and shoved a fresh sandwich at him.

They finished their peanut butter sandwiches and continued to do their homework into the night.

152

Chapter 25: Eavesdrop

With eyes the color of dollar bills and hair as dark as the black market, Pecunia Eve Windfall had a talent for skirting trouble. The less she did, the less people expected of her, and she liked it that way. That morning, as she overheard a commotion in the living room, she tiptoed to the end of the hallway to eavesdrop.

"I need you to get rid of it. *Now.*" Her mother's sharp words carried from around the corner.

"You realize I can't just *get rid of* my pet," Promise's voice shot back, her big brother's attitude impossible to miss, "Like, where's he gonna go?"

"Release it in the park."

"Mom, that's *animal cruelty.*"

"People let go of their emotions all the time," Madison chided, "You need to find a way to say goodbye to Greed."

"Well, what if I can't?"

"This isn't up for discussion," Madison's voice was escalating sharply, each word bitten off. "You need to get that creature out of our home."

"What if I don't want to? And what if I don't?"

"Then you're disrespecting your mother."

A silence hung in the air before Promise talked back.

"So what?" he challenged, his words trembling slightly, "What if I disagree because your opinion is dumb?"

The sound of rapid footsteps echoed, followed by Madison's voice, now an iron bark. "Don't you *dare* take that tone with me, young man."

Promise replied with something that Pecunia knew was only going to get him into more trouble.

"Watch your language!" Madison snapped. "I am your mother, and you will do as I say!"

Suddenly, blue light spilled around the corner, followed by bright white, a smack, and the sound of a chair being tipped over. It was followed by a red glow, and a mess of shadows, snarling Voidpet sounds, and something falling to the floor with a thud.

"Have you ever stopped to think that maybe *you're* the reason I have him in the first place?" Promise snarled. "You think I was just *born greedy*? *Who* do you think taught me there's no such thing as enough?"

Sounds of Madison sobbing ensued.

Yikes, Pecunia thought. *What a mess.*

Both Madison and Promise were what Pecunia would describe as 'extra', which meant that the fight had only just gotten started.

A sudden warmth beside her announced Volo's stealthy arrival. Her little brother slid next to her, whispering, "What's happening?"

"Promise is getting cooked by Mom," she whispered back.

"Ok."

"Shh."

Pecunia knew that Promise had been keeping his Greed for a few months now. For some reason, he'd stashed it in his closet instead of capturing it in a container. That either meant that Greed was too strong to be contained, or that Promise was too naïve to house it properly.

She figured it was most likely the latter.

Pecunia smirked to herself as she studied the intricate ring coiled around her middle finger, admiring the unassuming vessel containing her own little secret. Ever since she was a little girl, she'd paid close attention to how her dad stored his Sanctimony in his watch—and quietly executed the same technique using her favorite piece from her jewelry box.

One thing she and Volo had agreed on long ago: it was important to contain your Voidpets correctly.

Another thing they agreed on: Promise was foolish for getting caught.

Chapter 26: Something Park

Outside, the evening sky melted into hues of cotton candy. Wisps of distant void matter swirled lazily overhead, as the autumn sunset bathed the tree-lined street in a golden sheen. It was a rare evening where Madison had decided to cancel training, and the Windfall children were headed to the park, enjoying their first night off in a long time.

The children's footsteps crunched on fallen leaves, and the air carried a faint scent of sweet decay. As they ambled towards Something Park, the world seemed to slow down. Even in nature, void matter responded to the human mind, and painted the air with the colors of soft fascination.

Promise's Lonely bobbled beside him, looking at him fondly with her round googly-eyes. Pandora hummed a half-remembered lullaby over the steady rhythm of her boots and rustling leaves, while Pride trotted by her side like a loyal retriever. Pecunia skipped and twirled, her glossy hair catching the last golden rays of sunlight, and Volo walked with his hands in his pockets, staring out into the distance in deep thought. Streetlamps flickered to life as dusk fell, casting an ethereal glow behind the light of drifting void matter particles. The silhouette of Something Park emerged, its trees and roads blending into the twilight like watercolor. In that moment, their lives were simple. They were together on a perfect autumn evening, without a care in the world.

As they entered the park, now a good distance from home, Pecunia's eyes glimmered with mischief. She casually extended her hand, pretending to admire her nails. Suddenly, the delicate ring on her third finger began to shine with golden light. It unfurled in a swirl of inky void matter, coalescing into a form beside her. Sloth materialized, looking like a peculiar cross between a bloated slug and a sleepy puppy, complete with a snout. "Tada!" Pecunia sang, her voice brimming with excitement. Promise and Pandora froze mid-step, their jaws dropping in unison. Pecunia couldn't contain her glee at their shocked expressions. "Bet you didn't know I had a secret too!" she teased, sticking out her tongue. With a giggle, she scooped Sloth out of the air, cuddling him like an oversized, wiggly teddy bear.

Promise, having just gotten in trouble for his Greed, was not exactly thrilled with this knowledge. But he cared more about his little sister's joy than whether things were fair between them.

"What? There is *no way* you got away with that!" He said with an incredulous grin, "I think I've been outclassed as an evil mastermind..."

Pecunia cackled as she sprinted deeper into the park, carrying her pet Sloth in her arms.

"Catch me if you can, SLOWPOKE!" For a petite 12-year-old, Pecunia certainly had a big attitude, and a hearty belly laugh to go with it.

Promise chased after Pecunia, conjuring a stream of red void matter to fly after her in the shape of an abstract dragon. "Careful who you call slowpoke!" he replied, as they ran through the large meadow at the front of the park in a playful game of pursuit.

Volo, who was not involved in the conversation, decided to join in simply because he liked to run. He let the older two get a head start, and then sprinted up to Pecunia as fast as he could to race her.

Pandora smiled, continuing her leisurely walk as her siblings charged into the distance. It was during times like this that she noticed how close the four of them were. They could have easily resented each other, especially given the rigor of their homeschooling, but for some reason, they didn't.

As the sun dipped lower on the horizon, casting long shadows across Something Park, the Windfall siblings continued to play in the meadow. The sounds of their voices rang across the empty park as if they were truly suspended in a void. It was as if time had paused, allowing them a brief reprieve to just be children.

Volo's brown eyes widened. "Look!" he exclaimed, pointing skyward. A large swarm of Wonder emerged from the treetops and fluttered overhead. Their ribbon-tailed butterfly wings shimmered in the fading light, leaving trails of sparkling dust in their wake.

"I think some of them are vivid," he said quietly. "Those are rare."

Pandora nodded slowly, entranced by their beauty. Most Voidpets were black and white, but vivid variants came in different colors. The children paused to watched the Wonder disappear into the distance, marveling at the flecks of red, blue, and gold that dotted their inky formation.

The siblings ran around some more, making their way over to the Something Park Lake.

"Last one in owes me all their void matter!" Pecunia squealed, soaking her wool skirt as she led the charge into the cold water, toting Sloth in to float beside her. Volo cannonballed in after her, while Pandora bunched her skirt and waded in with Pride. Promise hesitated at the thought of getting wet, but reluctantly followed as Lonely nudged him into the lake.

"You owe me all of *your* void matter for saying that," he quipped back, before splashing her with a scoop of lake water.

Soon, they got tired and lay in the grass to dry off. As they laughed and looked up at the sky, they watched it fade from a canvas of vibrant pinks into a serene, open black.

The Void was a beautiful place sometimes.

Unfortunately, their reverie came to an abrupt end.

The sky boomed with a thunderous roar and screamed with green light.

The children leapt to their feet to face the source of the noise.

A worm the size of a train was circling through the night sky. Their apartment building was under attack.

Chapter 27: Nerves of Steel

The pale Nightmare swam through the air, sixteen stories above. Armored rings encased it from head to tail, gleaming in the moonlight as the creature twisted through the sky. It lunged at the building with the full force of its serpentine body, bludgeoning the structure like a battering ram. The creature's mouth, a series of concentric rings, turned to face them. Each set of jagged teeth glowed like a furnace, illuminated by its fiery interior.

This Nightmare dwarfed any they'd encountered. Four pairs of eyes ran down its length—a Stage 5, Pandora realized. The most powerful form, rarely ever seen.

Pandora's mind raced as she assessed the threat.

They faced two challenges: one, neutralize the Nightmare, and two, prevent the building's collapse. As she formulated her battle strategy, she thought of their childhood fantasy games: herself, the warrior, Promise the sorcerer, Volo the assassin, Pecunia the thief.

Promise, true to his role, excelled at manipulating energies from a distance. But he struggled with precision against moving targets and was weak at using void matter in its solid form. He was neither suited to protect the building nor defeat the Nightmare—Therefore, distraction would be his best utility, giving Pandora time to do both. She also knew better than to slight her brother by saying that out loud.

Pandora grit her teeth and barked orders.

"You take down the Nightmare," she told Promise.

She looked at the top floor of the building that the creature was bashing to rubble, then turned to face Volo and Pecunia.

"You two, stay back and find help," she directed. She knew the two little ones were tough, but refused to put them in danger.

Volo's reply was curt.

"We're finding our parents," he said in polite contradiction. He erupted into a dash and sped towards the building with Pecunia close behind.

No time to argue. Pandora had her own task.

She marched up to the base of the architecture, charging up her fists with sparkling white void matter, and planted her palms into the walls with all her might. Pride mirrored her, pressing its lion-like paws into the structure, and lending her its power.

The technique was called *Nerves of Steel*. Normally, it was about fortifying one's own body, but in this case, she was extending it to the building itself.

She'd never attempted it on such a scale, but her calculations suggested it should work. Her architectural knowledge told her that there was no need to reinforce the entire building—her job was to protect the core columns, and brace the top floor system from caving in.

Pandora's void matter surged through the building's skeleton. Steel beams groaned as her energy protected them, forming an invisible lattice of strength. She visualized the structure's weak points, directing her power with precision. Sweat beaded on her brow.

The top floors swayed dangerously with each impact from the Nightmare. Pandora clenched her jaw, doubling her efforts. She felt every tremor, every stress point. Her mind raced, calculations flowing as she adjusted her technique. More power to the eastern corner. Reinforce that load-bearing wall. Stabilize the roof before it caves. Pride augmented her strength, its pure metal energy merging with Pandora's. Together, they created a web of support that ran from foundation to rooftop. The Nightmare struck again, and Pandora staggered. But the building stood firm. Her plan was working—the structure now moved as one unified entity, bending and recovering instead of crumbling.

Seconds felt like hours. Pandora's arms shook, muscles screaming. Sweat poured down her face. The strain of holding an entire building together with sheer will threatened to crush her. But she didn't break. Another impact. Pandora gritted her teeth and ducked her head as dust rained on her from above. Her vision blurred. Still, she poured everything into her task.

Just a little longer. Just a few more seconds.

The fate of her family, of their home, rested on Pandora's fourteen-year-old shoulders.

Fortunately, Pandora wasn't one to buckle.

Chapter 28: 10k VM

Teleporting one's body was a highly advanced technique with unforgiving consequences. It was also the only way to reach a monster flying sixteen stories above the ground.

Promise felt his pulse pounding in his ears. This was his chance to use all the techniques that were forbidden in training. It was his chance to show his full strength and be a real hero for his family. He flexed his fingers in ritual, looked up at the Nightmare, and prepared his attack.

Pandora trusted him to take it down, and he wouldn't disappoint.

Promise did not have Pandora's stamina, nor did he have her strength. He lacked the dexterity of his little brother and the evasiveness of his little sister. However, he compensated for everything in raw lucidity—which, in his opinion, was the most important skill in the Void anyway.

The human body was made of void matter, albeit in a highly processed form. The further void matter was from its original form, the harder it was to manipulate—but it was not impossible. He bit his lip in concentration. Any person, including oneself, could be manipulated just like anything else. The ultimate boundary to push.

As he turned his energy inward and cast his focus on where he needed to be, streams of black vapor rose and escaped from his form. He repeated the mantras from training to focus his mind.

Solid, liquid, gas.

Matter is neither created nor destroyed.

As the behemoth Nightmare continued to lunge at the building, smashing its head into the walls like a wrecking ball, Promise stood still, letting the world go quiet. His pulse pounded louder in his ears, and the creature's relentless assault faded to background noise. As he focused his lucidity, the world seemed to slow.

The Nightmare was fully covered in a shell-like armor that ran down the full length of its annelid form. It was likely too tough to be slashed. Too thick to incinerate. But its insides? Vulnerable. One spot to strike. He visualized his target—the Nightmare's gaping maw, ringed with concentric rows of teeth—directing all his void matter into his hands as the rest of his body continued to fade into vapor.

He felt himself growing lightheaded and losing his vision as his form faded.

Seconds ticked. Time screeched to a halt as the moment arrived.

There was something oddly intoxicating about shortcutting through space and time.

This was what it meant to feel alive. To rewrite the rules of reality.

In a heartbeat, he was sixteen stories in the air.

He materialized right in front of the Nightmare's open mouth, holding a ball of crackling red matter as he gazed into the endless rings of teeth. As the black vapor materialized his form, he appeared frozen, like a pitcher before a throw.

Everything about the moment was pure adrenaline—the wind whipping through his hair, the dizzying height, the cavernous maw before him.

He slammed his arm forward. The ball compressed. Ecstasy ensued.

As Promise's vision began to fade to black once again, he saw a red shockwave exploding from his palm, barreling straight down the Nightmare's mouth. The blast zoomed. The air smelled like seared meat. Rings of red rippled down throughout the length of its form, as the flying creature roared a final cry and faltered towards the ground like a train breaking down and collapsing.

Oh yeah.

That was a good hit.

So that's what spending 10,000 void matter looked like.

Perhaps it was too much.

But it didn't matter anymore. It was done.

With no void matter left, Promise blacked out and started free falling from sixteen stories in the air. A serene grace washed over him as his consciousness faded.

There's no such thing as too much when you're playing to win.

Chapter 29: Golden Child

Volo noticed the red explosion as he reached the tenth floor of his crumbling apartment building. Having scaled the walls from the outside, he paused to observe, with one long saber anchored into the concrete from his wrist.

It seemed as though Promise had KO'ed himself, and the worm was still alive.

Understandable, he thought.

Stage 5 Nightmares were serious business.

As Volo spotted his brother plummeting from the sky, he launched himself off the wall with explosive force. Like a human bullet, he intercepted Promise mid-air, their momentum carrying them across the street. With practiced precision, Volo twisted in flight, driving his wrist saber into the concrete of an opposite building to arrest their fall. The blade bit deep, securing them in place with a jarring halt.

Years of disciplined training had allowed Volo to store vast amounts of void matter within his own musculature. He'd honed his abilities to focus entirely on enhancing his physical strength and dexterity, eschewing the flashier conjuring techniques favored by others. This philosophy, instilled in him from a young age, stemmed from the belief that conserving void matter was far more efficient than blasting it all over the place.

While Volo's conjuring abilities were limited primarily to the physical mutations he employed in battle, his approach gave him a distinct edge. By wielding void matter within his body rather than projecting it outward, he'd become a finely tuned instrument of compact power.

With unconscious Promise secured in one arm, Volo descended the neighboring wall. His saber, manipulated with expert control, cleaved through concrete like a diamond saw, guiding their controlled fall. This technique wasn't just effective—it was incredibly efficient. Generating his sabers cost a mere hundred void matter, and he could reabsorb them with up to 95% recovery—sometimes even 100% if used lightly. The entire rescue had cost him a mere 5 void matter.

Volo wasn't one to judge, however. He knew he was fortunate to have a passion for physical activity, which enabled him to develop a very different relationship with void matter. His heightened proprioception allowed him to contain his Voidpet in his own skeleton, and thus draw upon its anatomic powers.

As he set Promise down on the sidewalk, taking care to choose a spot far enough from the demolition rubble, he held a moment of quiet respect for his big brother. Volo had never seen a blast of such magnitude before, nor had he seen anyone successfully teleport in his 11 years of life. Despite his obvious weaknesses, Promise was a menace in his own right.

Volo quickly returned his attention to the incapacitated Nightmare that had crashed down into the pavement across the street from him. Its tremendous form lay twisted upon itself like a coil of discarded rope, now smoking with flames. He studied the runic eye patterns on its armor—nine of which had dulled to a lifeless gray. His gaze locked on the one that remained a pulsing, shining black, located towards the end of its tail. The one he needed to destroy.

As the massive tail began to lurch towards him like a possessed train car, Volo bolted. He flipped to the side, rocketed himself into the air with a VM powered leap, and landed in the center of the final eye marking, his fist touching down as his saber plunged deep into the center of the symbol. The Nightmare hummed like a dying engine and powered down.

As Volo pulled his saber out, a sandy substance began to spill from the cut. *Nightmare fuel*, he thought. This would be useful later.

Unfortunately, he didn't have time to sit around and collect the dust. The Nightmare was defeated. Pandora had stabilized the building. And Pecunia seemed to have made it up the building with no issue. But there was still no sign of their parents.

Channeling another burst of void matter to his muscles, Volo sprinted towards the base of the building again. He began to dash up the side of the wall, latching onto patios with appendages that sprouted from his back, bouldering over the stonework until he reached the sixteenth floor.

When he reached the window and crawled inside, he saw both of his sisters standing in the living room of their demolished apartment.

"Where's Promise?" Pandora asked.

"Sleeping on the sidewalk."

"Is he okay?"

"He's fine."

"Where's Mom and Dad?"

"We don't know yet."

The three of them dug through the rubble and cried out for their parents.

A few minutes later, they heard the elevator ding, and Promise limped over to join them. His white shirt was stained dark red.

"I can't believe..." he stopped to catch his breath, "...you just left me on the street," he said. He tried smiling to show he was well, but his mouth dripping with blood did not help his case.

"What happened?" Pandora asked.

"I just..." he said through strained breaths, "pulled off the greatest move of all time back there, did you see it?" He gestured out the window and propped his hand on the wall to stop himself from collapsing.

His forced smile quickly faded as he noticed the mood in the room. There was no sight of Madison or Broadway, and it was clear they had been searching for some time.

"Woah, did you guys see this?" Promise's face paled, suddenly pointing to the mirror as he walked through the entryway.

Volo and his sisters scrambled over to look—since none of them had thought to check their reflections mid-crisis.

A large circle was etched on the glass, slashed through with a diagonal line.

"No, I missed that," Pandora murmured, tracing her fingertips around the marking.

"Who do you think did that?" asked Pecunia. Since it clearly couldn't have been the worm.

"Maybe someone left us a clue," Volo offered, to which only a defeated silence followed. Even if it was a message from their parents, no one knew what to make of it.

Exhausted, they sat together amidst the rubble and flames. Promise coughed. He curled up on his side from his searing stomachache and fought to keep his composure.

"Pandora... are you mad at me?" Promise asked.

"No," she replied, "Not at all. It was my fault for telling you to fight the Nightmare alone."

"But I made that fight look so *easy, didn't I?*" he rasped, a weak smile spreading across his face.

"You're lucky you're alive," Pandora responded.

"I knew one of you was gonna get me," Promise said, slurring his words.

"Also, I'm broke."

Pandora was out of void matter as well, but she didn't mention it.

Promise's emotions cycled rapidly between pained laughter and distress. The toll of teleportation was evident in his disorientation and extreme fatigue. Volo sat stone faced. Pecunia started to cry, and clutched Pandora's arm.

Volo noticed the weight of responsibility setting on Pandora's face. Though she refused to show any emotion in that moment, her blank expression gave away her dissociation.

"They're not here, are they?" Pecunia whispered, her voice trembling.

Pandora swallowed hard, looking at each of her siblings in turn. Promise's pained expression, Pecunia's tear-stained face, Volo's stony facade. She took a deep breath.

"No, I don't think they are," she said.

The silence that followed was deafening. Even Promise's labored breathing seemed to quiet.

"What do we do?" Volo asked, breaking his silence. His voice was steady, but his clenched fists betrayed him.

Suddenly, the building groaned with the cracking of limestone, and Pandora stood up, her decision made.

"We can't stay here tonight. It's not safe." She said, "And they're not coming back. Not tonight, anyway—not here."

Promise struggled to sit up, wincing. "So, what's the plan, then?"

"Tomorrow. Tomorrow we'll figure out what to do next," she said, her voice stronger now.

"Let's go sleep in the park tonight." She said with a hollow smile.

As they made their way out of the demolished apartment, it occurred to Volo that they might never go back to the life they once knew.

Chapter 30: Tilde

Tilde was a 9-year-old student at the Institute's elementary school. She was Level 0, a fire-type, an Anger keeper, and, most importantly, an Aries. She believed in ghosts, and read her horoscope every day.

Today, it predicted disaster, and it was correct.

The shelter-in-place alarm blared through the marble halls of the Institute. Tilde wheeled herself to the dark window, her strawberry hair reflecting off the glass like a streak of flame in the night. Outside, small Voidpets scrambled for safety in the shadows of the school garden.

She checked the notification on her phone.

Another building collapse.

This time, it was a residential apartment nearby, on Something Park South, no less—a well-to-do street where famous people lived.

For a second, she felt relief that it wasn't a poor neighborhood. At least the victims of this attack might have had more void matter on hand to protect themselves with.

Still, she was saddened at the news. Her old home had collapsed from a Nightmare attack when she was a small child, and after being crushed under the falling debris, she suffered permanent injury to her legs.

"I hope you all make it out safe," she whispered, her soft hands clasping together as she shut her eyes in concentration. Her Anger Voidpet, a robust companion clad in a red scarf, curled up in her lap to reassure her, and nuzzled her with its baby dragon snout.

Tilde turned away from the window, holding Anger in her powder blue chemise. Her round face, usually sporting rosy cheeks, was solemn as she contemplated the disaster. She thought of what innocent children might have been orphaned or injured. Such was a common occurrence in the Void, as Nightmares were more likely to attack adults.

For the past year, Tilde had called the Institute her home. Her dorm room, a small single in a shared hallway, was a chaotic mix of clothes and school supplies. Her financial aid papers were scattered across the floor, mixed in with her paperwork for physical therapy, and her class schedule was buried in the heap somewhere as well.

Tilde let out a deep exhale, staring at the mess in frustration.

She didn't have the time, nor energy, to tidy up, and was up late struggling with another homework assignment that she was certain to fail.

She held two chunks of void matter in her hand.

As a fire-type, her task was to transform them into a small flame.

Tilde stared at the two little crystals, each pulsing with an ominous blue glow as if waiting impatiently for her to connect with them. She closed her eyes, trying to concentrate despite the chaos around her. *"Come on,"* she whispered, willing the void matter to transform. A tiny spark jumped between her fingers, then faded. Tilde furrowed her brow, frustration building.

Her Anger Voidpet stirred, reacting to her emotions. It looked up at her with encouragement.

"Thanks, Angy," Tilde murmured, taking a deep breath. She focused again. This time, she clenched her muscles and produced an animalistic growl as if she could convince the crystals to transform out of sheer fury.

Nothing happened.

Tilde let out a tremendous "UGH," and threw them onto the floor.

It didn't seem to matter what she did. She'd been up for hours past her bedtime, and there was no semblance of progress in sight. No matter how hard she tried, the Void didn't want to make her life any easier.

She turned on the TV and decided to watch her favorite comedy show instead.

Laughter was often the best medicine, especially this late at night.

Chapter 31: The Boy in the Dumpster

Luden usually slept alone in the park, but today, he woke up with company. From behind the safety of his iron bunker, he peered at the sleeping newcomers, a few feet away:

A boy around his age, with dark hair, wearing in a fancy black vest of some sort. He lay flat on his back, with a peaceful expression on his face.

A girl, perhaps also his age. She had long black hair that pooled on the grass like silk. And a ring on her middle finger. He thought she was pretty, but then felt weird for thinking that.

A taller boy. Wearing a different kind of collared jacket that he didn't know how to describe. He was tall enough to be an adult, but skinny enough to look like a kid. He was curled up on his side, and appeared to have been somehow injured from the night before. His breathing was shallow and he was shaking a bit, but he somehow looked dangerous. Perhaps it was the way his hands were covered in dark grit, or the way his long fingers remained tense, like claws.

A bigger brunette girl, also with the proportions of an adult contrasting with her childlike face. She looked exhausted and was snoring lightly, her hands clenched into fists. She lay sprawled on her back like a starfish, wearing a cream sweater and knit skirt. She smelled like cookies and cinnamon. He felt weird that he was close enough to smell her, and backed away. He suddenly realized he'd unconsciously assumed all their genders and also felt weird about that.

A few Voidpets lay sleeping beside the kids as well. It occurred to him then that all the Voidpets were quite beautiful, and so were the humans they were with.

Luden decided to crawl back behind the shelter of the dumpster and respect their privacy. His intrusive thoughts were out of control, and at this point, he just wanted to disappear.

He wondered if they could have escaped from the chaos he saw the night before.

But what if they were injured, or needed his help?

He froze, mid-crawl, unsure whether to respect privacy, or approach and ask if they were okay. His own Voidpet, Cringe, perched on his shoulder like an oversized, limbless gecko, froze as well.

The boy with black hair opened his eyes and sat upright, staring directly at Luden.

"Hey."

He had deep brown eyes that stared into Luden's soul. "I'm Volo," he said.

The last thing Luden expected was for one of the kids to wake up and introduce himself. He tried to speak but found himself at a loss for words. Panic set in, as he realized he was being perceived.

"Me? L-luden" he stammered, then realized that he sounded like a caveman. "I'm Luden - my name is Luden, if that's what you're asking."

Actually he never asked...

Luden didn't have any friends, and he was scared he blew his one chance at making a new one.

"Nice to meet you, Luden. Do you want to be friends?"

"Uh... do you?" Luden replied, unsure if Volo was interrogating him or making an offer.

"Yeah."

Luden felt a wave of relief. He didn't realize that's how people made friends. He thought there was some social dance he'd have to do or something.

"Oh, okay then, sure."

Volo smiled.

"Thanks for being my first friend, Luden," Volo answered with a little nod.

Luden felt another twang of panic. So this Volo kid was not normal, then. And from the sound of it, he had no other friends either. What if he was a serial killer? What if this was a trap?

Volo's eyes turned red, and he produced a thin, red blade that extended forward from his wrist like a rapier. Luden suppressed a shriek. Cringe fell off his shoulder in shock.

"Let's be transparent about our powers to establish a foundation of trust," said Volo.

"Do you trust me?"

Luden gulped. He thought for a minute before deciding that this was, in fact, a better outcome than being attacked on the spot, or perhaps ended in his sleep. Unfortunately, Luden did not have any significant powers of his own, and was unsure if his honesty would satisfy Volo.

"Uh... my skin oozes green goo?" Luden suggested, extending a hand to demonstrate.

"Woah, that's awesome!" Volo replied. His red eyes gleamed as they took in the sight of the goo, transfixed by its fluorescence, "What does it do?"

"Er... nothing, really," Luden murmured, before changing the subject to hide his embarrassment.

"There's void matter in the dumpster if you're hungry," he suggested.

A few feet away, the tall boy gasped awake at the mention of void matter. His bloodshot eyes blazed as he scrambled to his feet and dove into the dumpster with zeal. A hungry-eyed Voidpet slithered in after him.

The two girls stirred at the commotion, the bigger one's eyes snapping open. The smaller one yawned, her ring glinting as she stretched. "Where are we?"

"Why is Promise in the dumpster?"

"And who are you?" She asked, studying Luden in his bandages and tattered clothes.

"That's my friend, Luden." Volo explained, saving him from another awkward introduction.

"And that's my sister, Pecunia," Volo added, turning to face Luden.

Luden's heart raced as Pecunia and Volo both looked directly at him.

The tall boy, presumably Promise, emerged from the dumpster with a look of disappointment, holding six small crystals in his hand.

"This all you got, dude?" He handed the crystals back to Luden, who felt himself recoil at the intensity of Promise's icy stare.

Luden nodded, hoping not to upset him.

"Six bucks?" Promise frowned, hooking both thumbs into the pockets of his black jacket and starting to pace.

"We need more VM, ASAP."

Confused, Luden felt his own stomach growl, so he picked up one of the crystals and started to gnaw on them. All four of the kids looked at him in horror. The older girl politely intervened.

"Hey Luden... are you hungry?"

Luden nodded. Why else would he be eating void matter?

"Can I make you something?" she asked, reaching out her hand to accept one of Luden's crystals.

The girl's brow furrowed in concentration as she cupped both hands around the glowing chunk of void matter, ballooning it into an orb of white energy. As the matter shifted and stretched like taffy, the white glow slowly dimmed. Luden's eyes widened. The void matter settled into a textured beige disc, filling the air with the warm scent of freshly baked cinnamon.

"Tada!" She sang out triumphantly, holding up a perfectly formed cookie. Her sleeping Pride woke up beside her, flexing its silver wings in admiration. "It's cinnamon sugar!" she added, handing it to Luden.

"I'm Pandora, by the way. Thank you for sharing your void matter with us."

Fireworks went off on Luden's taste buds as he took a bite of Pandora's cookie. He didn't know it was possible to turn void matter into actual food, let alone something that tasted this good. Tears filled his eyes as savored the treat. Pecunia watched his delight and giggled, which made Luden's face redden.

"Luden, where do you live?" Pandora asked.

Luden pointed at the dumpster.

Promise raised an eyebrow. A hint of disgust flitted across his face, before his mouth stretched into a sideways smile. "You live in a dumpster? That's... actually kind of hardcore."

Luden's stomach lurched as Promise sized him up, his eyes a calculating, electric blue. These strange children's compliments made him uncomfortable, and he wasn't sure whether he wanted to believe them or just curl up and melt away. As Luden sat, processing his anxiety with his arms wrapped around his legs, Pandora and Promise turned to face each other, releasing Luden from their gaze. Their expressions darkened, as if snapping back to a harsher reality.

"So what's our move?" Promise asked, taking a seat in the grass. "We're broke. Mom and Dad are gone. Our home's a wreck. Do we just... go to the Institute for help?"

She furrowed her brow and held her chin in thought.

"If our parents worked their whole lives to keep us away from The Institute," she reasoned slowly, "we should at least respect that until we no longer have a choice."

Luden listened thoughtfully. It appeared they'd decided to jump into a family conversation in front of him, and didn't deem him a threat. His heart skipped a beat as he connected the dots. The red blast in the sky. The flying beast that collapsed to the ground. The crumbling building that healed itself with veins of light. If these kids had survived that scale of danger, then they were probably tough.

"You're right, Pandora." Promise said, his signature tone of absolute certainty settling back into his voice. "We just need to get our hands on as much void matter as possible, and then we're golden. Then we rebuild our house, find our parents, and build the life of our dreams in the Void. It's real simple, actually." He paused to look each of his siblings in the eye individually. "In front of me are the three most powerful people I know."

Then, his gaze turned to Luden. Promise paused, before breaking out into a smile that Luden couldn't quite characterize as either warm or cold. "And an expert survivalist who knows how to live under the radar," he said, disorienting Luden with another out-of-pocket compliment. "We can do *anything* we want now," Promise concluded.

Luden's mind buzzed with hesitations. He wasn't sure why he was randomly being included in their plans and resisted to urge to point out that their parents were probably dead. He didn't see how a handful of homeless children could build a house, but he decided to keep his mouth shut. Promise was even more scary awake than he was asleep, and Luden did not want to get on his bad side.

"There are empty buildings all over town," Pandora chimed, color returning to her face as she calibrated her goals to their new reality. "Let's go find shelter, and from there, we'll hatch a plan to get more VM," she said.

The younger two looked at each other in agreement.

In the distance, sirens wailed. "We should move," Volo said, helping Pecunia to her feet. "Luden, are you coming?" He asked.

As they stood up to leave, Luden had butterflies in his stomach. Though terrified, he agreed. For the first time, he wasn't alone.

Chapter 32: No Rules

With his parents gone and a new mission to man, Volo figured it was a good time to let out his Voidpet for some fresh air. As he extended his arms in a big stretch, a shadow emerged from his back like smoke. It slithered into the air as a pitch-black serpent with red eyes.

Pandora identified that the creature as a Lust—a powerful, rare species that was extremely difficult to tame.

"No wonder you hid that from us," Promise remarked with a snicker.

Volo chose not to react to his brother's comment. "Do we need to hide from The Institute?" He asked.

"No," Luden responded. "They'll wait for you to come to them."

The five children meandered through the city like ants in a maze. The Institute loomed in the distance, a block of white above their gray world. It was a landmark they couldn't forget. An ominous reminder of a world they knew nothing of.

"How do we pick which building to live in?" Volo asked. A simple question with complex answers.

"Well, there's structural integrity to consider," Pandora offered.

She looked at Luden, who shifted uncomfortably, unused to having his opinion sought. "Maybe somewhere with... hiding spots?' he offered.

"And the issue of Nightmares at night," Pandora added.

"We also *need* to pick somewhere nice," Pecunia said firmly, "like with comfy beds and clean water."

"And what about food, and—" Luden suggested, before Promise cut him off.

"All of that can be solved with void matter."

"What we need is a strategic outpost. Somewhere where we can take down as many Nightmares as possible, train hard, and build our wealth. All we need is a hunting ground—"

"But won't it be scary if there are Nightmares at night?" Pecunia interrupted.

Luden nodded vigorously.

"That's *exactly* what we want," Promise replied with a wicked grin. "It'll be safe to sleep in during the day, and that's all that matters. And at night, we let our prey come to us. That's when we get to work."

A silence settled on the group as they considered his proposal.

"Seize power first, and the rest will follow," Promise reiterated for anyone who might have missed his earlier point.

"Then we should go east," Volo said.

East was where Madison took them to train. East was far from the Institute, riddled with Nightmares, and a place where human communities were known to be few and far between. East made sense, and no one else spoke up to disagree.

The five children made their way to the nearest ghost train station with their Voidpets following closely. Hungry, exhausted, and covered in grime, they were whisked across town in an empty car, staring out the window as the afternoon sun lit a shining river beneath them. They rode the train until it screeched to a halt at the eastern-most terminal.

The Windfall siblings had never been to the east side of town before sunset and marveled at the colorful storefronts that seemed to stretch on for miles. The low-rise buildings looked nothing like the rows of polished limestone they were used to. The air smelled of aromatic spices and the sweet scent of empty tea shops. In a sea of neon lights, vibrant reds, golds, and brick, The siblings found themselves in a sensory carnival, a far cry from the subdued elegance of their former neighborhood. There was something that felt more like home about this new place, though they didn't know why.

"This place feels alive..." Pandora murmured.

As they walked, the siblings noticed dark shapes flickering at the edges of their vision, drawn to the currents of feeling that flowed through the neighborhood. Perhaps it was the sheer depth of human experience that was tangible in the air. The Ancient Americans who built this neighborhood long ago were dreamers, and it was no surprise that Nightmares were attracted to their memories.

They wandered until the sun went down, and Pecunia spotted a large doorway. The building, which had once been a hotel, beckoned them through glass doors with its bright golden lobby, glossy lounge and modern chandelier. The lights were all on for some reason.

"I like this one!" Pecunia started to run inside.

Volo grabbed his sister's arm and stopped her.

His combat instincts spurred into action as he noticed a horde of human-sized Nightmares behind the leather couches. Pandora and Promise were out of void matter and Pecunia wasn't passionate about fighting—so despite being the youngest, Volo assumed the role as the lead hunter of the team.

As Lust flooded back into his spine, Volo's eyes turned a deep ruby red. His two sabers unsheathed from the backs of his hands, and he did a 360 scan for danger.

"Looks like it's you and me, buddy," he said to Luden, whose eyes bugged out in horror.

"Everyone else, wait here a moment," he said. He slipped through the glass doors of the lobby and gestured for Luden to follow.

As Luden entered the lobby, he backed towards the door, clutching his tattered shirt. "They're... everywhere," he whispered. Green goo began to drip from his clothes and Cringe covered its eyes.

Outside, Promise and Pecunia pressed their faces into the glass to watch. Pandora flashed two thumbs-up in encouragement.

Volo felt time slow as he looked around. He counted 33 Nightmares in total. All of them Stage 2 Limits, which were no issue for him.

"Luden, cover my back?" he said.

His muscles flexed with the power of void matter, allowing him to rush at them with blistering force. In a multi-target battle like this, striking first would give him the upper hand before the Nightmares had a chance to swarm. He didn't want to ruin the furniture, so his first blade went behind the couch, parallel to the backrest. Three Nightmares dissolved to dust, while his left hand arced through the air and cut down two more.

28 left.

It was at this moment his siblings realized their mother wasn't watching, so they could spectate however childishly they pleased. Pecunia hooted and pounded on the glass.

"Let's go lil' bro!" Promise hollered with a fist pump, while Pandora clapped with glee.

Luden's eyes darted as he tried to keep track of which direction Volo's back was facing. Now that the Nightmares were focused on him, the rest of the battle was easy.

As another wave leapt at him from the shadows, he spun and cleaved his way through, taking out two, then four, then six at a time. It felt like one of those mobile games where you slice up fruits—which Volo thoroughly enjoyed on the rare occasions he got to play.

16 more.

His vision grew scarlet as time slowed further. Volo's technique was called *Seeing Red*, and it was granted to him by his Voidpet. At the cost of tunnel vision and a numbing of emotion, his agility and strength would continue to increase until he decided to power down.

One Nightmare leapt at him in what seemed like slow motion. He dodged, rolled underneath, and speared it from the back. Another lunged towards his feet, which he leapt over and sliced in half. As the remaining Nightmares began to climb up the walls, gearing up to rain down on him in an aerial assault, Volo leapt up to the chandelier and unleashed his final move. He first noted that Luden was safe by the door, out of range of his next maneuver—then, with the help of Lust, four alien stingers sprouted from his back, fanning outwards to vanquish each creature that pounced from the walls.

Three on the left, three on the right, four behind, and four in front. Each wave dissolved to dust as his stingers whisked through the room, pureeing the remaining Nightmares like a blender.

That was 33.

Volo dropped down from the chandelier, landing like a cat. He retracted his blades, absorbed the stingers back into his spine, and let the red run out of his eyes. Then, he trotted back to Luden and opened the door to his siblings.

He turned to face his sister with the hint of a smile, his face streaked with dark splatters of Nightmare fuel.

"I like this place too, Pecunia. I think it's safe now."

Luden stared at Volo, still processing the seconds that had flashed by before him. "That was... Is that normal for you guys?"

"What are you referring to exactly?" Volo asked.

As the team headed inside the hotel to gather the Nightmare fuel, Promise grabbed a melon candy from the empty reception desk. He wiped off the grime from the fight, unwrapped it, and popped it in his mouth.

Chapter 33: Nightmare Fuel

Promise breathed in the scent of Nightmare fuel. The smells of smoke and gasoline soothed him, and he crouched down to run his bare hands through the dust. He felt good. There was nothing better than profiting from the ashes of his enemies.

As he scooped up a handful of dust in one hand, the remaining particles of grime began to levitate around the room. At his use of *Singularity*, Greed looped with delight. A nucleus condensed above his palm and the particles raced to feed into it, swirling into the center like a mini black hole.

Nightmare fuel was crude void matter, which made it the easiest substance to reverse-channel. While it didn't respond to the human mind as obediently as it did in its purest form, it could be gathered and distilled with a human's lucidity—particularly the advanced lucidity of a Greed keeper.

Promise suppressed a laugh as he saw Luden's slack-jawed expression. It was fun having a spectator who seemed impressed.

He scooped another handful of dust to create a second black hole, and spun both out on his fingertips, accelerating the collection of fuel. The orbs glowed black and red, convulsing as they compacted the dust into crystals of void matter. Currents of particles filled the lobby as they streamed through the air to coalesce at his fingertips. Grime flitted off Volo's face, and dark stains lifted off the walls.

As the dust settled, Promise stood victorious, holding baseball-sized nuggets of void matter in each hand.

"330 VM." He announced.

He felt power course through his veins as he gripped the blue matter in his hands. His fatigue screamed at him to absorb it all for himself, but he knew that wasn't fair. Volo was the one who'd defeated the whole swarm on his own.

Promise contemplated despotism. None of the others could hold a candle to his lucidity, which meant he could claim every drop of void matter before anyone else could—or embezzle some whenever he pleased. Greed swirled faster, purring at this thought.

But it was Lonely's blink that finalized his decision. Promise considered his family an extension of himself, and therefore, he'd invest rather than exploit.

"We'll split it four ways," he declared across the golden lobby, "so we can fight better as a team." The two crystals reformed into four— each worth 84 VM, and he shared them with Pandora, Pecunia, and Volo. As he dropped the two remaining in Luden's hands, he lowered his voice. "Show me what you can do, and *then* we'll talk."

Promise looked down at Luden, before crushing his own crystal in his hand. The void matter melted into liquid, then evaporated into plasma, before disappearing into his palm. He smiled. It was up to the newcomer to interpret that as a boundary or as a challenge.

Luden nodded and put the two pieces of void matter into his pocket. He wiped his fingers on his pants as they continued to ooze with green goo.

The other three accepted the terms in silence. The Windfall siblings shared the understanding that they each brought valuable strengths in combat. They also shared the understanding that it didn't make sense to give Luden void matter if he couldn't do anything with it.

"Dinnertime?" Pandora took a seat on the leather couch and began to spin a white blob of 10 VM between her hands. She stretched and pulled it like dough, taking care to fold each piece repeatedly until the matter extended like a scroll.

Volo's eyes lit up at the sight of food. While summoning objects wasn't his forte, he mustered 3 VM into the palm of his hand and carefully kneaded it into a bowl. It was a little rough around the edges, but enough to collect the noodles as Pandora released her recipe from the air.

"Thank you, Volo," said Pandora. "Now what protein would you like?"

Pecunia interrupted with a rhetorical question. "Is all meat vegan because it's made of void matter? Or is all food meat because void matter comes from living things?"

Volo was too hungry to entertain her question. "Steak," he answered, handing Pandora a chunk of 5 VM to channel into bite sized cuts of beef. The scent of cumin, roasted garlic, and chili oil began to waft from the bowl as Pandora showed off her robust spice repertoire.

"Biang biang noodles are ready!" She sang.

The three younger children sat starry-eyed as Pandora used two more VM to create a set of wooden chopsticks. She added a fork for Luden, who was confused, and handed out the utensils. Promise watched the four of them devour the hand-pulled noodles like a pack of hungry animals.

For his own dinner, he conjured a cup of something that could be described as a caffeinated protein shake and slurped it alone in a corner. He wasn't one to share a bowl with someone who had been living in a dumpster—and not one to waste VM on things like chili oil. Not to mention, his stomach wasn't well enough to handle solid food.

Promise's mind raced as he yearned for nothing more than to charge back up with void matter. He couldn't sit still. The only way to stop thinking about his parents was to fixate on getting rich. The craving for void matter consumed him, making stillness an impossible luxury.

"I'll be back in the morning." he announced, standing up and striding towards the door.

"Woah there, not so fast mister," Pandora said, her words muffled by a mouthful of noodles. "You're still injured, and your battery is way low."

Promise bristled, shooting his sister a venomous stare. He bit back a caustic retort, as snark was too much effort in his depleted state. Instead, he simply continued to walk.

Pandora's sigh of resignation followed his footsteps. "At least take someone with you in case of emergency."

Promise paused, turning around to consider his options. Pandora clearly wasn't volunteering herself, as that'd mean leaving the three younger kids alone. Volo had earned his rest after securing their new base, and he didn't have the heart to rip his little sister away from the safety of the hotel. That left only Luden.

It was then that Promise realized the upside of their new headcount. Maybe the kid wasn't useless after all. "Luden, you're coming with me," he ordered, his voice piercing through the warmth of their little banquet.

Luden wiped the chili oil off his face. He jumped to his feet, his eyes wild like a raccoon that'd been caught in the trash, and scrambled to follow Promise out the door.

"See you later," Volo heaved another mouthful of noodles.

"Toodles!" Pecunia shoveled more steak in her mouth.

The doors swung closed behind the two of them, leaving the others to enjoy their meal in the hotel. Promise stepped out into the evening, feeling himself come to life as his lungs filled with fresh air. The cold breeze snapped his hair and pushed his jacket open, and his strides lengthened with purpose. Luden followed like a lost puppy, stumbling to catch up.

Promise grinned to himself as he felt the darkness grow around him. To him, adrenaline was a feeling of comfort, and sitting around made him uneasy. Danger was the only thing that balanced his blood chemicals.

He turned to Luden. "You have one job, okay?" Promise said to his new assistant. "All you have to do is run and get the others if I pass out."

Using 2 VM, he whipped up a 5-hour-energy drink and slapped it into Luden's hands. "And don't fall asleep."

Luden nodded.

"Got it?" Promise asked again, looking Luden in the eyes to make sure he was listening.

"Yessir," Luden replied curtly, before covering his mouth in embarrassment. Promise suppressed a laugh as he noticed Cringe covering its mouth too. Luden's self-esteem was so pitiful, even his Voidpet was embarrassed.

Emboldened by the presence of a weaker individual, Promise's malaise faded to the back of his head. He unleashed a current of void matter from his hand, all 80 he had blooming out of his palm in a stream of viscous red. He debated using black or blue to lower his burn rate, but decided that tonight, he was in the mood for red. He had a new technique in mind to try for frugality, anyways.

As his matter radiated in the darkness, the sound of Nightmares rattled to life. Under the light of red, Promise led Luden into a narrow alley, flanked by towering brick walls. Rusty fire escapes zigzagged up the buildings, and overflowing dumpsters lined one side.

"Up there," Promise pointed to a fire escape landing about two stories up. "You'll have a good view."

Luden hesitated, eyeing the rickety metal stairs. His eyes gravitated towards the row of dumpsters beneath them, and he looked at Promise as if asking for permission.

"I mean, if that's what you prefer," Promise said, noting Luden's relief as he climbed to take shelter inside a fortress of urban waste.

"Head down, eyes up. And remember—"

"Run if you pass out. Got it," Luden finished, peeking over the dumpster's edge.

"Perfect," Promise nodded, turning to place his Lonely in the dumpster beside Luden. Red void matter encircled his right hand as shadows stirred in the darkness beyond. "Oh, and don't try running before I'm done," he added. "Don't want you to get hurt."

Luden chugged the 5-hour-energy and mustered a thumbs-up. He closed the lid on top of himself and descended into the sea of bags.

Chapter 34: For Profit and Glory

Luden found the smell of rotting takeout to be oddly comforting. He peered through a gap between the lid and the rim, heart pounding as he prepared to watch the battle unfold. On his shoulder, Cringe inched its face closer to the gap to watch.

He noted that this was Volo's *older* brother, and shuddered at what that might have entailed about his abilities.

Promise stood in the alley, a beacon of red light with the dot of Greed hovering behind. His void matter flickered like a living thing, hungry and wild in the night. The shadows at the end of the alley began to move. Nightmares. Dozens of them, pouring into the alley in a milky flood. Promise didn't flinch.

He reacted with a slash, directing the thinnest thread of red to slice through the air like a wire saw. The low-level Nightmares evaporated to dust on contact, their residue combusting into flames as it sprinkled to the ground.

"Low battery mode," Promise shot a smug look at the dumpster.

Luden wasn't sure what that meant but continued to keep an eye on Promise's safety.

In Promise's left hand, he performed the same black hole technique that Luden had remembered from earlier. The dust from the invisible stroke flew straight into his palm and slowly converted into void matter that could fuel his offense. Meanwhile, his right hand continued to conduct threads of razor-thin void matter at the onslaught of Nightmares.

Luden found himself studying the variety of Nightmares. Some were the shape of insects, birds, and animals. Others were shaped like uncanny humans, like the ones Volo had fought earlier. Both kinds came in all different sizes and were covered in runic markings that looked like eyes. The small ones had only one pair where their eyes should be, while the bigger ones had two.

The eyes appeared to be their spots of weakness. As soon as Promise's VM touched them, the small Nightmares puffed into thin clouds of dust, while the larger ones clunked to the ground and emptied like bags of sand. As the barrage continued, the relative size of attackers was increasing. Luden felt a sense of impending doom and worried that things would get out of hand.

A lull in the battle allowed Promise to pause, taking a moment to recalibrate. Tired of dual wielding techniques, he let his Greed swallow the black hole in his left. He directed the creature to fly around the alleyway, collecting dust with the magnetism of its own little form. With a flick of his free hand, he tossed back a shot of espresso, and wiped grime from his face with the back of his hand.

Promise's eyes glinted with a predatory light as he surveyed the carnage around him. "Still alive in there?" he asked the dumpster. Luden stuck out a thumbs-up.

Luden was having a surprisingly okay time spectating from the safety of his bunker. He watched Greed take over the black hole with fascination. He didn't know you could do that—but then again, there was a lot he didn't know. Inside the dumpster, Luden and Cringe were both exuding green goo together, and he wondered if humans and their Voidpets shared their powers somehow.

Greed began to transform as it zoomed around the alley. First, it sprouted little arms and legs, which broke into a run as its body streamlined. Then, its face elongated and tapered into that of fox. Its short tail blossomed into a much larger one with a new set of eyes.

Promise started laughing as he admired his companion's evolved form. Greed leapt into his outstretched arms and climbed onto his shoulders, purring as it delivered a fresh shipment of distilled void matter.

"Who's a good boy?" he said to his Voidpet, nuzzling his face into the little fox.

"You're such a good boy, yes you are."

Luden blinked, unsure how to feel about Promise cooing at his pet. He felt like he was intruding on a private moment and wanted to look away—but remembered his mission and kept watch.

As Promise looked up to face the next wave of Nightmares, his expression was something beyond arrogance. He tilted his head, ran his tongue across his lip, and shredded the next wave of foes in a whirlwind of black and red. Fire raced along the edges of the alleyway, and black stains settled into the brick, up to three stories high. The air smelled like gasoline, and he appeared to shudder with satisfaction. Luden learned why earlier had been considered 'low battery mode'.

"It's good to be back," Promise mused to Greed, giving the fox a little head scratch.

No wonder he loved his pet so much.

From that point on, the rest of the combat was on another level. As the hours wore on, the Nightmares grew larger, more grotesque. Promise met each new challenge with a savage grin. Luden found himself in awe with each successive victory, almost forgetting to be terrified. At one point, a particularly large Nightmare—easily twice their size—lumbered into the alley and grabbed Promise with its claw, wrapping its giant fingers around his whole waist. In a motion too fast for Luden to follow, Promise disappeared from its grip and ended up above the behemoth's head. As he descended, a red disc of matter sliced down through it like it was made of paper.

"Did you see that?" Promise called out like a kid who'd done a cartwheel. Luden weaseled another thumbs-up out of the dumpster.

Despite his wealth replenishing, Luden noticed that Promise's physical stamina had depleted rapidly. He coughed and struggled to keep his balance, his stance faltering as his void matter quivered beside him. Promise stumbled, out of steam. He leaned against a wall, breathing heavily.

It was then that the crack of dawn lit up the alleyway, and Luden realized he'd been sitting in the dumpster for hours. He decided it was appropriate to emerge, given that the sun was now rising, and Promise appeared to be on the verge of losing consciousness. Lonely wriggled out after him.

"Hey, um... are you okay?" Luden asked, approaching slowly.

Promise looked up, his facade flickering as his voice cracked. "Yeah, just... give me a sec." He staggered to collect himself in the aftermath of the battle.

Luden tried to express his admiration over small talk. "Man, you were great out there... I hope when I'm your age I'll learn how to protect myself like that," he said, scratching his head.

Promise paused. His eyes narrowed, as he processed what Luden had said. "How old are you, Luden?"

"Um, I'm 12," said Luden, suddenly paranoid that he might have offended his new mentor.

"When's your birthday?"

"Uh... June?" Luden said. "...24th, I think?" He added, unsure how to respond, or when his actual birthday even was.

Promise snorted. "You've got a few months to catch up, king."

"Huh?"

"Dude. I'm 13."

Luden was confused. The way Promise carried himself, his height, the expensive clothes he wore. There was no way they were the same age.

"Look, I've been training every day my whole life, okay?" Promise cracked his knuckles and fixed his jacket with a shrug. "Just follow my lead, and you'll get there in no time."

"You're a champ, you know that?" Promise smiled at Luden with a jaded look, grinning as blood dripped out of the corner of his mouth, "We should do this more often."

"Oh. Well, thanks?" Luden offered, unsure if the compliment was meant for anything other than his unquestioning obedience. "And uh, thanks for not hurting me, by the way—"

"Why would I ever hurt you if you're not a threat?"

Promise's arm draped over Luden's shoulders, and he couldn't tell if it was for keeping his balance or as a subtle reminder of who was in charge.

Luden realized he was now more terrified of a human than he was of any Nightmare. He couldn't shake the feeling that he'd just made a deal with the devil—but somehow, with all the dangers that lurked in the Void, that feeling gave him some comfort.

As the sun began to creep back up the horizon, the two boys made their way back to the hotel.

Chapter 35: Takeout

Char smashed the snooze button on his alarm clock as it rang out for the fourth time. *6:45 am.* If he didn't get out of bed by the next ring, he'd be late for cram school.

"Get up, bozo," his big sister Dyna hollered from the bathroom, already dressed and doing her makeup.

"Shut up, loser!" Char yelled, loud enough to wake himself up.

He rubbed his eyes and clambered out of bed. In his hurry, he accidentally displaced Envy off the foot of the narrow twin bed that they shared. The small Voidpet fell to the ground with a tremendous THUNK, dropping like a bowling ball before waking up and levitating itself into the air.

Envy screeched, and head-butted Char in the rear.

"Agh, sorry bud," he muttered, "we're gonna be late."

He grabbed his yellow T-shirt off the floor, put on a pair of blue shorts over his boxers. He sprayed his clothes down with drugstore deodorant to mask the pungent smell of frying oil that clung to them.

Next, he shoveled a stack of textbooks into his backpack. He hated the way the books jutted through the corners of his bag, his zippers breaking at the seams to contain them. Unfortunately, Char didn't have the money to waste on a new backpack, so it'd have to do. His parents could barely afford the Institute, and he was banking on cram school to score a big scholarship.

As a small 10-year-old, Char's book bag weighed almost as much as he did. As he hoisted it onto his back, he walked slightly hunched to keep his balance, resembling a leggy turtle.

Dyna waited for him by the door, her foot tapping as her Jealous perched on her shoulder. She wore her hair in loose braids and sported a trendy white halter top, which Char noticed with disdain. He tallied the work hours her outfit represented—hours their parents spent sweating over hot stoves while Dyna played dress-up with designer knockoffs.

Together, they scurried to cram school, stopping to grab bacon-egg-and-cheese bagels from a coffee stand on the way. The side of the cart held a stack of newspapers, and Char spotted a headline about a collapsed building in the wealthy district—a tragedy for the city, its beautiful limestone now rubble.

Good, he thought, his mouth full of bagel as he hurried along his commute. *Anything to level the playing field.*

They arrived at 6:59 am on the dot, scrambling down the stairs into the windowless basement of a narrow brick building, just in time for class to start at 7. Dyna headed into the advanced classroom, while Char took his seat in the intermediate session.

Class that day was a lecture on VM theory. A series of multiple-choice practice tests. Questions about ancient history, abstract math, and the taxonomy of Voidpets. Nothing on modern history or anything practical, of course. Since this was a budget class.

The Sonder teacher held a piece of chalk in its tail and scribbled diagrams on the board. While the instructor droned on, Char found himself doodling a chessboard in his notebook, playing an imaginary match to pass the time. The class moved a bit slow for his liking, but beggars couldn't be choosers when it came to education.

As Char finished his test early, he zoned out to stare at the Institute posters on the wall. They depicted a gleaming white castle surrounded by picturesque gardens, floating on a rock over the city. He wondered what it was like to belong there.

One day, I'll be looking down at this dump from up there.

There were two known ways to get into the Institute. First was making it through the high school entrance exam, which is what Char fully intended to do. Second was being recruited as a young child. For

that, spots were few, and you had to live on the west side of town.
Envy clenched on his shoulder as Char thought of how unfair it was.
The west side of town was exorbitantly expensive—which left kids like
him even further in the dust.

When class ended at 10:00 am, Char and Dyna began the more
grueling half of their day. They walked to the local food court, carrying
their book bags to the dumpling stall where their parents worked.

A far as Char knew, there were two types of people in the Void:
those who didn't need to work for Voidpets, and those who did.
Char's world belonged to the latter bucket—so he put on his apron
and got to work.

The little stall buzzed with activity, as wild Voidpets lined up to
purchase takeout. Steam billowed from huge pots, carrying the aroma
of pork and chives. His mother rolled out dough, his hands a blur as he
kneaded and shaped it into little circles. His father stood at the fryer,
sizzling batches of golden, crispy dumplings.

While Dyna took the shift at the cash register, Char took his place at
the prep station, his hands moving like a machine as he chopped green
onions and minced garlic. He'd always been good with knives. He'd
often daydream about learning to fight, imagining himself wielding the
blade with the same precision in combat. The rhythmic thud of his
knife on the cutting board blended with the sizzle of the fryer, and he
passed the time in a state of autopilot.

Out of the corner of his eye, he noticed an irregularity. A human
girl stood at the front of the line, amidst the sea of Voidpet customers,
and placed a large order for 10 dozen dumplings. His gaze gravitated
towards the girl, who couldn't have been much older than him. With
glossy hair, green eyes, and a magical voice that cut clear through the
humdrum, she seemed ethereal—like a princess from another reality.
He had no qualms about stacking girls against each other, and decided,
for certain, that she was much cooler than his dumb, ugly sister.

He wondered if she planned to eat all 120 dumplings by herself, or
how she could afford to pay for that many. Where was she from? Why
was she here?

Char's eyes widened as he witnessed an act of magic before his eyes. The girl held out her palm, and materialized an entire crystal of void matter in the palm of her hand. She handed it to Dyna with a little giggle, who weighed it on the scale to verify that it was, indeed, the whopping sum of 50 VM, and stepped back to wait in the pickup line.

Char itched to say hi, but stopped himself. Stepping out of a food stall in an apron and gloves was no place to make a first impression. He thought of slipping his number into her takeout box, but he was 10 years old and didn't have a phone.

As Dyna passed her order ticket to the back, she rolled her eyes at Char and shook her head, unamused with her brother's fascination. He ignored her, grabbing the ticket to read what it said.

Number #113: Order for Pecunia. $5/dozen set x 10.

Pecunia, he mouthed to himself. What a strange, beautiful name.

From the kitchen, Char's parents didn't seem to notice a thing. They moved through their routine in silent efficiency, too tired for conversation. His mother's eyes were heavy-lidded as she folded rows and rows of dumplings, racing to finish the 120, and more. His father's shoulders slumped as he flipped the frying pans and filled takeout boxes. His Apathy stood in the back, a sturdy, donkey-like creature eating leftovers out of the garbage can.

As Char thought of Pecunia, his picture of the future began to shine all more the bright. He imagined himself getting into the Institute, where he'd develop magical powers of his own, befriend students like her, and be done with monotonous labor for good.

In that moment, he vowed to become the very greatest, like no other. He'd work his way to the top and get out of here—no matter what it took.

Chapter 36: Spoils

Promise spread his arms over the back of the couch and kicked his legs up onto the glass coffee table. He glanced at Luden, who had somehow fallen asleep on the floor, and closed his eyes, letting Greed curl up on his stomach. He relished the feeling of fresh void matter coursing through his veins; the rush of victory overpowered his exhaustion.

There was a *ding,* and Pandora stepped out of the lobby elevator. Volo followed close behind.

Promise rolled his head to face them. "Have a nice night?" He asked.

"Oh it was alright," Pandora responded, her smile weary, "we just cleaned out the hotel."

She placed a soccer-ball sized crystal in the middle of the coffee table, which looked like at least 1000 VM.

Promise raised his eyebrows. "Not bad."

"There's more upstairs," Volo said. "We left it for you."

Promise nodded. He knew that Pandora and Volo had to scoop up the Nightmare fuel with their bare hands to convert it—and was impressed that they even bothered to at all.

Pecunia entered through the glass doors with a plastic bag stuffed full of takeout.

"Second dinner!" She exclaimed, opening the bag on the table to reveal ten foam boxes, unleashing the aroma of chives and fried dough. An array of disposable utensils clattered to the table.

Pandora and Volo lit up with delight as they snapped open their wooden chopsticks. Promise reached for a pair, figuring he could use a bite as well.

"Did you know there's a food court nearby?" Pecunia said, brimming with energy as she spread the boxes across the table. "They've tasty stuff for cheap!"

"You're bright eyed and bushy tailed, aren't you?" Promise remarked, noting his little sister's exuberance.

"I just woke up!" Pecunia giggled.

He looked at Pandora and Volo, each covered in grime, their eyes dull with fatigue as they wolfed down the dumplings. He didn't need to ask to know what happened—Pecunia had clearly gone to sleep while the other two went to work.

"7 floors, 210 rooms," Pandora said, as if reading his mind. "All clear."

Promise nodded, unsurprised. He was certain they'd fought with tireless precision, ensuring the hotel remained hospitable by the end of their massacre. Pandora and Volo were always thorough.

Pandora polished off her first dozen dumplings, and reached for the large VM cluster on the table. She channeled white metal into her fingers to crack it in half, handing one piece to Volo.

She looked at Promise, and spoke with measured words.

"From here on out, let's each keep what we earn for ourselves."

Promise's eyes darted to the side as he pondered, confused. He'd earned far more than 1000 VM from his solo night out, so she was selling herself short by choosing not to split the pot. Perhaps she'd underestimated his haul? Greed growled, betraying his suspicion.

"Why?"

Pandora looked him in the eye and spoke slowly. "Because I know you. And I'd rather I make that decision out loud before there's any room for you to make the same one behind my back." She shot him a sugary smile before digging into another box of dumplings.

Well then. Promise hesitated, then shrugged in agreement.

"Valid."

They ate in silence for a few minutes. Volo, yawned, and Pandora noted it was a good time to go to sleep.

After packing up the remaining dumplings for Luden, Volo scooped his sleeping friend onto his back. Then, the gang took the elevator up to the 7th floor.

The hallways were splattered with Nightmare fuel, which Promise quickly collected by walking through with a wave of his hand. The rest of the group peeked into each hotel room, all the locks having been dismantled by Volo's blades earlier that night.

"Dibs on the executive suite," Pandora said, her lips pursed in a neat smile as she opened door 701.

"Don't worry, there's another one," she added, opening 711 for Promise before he could consider protesting.

Volo and Pecunia settled on a double room, 725, and decided to share it for safety. Luden, his eyes fluttering open, volunteered himself to take the sofa bed beside them.

"You know there are like two hundred rooms in this hotel..." Promise said.

"But we'd rather have a sleepover than be alone," Pecunia responded.

Promise couldn't relate. "Suit yourselves," he said with a yawn, before slipping off to his private suite.

It was 12:00 pm, noon—which, according to their new schedule, was now their new midnight.

With the sun at its peak in the sky, each of the children shut their blinds and headed to sleep in their empty hotel beds. They quickly fell asleep as their tired muscles finally let out a sigh of relief, and even Pecunia quickly drifted back to bed.

Though dark days lay ahead, at least they had made it through this first one.

Chapter 37: Hyphen

Hyphen froze as she stepped out of the shower in her bathrobe, her springy curls still slick with water.

A Nightmare, inside the Institute.

It looked like a large cockroach that kept getting bigger. As she stared at it, her eyes locked in a terrified fixation. There were little minions spilling out of its back, scurrying into the corners of the bathroom.

Hyphen found herself unable to move. Her pet Anxious was shivering in her arms, it's saucer-like eyes extra wide—at age 9, she had no training against Nightmares.

"Tilde?" she cried out to the shower stall next door, her voice trembling.

Tilde heard her friend's cry and quickly finished rinsing off. She shut off the water and called out, "What's going on?"

"There's... There's a Nightmare!" Hyphen's voice was shaking. "It keeps getting bigger!"

Tilde took a deep breath. "Okay, I'm coming. Can you toss me my clothes?"

Hyphen tossed a blue dress over the stall divider, where Tilde dried off as best she could and changed into it. She carefully transferred to her shower wheelchair, gripping the safety bars. "Hyphen, you're going to be okay," Tilde called out as she wheeled out of the stall. "Remember your breathing exercises!"

The cockroach Nightmare was now the size of a small bird. "Get on the sink," Tilde instructed.

As Hyphen retreated to higher ground, Tilde wheeled forward. Anger materialized in her lap, growling at the intruder.

"Ready, Angy?" She said, and the little Voidpet grunted.

Tilde hurled Anger forth in a blur of red. The pet slammed into the Nightmare, sending it skidding across the floor, stunned. Tilde herself followed up with a battle cry, steamrolling it with her wheelchair. The cockroach melted to dust, its legs flailing as it disintegrated.

"RAHH!" Tilde exclaimed, with a victorious pump of her fists.

"What about... all the little ones?" Hyphen asked, standing crouched on the sink.

Tilde was confused. "What are you talking about?"

"You don't see them...everywhere?" Hyphen answered, still shaking.

"Nope."

Hyphen thought that was odd. Tilde wasn't one to lie.

"Tilde... I'm still seeing all these little roaches scurrying all over the place," she said. "Can you see them too? Or is it just me?"

Tilde frowned. "I think it's just you. Are you okay?"

"Yeah, I'm fine," Hyphen replied, choosing not to climb down from the sink just yet, "maybe it's just some Nightmare spell, or like, I don't know, something in my head."

Tilde scooted closer to her friend, her brow furrowed in concern. "Hyphen, do you want to talk about what you're seeing?"

Hyphen shook her head, her eyes still darting around the room. "Not really. I just... need a minute."

"Okay," Tilde said softly. "I'll be right here when you're ready." The bathroom fell silent except for the drip of the shower and Hyphen's uneven breathing. Hyphen wrapped her arms around Anxious, whose shuddering gradually slowed as she closed her eyes.

Tilde waited patiently as Hyphen rocked on the bathroom sink, her head tucked into her knees, shoulders heaving as she fought to control her breath.

Tilde was going to be late for class again—but there were more important things in life than her attendance record that day.

Chapter 38: Divide and Conquer

The sun dipped below the horizon, bathing the city in blue twilight. As the clock struck 8:00 pm, a new day began for the four siblings and their newfound friend.

Pandora stood by the window, her eyes scanning the darkening streets. She'd inherited her mother's passion for planning, and over the past week, her skills had served as the group's lifeline. In the absence of parental guidance, Pandora had stepped up, creating a rotating buddy system to ensure everyone learned to work well together. Through trial and error, she'd discovered the value of rest days and keeping battle teams lean and agile, with two-person squads proving to be the ideal configuration.

Tonight's plan followed the schedule she'd established: she'd take Pecunia on a hunt, leaving the three boys to handle meals and base security. As Pandora reviewed her strategy in her head, Pecunia's voice broke through her thoughts.

"Can we dress up for our mission?" Pecunia asked, her emerald eyes twinkling.

At first, Pandora was taken aback. Dressing up seemed frivolous given their circumstances. But given what remnants of girlhood remained in their new reality, that this small indulgence seemed fair.

A smile tugged at Pandora's lips as she nodded. "Why not? Let's see what we can do."

The sisters stepped into the bathroom of Pandora's suite and flicked the light switch on. Pecunia let Sloth out to sit in one of the sinks, while Pride put its paws up on the countertop.

Pandora looked at her reflection in the bathroom mirror, then back at Pecunia, awaiting her little sister's verdict. Her own attire—a simple cream turtleneck, a knit skirt, and black pantyhose underneath—was now marred with dirt. Pecunia wore a similar ensemble, though her turtleneck was sleeveless, and her garments remained unscathed. A pang of sorrow struck Pandora as she remembered their abandoned wardrobe in the old apartment. Fabricating new clothes from void matter was both too challenging, and too costly.

Pecunia scrunched her nose as she toyed with the fabric of her cashmere halter. She posed in different angles, angling her shoulders as she studied her silhouette in the mirror.

"Hmmm..." she said with a pout, "I actually think our outfits look perfect already!"

Pandora felt bittersweet relief. She wasn't sure if her sister actually thought that, or if she was sparing Pandora the embarrassment of admitting they had nothing else to wear.

Pecunia's face flickered to life with an idea. "How about we do our hair and makeup instead?"

Pandora grinned. That, she could manage.

She channeled three blobs of void matter into her hands, and shaped them into little accessories: first, a metal cylinder of lipstick, second, a silver-toothed comb, and third, the metallic shell of compact blush.

Pandora did the math. *9 VM. Essentially a convenience store haul.* The price tag was more than justified by what a little bit of fun could do for their morale.

They sat cross-legged on the bathroom floor, the three new creations spread between them. They were nothing fancy, but enough for a mini makeover.

"Here, let me," Pandora said, carefully applying a hint of blush to Pecunia's cheeks. As Pandora dabbed on the pink powder, she noticed how it seemed to meld with Pecunia's skin, its colors subtly shifting with her expressions in a way no ordinary makeup could.

Pecunia giggled, then took the lipstick, dabbing a coat of coral sheen into Pandora's lips.

As they took turns combing each other's hair, they shared memories of watching their mother get ready for events, trying to mimic her graceful movements.

"Remember when you used all of Mom's lipstick to draw on the walls?" Pandora laughed.

"Remember when Volo thought it was candy and *ate it*?" Pecunia added, and they both burst into laughter.

"Remember—remember when Mom wouldn't let Promise bleach his hair, so he started putting lemon juice in it?" Pecunia snorted.

"*You* wanted to bleach your hair too!" Pandora exclaimed, "*You* did it with him!"

The sisters cracked up and shed a few tears as they reminisced on the bathroom floor.

When they finished, they looked in the mirror. Their clothes were the same, but their faces glowed with a touch of color, shimmering in the dim light. Pandora studied their reflections in the large glass of the presidential suite—two small figures in a frame far too large, as if the world had suddenly expanded around them. Her eyes began to water as the uncanny scene cracked a dam within her. Despite her effort to maintain morale, there was no escaping the truth that they were now on their own.

"Things may be different," Pandora mustered a motivational statement as she squeezed her sister's hand, "but who we are will never change."

Pecunia produced a broken giggle as her eyes also began to brim with tears. "You know, if life were a movie, I'd tell you that line was cheesy."

Pandora's cheeks reddened, but before she could respond, her little sister wrapped her in a bear hug. "But I like cheese," she sniffled, nuzzling her face into Pandora's sweater, "You made me feel better."

With a shared smile, they linked arms and headed downstairs with their Voidpets, ready to face the night together.

The cool air nipped at their skin as they stepped out into the dark. Pandora's eyes scanned the horizon, searching for potential hunting grounds. In the distance, a large structure loomed against the starry sky. She nudged Pecunia, pointing towards the wide building.

"Is that...?" Pecunia started.

"A stadium," Pandora finished, her lips etching a smirk. "*Bingo.*"

As a team of two, she and Pecunia excelled at ranged combat. A large space would amplify their advantages—even more so if there was elevated ground to utilize.

"Race you there?" Pecunia challenged.

Pandora cackled. "You're *on.*"

The sisters took off through the empty streets, their Voidpets rushing alongside them. Pride's silver form bounded in the moonlight, while Sloth hovered lazily.

As they approached the stadium, its enormous silhouette grew more distinct. Faded signs and weathered walls hinted at its former glory. Pandora's mind churned with tactical possibilities as they breached the entrance.

"Ready?" she asked, glancing at Pecunia.

Her sister nodded.

"You go up to the bleachers and get into position, okay?" Pandora said. "Lay low and back me up when things start heating up. Sound good?"

Pandora knew how her little sister functioned. She avoided getting her hands dirty for as long as she could, but loved to come in at the last minute to save the day. She was best utilized as a late-game trump card.

"You betcha!" Pecunia responded, before hurrying off to the nearest staircase and climbing up high.

She pushed open the rusty gates and stepped onto the field.

As Pandora marched onto the baseball field, floodlights suddenly blazed to life, bathing the night in harsh white light. She instinctively dropped into a defensive stance, eyes scanning for threats. Without warning, the stadium's ancient sound system crackled to life. A jaunty tune began to play, echoing across the empty stands. Brassy trumpets blared out a cheerful melody, accompanied by the steady rhythm of drums and the warm tones of trombones. The peppy, old-fashioned fight song filled the air, its upbeat tempo a stark contrast to the eerie silence of the abandoned city.

Perhaps it was the void matter in the air reacting to her excitement.

Pandora focused herself, as Pride broke into a run by her side. She thought of how Promise would kill to be here right now: standing in the middle of this gigantic stadium, under the spotlights, music playing—but that was too bad for him, because this arena was for her and Pecunia tonight.

Pandora shouted over the music, into the night.

"Alright, let's go!"

In one strong motion, she enveloped her fist in luminous white matter. As she slammed it into the ground, a boom resonated across the stadium floor. The impact stirred the nearby Nightmares, their hisses and growls erupting from beneath the bleachers. Above, Pride unfurled its metallic wings and took flight, poised to protect her from the looming threats.

Pandora liked to warm up with close combat. She settled into a wide stance, holding her fists in front of her face, channeling void matter to encase them like metal gloves.

The first wave of Stage 1 and Stage 2 Nightmares charged at her, a writhing mass of shadows and teeth. Pandora met them head-on, her reinforced fists connecting with satisfying thuds. Each punch sent shockwaves through the air, disintegrating smaller Nightmares on impact.

A versatile attacker, Pandora's style was a combination of explosive strength and tactful conjuration. There was hardly a creature in the Void that could hold up to her punches, and those who did would face the blazing fury that came next. Pandora bludgeoned through the fray, her movements a well-rehearsed sequence of strikes and parries. Void matter glowed in her fists and forearms, constantly reinforcing their strength.

As a particularly sturdy Nightmare managed to absorb the force of Pandora's iron punch, its body bracing against the impact like an armored boar, Pandora activated her special technique—laser precision, two fearsome beams of red that blasted from her eyes, blazing through its solid defenses like a hot blade through ice. The Nightmare howled as it disintegrated, leaving nothing but wisps of shadow in its wake.

Pandora fought with concise motions, and preferred to hold her ground. She pivoted on the spot, never giving an inch of territory. Her eyes darted from one threat to the next, calculating each move with cold efficiency. When a pack of Nightmares tried to overwhelm her with sheer numbers, she slammed them with a wall of white, buying herself a moment to catch her breath and reassess. Pride backed her up with a blast of lasers from above.

Fast or slow, near or far, Pandora didn't care. Anything that could take a punch would be vaporized by lasers, and anything that escaped the lasers would soon meet the business end of fist. Her only weakness was whatever was behind her back.

She barely noticed the Stage 3 Nightmare lumbering towards her from behind—a large Limit that looked like a three-story-tall humanoid. Its alien form towered over her, its faceless head elevated atop a serpentine neck, with each of its hands fused to an appendage resembling a spiked bat. Six runic eyes dotted its body—one on each bat, two on its torso, and two on its head.

As Pandora spun to face the new threat, her foot caught on uneven ground. She nearly tripped as she steadied herself from the first blow, her fist dispatching the first eye as it collided with a swing from the creature's bat. With lightning speed, she fired her lasers. They took the two torso eyes in rapid succession, before neutralizing the eye on its second bat.

As Pandora calculated her next move, the Nightmare countered. Its neck arced backwards, the two remaining eyes on its head swerving out of range from Pandora's lasers. With one arm, it swatted at Pride, keeping her aerial reinforcements at bay. The other arm swung towards her, its blade glinting in the harsh stadium lights.

Pandora activated *Nerves of Steel* to defend herself, knowing she couldn't dodge in time—

Suddenly, The looming attacker disintegrated with the sound of two thundering *cracks*.

From the bleachers, Pecunia crouched over Sloth like a sniper, the creature's mouth wide open as smoke trailed out if its maw. She pumped her arm triumphantly and cheered, her voice ringing out across the stadium.

"Did you see that?" Pecunia called out.

Pandora beamed at her sister with pride, her heart swelling with affection. There was something about it being just the two of them that really made Pecunia come into herself.

The downfall of the Stage 3 seemed to trigger a frenzied rush of minions, which surged forth en masse to overwhelm Pandora. In response, Pecunia adjusted her grip on Sloth, sporting a nasty grin. The Voidpet seemed to feed off her energy. As Pecunia's confidence surged, Sloth's form streamlined, and a single wing unfurled from its back.

With a clicking sound, she lifted Sloth and locked her aim. The pet was now something of an automatic firearm, rattling rounds of tiny crystal bullets as Pecunia walked closer to the center of the field. The air filled with a staccato of shots, each one finding its mark with uncanny precision. Nightmares fell left and right, unable to close the distance between themselves and the deadly duo.

Pride screeched in the sky. Trumpets blared from the loudspeakers. The stadium lights flashed red, white, and blue, triggered by some ancient programming meant for holiday games.

Pecunia whooped with gusto as she aimed Sloth's mouth all over the place, raining diamonds on what remaining foes scampered to retreat.

As the last of the Nightmares dissolved into dust, the stadium fell quiet. The trumpets faded, leaving only the soft hum of the floodlights. Pandora and Pecunia stood back-to-back in the center of the field, breathing heavily but grinning from ear to ear.

"We should head back," Pandora said, glancing at the sky. "It's getting late, and I'm curious to see what kind of trouble the others have gotten into."

Pecunia nodded, stifling a yawn. "Yeah, I just hope we don't have to eat Promise's cooking," she said.

She stuck her tongue out and made a *bleh* face, in response to which Pandora chortled.

"I wouldn't be surprised if the lobby was on fire."

They stopped to scoop up as much Nightmare fuel as they could carry. Then, they headed out. The sisters walked side by side, enjoying each other's company in silence as they recuperated their energy from the battle. When they finally reached the golden doorway of the hotel, they could hear muffled voices and the sound of activity inside. Pandora and Pecunia shared a look. Something about the hotel was starting to feel like home, even though they couldn't quite explain it.

To their surprise, Luden opened the door for them with a polite bow. He escorted the sisters past the elevators, up the stairs, and into a large banquet hall.

An extravagant feast awaited on the table—rice bowls topped with cuts of fresh fish that glistened like jewels, crispy duck with steamed buns and garnishes, braised beef shank with steamed vegetables, a whole steamed sea bass drizzled in colorful herbs and spices, little slices of toast covered in caviar and sea urchin.

Volo stood in an apron, arranging his dishes across a circular banquet table in the center of the room.

"Dinner is ready," he said.

Pandora and Pecunia stood in the doorway, mouths agape. The banquet hall was transformed, with soft lighting and the aroma of a delicious feast filling the air.

Against the back wall was an elevated stage, with two golden sculptures adorning the walls. On the left, Wrath, and the right, Estrangement, guarding an intricate bench that stood between them. Promise lounged sideways on it, lost in thought, but then sat up to greet them.

"Welcome back, ladies," he drawled, swinging his feet to the ground and standing up on stage. He walked down slowly towards the dining table.

"We were worried the food was getting cold," he added.

Pecunia's mouth watered, and she rushed to take a seat at the table.

"I... what?" Pandora stuttered, her eyes wide with disbelief, "How much did this cost?"

Volo shrugged.

"It wouldn't be polite to disclose that to our guests now, would it?" Promise said to Luden and Volo, flashing Pandora a simper as he pulled out a chair and took a seat opposite from his sister.

Pandora's eyes remained skeptical, but she took her seat and expressed her thanks.

"How thoughtful of you boys to prepare this surprise for us!" She stated, clasping her hands together and holding them close to her chest, "Thank you *very* much for this lovely meal!"

Volo took off his apron and took a seat next to Pecunia, and Luden shyly pulled up a chair on his other side. The four sat next to each other on the large circular table, leaving Promise alone on the opposite side.

Luden's eyes turned into saucers as he took in the banquet before his eyes.

"I've never seen anything like this before," he whispered to Volo, who smiled back in appreciation.

"Shall we?" Pandora asked, and they all dug in. Pandora built herself a robust duck bun, and Pecunia snatched up a mini kaisen don. Luden gingerly claimed a bowl of soup, and Volo cut himself a hearty portion of steamed fish.

Promise patiently sipped his water as he waited for the others to choose their favorites. He eyed the others with satisfaction before reaching for his slice of caviar toast.

The four sitting next to each other chittered with some small talk between bites.

"How was girls' night?" Volo asked.

"It was good!"

"Were there any tough Nightmares?" said Luden.

"Nah, they were all easy-peasy!" Pecunia boasted.

"Only because you saved me!" Pandora giggled and pat her sister on the head.

"Seriously?" Luden wondered aloud, "Is it always this easy to beat the bad guys?"

"Heh. I guess most good guys don't have it this good," Pecunia teased.

They laughed and continued to chow down.

Minutes passed as the team feasted in glory. Then, Pandora broke the silence.

She dabbed her mouth with her handkerchief, then took a deep breath, looking up from her plate to confront Promise.

"So. Why the feast tonight?"

He met her gaze with a cold stare, a lopsided smile spreading across his face.

"Well, I'm glad you finally asked," he said.

Chapter 39: Big Dreams

Promise's gaze swept across the table, surveying the remnants of their feast. The others sat satiated, conversation dwindling into content silence.

"So," he began, "what'd you think?"

"It was *delicious*!" Pecunia beamed. "You made all my favorites!"

"That was fun. I like cooking," Volo answered.

Luden mumbled a flustered "Thank you" through a mouthful of food.

Pandora, however, eyed Promise warily. "It was wonderful, but... why? Why go to all this trouble?"

Promise's lips curled into a smile. "Why not? Don't you think we *deserve* it?"

"But the price," Pandora pressed, "this must have cost a lot of void matter..."

"Mmhm," Promise leaned forward, baiting her to continue. "And so what?"

Pandora hesitated, choosing her words carefully. "We need to be practical. Conserve our resources. We can't afford to—"

"Can't afford?" Promise mused, his tone feigning confusion. "And why is that?"

"Because we're children living without supervision? Because we don't have much to spare?" Pandora feigned confusion back.

Promise flashed a toothy grin as Greed leapt up to perch on his shoulder.

"And that, my friends, is the crux of the problem."

He leaned back in his chair, twirling his fork between his fingers. "Right now—under this program... we're living paycheck to paycheck, doing grueling, manual labor." He gestured with the utensil, emphasizing each word. "It's enough to survive, sure. But that's the *problem*."

"Wait, but how is that bad?" Luden asked, his voice small. "We have food, shelter..."

Promise's hands gripped the table. He stood up and leaned forward.

"Because we should want *more*."

The lighting dimmed, his void matter creeping up the walls and covering the lights. Promise's eyes gleamed in the low light as he continued.

"Think about it. We have powers beyond imagination. We've survived when others haven't. Are we really destined to scrape by, day after day, fighting just to stay alive? Is that what we really want for ourselves? For our future *children*?"

He began to pace around the table, his voice rising. "We could be builders, not scavengers. Leaders, not survivors." He paused behind Pandora's chair, placing a hand on her shoulder. "Imagine never having to worry about void matter again. Imagine rebuilding this city to be even greater than it ever was, full of every new thing we can possibly dream of."

As he stood behind her, Pandora noticed the presence of his newly evolved Greed, whose tail brushed against her as he spoke.

"Imagine being able to find Mom and Dad, and show them all that we've done—show them who we really are."

His tone darkened as he addressed Volo and Pecunia.

"Tonight, we dined like kings and queens—" he paused.

"Because it's time for us to start *acting* like royalty."

Promise raised his hand, and a stream of dark red liquid materialized, swirling through the air like a ribbon. It separated into five tendrils, each pouring into their empty wine glasses.

"Um, what's that?" Luden asked, eyeing his glass warily.

"Pomegranate juice," Promise flashed a look of innocence, "the fruit of the underworld," he added with a wry nod.

He returned to his place at the head of the table, raising his glass. "To our future empire," he declared, his eyes gleaming with an unsettling certainty.

Pandora hesitantly raised her glass, her eyes meeting Promise's. "To our *future*," she said pointedly. The others followed suit, silence settling over the room.

Promise took a sip from his glass, closing his eyes as he downed the full glass of pomegranate juice. He savored the silence, the low light, then continued to speak.

He propped his elbows up on the table and interlaced his fingers. "I have a new plan."

"And what might that be?" Pandora asked, her voice steely as Pride paced behind her.

"We can't keep wasting our time fighting in the streets. We need to earn void matter in way that *doesn't* involve violence—"

A hopeful smile spread on Luden's face before faltering with confusion—

"Because physical labor doesn't scale."

"What do you mean?" Volo asked.

"Heh. Well maybe for you, it does," Promise shot a glance at his brother before explaining, "But the rest of us—we've been pushing ourselves to our limits every hunt, and we're only left with a few hundred VM after our expenses."

"That's still a lot...?" Luden ventured, trailing off as he waited to be countered.

Promise pounced on the rhetorical set up. "Anyone know how much it costs to attend the Institute?"

"Fifty thousand VM per year," Pandora replied instantly.

"Anyone know how much to buy a place next to Something Park?"

"Between one to ten million, maybe twenty."

"And what about building a sixteen-story structure in the middle of the city, like our old home?"

"I'd estimate that as at least a hundred million VM project," said Pandora, matter-of-factly.

Promise and Pandora locked eyes and began to share a mutual understanding.

"You get it now, right? There's no way people got those levels of resources by hunting monsters all day." Promise said slowly. "That doesn't add up. There's got to be another way."

"Well that's not exactly a *plan*," Pandora huffed, "but you have a point."

"To do that, we'll need to gain knowledge in addition to just training," Pandora muttered. "We'll need a better understanding of how things work in the Void, so we can get smart instead of just getting by."

"Exactly," Promise snapped his fingers. "We need to *create* value, not just pick up scraps. That's how we build our power."

"Sounds good," Pandora shrugged, then tilted her head. "So what's your grand idea?"

The lights went back to normal as Promise's intensity melted to reveal a sheepish face.

"Hey, don't look at me," he said, putting his hands up.

"I'm 13."

The room fell silent.

Two seconds later, Pandora burst into melodious laughter and slapped her knee. Promise looked at her like he'd been caught with his hand in the cookie jar.

"Hey!" He protested like a small child, "I thought we took turns finishing each other's bad ideas!"

Pandora snorted and shook her head. "Since when have *you* ever done something *bad* that *I* said?"

"I literally blew up a giant worm for you."

"I helped," Volo interjected.

"Ok, fair."

Suddenly everyone was giggling at the absurdity of the conversation, and even Luden allowed himself a chuckle.

Pandora tapped her chin. "So we need to gain knowledge... but how? Maybe we can search for a local library and set up a base there?"

Pecunia shifted in her seat, her eyes lit up with guilty glee. "Well you know, I've always kind of wanted to go to the Institute."

Her words hung in the air as she quickly added, "I mean, it's just an idea. We don't have to—"

"Me too," Volo interjected, his gaze fixed on Pecunia.

Pecunia's cheeks flushed, caught between her burning curiosity and the weight of suggesting something potentially taboo. She glanced nervously at Pandora, her fingers twirling a long lock of hair.

"Ew, I'm not going to *school,*" Promise made a face and leaned back in his seat. "Literally the *one* good thing about no parents is *no school.* You really want to ruin that too?"

"I mean at this point, the Institute might be our only option to educate ourselves on the workings of the Void..." said Pandora, biting her lip in thought.

Luden nodded silently in agreement.

Pecunia guffawed at Promise, emboldened by the support. "You can keep playing hooky by yourself, then!" She teased, "Everyone else is coming with ME!"

"Heh. Meanwhile you have fun saving up 200,000 VM by yourselves and giving it away," Promise retorted. "With that kind of money, I'd rather just get myself a sports car."

"Can it be red?" Volo asked, getting excited despite himself.

"Wait, wait," Luden interjected, looking confused. "What's a sports car?"

Promise started cracking up. "Skip school with me and I'll show you."

"Gee, then how can I refuse?" Luden replied, impressing himself with his banter.

"Hey, I thought you were on our side!" Pecunia protested.

"I'm on the side of whoever's least likely to get us all killed," Luden replied, putting his hands up with a grin.

Pandora dropped her jaw in surprise. "And out of all of us, you picked Promise???"

"Sports car trumps survival." Volo deadpanned.

The rest of the night devolved into jovial shenanigans.

Chapter 40: Windfall Inc.

As months went by, Luden slowly adjusted to his new life.

Promise and Pandora naturally fell into the roles of stand-in parents, and it was with the younger pair that Luden felt most at ease. Together, the three of them could just be kids, playing through their strange world.

One night, the trio trudged back to their room after a hunting mission. As usual, Volo's clothes were splattered with the inky residue of vanquished Nightmares. Meanwhile, Luden and Pecunia's fingers were sticky with snack residue—spectators to the night's battle. Despite his inaction, Luden felt drained, the secondhand adrenaline of watching Volo fight leaving him unexpectedly exhausted.

They settled into their respective sleeping spots in their seventh-floor hotel room: Volo and Pecunia in their beds, Luden on the couch. The heavy blackout curtains were drawn tight against the midday sun, plunging the room into an artificial twilight. A thin sliver of light seeped through a gap in the fabric, a reminder of the inverted world they now inhabited. As Luden heaved a huge yawn and adjusted himself on the couch, Volo's voice broke through the manufactured night.

"Luden, do you ever miss your old home?"

"No, not really," Luden replied, his words small in the vastness of the dark.

The silence that followed felt heavy, prompting Luden to elaborate. "I... I lived in that dumpster for as long as I can remember. There's nothing before that, really."

"Oh, okay," Volo said, his tone neutral. He was comfortable with silence and embraced the pause.

"Do you like it here?" Volo asked.

Luden's reply came with a smile that no one could see. "Well, I mean, yeah, how could I not?" The words tumbled out with gratitude and lingering disbelief. He'd gone from being homeless and alone to living in a luxury hotel with what felt like family.

But in this perpetual sleepover, reflections were commonplace, and he felt compelled to confess.

"I just... sometimes I feel like I don't belong here. Like I'm a fraud for mooching off you guys."

From the darkness chimed Pecunia's melodic scoff. "Everyone's a fraud," she declared, her voice laced with a tongue-in-cheek glee.

"No, not everyone," Luden countered softly. "You guys are the real deal."

His earnest words invited a pensive quiet to settle over the room. In the silence, Luden's mind wandered to the Windfalls' achievements. While his own past had been defined by simply getting by, the four siblings had quickly mastered survival, and were now leveling up their skills with a fervor that left him in awe.

Pandora had already conquered the local library and refurbished it into a makeshift café for Voidpets. Promise pushed the boundaries of lucidity daily, adding complex substances like oil and electricity to his repertoire—all with his heart set on rebuilding his old home. Pecunia, with her keen eye, was constantly scheming new opportunities, and Volo stood as their vigilant defender, securing their ever-growing territory.

"Nah," Pecunia blurted, and Luden could envision her nose scrunching in the dark. "I feel like we don't really do anything. If anyone's doing real work, it's you!"

Her words brought a flush to Luden's face, invisible in the dimness. Determined to make himself useful, he'd taken on the role of hotel cleaner. As the self-declared weak link, he pushed himself to go above and beyond, clinging to his humility like a lifeline.

"No, come on, don't say that," he protested, wiping a thread of goo from his hands. "I know you guys are doing all the important stuff."

"That's not true," Volo's quiet voice drifted from his bed.

"Not me!" Pecunia declared, her tone oddly proud.

Luden disagreed. "Pecunia... come on... didn't you singlehandedly earn a *million* void matter yesterday?"

"Yeah, but it was a scam!" Pecunia slapped the bed for emphasis and began to cackle with delight, "I didn't do *squat*!"

"I mean, you worked hard to make those golden rocks, and you came up with really clever marketing for them..." Luden mumbled. "Not everyone can sell *Tabloons* for 100k a piece. That takes talent."

Pecunia snorted. "I just got lucky that some rich Voidpets wanted to sport them as a status symbol. That's got nothing to do with me," she giggled.

Luden sighed. Pecunia was just as brilliant as the rest of her family, but of course, she'd never admit it.

"Well at least Promise and Pandora are doing serious stuff, you can't deny that," Luden persisted, to which the others murmured in concession. Luden gazed into the darkness with Cringe curled on his chest. The Voidpet offered a brooding blink.

"I don't know," Luden sighed, "I just sometimes don't get why I'm here. Like I did nothing to deserve this, and I'm intruding on your family..."

Pecunia's laugh swept away the gloom. "I mean I literally do nothing and feel *fantastic* about it," Pecunia guffawed.

Her voice softened. "But Luden, you deserve nice things, and you're not intruding. You know you're basically family now, right?"

Luden's throat tightened as her words sank in. A part of him yearned to accept her words, but doubt lingered in his chest.

Sensing his unease, Pecunia changed tack. "Luden, wanna know what's *really* fake?" she piped up, a devious edge creeping into her tone. "Promise's *eyes*."

"Huh?" Luden was confused.

Volo's matter-of-fact explanation followed. "He made contacts out of void matter and basically glued them to his irises."

"Yeah, and he was like, crying for *days!*" Pecunia added with a cackle that echoed off the walls, "Mom lost her *mind* about it!"

Luden's bewilderment grew. "What's that got to do with anything?"

"I'm just saying," Pecunia explained, her giggles punctuating her words, "that people aren't all they're cracked out to be. Everyone's faking something. So don't count yourself out so much."

Luden considered, but he didn't think the anecdote was a fair parallel. "I mean sure his eyes might be fake, but like... he made a *smartphone* yesterday," he murmured, still in disbelief.

Pecunia's laughter, a singsong trill, filled the room once more. "So what? The phone didn't even work! It melted!"

The image of Promise holding his liquefied creation triggered snickers from Volo. But Luden remained solemn, the scene reminiscent of his own goo-oozing hands.

A disquieting thought crept into Luden's mind. There was something disingenuous about how they could compliment him as 'hard working' and 'awesome' yet howl with laughter at the mistakes of someone who was clearly a generational prodigy.

The contradiction festered.

"Are you really making fun of him for doing something *that* impressive?" Luden's voice was fragile, his own vulnerability seeping through. "What... does that mean you guys think of *me*?"

The laughter died down, replaced by a thoughtful silence. Volo's voice, when it came, was sincere.

"Humor is a good thing," he spoke slowly, his words carefully chosen. "We don't think any less of him for it."

Volo paused, his tone growing pensive. "Laughing at our humanity is not discounting our effort."

His words lingered in the air, a pious counterpoint to the earlier jubilance. Luden lay still, letting his next thoughts brew in the solitude of his own mind. The room fell quiet, save for the soft breathing of his friends.

As sleep began to claim him, Luden drifted off in a curious new state of mind. The Void was an absurd place, and somehow, he had ended up here with the Windfalls, swept up in their plans to build a corporate empire from scratch. With the rest of his life ahead to live, perhaps it was better to start enjoying it sooner rather than later.

Part III:
The Layers

Chapter 41: Zero

Ideas exist in opposition.
Favor implies burden. Motion implies stasis.
Existence begets absence; intention creates abandon—
And where there is One, there must be Zero.

Chapter 42: Freshmen Again

As Hyphen approached the university quad, she was greeted by an enthusiastic chorus of "SURPRISE!" Her friends were gathered around a small picnic blanket, adorned with a homemade banner that read "Happy 18th Birthday, Hyphen!"

Tilde zoomed through the air, practically tackling Hyphen with a bear hug. "Happy birthday to my BESTEST friend in the whole Void!" she exclaimed, floating on a pink trail of void matter.

Alt stepped forward, his hands balancing a small cake with the help of lilac tendrils. "We made this for you," he said with a shy smile. "Well, Tilde baked it, and I decorated." The cake was adorned with swirling patterns of frosting.

Char grinned, producing a small gift box from behind his back. "And this is from all of us," he said, handing it to Hyphen with a flourish.

Hyphen's eyes welled up with happy tears as she opened the box to find a delicate charm necklace. Each gold charm represented one of her Anxious, perfectly capturing their worried little expressions.

"You guys," she sniffled, "this is amazing. Thank you so much!"

As Char helped her put on the necklace, her Voidpets swirled around seemingly approving of their miniature representations. For some reason, none of her Anxious (or *Anxi*, as she affectionally coined for the plural) liked to evolve. Instead, she kept finding new ones showing up at her door. The whole pack trailed behind her like floating exclamation points as she grinned from ear to ear.

At the back of her neck, she heard the clasp click together between his fingers and felt a small leap in her chest. She was touched by the thought of how much everyone cared for her.

"Alright, birthday girl," Tilde said, as everyone took a seat on the picnic blanket. "Make a wish and blow out your candles! Then we can stuff our faces with cake and talk about our plans for the year."

Hyphen closed her eyes, made a wish, and blew out the candles. As her friends cheered and began cutting the cake, she was overwhelmed with gratitude. September 5th also marked the start of her freshman year—now at the Institute's University, and her friends had made their first day of school all about her. What better way to start the semester than celebrating with the people she loved most?

Hyphen and her friends devoured the cake, and then settled into the quad, the excitement of the surprise party slowly giving way to a more relaxed atmosphere. While Alt pulled out his notebook to sketch, his tendrils wielding multiple pencils like extra fingers, Char leaned against a tree, passing a royal blue blob of VM between his hands like a tennis ball.

Tilde's wheelchair was parked as she returned to hover a few inches above it, her legs transformed into a ghost-tail of VM. For a second, her torso hovered atop nothing but rose-colored smoke. Then, the trail faded and coalesced back into legs.

"YOW," she chirped, as she dropped back into her chair with a thud. "I'm still workin' on this whole flight thing," she admitted, her cheeks pink as she fixed her coral hair.

Hyphen beamed as she adjusted herself on the blanket, pulling her book bag close. "Tilde, I will still never get over how you can *fly* now."

"Heheheh," Tilde guffawed, before popping a modest shrug, "It takes all my focus and burns a ton of VM though, so I can't do it all the time."

"Still, you're incredible," Hyphen gushed, nudging her best friend with encouragement.

The next thing she knew, an ethereal blob of energy emerged from Tilde's chest, materializing in the grass as Anger's Stage 3 form. The scarfed Voidpet, now almost half as tall as Tilde, had the comical stature of a hand puppet. While its top half resembled a dragon, with both fearsome jaws and claws, its bottom half puddled into the ground with no legs.

"You're incredible too, Angy," Hyphen cooed, opening her bag to feed the Voidpet a cookie.

"So, what extracurriculars is everyone thinking about?" she asked, dusting off her hands as she turned to face her friends. "I know Professor Bool's got a poker club, String's hosting meditation retreats... and Professor Esse's doing that leadership summit thing!"

"I'm telling you guys, the Windfall corporate internship is where it's at," Char insisted, clearly having given a lot of thought to the topic. "I heard there's free coconut water at the office, and they pay you a boatload for doing nothing!"

Tilde rolled her eyes, dropping to the blanket with a soft thud as she hoisted herself down from her wheelchair. "Come on, I'm not going to sell my *soul* for coconut water. You literally hate them, why would you work for them?"

"I mean, what's your game plan for not being *broke* this semester?" Char prodded, tossing his ball into the air, "The academic programs don't pay, and it's not like our aid packages cover the rising cost of our void matter expenses." He caught the ball with his hand encased in a liquid blue claw.

"I've got my sights set on doing non-profit Voidpet research with Professor Invidere," Tilde declared with a puff in her chest. "Did you know there are 96 Vivid variants of Voidpets? That's kind of nuts! Like, I've only seen a handful of them in my whole life!"

"That doesn't answer my question," Char quipped, rolling his eyes as he sat back down.

Alt looked up from his sketchbook, a slight frown on his face. "I don't know, Char. I feel like void matter isn't as important as doing something you're passionate about. I'm with Tilde on this one. I'm personally just planning to paint more, and I'll figure out how to get by on less."

As Char's skepticism drifted to face Alt and his sketch, his eyes suddenly bugged out in horror.

"Dude, why are you drawing *Volo*???" Char demanded, slapping his hand to the ground, aghast.

"Yo, chill!" Alt protested, his sleeves scrambling to cover the half-finished artwork as his face turned red, "We're in a portrait class together, Professor String paired us up for the assignment."

"Well then make it more realistic, he looks worse in real life," Char harrumphed.

Tilde leaned forward to investigate. "Honestly, I think Alt's got it pretty spot on," Tilde said matter-of-factly.

Hyphen giggled at the silliness of the conversation and sought to redirect it back to the original subject. "Char, I'm with you on the internship, I think that's what I'll be applying for as well. And I really hope we both get it together!"

Char nodded, a small smile returning to his face as he looked at Hyphen. The two of them tended to be on the same page when it came to career and academics, and it was fine that not everyone else was. She decided, again, to steer the subject to something they could all relate to.

"So," Hyphen pretzeled her legs, her collection of Anxi settling around her like a cluster of worried balloons, "Are you all ready for our first Nightmare mission? I heard it's coming up soon!"

"Oh, HECK yeah I am!" Tilde cried, a pink ball of matter forming around her fist.

"Oh, I was *born* ready," Char grinned at Tilde, their camaraderie returning at the thought of combat. Now that students were expected to be at least Level 3, proficient in manipulating at least 1000 VM, the possibilities for magic and mayhem were exponentially greater.

Alt nodded, his tendrils curling protectively around his sketchbook. "Yeah, I think we've got this. Thank goodness we get to pick our own groups for this one, right?"

Hyphen nodded. "I wonder what the objective will be," Hyphen's brow furrowed in thought. "Maybe a research mission? Or Void exploration? Or just straight-up Nightmare extermination?"

"I don't care as long as I get to KICK BUTT!" Tilde huffed, punching her fists out in a silly dance.

The group giggled.

In some ways, they all had changed, but in others, they were exactly the same.

Chapter 43: Alone Time

Luden still hadn't gotten used to living in a penthouse—especially one that was on the 104th floor.

As he entered the living room of 212 Something Park South, he felt his stomach lurch. The view was dizzying, and he was afraid of heights. Unfortunately, he hadn't had the guts to admit that and agreed to room there with the Windfalls.

That morning, he entered the apartment alone to retrieve the forgotten book bag. Luckily, his new place was only 5 minutes from school. As he rummaged through the couch pillows, careful to face away from the floor-to-ceiling windows behind him, he suddenly heard the door click.

Luden froze in place as Pandora walked in, Cringe falling to the floor with a dramatic plop.

"Oh, hello there!" Her voice twinkled, the scent of cinnamon wafting in with her arrival. She strode into the room in a steel blue peacoat, clutching a warm drink in one hand and a large tote bag in the other. Atop her head was a matching sun hat, adorned with a neat ribbon of blue.

"Oh, uh, hi Pandora," Luden stammered, embarrassed to be caught in the act of his negligence, "I just, um, forgot some stuff at home. Well actually like... all my stuff," the words rushed from his mouth as he felt goo bead at his brow. Pandora had insisted on funding his college tuition, even though he had nothing to show from his high school education. He didn't want to waste any more of the Windfalls' money and hated to let himself bumble in front of them.

Pandora giggled, heading straight for the kitchen. "Well it's a good thing we live right next to campus now!"

Luden's shoulders relaxed as Pandora's attention turned from him to the fridge. Though Pandora herself had graduated early from college as valedictorian, she didn't seem to hold anyone else to the same standard.

"Just don't tell anyone I took these, hehe," she said, popping a goofy wink as she grabbed a tub of cookies from the fridge. She turned on a dime and was gone from the apartment as quickly as she came. Outside the window, Luden saw Pandora soar away on the back of Pride—now a majestic dragon with four wings and a lion's mane.

He breathed a sigh of relief. Even though the Windfalls were practically family at this point, he still found himself standing straighter whenever they were around. As he turned his attention back to the couch, he found his bag, sandwiched between two of the seat backs.

Thank goodness!

Unfortunately, as he examined his crumpled bag, he realized that his phone and student ID had both fallen out. *Oh, bother.* Luden shook his head in frustration as he started to remove the couch's seat cushions one by one.

Suddenly, another sound clacked from the door, and it swung open. As Promise strode into the apartment, Luden felt his bones lock in place. The guy was already a menace at 13, but he was even worse at 21.

Promise was dressed in black from head to toe, his clawed fingertips visible through gloves that he never took off. He wore a coat that split into three long tails, each flowing through the air with a life of their own. The most striking part of his ensemble was a gold belt buckle, shaped like a Greed in the shape of a stylized W.

"Luden! What are *you* doing here?" he asked, his dry voice reverberating across the expanse of the apartment.

Luden felt his heart beat faster as he fumbled for an explanation. Though Promise was like a brother, there was still an edge to him that made it uncomfortable to be alone in his presence.

"Uh, hey Promise," Luden stammered, feeling his voice weaken, "I just forgot my book bag."

Promise's stride faltered.

"You forgot your *whole bag*?" He asked, before doubling over with laughter.

"Yeah kind of," Luden managed a self-deprecating smile.

Promise couldn't stop laughing as he propped himself over the kitchen island. He wiped a tear from his eye. "That's *gold*."

"So, uh, what are you doing here today?" Luden asked, trying to make friendly conversation.

"Well..." Promise's eyes looked up through his brows as he held his hunched position, "This is usually my alone time. In, well, you know... *my house*."

As he said that last part, his smile twisted with satire, and Luden felt his blood go cold. Promise's expressions often straddled the line between facetious leer and child-like delight, and Luden couldn't tell the two apart. What could have been a simple statement of fact could just as easily be construed as a not-so-subtle reminder of who was living rent-free in whose skyscraper.

"So are you done attacking the couch, or what?" Promise pressed, his playful tone seemingly unaware of the weight of his words, "Cause... that's my spot."

"Uh, I still haven't found my phone yet, sorry," Luden said, shuffling to check behind another pillow.

Without warning, Promise snapped his fingers from the kitchen island. All the cushions erupted into the air, one of them nearly hitting Luden in the face.

Luden leapt back at the sudden action around him. As the cushions hovered in place, his missing belongings separated from the mess and floated into his bag. Then, Promise flipped his hand, commanding the pillows to smash back into the couch into their rightful positions.

"There you go, bud," he quipped, before strolling up to the couch and plopping the full length of himself on it.

On the couch, Promise took out his phone to text, leaving Luden stunned.

The 'psychic' ability to move regular objects—ones that weren't freshly formed from void matter—was one of those highly advanced techniques that put him in a league of lucidity above everyone else.

"You got anything else to do today? Or are you just going to stand there and watch me?" Promise's eyes wandered to Luden, who was staring, slack jawed. In his other hand, he summoned an iced beverage, absently guiding the straw into his open mouth.

Luden managed a meek laugh. "Haha yeah, uh, thanks! I'll see you around."

As Promise sprawled on the couch, Luden noticed the dark circles under his eyes, the tension in his shoulders. He often seemed spaced out these days, as if having conversations in his head. Sometimes, Luden felt bad for him.

Ever since he dropped out of high school, Promise became somewhat of an enigma. He didn't take part in the memories everyone had made together at the Institute. He didn't have hobbies, he didn't make friends, and he spent far more time by himself. Meanwhile, he had gotten significantly more powerful, and no one was around to witness how.

Luden hesitated at the door. He thought back to when their whole family would drive to the Institute together, and the wild first week of high school where they teamed up for that game. Even those hooligan days when they were running around hunting Nightmares out east. Promise had once had straightforward goals—protecting his family, hunting Nightmares, and earning VM so that they could all live well— but now it was impossible to tell what was going through his head.

There was a question he'd never thought to ask any of the Windfalls before but felt inclined to ask today. It was the first time he'd been alone with Promise in a while, and the concern simply came rolling off his tongue.

"Hey Promise, um, are you... doing okay these days?" Luden asked.

Promise tilted his phone down, consuming Luden with his ice blue stare. An off-kilter smile spread across his face, his pointed canines glinting as he ran his tongue across the edge of his teeth.

"I've never been better," he replied, holding his gaze on Luden as if entertained by the consideration.

"Sweet of you to ask, though," Promise added, a cloying look forming as his eyes drifted back to his phone.

"Oh, uh…" Luden smiled half-heartedly as he flashed an awkward thumbs-up. "That's great then!"

He backed out of the apartment, fumbling with the doorknob behind him as Promise's unnerving response hung in the air. He couldn't shake the feeling that something was off with his old friend.

The elevator ride down was a nerve-wracking blur, but soon, the picturesque view of the Institute floating in the sky snapped him back to reality. As he stepped out of the lobby, the midday sun warmed his face, washing away the chill he'd felt in the penthouse.

Luden checked the time on his phone, realizing he'd spent more time upstairs than he'd intended. He quickened his pace, making his way down Something Park South. The Institute wasn't far, but he'd have to hurry to make it to class on time.

As he jogged up Ghost Road, he was greeted by the familiar sights and sounds of campus life. Voidpets milled about, some students rushed to class, and others congregated in small groups. Luden passed groups of university students headed in the opposite direction off campus, likely off to an early lunch. Among them were new faces from his college classes, as well as a few familiar ones from high school.

"Hey there, Luden!" Dyna sang out with a wave as she passed by.

A few groups behind her was Verve, who stopped to give Luden a hug. "Luden!!!! *Love* the new look," she said in a sing-song voice, tugging at the sleeve of his new linen button down.

"Thanks Verve," Luden replied, flustered by the compliment as he adjusted his newly recovered backpack. "Enjoy your lunch!"

As he hurried across the courtyard, he passed Tilde waving at him, and he waved back.

Luden felt a smile return to his face, knowing that he'd at least kept up some friendships since first attending the Institute. People were nice to him. He was popular. And he had no idea why.

Luden picked up his pace, hoping he wouldn't be late for Professor String's next lecture.

Chapter 44: Secret Recipe

Pandora was en route to her favorite café.

She dismounted Pride, recalling the Voidpet back into her coat sash, and carried her box of cookies towards the shop. As she pushed open the door of Pandora's Bread—the café named after herself, of course—the familiar scent of freshly baked goods enveloped her. The aroma sang of warm bread and cinnamon, harmonizing with floral notes from locally sourced lavender in their signature scones.

The cafe's interior was a soothing oasis amidst the concrete city. Warm light filtered through gauzy curtains, casting a gentle glow on the polished wood tables and plush, mismatched armchairs. Potted herbs lined the windowsills, their fresh scent mingling with the bakery aromas. Soft, acoustic melodies drifted through the air, punctuated by the gentle clink of porcelain cups and the low hum of conversation.

What was once a small business she started in high school had blossomed into a chain with multiple locations throughout the city. The Something Park South location was the closest to her home, so it served as the flagship store and the main test kitchen. Despite its growth, each location was designed to maintain the cozy, intimate feel of a neighborhood bakery.

Today, she'd brought a special batch of test cookies, carefully crafted in her home kitchen. Golden-brown and studded with amber flecks, they were a brand-new recipe, featuring an ingredient called Dopamine. She'd surveyed her customers, and this was their top request.

The human body produced its own dopamine, of course. But the substance that Voidpets called Dopamine was different. It was some sort of natural mineral that apparently tasted like heaven and could be found as a raw material in the Void. Luckily, Volo been able to find her a sample from one of his field missions.

Pandora opened the box and took a small bite, just to double-check they were still good. To her human taste buds, it was pleasant enough—a mild sweet, with a hint of something savory. Meanwhile, her belt containing Pride tightened with anticipation as she chewed.

"Alright, alright," she laughed, breaking off a small piece for her companion. The tip of her sash yawned into the maw of a beast, and Pride snatched it up, widening its eyes in bliss before shrinking back into a ribbon. Pandora smiled, glad her recipe seemed to be on the right track. Volo said Voidpets went wild for Dopamine, so she was hoping that this new treat would be a hit.

A Merry Voidpet peeked out from the kitchen, standing even taller than Pandora in a crown of hibiscus flowers. As a Saccharine Vivid, her full body was pink, along with her flared crest that fanned out like five bunny ears.

"Hello, Peach! The new sample recipe is ready!" Pandora sung, handing the box to the café's manager.

"Oooh, yum yum Pandora!" Peach took the box into her tiny paws, turning into the kitchen with a swish of her fluffy tail. "They smell scrumptious, dear!" the Voidpet said, taking a big whiff of the box.

"Oh, and—would you like anything to eat while you work today?" Peach poked her head out to ask.

"May I please get a large pumpkin spice latte and a passionfruit kouign amann?" Pandora recited perfectly, her request all smiles.

"Sure thing, darling!"

"Thank you, Peach!"

Pandora slipped some extra void matter into the tip jar with a big wink. Peach was one of her top-performing employees, and she was always thankful to the Merry for delivering consistent customer service. Even though Pandora had quietly lowered wages to fit more workers onto the staff, she still did her best to make sure those under her leadership felt cared for.

As she turned away from the counter, Pandora's heart skipped a beat. Settling into a corner booth was Professor Cogito, his dragon mask gleaming in the soft light. He arranged a stack of papers as he set down a large mug of tea.

Pandora's heart swelled. To see her former professor—perhaps the most esteemed intellectual in the Void—choosing her cafe as his workspace was the highest compliment. A testament to the atmosphere she'd worked hard to create.

Pandora beamed as she caught his eye. The professor gave a slight nod, the eyes of his mask crinkling in what she hoped was a smile. She resisted the urge to go over and ask if he needed anything, not wanting to disturb his concentration. Instead, she made a mental note to have Peach bring him a fresh pot of tea later.

Meanwhile, she thought with a sigh, some others were not such diligent workers.

'No idea,' or 'don't care,' were the responses she'd get when she asked Promise about logistics or financials. So, it was Pandora who was left with the job of making sure their empire was still making money.

She sought out her favorite booth by the window, sinking into the well-worn leather seat. The table was crafted from reclaimed wood, its surface bearing the gentle rings of countless cups and plates. Pandora took a moment to breathe in the calming atmosphere she'd created, relishing the warm steam of pumpkin spice that tickled her face.

There, she pulled out her laptop to begin her afternoon work session. In the comfort of her booth, Pandora sifted through emails from customers, unpaid bills, and a world of other operations. The Windfalls had lots of businesses to look after, and she was the one responsible for managing them all.

Surrounded by the warmth of her café with the aroma of her pumpkin spice latte wafting up from her mug, Pandora felt herself slip into a state of flow. In this familiar sanctuary of her own creation, no email was too daunting, no spreadsheet too complex.

Here, in her element, she felt invincible.

Chapter 45: Pandora vs. Promise

Luden unloaded onto the couch after a long day of school. Volo plopped into the cushions beside him, and Pecunia kicked her feet up onto the chaise to recline. Pandora, having just gotten home from a day of work, stood by the window, admiring the skyline.

The floor-to-ceiling windows yawned before them, filling the room with golden hour light. As he let the couch absorb him, Luden felt like he was living on a cloud. Perhaps the 104th floor was something he could get used to—if he just didn't look down.

Unfortunately, the moment of peace was short-lived.

Promise entered the apartment, and pandemonium ensued.

"*Pandora*. What did you *do*—"

"What?" Pandora immediately cut him off with a curt snap.

"Where did the yellow cookies go?" He demanded, advancing toward the window where she stood.

"I sold them at my cafe...?" She answered with a skeptical tilt of her head.

"But I was *eating* them." Promise said, matter-of-factly.

"Well, they weren't for you," Pandora retorted with pursed lips.

Before Luden could predict what could happen next, Lonely materialized on the couch beside him. Promise extended his arms, still striding towards his sister, and willed his gloves to dissolve into smoke.

In the next second, a metallic clash pierced the air, and he had blinked across the room in front of Pandora, smoke trailing in the wake of his lunge. Pandora's fists were coated in a pearly glow, gripping his forearms to restrain his outstretched claws. Before Luden could process what was happening, the two siblings were locked in combat.

Promise's demeanor resembled that of a wild Voidpet. His three coat tails bristled like actual tails, and his grin fully bared his pointed canine teeth. They were both visibly shaking to overpower each other, and the smell of hot metal filled the air.

"Woah there, what's your deal?" Pandora was flabbergasted, and so was Luden.

Now in their early 20s, the Windfalls developed a taste for sparring like children. While combat was once a survival necessity, it now seemed like they were itching to brawl out of boredom.

Promise's voice was a melodramatic rasp, "I want them *all*."

Pandora rolled her eyes. Though Promise had a habit for histrionics, this reaction seemed overdramatic, even for him.

"You mean ...the *cookies*?"

Promise pushed harder, and Luden saw Pandora's image begin to flicker. Little glitches percolated her arms, while an unhinged grin revealed Promise's inner power trip. Luden suddenly wondered if it was possible to manipulate the void matter inside another person, and he feared that the answer was yes.

As he nearly willed Pandora to buckle, she countered with *Nerves of Steel*, reinforcing herself with a white aura from head to toe.

"Oh, don't even try me. *That's* a dirty move," she snarled, gripping his arms tighter and pushing him back. Clearly offended, she retaliated with an explosive shove, launching her brother out of the penthouse window with a trail of shattered glass.

"Oof. Savage," Pecunia mused, her eyes following Promise's trajectory through the sky.

Luden was now inching towards panic mode, unsure at how such a fight had escalated.

"Should we, like try to maybe stop them, or...?" he asked, as a wind blew through the now open window. His voice trailed off with fear, knowing he was helpless to intervene.

"Nah," Volo said, spreading his arms back on the couch. As he kicked up his legs, Luden noticed the hint of a smile form on his face. "I've always wanted to see 'em fight."

Luden looked at Pecunia, who shrugged and nodded. "Ok then."

After admiring her handiwork, Pandora began to charge out the window. She leapt out, appearing to free-fall off the edge before Pride surged into the air, carrying her skyward on its back. The silver dragon soared forth with a battle screech.

Before Pride could snatch Promise out of the sky, he was back in the house. He crouched before the broken window, shrouded in a trail of smoke and floating glass.

"*Hey Pandora,*" he taunted, charging up an orb of matter as he straightened, "*behind you.*"

As Pride maneuvered Pandora with a graceful loop through the air, Promise hit them square on with a beam of red. It fully engulfed Pandora and her whole Voidpet before pummeling the sky, sending shockwaves rippling through the clouds. He stood there sustaining the blast, a villainous laugh rising as he stumbled backwards to keep his own balance.

Luden's eyes expanded like saucers as time seemed to slow. He had suspected something was off with Promise, but he didn't expect him to delete Pandora outright. He looked at Volo, who seemed to be enjoying himself on the couch, and then at Pecunia, who was now on her phone.

Luden gulped. He'd postpone his panic until they were panicking too.

Seconds later, the blast petered out. Pride remained intact, fully aglow with Pandora on its back. Her own aura was blazing white, so much so that it hurt to look her direction, and they emerged from the attack unscathed—albeit pushed back a few hundred feet.

Promise cracked up hysterically, seemingly amused at what had happened. He spread both hands, admiring the electric power that surged around them, and instantly summoned two inky streams.

"Not bad, right?" Promise shot a simper towards the couch, where Luden and the others sat watching him like afternoon TV.

He began to gloat at her, though she was too far away to hear. "What's the matter? Fire too easy for you now?" His grin was wide, and the air around him crackled with energy.

He flexed his hands, multiplying the void matter in a surge of electric blue. "Let's see how you do with lightning," he jeered, as if imitating a cartoon villain.

With the full leverage of his wingspan, he hurled them towards Pandora, casting bolts through the afternoon sky.

Despite the force of his onslaught, which thundered through the air for miles, all he could do was push Pandora back a few hundred feet as if he were poking her with a stick. His hand movements remained deliberate while the rest of him staggered, fingers locking into place while his willowy form faltered under the force of his attacks.

Luden felt lightheaded as he clutched the edge of his seat. The Institute floated at the corner of their view, and it dawned on him that a slightly misplaced angle could have sent any of these blasts right into the school.

"*Ready for round two*?" Promise jeered out the window as he charged up a new move. As the fox part of Greed jumped up to his shoulder, its three hydra heads spiraled around his arm, culminating at his fingertips with each pair of jaws spread wide open. A cosmic orb bloomed in front, filling the apartment with a furious gust of wind.

Luden clutched his bag to keep it from flying out the window. "Should we stop him *now*?" he yelled at Volo over the wind, who thought for a few seconds before deciding it was finally acceptable to intervene.

Before the attack could unfold, Volo was behind his brother, restraining him in a measured chokehold. The onslaught now over, Pandora and Pride coasted back to the apartment.

"*Heyyyyy*, come on, I was about to get her," Promise slurred before passing out, his Greed powering down with a disappointed hum.

"Not even close," Pandora landed with a haughty chuckle, crossing her arms as she let down her shield with a huff.

Luden grabbed an extra bandage from his bag, realizing he needed reinforcements for the volume of goo that was oozing from his hands. He was glad everyone was okay, and things appeared to be cooling down.

"Did he just want... more *cookies*?" Luden asked.

"Yeah, I guess," Pandora mused, planting her hands on her hips as she glanced to the side in thought.

Luden found himself itching to break the silence that stretched before them. "Was there anything... special in those cookies?" he asked.

Volo shook his head. "It was just Dopamine. A natural mineral," he explained. "Voidpets like it."

Pandora shrugged. "Guess he just really liked my recipe!"

She then held her hand to her chin, her voice suddenly skeptical. "Or maybe he had some reaction to the cookies...?" Pandora asked, her eyes narrowing. "I mean, the rest of us can eat them just fine..." Pandora muttered.

"He's fine," said Volo, flatly. "He was messing with you."

"Are you sure that was all it was?" Luden asked, suddenly finding himself emboldened to ask questions now that Promise had been neutralized.

"Yes." Volo asserted. "He made a scene for attention."

Volo scoffed with amusement before adding, "Dopamine isn't the kind of thing that hijacks your mind. If anyone chooses to act up, that's on them."

The group looked around at each other, and Pecunia finally looked up from her phone.

"I mean you guys were just play fighting, right?" she said, puckering her lips to the side. "Plus, the cookies *were* really good."

Volo looked at Pandora, who frowned, and then brightened up. "Yeah, I guess you're right."

Volo lifted Promise's unconscious form onto his back, carrying him off to his room. Pecunia returned to her phone, while Pandora opened a book by the shattered window, unbothered by the draft.

"Oh, don't worry, he'll fix it when he wakes up," Pandora reassured, noticing Luden's worried expression. "He should clean up after himself."

Luden sat, confused. His mind reeled, trying to process what he'd just witnessed. The erratic display of power, the enthusiasm with which they nearly destroyed their own penthouse—still felt surreal despite how long he had known them. As children, the Windfalls were already extraordinary. But as adults, they weren't *just* talented. Their actions now held the weight of catastrophic consequences, and it was not only himself, but the rest of the Void who seemed to be at their mercy.

He glanced at his hands, where a thin film of goo had collected. The gap between him and the others had never felt so vast.

Luden opened his mouth, wanting to say something, anything, about the absurdity of what had transpired. But looking at their unperturbed faces, he realized they probably wouldn't even understand his concern. To them, this was just another Tuesday.

Luden didn't even know if it was worth sharing that he was worried about Promise. The guy had always been an enigma to him, and their power gap only made things more confusing. Did he act out as a cry for help? Or had he gotten so out of touch that this was now his idea of a good time?

With a sigh, Luden decided to focus on what he could control. He had homework to do, and he figured it was best to get started before the day got too late.

Chapter 46: Pandora's Bread

Pandora couldn't believe her eyes. As she went to grab her coffee at Pandora's Bread that morning, her jaw dropped at the size of the line. This wasn't just busy—it was a madhouse.

She'd received an email from Peach saying the sample cookies were a hit. But "hit" didn't begin to cover this.

As she ventured up the line, the scene looked surreal. It appeared word of the cookies spread, and Voidpets were going hog wild. Species of all kinds crowded the sidewalk. Greeds had brought their whole families, pawing at the windows with want. A clan of Gluttony jostled for position near the front.

But Pandora felt a weight in her chest as it dawned upon her that they weren't just eager—they were agitated. Anger Voidpets waved fiery fists, holding signs where the "Br" in "Pandora's Bread" was crossed out and replaced with "D." Anxious chattered in packs, commentating on the chaos, while an Apathy rammed the door repeatedly.

Pandora squeezed through the crowd, slipping into the store. Peach greeted her with a weary smile, but the Merry manager was clearly overwhelmed.

"We're sold out," Peach explained, voice hoarse from repetition. "But they won't leave."

The café was in disarray. Glee bounced off walls while Grumpy refused to budge from their seats. At the counter, a regular Greed rasped, "Give me ALL of them."

At the customer's words, Pandora's mind flashed to Promise.

Was this how the cookies had affected him?

Peach pulled her into the kitchen for an emergency meeting. "They're boycotting until we restock," the pink Voidpet said, her fluffy tail bristling with concern, "They won't order anything else."

Pandora tried to stay positive. "We'll be back in stock tomorrow! Let's just focus on recommending alternatives for now."

But Peach shook her head, her snout twitching with urgency. "No. They don't want anything else. We NEED more, NOW."

Pandora suddenly realized that the staff must have eaten the samples too. The urgency in Peach's voice suggested that the manager herself needed more cookies, NOW.

Pandora gripped the brim of her hat, mind racing. "Alright, we'll move fast then. I'll grab Volo and we'll whip up another batch in the kitchen. We can have more cookies ready in no time." Peach's eyes widened in panic. "Wait, no! Please, don't go!" Her little paws flailed, gesturing towards the front of the store. "What am I supposed to tell them? They're not exactly in a patient mood!"

Pandora paused, taking in Peach's frazzled state. The usually composed Voidpet was twitching with stress. "Okay, okay. You're right. I'll stay here and help keep things under control. We'll just call Volo."

She pulled out her phone, dialing quickly. "Hey Vo? Yeah, it's me. We need a favor. A big one. How fast can you get your hands on a large quantity of Dopamine? ...Yes, that Dopamine. It's an emergency."

***

As night fell and they finally closed shop, Pandora leaned against the wall, exhausted. The day had been hectic, and she wasn't sure if this was the direction she wanted her business to take. After all the rowdiness, the customers had finally eaten their fill and gone home. While the cookies had brought in record sales, Pandora realized it was the first day she hadn't enjoyed being in her own café.

Pandora looked at Peach, who was slumped over a table, her five ears drooped with fatigue. "Thanks for all your great work today, Peach," Pandora said softly. "Get some rest—you've earned it." Peach nodded wearily and shuffled out, leaving Pandora alone with her brother in the café.

Pandora sighed, pondering the aftermath of the day's chaos. In the span of the afternoon, a Disdain journalist had published an article about Pandora's poor management skills. A Wrath had flung the napkin dispenser out the window when his card declined. Tables were askew, napkins littered the floor, and her usually beautiful midday oasis was looking like a mess.

She placed her hands on her hips, trying to decide what to make of the situation.

After a moment, she turned to Volo. "Do you think there's anything wrong with this new flavor we're selling?"

Volo shrugged, his face impassive as he leaned against the counter. "Everyone likes dopamine. It's natural."

"But... is it healthy?" Pandora asked. She couldn't tell if she was looking for reasons to shy away from the demand, or if there was a genuine ethical dilemma at stake.

"It should be healthy in moderation," Volo responded, "It's just upsetting when you can't get it."

"Is that... well documented in peer reviewed research?" Pandora prodded, still skeptical.

Volo looked at her to explain, his dark eyes stoic in the dim of the evening. "Dopamine isn't a toxin. It's an essential vitamin for Voidpets. Lots of emotions need it to function."

"The Dopamine in our cookies isn't doing anything harmful to them," Volo continued, his voice calm as he strolled towards the coat rack in the back of the store. "It's just registering with their natural reward system. That's why they're eager to keep eating them. Their bodies are saying it's good, so they'd like more."

Pandora nodded, still not fully convinced. "But is 42 grams... too much?"

"That depends." Volo paused, considering. "It's not about the amount, exactly. It's about balance. It's only a problem if it's their only source of happiness. And if that's the case—it's not your fault."

"What about Promise though?" Pandora asked, her face furrowing as she recounted her battle from earlier, "Are you sure the cookies didn't do something to him?"

Volo looked at her, unsympathetic. "That's how he behaves when he doesn't get what he wants."

Pandora realized that Volo might have understood their brother in a way she didn't. Though she and Promise were practically best friends as children, Promise and Volo had gotten closer with age. As adult men, there was an unspoken bond between them that felt somewhat foreign to her. She felt a pang of guilt for having drifted from them—for not being around to understand where their heads were at.

"Again, not your fault," Volo said, as if reading her mind.

As he finished speaking, Volo stopped to check the silver watch on his wrist. The flour and cookie dough smears disappeared from his cuffed shirt sleeves as he cleaned himself with a ripple of void matter. Then, he pulled his tuxedo coat from the rack and slipped it over his shoulders.

"It's just science. I wouldn't worry," he said, before disappearing into the night.

Pandora was still conflicted. She felt solace knowing she hadn't harmed any of the customers, but still didn't like the behavior she had witnessed as a result. Usually, Volo was the sibling she trusted the most when it came to matters of ethics, but as he got deeper into his medical studies, he'd gotten more detached. His words were reassuring, yet clinical—as if in learning to heal bodies, he'd learn to see them more as machines.

As Pandora locked up the café, her mind was a whirlwind. The day's chaos had left her drained, but more than that, it had shaken her confidence in her business decisions. She needed perspective, and an outlet to talk about her dilemma.

Luckily, she had two more siblings to consult.

***

When she arrived back at the apartment, she opened the door, relieved to see a familiar sight.

On the couch, Pecunia was sprawled over Sloth in her pajamas. She lounged on the Voidpet like a giant pillow, its plump body soft in slumber. Phone in one hand and pink drink in the other, Pecunia looked up as Pandora entered, a mischievous grin spreading across her face.

"There's my *superstar* sister!" Pecunia sung, stretching herself up with a celebratory wiggle. "I heard your café was THE hottest spot in the Void today."

"I made you this to celebrate," Pecunia smirked, reaching for the second glass of sparkling punch. She slid the drink across the smooth surface of the coffee table, pushing aside her unopened psychology books.

Pandora smiled, sinking down next to her sister. She heaved a big sigh as she sipped the fresh flavors of grapefruit and pear. "Thanks, Pec. It was... an interesting day for sure."

Pecunia rolled her eyes, playfully swatting Pandora's arm. Her diamond bracelet jingled with the movement, "Girl, don't *even*—"

"You weren't there to see it," Pandora shook her head, her whole face weary. "The Voidpets were going wild, they left the café a mess."

"Pandora," Pecunia interrupted, her voice taking on a mock-serious tone. "That's what we call *happy customers*." She leaned in, green eyes sparkling. "Don't self-sabotage."

"It just—it didn't feel as good as I'd hoped," Pandora confessed. "The customers were acting up whenever we ran out, and I found myself spending the whole day worrying what could go wrong. I'm just not sure if this is how I imagined my café succeeding..." Volo had convinced her that there was nothing medically harmful about the new flavor, but Pandora still didn't feel ready to celebrate.

"Oh Pan, I'm sorry," Pecunia's playful demeanor softened into a sympathetic pout. Pensive, she set her drink down, the ice clinking against the glass.

"You weren't actually in *danger* at any point though, were you?" Pecunia asked, with a skeptical frown.

Pandora paused, considering. "No... no, it was just rowdy, that's all."

Pecunia nodded, wrapping her arms around her knees as she processed Pandora's words.

"Hey," she said, tucking a strand behind her ear, "You've always been, like, the responsible one, right? The planner behind the scenes, the one looking after the rest of us. You're always keeping an eye out for danger, making sure no one gets hurt."

Pecunia's voice bubbled into a misty tone, "And now you're having fun doing something you *love*. It's a wild ride, you're suddenly in the spotlight, getting lots of attention—and you're just not *used* to it."

Pandora gulped. She hadn't thought of it this way before. "Well, I mean, I..." Pandora trailed, unsure what to say.

"Like, Pandora. You're *literally* indestructible," Pecunia gestured with a jiggle of her diamonds, "You can walk through lightning and fire, and you built a *steel skyscraper* with your bare hands. Don't let some silly cookie drama get you down."

Pecunia leaned back, her glossed lips pursed into a clever smile. "This *honestly* sounds like a classic case of impostor syndrome. You feel thrown off by a new kind of success, and you're looking for reasons to convince yourself you can't handle it."

Pandora was taken aback, her mind reeling. Could Pecunia be right?

She placed a hand on Pandora's. "Maybe instead of worrying so much, ask yourself why you're so quick to doubt a good thing when it happens to you."

Pandora felt stunned, her sister's words echoing in her head. The idea that her doubts might be stemming from her own insecurities was not something that had crossed her mind.

But even as she considered this, another thought nagged at her. She remembered that Pecunia was, well... *Pecunia*. The sister with the most questionable morals in the family. The one who could talk her way out of anything.

Pandora took a deep breath, forcing a smile. She leaned in to hug her little sister, inhaling her familiar scent of vanilla and chamomile. "Thanks, Pec," she said softly. "You've given me a lot to think about."

As she pulled away, Pandora stood up, smoothing down her skirt. "I think I just need time to process. I'm going to go lie down."

Pecunia nodded, already reaching for her phone again as she sunk back down into Sloth. "Just get some sleep. You'll feel better in the morning."

Pandora made her way down the hallway, somber as her inner turmoil continued to churn. As she passed Promise's door, she paused. A sliver of light peeked out from underneath.

She hesitated, her hand hovering near the door.

One more sibling left.

***

To think that Promise was her last resort for an ethical dilemma was not reassuring, but she was out of options, and still feeling desperate for advice.

She took a deep breath and knocked softly on Promise's door. The sound echoed in the quiet hallway.

The door moved open for her on its own, a whisper of void matter at work. A strong scent—was it sandalwood and bergamot? —hung in the air, and Promise stood in front of the mirror, preening at his own reflection.

"Is there some party I didn't get the memo for?" Pandora asked, taking in Promise's outfit, paired with his apparent use of cologne. She realized that both of her brothers were dressed to go out for the night.

Promise looked up at her through the reflection in the mirror as he adjusted his belt. "You always need an invitation to have fun, don't you?" he replied with a look.

A silence hung in the air, heavy with the unanswered question. Pandora shifted her weight, mustering up the courage to break the ice.

"So, about our little battle yesterday..." Pandora began, her voice barely above a whisper. She cleared her throat. "I think I owe you an apology."

Promise scoffed, running his fingers through his now platinum blonde hair. "I started it. You had a good time. What's the problem?"

Pandora shuffled her feet, her gaze dropping to the plush carpet. "I'm worried you might have had some kind of reaction to my cookies."

Promise turned to face her, his expression enthused with sarcasm. "You don't *say*???" He cocked an eyebrow. "How did you figure that one out, genius??"

Pandora looked down, sheepish. Her fingers played with the hem of her shirt. "Things got wild at the cafe today." She paused, gathering her thoughts. "The customers wouldn't stop demanding more cookies and making a scene."

Promise's eyes widened with interest. "Well," he said, turning to fully face her. "I, for one, *loved* them."

Pandora took a deep breath, her brow furrowing. "But is it still ethical to serve these to customers? I think it's clear that Dopamine can have some unpredictable side effects."

Promise thought for a moment, his fingers drumming a silent rhythm on the dresser. "I mean, I felt fine eating it. If they want it so bad, just feed it to 'em," he replied with a shrug. "Put, like, a nutrition label on it so they know."

He put on his gloves with a flourish and flashed a toothy smile. "Problem solved."

Pandora's frown deepened. "Is that enough...?"

Promise's response was quick and confident as he gestured to read an imaginary label in the air, "42 grams of Dopamine. Boom. Now they know what they're getting into."

"What if they don't read it?" Pandora pressed, unsure if he was joking or serious.

"Well. Sometimes you just have to let people make their own decisions." He bit his lip and shrugged. "Some people want to pay for momentary pleasure, and that's their call. Really just comes down to different customer motivations."

"Hmm... okay then," Pandora nodded slowly, somehow feeling defeated. Everyone was telling her that there was nothing wrong with selling the cookies, but she realized she was still yearning for a reason to get them off her plate. "I'll be honest, Promise, I still feel uncomfortable despite it all, and I don't know why."

Promise's tone suddenly dropped from sarcastic to reassuring.

"Hey look, Pandora," he placed a gloved hand on her shoulder, "I totally get it. It's not what you want for your brand. That's an important value to respect." He paused, letting the words sink in as Pandora nodded with relief.

"Not every choice has to be about money." He met her gaze, a rare gentleness in his voice. "You're allowed to have preferences, even if you don't have perfect moral justifications for them." Promise gestured out the window, where the cafe stood a hundred and three stories below. "Remember, Pandora's Bread has *your* name on it. *You* set out to serve people a sophisticated, cozy experience—" Promise spoke slowly, with emphasis on each descriptor, "—not one of rapture and instant gratification. You shouldn't have to serve *anything* you're not comfortable with."

As he finished speaking, the tension in Pandora's shoulders visibly eased. For the first time that day, she felt truly heard and understood.

"You're right," she gushed, feeling grateful for his advice as relief flooded back into her chest, "I really *would* feel so much better just not having those cookies at my cafe. That's not what I wanted Pandora's Bread to be about, and I just needed to hear that out loud."

But her smile faltered slightly. "I just feel so terrible letting down all the customers, and the missed opportunity…"

Promise's reassuring smile didn't waver as he guided Pandora towards the door, placing a steady hand on her back. "You have nothing to worry about, Pandora," he crooned, his voice low and chilling, "I'll take care of it."

It was in this moment that Pandora suddenly felt how much taller her younger brother had grown, now standing almost a whole head above her. As he brushed past her and walked out, his coat tails slithered behind like a pack of hungry snakes.

"Wait, where are you going?" Pandora asked.

He turned his head just enough for her to catch a glint in his eye.

"To solve your problems."

Chapter 47: McGreedy's

Alt was torn. He cared about the environment, but he was also broke, and couldn't decide where to eat.

"Alright, let's hear both sides," he sighed, as the friend group made their way off campus for lunch.

"Ok, I know you guys might not be with me on this," Hyphen began, already bracing for defeat, "but I just feel like Pandora's Bread is the way to go. They just banned Dopamine in their pastries, which is a good sign that they're thinking responsibly about their ingredients."

Alt didn't know what Dopamine was or why it was bad for you, but he figured that anyone who was thoughtful enough to ban it must be the conscientious type.

"Makes sense," he said, "I think that's a smart way to think about it. I want to eat somewhere I feel like I can trust their food."

Tilde and Char, on the other hand, were begging to hit McGreedy's. The brand-new restaurant was all the rage.

"Are you kidding me? How can you not want to try the Dopamine donuts?" Char asked, her wheelchair now gliding effortlessly on Ghost Road.

"A.k.a. Mickey G's Double Ds!" Tilde grinned with her mouth open.

"Also, come on, we've even got student vouchers to cut the line this week!" Char added, "The line's been out the door since they opened, and we don't wanna miss our chance."

Hyphen grimaced. "But like... it's called *McGreedy's*. Their logo is literally a Greed with a smiling tail."

"And I don't know how I feel eating somewhere that uses polystyrene," Alt said, shaking his head. "That's really bad for the environment."

"Yeah, but it's cheaper and more accessible," Tilde frowned. "Pandora's Bread prices aren't affordable to most students."

"Like, I can't afford a 20 VM salad," Char jumped in to back her up, "At least McGreedy's is honest about what it is."

Alt was still distraught. He realized he also couldn't afford to eat at Pandora's Bread again this week, and the point about the student vouchers was valid.

"Also," Char said, lowering his voice to deliver his final blow, "Did you read the news? I heard the Voidpets are *boycotting* Pandora's Bread. It's kind of messed up to eat somewhere if they're in the middle of protesting a cause, right?"

Alt weighed Char's words carefully. Perhaps the environment would have to take one for the team today. With that in consideration, the reasons to eat at McGreedy's now outnumbered the reasons to go to Pandora's Bread.

"I guess you're right," Alt sighed, resigning himself to polluting both his body and the planet.

The group soon approached McGreedy's, the line stretching far beyond the entrance. Char's eyes gleamed with excitement as he brandished his student ID.

"VIP treatment, coming right up," Char grinned, leading them to the front.

The restaurant loomed before them, a whimsical castle complete with a moat. Alt shook his head at the over-the-top design, even as a part of him admired the commitment to the theme.

A burly Greed, decked out in a security uniform, manned the entrance. His fox snout scrutinized their IDs with exaggerated seriousness before dramatically sweeping aside the velvet rope with a snaky tail.

"Your kingdom awaits," the bouncer intoned, managing to keep a straight face.

As they entered, Tilde let out a delighted giggle. "I feel like royalty already!"

Char was practically bursting with enthusiasm. "See? I told you guys this place was LIT!"

While the outside looked like a castle, the inside looked almost like an arcade. On the wall was a huge, colorful sign explaining that McG's DDs rotated flavor sets every week. A chibi cartoon of a doe-eyed Greed clutched its paws to its face, with a speech bubble saying, "Every week is a new adventure!" Meanwhile, another cartoon fox denoted that the establishment was hiring.

They approached the counter, where a giant menu board displayed the day's offerings.

Today's flavors:

Strawberry Swagger

Champion's Cheesecake

Matcha Millionaire

Jasmine Jackpot

Alt cracked a smile at the goofy names. He liked the creativity and was quite surprised by the diverse flavor selection—McGreedy's was lowkey cultured. But his eyes were immediately drawn to the nutrition label prominently featured next to the McG's DDs: 76 grams of Dopamine.

"Is that... unhealthy?" Hyphen asked, trying to recall if Professor String had said anything about Dopamine.

"Nah," said Tilde, "I think it's just a vitamin."

Alt didn't really know what a gram was, or at least, how to visualize one, but he figured it couldn't be that bad since the donuts were quite small.

Hyphen, ever the voice of reason, suggested, "Why don't we get the set of four to split? There's a 25% discount."

As they placed their order, the cashier—a tiny Greed in a little suit—handed them a ticket. "Don't forget to try McGreedy's Grabs!" it chirped, gesturing to a gaudy roulette wheel nearby.

Tilde's eyes lit up. "YO, I've got this!" She scooted over and gave the wheel a mighty spin.

The group watched, breaths held, as the wheel slowly came to a stop. Suddenly, lights flashed, and a triumphant jingle played.

"SCORE!" Char shouted, pumping his fist in the air. "We got the EPIC prize!"

They'd won VIP passes for a week, complete with a streak bonus for daily visits. Alt raised an eyebrow, impressed despite himself.

Their prize included additional vouchers for 'McGreedy's Goods.' Alt was touched when the machine dispensed a tiny flower necklace for Sad. Char was bouncing off the walls with the 'legendary' spiked collar he got for Envy.

When their donuts arrived, the group divvied them up with the seriousness of medieval lords parceling out land. Tilde claimed Strawberry Swagger, Char predictably went for Champion's Cheesecake, Hyphen's eyes locked onto Matcha Millionaire, leaving Alt with Jasmine Jackpot.

As they bit into their treats, a wave of bliss washed over the table. Their Voidpets began to dance, feeling the euphoria emanating from their keepers.

Alt took a bite and almost forgot he was depressed. The jasmine flavor bloomed on his tongue, perfectly balanced with the donut's squishy chew. For a moment, the world seemed a little brighter. He was with his friends, sitting in a castle, on top of the world.

He glanced around at his friends, all equally enraptured by their donuts. Even Hyphen, the most skeptical of the group, was wide-eyed with delight.

"You know," Tilde mused, licking a spot of glaze from her finger, "think about all the PLANTS we're saving by not having any vegetables for lunch!"

Alt nodded, surprising himself. Tilde had a point—sort of. Over-farming was a real issue, even if this wasn't exactly solving it.

As the flavors danced on his palate, inspiration struck. Alt could already envision his next painting: an abstract visual of the flavors, whirling across the canvas in streaks of gold and yellow.

Maybe McGreedy's wasn't so bad after all.

Chapter 48: Sigma Psi Alpha

Pecunia closed her eyes and smiled as she entered the Sigma Psi Alpha sorority house. The space was her sanctuary, a place to retreat when the bustling energy of the Windfall penthouse became too much. She glanced at the elegant script adorning the wall:

Σοφία Ψυχής Αταραξία. Sofia Psyches Ataraxia.

"Tranquility is the wisdom of the soul," she hummed, letting the words wash over her. The sorority's focus on self-care had initially drawn her in, but more importantly, their lavish mansion had sealed the deal.

Her siblings had expected the penthouse's 9,000 square feet to be plenty, but it still felt like a zoo with the whole family running around. Luden and her two brothers had come home late last night, disrupting the sanctity of her sleep. Meanwhile, Pandora was up first thing in the morning, making a ruckus on the phone.

The sorority house on the other hand was a pastel paradise. Soft-hued Voidpets lounged about—a white Curious with sweeping peacock tails purred nearby, while the house's pet, a tiny pink Glee, was curled up on a cushion. Scented candles and lush plants added to the tranquil atmosphere, filling the air with notes of amber and vanilla.

Dyna was already there, sitting crisscross in an armchair. She wore a tank top and sweatpants, her black hair cascading in two loose braids. She was digging into a brown takeout carton from Pandora's Bread.

As Pecunia sank into the plush couch, Dyna playfully tossed a small decorative pillow her way. "Catch!" Pecunia grabbed it mid-air, laughing as she hugged it to her chest.

Leaning back, Pecunia relished the quiet afternoon. The soft fabric of the throw pillow was cool against her skin. A gentle breeze from the open window carried the scent of fresh grass from the garden outside, mingling with the aroma of Dyna's lunch.

"Ooh, whatcha eating?" Pecunia asked, eyeing the takeout box.

Dyna grinned, holding out the carton. "Pandora's new quinoa bowl. Want some?"

Pecunia leaned forward, snagging a forkful. The flavors burst on her tongue—nutty quinoa, tangy feta, and the bright pop of pomegranate seeds.

"How's the intern recruiting going?" Dyna asked.

"Oh, you know, they're going alright," Pecunia answered with a modest smile. Her job post had caught the eye of all the top students at the Institute—including Dyna's own little brother.

"Did you find what you were looking for?" Dyna asked, taking another bite of quinoa.

Pecunia shrugged. "Yeah, like, we got plenty of strong students to choose from, the hard part now is getting one past my brother," she teased with a little eye roll, and Dyna giggled back. Venting about siblings, particularly troublesome brothers, was one of the many little bonds they shared.

The Curious did a big stretch before padding over to curl up at Pecunia's feet, its peacock tails fanning out across the polished hardwood floor. The girls sat in comfortable silence, the only sounds the soft jazz music playing from ambient speakers and the occasional rustle as Dyna reached for another bite.

The tranquil atmosphere was broken by the sound of footsteps on the stairs. Verve emerged, dressed in a black tube top and denim shorts. A baseball cap perched atop her honey-brown hair, which fell in two long pigtails down her back. She sauntered down the stairs humming a popular song, and Pecunia and Dyna joined in, their harmony rehearsed over shared car rides and karaoke nights.

"*So*, Ladies—" Verve began, the words melodic on her tongue, "what are we thinking for our next *charity* event?"

Pecunia shrugged. She hadn't thought to plan anything.

Dyna perked up, setting aside her takeout box. "I was thinking we should do a formal this time! Something classy, with ball gowns and all."

Verve's eyes lit up, a sly smile spreading across her face. "Ooh, that's *perfect*."

"Yeah, I'm just not sure about the venue," Dyna continued, fiddling with the elastic of one of her braids. "I feel like we should do something outside of the sorority house."

Verve nodded, smirking as she turned to Pecunia. "I think I know *just* the place."

Pecunia felt herself sit straighter. She knew that look in Verve's eyes.

"Hey Penny, hear me out..." Verve's voice dripped with sugar as she strolled to the couch and placed a hand on Pecunia's shoulder. The tropical notes of Verve's perfume were disarming, but Pecunia predicted the ask that was about to follow.

"Let's suppose..." she paused, glancing at Dyna, "We do it on the rooftop of *your* place. That view from the 104th floor would be *breathtaking*."

Pecunia scoffed. "There's no way—"

"Come on, think about it," Verve pressed, her voice honeyed as she perched on the arm of Pecunia's couch. "I can't imagine *anywhere* better. It'd be the talk of the campus for *weeks*." As Verve spoke, she absentmindedly played with a strand of Pecunia's hair, an idyllic gesture of friendship that contrasted with her persistent words.

Pecunia felt a flicker of annoyance. "Promise would *not* want random people showing up in his house," she said flatly, then added with a hint of snark, "Why don't you ask him yourself?"

Verve pursed her lips, a flash of malice fleeting across her eyes. "Oooh, you're right, I *so* should!"

The girls exchanged tense looks, their eyes narrowed with unspoken challenge.

As Pecunia and Dyna's eyes met knowingly, Dyna jumped the break the tension. "You know," she said, lowering her voice as if sharing a secret, "I think Volo's been planning a gala to celebrate something he's been working on. Maybe we could work off his idea and put on some sort of auction to go with it. I think he already has a guest list and a venue in the park."

Pecunia felt relief at the change of subject, grateful for Dyna's intervention, though she suppressed a frown. She had heard nothing of the sort from Volo herself.

"An auction could work," Pecunia shrugged, warming to the idea. "We could showcase some of the art students' work. It'd be a great way to support local talent."

Verve regained her composure without skipping a beat. "I *love* that! We could even get some of the wealthier *alumni* involved. I bet they'd love to show off by bidding on student art."

Pecunia remained quiet as an idea dawned on her. Her family needed to donate for tax write-offs, and Pandora had tasked her with figuring that out. This could be the perfect opportunity to nail two birds with one stone...

As the conversation continued, Pecunia found herself retreating into her thoughts. The dynamic between the three of them had always been complicated. She was the newcomer to this friendship, acutely aware that Verve and Dyna had been best friends long before she entered the picture. Their whispered conversations and inside jokes were a constant reminder of her outsider status.

In many ways, their friendship felt like a political alliance. There was an undeniable "cheerleader effect" when they were together—people gravitated towards them, drawn by their combined charm.

Verve, the business student, was cunning and charismatic, an unabashed go-getter who always seemed to be working an angle. Dyna, on the other hand, was quieter but no less clever. She was rarely direct about what she wanted, but Pecunia could tell she was always scheming behind those big doe eyes.

And then there was Pecunia herself, caught in the middle. She wasn't blind to the way Verve and Dyna vied for her favor, each trying to align themselves more closely with the Windfall name. It gave her a certain power, knowing she held dirt on them both.

Suddenly, Pecunia's thoughts were interrupted by a Nightmare slithering in through the window.

As she and Dyna leapt backwards in their seats, Verve had jumped to her feet, already on it. The serpent stopped in its tracks, speared through the head by a metal kunai that had had been cast from Verve's hand. Her eyes glowed with snake-like slits of her own as Disdain's power coursed through her, before dimming back to normal.

Verve brushed the residual VM from her hands as the creature dissolved to dust, before looking at the other two with a goofy grimace of disgust. The tension in the room evaporated as each girl's attention was now turned to the squashed intruder.

"*Ew*," Pecunia said. They dissolved into giggles.

Despite everything, they were still her two best friends.

Verve sat down on the couch and leaned backwards into Pecunia, laughing as she turned to the side and propped up her legs. Dyna breathed a sigh of relief, before changing the subject to vent about her home life and ailing parents.

It dawned on Pecunia that it was only during times of peace that things were laced with an invisible tension.

Ironically, their bond was strongest when danger was eminent. Through stressful exams, dramatic breakups, family troubles, and even Nightmare hunts, the trio had supported each other unfailingly. The higher the stakes, the more Pecunia could count on those two to have her back.

Chapter 49: Wild Rejection

Char could not believe his eyes. He read the paper over and over, not believing what he was seeing.

Thank you for your interest in Windfall Inc.

Unfortunately...

No good news contained the word "unfortunately".

He had been rejected from the internship.

The white page trembled in his hands. Black ink blurred as he blinked rapidly, processing the information. The bustling sounds of the common room faded into a dull hum as his mind raced.

There was just no way. His GPA was perfect. His extracurriculars were outstanding. He was at the top of his class, and there was simply no reason he wasn't qualified for the job. And yet, he hadn't even made it to the interview.

What did he work so hard for? For the past four years, he'd commuted to school for nearly four hours a day. He did all the chores at home. He cooked for his parents now that they were getting too old to work. He barely got enough sleep, did his homework on the subway, and still had time for combat training.

The weight of his sacrifices pressed down on him, making it hard to breathe. The familiar scent of the common room—a mix of old books and coffee—suddenly felt suffocating.

There were no other corporate opportunities available that he knew of, and he couldn't bear to work in service after studying for years to escape it.

Char wasn't one to cry, but his eyes prickled with impending tears. A lump formed in his throat, threatening to choke him.

He wanted to turn invisible. Or fight someone. Or both.

Envy grew heavy, growling to protect him.

How could this be fair? What other students could they possibly have picked?

The common room door creaked open. Hyphen's face fell as she walked in and saw his expression. What was clearly a look of joy was now brimming with worry. She rushed forward to hug him wordlessly.

Of course.

She got the job, and he didn't.

That didn't need to be said.

His best friend would be working for his worst enemy, and he'd been tossed aside like trash.

Char wanted to be alone. He didn't want to see Tilde or Alt today, and hated that they had the audacity to be here.

Tilde sat wordlessly in her chair, silently removing a fox-eared headband from her head. Clearly, she was thrilled to have gotten hired at McGreedy's, and was trying to mask her joy as a poorly conceived gesture of solidarity. The rustle of the headband being set aside was painful in the silence.

He looked at Alt—who was broke and unemployed—and realized that the two of them were now in the same boat.

After all his hard work, he'd ended up in the same place as someone who wasn't even trying at all.

As Char ruminated in his rejection, the whole common room felt cold. The couches seemed hostile, the bookshelves looked down in judgement, and the lamps glared.

He felt a sense of restlessness, like some dark power was emanating out of him. He wasn't feeling good. He didn't know what it was or why, but he knew he needed to get out of here before something bad happened.

"Hey guys, I think I need some fresh air, I just need to be alone." His voice sounded distant, even to his own ears.

Hyphen didn't protest, but looked at him with concern. Her fretful gaze followed him as he stood up.

Char blundered out of the common room, feeling lightheaded as his footsteps hastened. But it wasn't just the common room that was cold—it was everywhere.

He ran faster and faster, trying to escape the chill, but it only intensified and followed him. The hallways blurred past, faces of other students melting into indistinct shapes.

Before he knew it, he was outside in the school garden.

The sky was gray, the grass looked colorless, and a cruel wind swept through the air. He fought to catch his breath, his lungs burning with each inhale. He wanted to scream out and shout, but his whole body felt like heavy metal. Suddenly, Envy screeched with a metallic roar.

A strange wild Voidpet was floating a few yards in front of him, this one, a bizarre brown sea creature with appendages protruding from its front and back. From the look of its face and posture, it almost looked like it was being impaled by its own fins.

No wonder.

It was a wild Rejection.

Rejection called out with a haunting cry that sent shivers down Char's spine. The little creature curled up in ball, shrouding itself in an aura of cold. Char's eyes widened, unsure if it needed help or if it was about to attack.

Apparently, it was the latter.

As the Rejection unfurled, currents of matter began to swirl, before raining towards Char like bullets of icicles. The air whistled as ice cut through. Luckily, Envy positioned its metal body to protect him, swatting the projectiles with its iron claws. A chorus of shatters rang out across the garden.

Char's heart was racing, pounding so hard he could feel it in his throat.

Hostile Voidpets were powerful and rare.

Like all Voidpets, they were intelligent. Their bodies were made of pure void matter, and lucidity came naturally to them. However, their aggression meant that they were ready use the full force of their abilities in combat, which meant that a dangerous battle was about to go down.

Unlike Nightmares, however, it was possible to befriend them. If you could defeat a hostile Voidpet in battle, there was always the chance that it'd join you as a powerful companion.

Envy suddenly dissolved into pure energy, rushing into Char's chest and filling him with a new strength. The sensation was electric, sending tingles through his entire body.

That meant things were serious. *The battle was on.*

As mist began to form at the Rejection's mouth, Char's left hand bloomed into an energy stream of royal blue. It formed into a giant Envy claw, which reflexively lashed to deflect a gust of icy breath from the hostile Voidpet. The collision of ice and energy created a misty explosion in the air. He felt his arm weaken as the chill drained his energy, but it was nothing he couldn't handle.

Fighting felt better than being sad, and Char felt his motivation surge as he charged his first offensive play. The familiar rush of adrenaline pushed away the lingering feelings of despair, and his strategic mind sprang to life as he seized the opportunity to use his signature opening.

A metallic orb swelled in the palm of his clawed hand, pulsing as it coated itself in a layer of destructive spikes. The energy crackled and hummed as it grew. When it ballooned to nearly his full height, Char cast it toward the Rejection, where it slammed the Voidpet backwards into the bushes with a thunderous crash.

Wrecking ball. A powerful metal type technique that was perfect for catching opponents off guard.

The disoriented Rejection popped out of the bushes, rearing its head to strike with another blow—this time forming an energy beam that spanned out of its mouth to strike Char. His Envy hand leapt to his face for defense, blocking the attack as Envy's form took the damage of its icy devastation. The impact sent shockwaves through Char's body, rattling his teeth.

He'd avoided a critical strike to the face, but he could feel his stamina draining as Envy's fatigue began to set in. He had to end this battle fast, before the wild Voidpet got the best of him.

Char opened his right hand, which beckoned a sparkling nucleus of royal blue. The energy whirred, casting a radiant glow on his face. With his clawed hand ready for defense, he pitched it forth like a football. It collided with Rejection in a shower of starry particles, the impact creating a spectacle of light and sound.

Alloy Burst. His bread and butter move.

With Rejection now lying in the grass, neutralized by the attack, Char seized his chance. He ran up to the creature, curled up on the ground, and began to rummage through his pockets. The sound of his frantic searching seemed loud in the sudden quiet following the battle.

To befriend a Voidpet, it was best to have a container that it could bond with.

Char was struggling to find anything in his pockets other than bits of VM, but then Envy materialized beside him with the rejection letter in its hand. It crumpled the paper into a ball, before extending it out to Rejection's snout. The rustle of the paper was oddly loud in the stillness of the garden.

Rejection sniffed the paper ball. Its nostrils flared, as if taking in the scent of Char's disappointment and frustration.

The little sea creature looked up at Char with sad eyes, and then back at the paper ball. The moment stretched, taut with anticipation.

Char wasn't sure if the paper could properly contain the Voidpet, and was prepared to leap back into battle if need be.

But slowly, the brown Voidpet faded into blue energy. It meandered around Char, filling him with a wave of frigid melancholy, before streaming into the paper ball and disappearing. The air around him vibrated with the transfer of energy.

The icy dread was as gone as quickly as it had come, and Char was left with a newfound awareness over the physical sensations of despair that had taken over his body. His limbs were heavy, his chest tight.

So that's what Professor Cogito meant by *'distilled emotions'*—when he said that Voidpets were not born from emotions themselves, but from ones 'distilled' into cognitive understanding.

He was still undeniably devastated about the internship, but at the same time, he was awestruck.

He had captured his first hostile Voidpet—a Vivid one no less.

Char stood there in the garden, the crumpled paper ball warm in his hand as the world slowly regained its color around him. The wind had died down, and he could hear the distant chatter of students and the rustle of leaves. He took a deep breath, the scent of grass and earth filling his lungs, grounding him in the moment. Despite the lingering ache of rejection, he managed a small smile.

Chapter 50: Counting Stars

Deep house music blasted in Volo's ear pods as his blades eviscerated another Nightmare. His eyes were ruby red as he slid down the length of the behemoth's spine, carving down two stories of pearly flesh in a downward aerial strike that carried him back to the sidewalk. Another Stage 4 down.

Beside him, he saw a soundless of ripple of splatters as Promise dispatched a wave of small ones—with a convenient psychic shred as opposed to setting them all on fire.

While Lust was fully merged with Volo in combat, Promise's Greed was having a field day in fox-form, prancing through the battlefield like it was a buffet.

When they had cleaned up the last of the wave, Volo made his way to the bleacher of stairs in the middle of the square. As his brother followed, he paused his music and took out his ear pods.

"172," Promise boasted with a grin, his voice echoing slightly in the empty square.

"180," Volo replied, allowing himself a rare smirk as his brother's faltered slightly.

They sat on the stairs of Neon Square, where the only sounds were their heavy breathing, and the soft clicking of Greed lapping at the dust. A small bead of sweat dripped onto the floor. Beneath the billboard screens, they were cast in an artificial light of reds, whites, and blues.

Volo reached for another beverage from the cooler between them. With a clink and a pop, he opened the sparkling electrolyte concoction and sipped it. Hydration was something they never thought about as kids, but it made a difference in these battles.

He passed one to Promise, who gratefully accepted and downed the whole can.

"Thanks bro," he said, exhaling as he wiped his mouth with the back of his hand.

Volo turned to Promise, who had just smeared black grime all over his own cheek. The inky smudge on his olive skin made for a comical portrait.

"Still not used to close combat, huh?" Volo quipped, as Promise's eyes widened to examine the back of his hand. The realization dawned on his face, visible even in the dim, flickering light.

Promise spat a swear word, the harsh consonants echoing off the nearby buildings. He suddenly remembered that his metal hands were stained from spearing Nightmares. He reverse-channeled the dirt away with a humble laugh, and then crushed the empty can in his hand.

"Old habits die hard," he grinned, his eyes staring out at some far away billboard.

Volo thought about it. As a kid, Promise attacked with storms of fire and liquid. He showed no mercy to his surroundings, unafraid to bring down dilapidated buildings along with his foes. Now, the buildings around him tended to be ones that he owned. His tactics cleaned up. His style grew closer to Volo's, with deliberate hand strikes and telekinetic control.

"Did we bring any more?" Promise asked, digging through the cooler and realizing that it was now empty.

"No." Volo breathed a small laugh, "Should we have?"

Luden had volunteered to tag along with an extra cooler, but Volo had declined. He didn't think this was the kind of excursion that warranted an audience, and the thought of their kindhearted friend amidst this carnage seemed somehow wrong.

"Nah," Promise responded, void matter already forming two fresh drinks in his hands before he passed one to Volo. The cans materialized with a soft hiss, condensation immediately forming on their cold surfaces.

Volo popped the can to take a sip, but nearly spat it out. "Dude. This is all sugar and caffeine," he exclaimed, shaking his head with an incredulous chuckle. The taste lingered in his mouth, drowning the flavors of the crisp electrolyte drink from earlier.

Promise cackled with mischief as Volo smiled. He had made his point about hydration enough times already, and he didn't need to deprive his brother of a good time.

Volo withdrew into his thoughts as they sat together in comfortable silence. The ambient noise of the city at night—distant hooting of Voidpets, the hum of neon signs, the occasional gust of wind—created a soothing backdrop to their rest.

Gone were the days of killing Nightmares for self-defense, or even money. Now, it was just about getting a good workout.

Promise's lifestyle had grown increasingly sedentary, which wasn't good for his health. But he hated cardio, and this was the only way. Hunting for sport was the only thing that got him out of the house. Volo could see the difference in his brother's physique—still strong from years of combat, but now even more slight than before.

In some ways, these outings were the few moments of normalcy that Promise got to enjoy. It was almost as if the brothers were simply loitering on the couch, cooling off after an evening of sports or video games.

Volo propped his elbows on his knees, leaning forward to take in the full spectacle of Neon Square at night. The giant screens flickered with surreal colors, their original images obscured by abstract distortions from prolonged exposure to void matter. In the sky, an Estrangement danced through the night like a dragon of eastern legends.

In the middle of it all, Promise and Volo sat out of place in formal clothing—Volo in a wool tuxedo, and Promise in his black tailed coat.

Dressing to the nines seemed counterintuitive for a workout, but there was a practical reason for it: confidence made for potent Nightmare bait. With an attitude of leisure, abundance, and a modest headcount of two, you had a recipe that compelled Nightmares to attack in droves. Volo had observed that his family seemed to encounter far more Nightmares than anyone else at school, and quickly connected the dots over the course of his research.

"You ever think about Madison and Broadway still?" Promise asked, his question piercing through the clear of the night.

Volo was surprised. Promise was dismissive whenever Pandora brought up the subject of their parents, so it was uncharacteristic of him to suddenly mention it. Even more so was his choice to call them by their first names.

"Yeah, of course." Volo replied, his voice soft but sure in the cool air.

"Well Pandora's turning into Madison," Promise snarked, his smile colored with a hint of sadness. The melancholy in his voice was unmistakable, though it was layered beneath a sigh of acceptance.

"I mean, I don't blame her. I get the trauma and whatnot," he said with an eye roll, "it affects all of us."

"But I think that means we need to level up."

"Really?" Volo was not following the logical conclusion. But he leaned forward with curiosity regardless, accustomed to the roundabout way Promise structured his arguments.

"Yeah, like go check out those next layers and stuff. See the world." Promise shrugged as he set down his drink, his can making a hollow sound as it hit the step.

"Get some fun back into our lives, you know? Do something *stupid*," his eyes flashed as he emphasized the last word.

"Is it really stupid to look for our parents?" Volo's voice was blunt against the hum of the city.

"It's *slightly* stupid to go looking for the gateway to the next dimension that maybe doesn't exist," Promise clarified, his tongue in cheek.

"Sure." Volo nodded, his eyes fixed on the dancing Estrangement in the sky.

"Volo, you know I'm not going to live forever, right?"

Volo raised an eyebrow. Something about the way he said this implied more than he was saying outright. He studied Promise, suddenly scanning his movements and body language.

"I mean, everybody dies," Promise followed up, breaking the tension with a sarcastic raise of his brows, "and we're not going to be young forever."

"I think I'm happy with what I've achieved here. I'm not done, obviously, but I'm happy with it." Promise's voice was strangely wistful as he looked into the distance, as if he was looking back on a long life rather than looking forward to one.

Volo nodded, masking his skepticism. It was nice to hear Promise express gratitude for something, and he sounded sincere.

"Like, our donut shop slapped *so* hard," Promise said with a devilish grin.

Volo laughed in agreement. Their new restaurant was certainly an absurd stroke of brilliance. Even Pandora was impressed by their cunning solution, despite being the one who got trolled. The memory of their sister's shock, followed by her grudging admiration, brought a smile to his face.

"You?" Promise's question hung in the air, an invitation for Volo to share his own gratitude.

"I've got stuff going on. I've started a little charity thing. And I'm still trying to be a doctor and stuff," Volo shrugged, the monotony of his school life seeming a little out of place for this conversation, "But at the end of the day, I want to explore the Void."

"I want to learn more about how the world works and what's out there." Volo's voice was deep, his eyes fixed on the swirling colors of the billboards.

Promise nodded.

"You gonna build another tower soon?" Volo asked, lobbing a casual question to continue their banter.

"Honestly probably not," Promise admitted with a chuckle. "It was more for vanity than anything else. It's not like we've even managed to fill all 100 floors." He made a face as he examined his hand, shrugging as he sported a frown of nonchalance.

"You think you wanna be a dad someday?"

Volo raised an eyebrow, processing the unexpected question.

"Never thought about it." he replied.

"Well, I do." Promise's voice was sharp with certainty.

"Why?"

"It's like... the one thing every billionaire has in common. You know?" Promise grinned comedically, "Like it's a celebration of life. An acceptance of absurdity."

"Sending someone out to live... just for the heck of it," he moved with a low chuckle as he said this, looking up at the stars with a sort of peculiar contentment.

Volo found the topic unfamiliar, but intriguing. The evening felt surreal, as if they were having their reflection in some sort of twilight dreamscape. The stars were eavesdropping, twinkling in the space above the neon-lit square.

"Putting a life into the world to experience it all. All the drama and emotions and whatnot. You do your best to treat 'em right and all, but in the end, you're still signing 'em up for the whole package. Because you decided yourself that the journey was worth it."

Promise exhaled a deep breath, "And you make 'em live with your legacy. All your errors, your baggage. Because that's what we all do. No matter how responsible you are. No one lives without a past."

"It's a relinquishment of control. An offering to entropy."

"And those who release control are the ones who control the future."

Promise's words seemed to echo in the empty square, the rhythm of his words coloring the night like an abstract poem.

"What are you *saying*, bro?" He laughed, the levity of his words anchoring them back to earth.

"Look I'm just getting old, man," Promise cracked a coy grin, "just saying weird stuff. Just being dramatic." He bit his lip.

"What are you, 21?" Volo asked.

"About to turn 22."

Volo scoffed. "You're still young."

"Nah, Volo, you don't understand. I already feel like I'm dying." Promise lay back and started chuckling. He closed his eyes, and spread his arms across the stairwell.

Volo picked up the energy drink and swirled the liquid inside the can. "Maybe it's 'cause of this."

Promise cracked up, the sound echoing off the buildings and filling the square with unrestrained joy.

"Volo, you kill me," he wheezed, clapping his metal hands together with a sharp ring.

They sat there in the night, their conversation petering out as they recovered from their workout. Greed continued to slurp dust, the soft sounds a constant background noise. The billboards overhead cycled with different colors, painting the brothers in ever-changing hues, and the air was cool against their skin, a welcome relief after the heat of battle.

Volo didn't mind the quiet.

Rest was good.

The journey was more important than the destination.

Chapter 51: First Mission

Tilde's heart pounded in her chest as she swooped through the air, narrowly avoiding the razor-sharp claws of the Stage 2 Nightmare. The creature was a terrifying sight to behold—a werewolf-like abomination with a humanoid body and a snarling canine head. Its piercing eyes, two on its head and one on each clawed hand, seemed to follow her every move. A long tail lashed out behind it like a whip, its rings of spiny studs promising agony to anything in its path.

Her wheelchair, her lifeline, sat tantalizingly across the street. So close, yet so far. Tilde's eyes darted between the Nightmare and her chair, her mind racing to formulate a plan.

Their first expedition was supposed to be simple. Their task: gather primary resources about the plays performed in the ancient civilization's abandoned theatre district. Unfortunately, they found themselves in the middle of a chaotic battleground a little earlier than expected, woefully unprepared.

Across the street, Char wrestled with a burly, orc-like Nightmare, his muscles straining against the creature's inhuman strength. He was holding his ground, determination etched on his face, but victory remained out of reach. His powerful Envy claw was doing everything it good just to protect him, unable to land a single strike.

Not far from him, Alt found himself in a surreal slap-fight with a worm, his tendrils whipping furiously at the creature as Sad cowered behind. That battle was not going anywhere.

In the center of it all stood Hyphen, frozen like a deer in headlights as her eyes darted from friend to friend. Suddenly, a giant spider descended before her, its multiple eyes reflecting her terror. While a plume of void matter supercharged her weakened leg, all she could do was run away, her Anxious army barely holding off the arachnid onslaught.

The air was charged with panic and the metallic tang of Nightmares. Chaos reigned supreme, and Tilde realized with a sinking feeling that none of them really knew what to do. Technically, they were qualified to handle Stage 2 Nightmares, but without any real-life battle experience, they were floundering.

Tilde's lungs burned, her flight stamina rapidly depleting. She knew she had to reach her wheelchair, stat. With a voice hoarse from exertion, she cried out, "Angy, CROSSFIRE!"

Her loyal Voidpet sprang into action, fists wreathed in flame. It smacked the werewolf Nightmare with a left and right hook to the face for a decent chunk of damage. But their victory was fleeting. The Nightmare's retaliatory swipe sent a wave of fatigue crashing over Tilde, a blunt reminder of the connection between human and Voidpet.

Rage fueled Tilde's next command: "FLAMES OF FURY! GO!"

Anger's body erupted into a living inferno, charging the Nightmare with reckless abandon, and pummeling it with a storm of jabs. The fire burned bright in the night, illuminating the concrete around them. Seizing her chance, Tilde zoomed through the air in a beeline for her wheelchair. Her breath came in ragged gasps, sweat beading on her brow.

Just as victory seemed within grasp, the Nightmare's spiked tail lashed out. The impact slapped Anger through the air, and Tilde's world spun. Nausea overwhelmed her—a physical manifestation of her Voidpet's damage.

Anger roared with determination, reeling as it recovered from being swatted away. Suddenly, Tilde's eyes lit up as she noticed the distance between them.

"Now! DRAGON BREATH!" Tilde bellowed, as Anger puffed up with a tremendous inhale.

The column of flame that erupted from Anger's maw illuminated the street, painting stark shadows that revealed the full extent of the chaos around them. The Nightmare scampered away into the darkness, leaving behind an ashy smell.

Ugh. That was close.

Relief washed over Tilde, but it was short-lived. As she surveyed the ongoing battles of her friends, a new terror struck. Giant hands seized her, ripping her from the safety of her wheelchair. The world blurred as she was hurled through the air. Wind whistled past her ears as she urgently conjured her ghost tail.

A neon billboard loomed before her, its garish colors zooming into view. Tilde braced herself for impact, her flight slowing her trajectory—but not enough to prevent the collision. With a resounding crash, she slammed into the sign five stories above the ground. Sparks flew, and the smell of ozone filled the air as the damaged screen flickered.

Dazed, Tilde clung to the edge of the billboard, suspended between earth and sky. Below her, the battles raged on. Alt continued his futile dance with the worm, while Char seemed to be gaining the upper hand against his brutish opponent. Hyphen, meanwhile, was being overwhelmed by spiders from all directions, her army of Anxious struggling to hold them off.

All of a sudden, Tilde felt a soft thud next to her hands. She looked up to the edge to see two leather dress shoes, continuing her gaze upwards to take in the full height of a man in a tuxedo. He extended a hand towards her, and she quickly glanced up to see his face.

Tilde almost fell off the billboard in disbelief.

Was that ... *Volo* from school?

As Tilde's fingers began to slip, Volo grabbed her by the wrists and pulled her upwards in one swift motion. As her ghost tail reformed into legs, he casually swung her onto his back like a bag, securing her with a wrap of his pet's stinger.

Volo balanced comfortably on the edge, but Tilde's stomach lurched as she looked down to a dizzying drop. There was a set of bleachers in the middle of the square, where another man sat and waved from below.

Huh?

Tilde clutched Volo's back as he ferried her down to safety. He jogged along the thin edge of the board, before climbing down the side of a building, deftly clambering across its windows and grooved surfaces.

She blinked as she noticed a familiar face grinning back at her from a few yards away. She didn't see him around much since he dropped out of high school, but there was no mistaking Promise. His sprawling height, languid mannerisms, and crooked smile had all remained the same, just as when she had dueled him four years ago.

"Whaaaat?" Tilde mumbled, still on Volo's back, weak with fatigue.

"Hey Tilde," Promise sung with a wiggle of his fingers, now covered with some sort of metallic glove.

Tilde suddenly gawked as she met the red eyes of one of his Greed's hydra tails. The little fox froze from its restful position in Promise's lap as if caught in some unbecoming act, and sheepishly sprung to its paws to assume a position of dignity.

Was that Ed? The Infernal Greed?

Her manager at McGreedy's?

"Hello Tilde," Ed said with a polite nod.

"Uh, hey Ed," Tilde replied from Volo's back.

Well, that was awkward.

"Are you okay?" Volo asked, turning his head slightly to address Tilde.

"Mmhm," Tilde groaned. She felt fine, but she suddenly began to worry for everyone else. Where were Char, Hyphen, and Alt? And where was Angy?

"I just need to find my friends," she murmured, "need to make sure they're okay."

Volo nodded.

He sprinted towards the theatre district with Tilde on his back. Promise walked leisurely, not far behind. The billboards and concrete all blurred together as Tilde held on for dear life, hoping not to fall off.

As they rounded the corner, they saw Hyphen and Alt standing back-to-back in the middle of a street. Anger stood between them, battle ready with fists of flame. Their faces were tense as their void matter glowed warily, their foes having retreated into the shadows at the sound of footsteps.

Hyphen's face lit up with relief when she spotted them. "Oh, thank *goodness*!" she cried out, her eyes brimming with worried tears.

Alt slumped to the ground, exhausted. "This Broadway mission was a lot harder than I expected."

Volo located Tilde's empty wheelchair among them, and set her down in it. "Where's Char?" she asked.

A muffled cry drew their attention to a nearby alley. Char was pinned against a wall by a Nightmare, its claws inches from his face.

Before Volo could dart forward to intervene, the Nightmare froze mid strike. Promise's hand had snapped forward, and the Nightmare slowly reeled to the ground, yards away. Char stumbled forward, gasping for air. Volo ran to his aid.

"You okay?" Volo asked, bracing him before he could fall.

Char nodded weakly. "Yeah... thanks."

Meanwhile, the incapacitated Nightmare was still moving.

As her friends were still recovering from the shock of battle, Tilde noticed an unsettling scene unfold. Promise held his hand in the air, as if trying to move the creature like a puppet. Its body glitched, as if fighting against some unseen force, and he flexed his hand in retaliation. It tried to stand up, a strangled screech escaping its throat, before crumpling back down to the ground.

Suddenly, Promise's eyes lit up as he spotted Hyphen, and the Nightmare burst into dust like a forgotten toy.

He strode over to her, a playful grin spreading on his face. "Well, if it isn't my *favorite* intern!" His voice rung with charisma, blissfully ignorant of the fear ridden atmosphere. "Excited to start tomorrow? I've got a feeling you're gonna *crush* it."

Tilde blinked, surprised by the interaction. She wasn't the only one who'd run into her boss today, it seemed.

From the corner of her eye, Tilde noticed Char. He was still catching his breath from the Nightmare attack, but his eyes were fixed on Promise, his face etched with a deep scowl.

Hyphen, flustered by Promise's attention, tucked a turquoise curl behind her ear. "Oh, um, yes! I'm looking forward to it!" She glanced around at the aftermath of their battle. "But I have to admit, I didn't expect to face four Nightmares on what was supposed to be a simple research mission."

"I wasn't prepared for all this fighting..." she said with a nervous laugh, "I was just excited to learn more about Broadway's history!"

Tilde was still processing the haunting means by which Promise disposed of the Nightmare, but her ears perked up at the name of her favorite actor.

"Gee, I really wasn't paying attention when they explained this assignment," she gushed, "so that's what this mission is about? I haven't heard that name since Broadway Windfall's show got cancelled!"

A silenced followed, as Promise's smile faltered.

Both Promise and Volo both turned to her with the same look.

"Huh?" Tilde's eyes narrowed in confusion, "Do you guys not know who that is?"

Realization dawned, and she clapped a hand over her mouth. "Oh! I never made the connection... You have the same last name!"

Volo's expression remained neutral as he directed his gaze to Hyphen. "Did you say 'Broadway'?"

Chapter 52: Broadway the Avenue

"This whole street used to be called Broadway, back in the ancient city," Hyphen said, her arm sweeping across the expansive avenue that stretched from the theatre district to Neon Square. The cracked asphalt glimmered under the flickering neon lights, hinting at its former grandeur.

Volo and Promise exchanged glances.

Volo's posture stiffened, his voice suddenly firm. "Has that always been common knowledge?"

"Oh, no no," Hyphen replied, her eyes sparkling with excitement at the chance to share her expertise. "It's a recent research breakthrough! They pieced it together from an expedition here, just before ours." Her words tumbled out rapidly, carried by her enthusiasm.

Volo turned to Promise, his face masking a storm of thought. "How is Dad named after a street no one knew about until now?"

Promise's shoulders rose in a lazy shrug. "Maybe it was just a common name in his generation."

Hyphen's eyes widened, her breath catching in her throat. She fidgeted with the hem of her skirt, torn between her eagerness to share knowledge and her uncertainty about intruding on family matters. She wanted to share everything she knew, but had to be careful not to cross a line with her future employer.

"Maybe he immigrated here from Layer Two?" Hyphen suggested, tentatively. "Did he ever talk about where he's from?"

"No," Volo responded.

Promise's gaze locked onto Hyphen, his eyes gleaming with newfound interest. "What's on Layer Two?"

Hyphen took a deep breath, steadying herself. "Layer Two is the Daydream Fields, the Realm of Places," she explained, her voice taking on a lecturer's cadence. "It's a dimension of existence where souls are formed from spatial memories."

"You know how Voidpets are formed from emotional language?" she continued, gesturing to her tiny Anxious nestled in her hair.

Volo nodded, his eyes never leaving Hyphen's face.

"Well, it's kind of like that, except instead you have people who are formed from *places*," Hyphen elaborated, her little hands animating as she spoke.

Tilde leaned forward in her wheelchair, her brow furrowed in confusion. "Wait, how does a place turn into a person?"

"It's the memories of the names," Hyphen replied, her voice softening. "Like, I'm sure if you meet them, they'll just seem like regular people, but that's the myth of how they came into being."

"And since there are so many places in the world—across space and time—that we've never been to," she said wistfully, "we wouldn't be able to make sense of it all anyway."

Volo looked pensive. "So Broadway is known for its theater district here?"

Hyphen nodded.

Tilde's face suddenly flushed a deep crimson as realization dawned. "Wait, so is Broadway Windfall your DAD?" she blurted out, her voice cracking with excitement.

Char's jaw dropped in exasperation, but Volo answered kindly, "Yeah, he is."

Tilde's face turned tomato red, her freckles almost disappearing against her skin. "Wait, so can I get his autograph?"

"He's not around anymore," Promise said, his voice laced with a hint of cruel satisfaction.

"But you can have *mine* if it's any solace," he added, causing Tilde to squirm further.

Alt stifled a yawn, his eyelids heavy with fatigue. "So how would someone immigrate from Layer Two?" he asked, his words slightly slurred. "I heard it's almost impossible to go down, and even harder to go back up."

Hyphen's shoulders slumped slightly. "That I don't know," she admitted, her voice tinged with disappointment.

Suddenly, Char's voice cut through the night air, sharp and clear. "I know of a way."

All eyes turned to him, the air ripe with renewed curiosity.

Promise's eyebrows shot up, betraying his interest. Even Volo leaned in, his calm wavering.

Char paused, savoring the moment. He held everyone's attention. Even Hyphen could tell that the Windfall brothers were now wrapped around his finger, hanging on for his next words. A smirk played at the corners of Char's mouth as he met Promise's wild gaze.

"But that's a story for another day," Char said, his voice cool and deliberate. He straightened up, wincing slightly from his earlier tussle, but his eyes gleamed with satisfaction.

Promise's eyes were daggers. He'd been got, and he wasn't happy about it.

"What?" he snapped, unable to mask his frustration.

Hyphen winced as Promise's hand clamped down on Char's shoulder.

"This is my *dad* we're talking about," Promise said slowly, as the air around him seemed to crackle with a dark energy.

Hyphen's stomach churned, not liking where this was headed. Her Anxi began to squeak, and she stepped backwards in embarrassment.

Char chuckled, unfazed as he parodied Promise's signature nonchalance. "Look, it's getting late, and we've all had a long day. Besides..." he added, his tone sharpening ever so slightly as he wiggled his eyebrows, "this isn't the kind of information you give out for *free*."

Volo's eyes flared red, studying Char with newfound intensity as Promise slowly released him. The challenge hung in the air between them.

Tilde looked from Char to the Windfall brothers with a gulp. "Um, maybe we should call it a night?" she suggested, her voice cutting through the tension.

Hyphen nodded eagerly, relief washing over her face. "Yes, let's head back. We can discuss more... another time."

Promise scoffed. He scanned the whole freshman group with a look of disgust, before fixing his gaze straight onto Hyphen. It lingered on her for a second before his frown twisted into a smile.

"I'll see you tomorrow, Hyphen," he crooned with a little wave, which made her stomach knot with anxiety.

He turned on a dime and stalked off into the night, his coat sweeping behind him like a trio of agitated tails. Volo gave a foreboding nod. He put his hands in his pockets and left with his brother.

As the group began to disperse, a twitch of fear crept into Char's triumph. He'd turned the tables on the Windfalls—but Hyphen feared for what he'd have to do to maintain his position.

The lights of Neon Square flickered overhead as they made their way back, casting ominous shadows behind them.

Hyphen was deeply worried for her best friend. The Windfall brothers were probably the last people in the Void she'd want as enemies, and she found herself fearing for Char's safety.

Why would Char bluff about their father just to get a reaction out of them?

She understood the rivalry, but that was just reckless and mean.

Her stomach churned as she headed back to campus, thinking about what her next day at work would entail. It seemed like things were about to get ugly.

Chapter 53: Coconut Water

Hyphen's stomach fluttered with nerves as she stood in the glass elevator, ears popping as it ascended to the 100th floor of Windfall Tower. The view was breathtaking—she could see all of Something Park stretching out below, and the Institute's gleaming spires in the distance.

She wanted to be as professional as possible for her first day of work, which is why her entire fleet of Anxi was contained in her head. The chattering little dinos were nowhere to be seen, tucked away in her mind in the form of pure energy.

Unfortunately, this was rather overwhelming.

In the sky-high waiting room, her head was screaming with Anxious clamor. As the frantic little Voidpets sought to escape into reality, unaccustomed to being packed inside all at once, the worried chatter of her Voidpets completely overwhelmed her thoughts. She tried to shake off scenes from the previous night: spiders crawling behind her eyelids, Tilde flung from her chair, Char overpowered in the alley, Alt hounded by that big worm.

To make matters worse, all her friends had warned her to be careful today. The Windfalls were officially *not* to be trusted, especially after their late night stand off with Char. Those final moments in Neon Square replayed in Hyphen's mind—the tension in the air, Promise's sudden shift from charm to menace, the way Char had stood his ground. It had felt like the prelude to something bigger, something dangerous.

Hyphen resisted the urge to bury her face in her hands or curl up into a ball, and instead began to fidget. Her fingers traced patterns on the arm of her chair, tapping out a nervous rhythm. She tried to focus on her breathing, but each inhale seemed to bring a new wave of fear.

The eerie beauty of the waiting area only intensified her discomfort. Glass windows stretched from the floor to the ceiling, with view so surreal it made her dizzy. Sleek, furniture lined the space, all clean lines and muted colors.

The glass door to the reception area swung open.

Promise held it open for her, glowing like a kid in a candy shop, his face alight without a single drop of malice. He was wearing a plain black hoodie, looking oddly disarming compared to his usual getup.

"Hyphen!" He beamed, his blue eyes crinkling into a smile.

"Where did all your Anxious go?" he suddenly asked with a curious frown.

"Oh, I..." Hyphen blushed, surprised he even knew, "Wait, how do you know about them?"

"How could I not remember from yesterday?" he grinned.

She blushed, surprised he remembered. "Well, I just... I thought it would be more appropriate to keep them contained for work."

"Naw, come on, I love those little guys," Promise beamed, as Hyphen noticed the pointed teeth at the corners of his smile. "They're welcome to roam the office."

As he said this, his two metal hands pulled out a box from behind the door, which was filled with colorful fidget toys. "A gift for the whole gang," he said, jiggling the box as Hyphen cautiously summoned her Anxi out one by one.

Promise's eyes met Hyphen's as she wavered in disbelief. The rattle of the colorful toys and his casual, sunshine demeanor stood in a disorienting contrast to the haunting sterility of earlier.

"Look, I *chose* you because you're the smartest student in the Institute," he spoke slowly, his lowered tone sending chills down her spine as she shuddered at the compliment. "So now it's time to cut yourself some slack."

As the Anxi claimed the fidget toys and began to wiggle off into the office with caution, Promise put away the empty box and nudged his head for her to step inside.

"Come on, let me take you on a tour to get you comfortable."

As they entered the office floor, Hyphen's senses were immediately overwhelmed by the luxurious office space. The air felt clean, with a soothing hint of eucalyptus. Ambient lighting bounced across the polished surfaces, creating an atmosphere of sophistication.

"All for you," Promise said, opening a stainless-steel fridge with a glass window. Inside, neat rows of pink coconut water bottles glowed invitingly. The cool air wafting out carried a hint of tropical sweetness.

As they moved through the different lounges, Hyphen's eyes widened at each new vista. From the south-facing view, sunlight poured through, bathing everything in a bright sheen. In the west, water glittered in the distance as it poured off the edge of the city island.

Finally, they reached the north quarter. "Now this," Promise said wistfully, "is my favorite spot."

The view of Something Park stretched out before them, a lush green oasis amidst the urban landscape. They were back at the front of the building, with the same magical view of the Institute and Ghost Road. Here, Promise showed her to a sleek desk of dark wood. A brand-new laptop sat waiting, its surface gleaming in the natural light.

As Hyphen settled in, she felt a profound sense of peace wash over her. The space was so beautiful, so tranquil, that the idea of leaving at the end of the day seemed to pain her. For the first time that day, her anxiety melted away, replaced by a desire to soak in every moment.

"Your job is simple," he explained. "Just read my emails. Then, you either delete them or forward to Pandora."

Hyphen nodded, awaiting more instruction, but there was none.

"Under what... um... criteria shall I determine how to classify the two categories?" she ventured nervously, her words coming out a bit convoluted in her attempt to sound professional.

Promise scoffed. "Hate mail, delete," he gestured to one side with a silly frown. "Crisis, Pandora" he gestured to the other with an open-mouthed grin.

"Anything else, just let it sit. You don't even have to respond," he dropped a shallow laugh.

"Otherwise, just work on whatever ideas interest you." He drummed his fingers on her desk, and shot her an encouraging smile, "I'll fund 'em if they're good."

Hyphen nodded.

"Any questions?" Promise asked.

"I'll get started and let you know!" she replied, still trying to process her assignment.

"Great. And I'll be right over here if anything comes up," he said, heading to a corner desk a few feet away, where he propped up his feet and began to scroll his phone.

Hyphen was stunned by how easy it sounded.

And the pay was 50 VM an hour!

She didn't dare question it.

But a worry still nagged. What was the catch? Why was he paying her to do this simple job, in an atmosphere of luxury? Why was he being so nice?

Anxious thoughts crept back, and she fought to keep them at bay. Was he going to blackmail her? Slowly escalate the workload? Plan an attack, or request dangerous favors? What if this was all a ploy to get information out of Char?

She knew to be skeptical of the Windfalls, but at the same time, she really wanted to believe they were just truly nice people.

Out of the corner of her eye, Hyphen noticed a small Voidpet hobble up to her feet. While shaped like a small, round, bean, it was quite a bit larger than any of her Anxi, and she suddenly realized that it had to be Promise's Lonely. It looked up at her with big googly eyes, before eagerly licking her leg.

"Hey there!" Hyphen giggled, feeling a wave of comfort return as she greeted with the familiar Voidpet. She still remembered the Lonely from the third day of high school, back when she had fed it a granola bar from her backpack. The Lonely bounced, as if asking to play, but Hyphen needed to get started on her job.

"Sorry pal," she gave it an apologetic smile, returning her attention to her work.

After an hour of getting settled, Hyphen finally mustered the courage to mouse her way to the kitchen for some coconut water. To her horror, the Anxi had already gotten into the fridge, and there were empty bottles everywhere. Her heart raced as she realized she'd already made a mess within her first hour of work. As she scrambled across the kitchen to collect the empty bottles, she nearly bumped into Promise.

"I'm SO sorry," she gushed, immediately tripping and sending empty bottles clattering to the floor them.

"Hey, hey, it's okay," he said softly, helping Hyphen to her feet. With the wave of his hand, he floated the bottles into the air, crushed them gently, and tossed them into the recycling bin.

"Don't sweat over coconut water," he assured her. "Your comfort is worth a lot more than any of this," he said, gesturing to the kitchen snack area. "I want you to relax and have a good time at work, okay?"

Hyphen nodded, feeling taken aback. The truth was, she wasn't very good at relaxing, and she wasn't convinced that having a good time could be part of her job.

"I'm sorry Promise, I—" she stammered, her cheeks flushing as she realized she was now embarrassed of being embarrassed.

"You have nothing to apologize for," he replied, looking down at her quizzically.

"Sorry—" Hyphen said again, before her hands leapt to her mouth.

"You can say sorry as much as you like. I'm not counting," he grinned, handing her a fresh bottle of coconut water. Hyphen accepted with sweaty palms as Promise paused to study her.

"Sorry, I just have a bit of anxiety..." Hyphen stammered, looking away.

"Oh, do you really?" Promise's tongue tucked behind his grin as his eyes drifted to the horde of Anxi playing behind them. But his face fell solemn as he noticed her shameful grimace.

"Look, I know what it's like to... feel like you're never enough and all that," he ventured with a flippant wave. "So, I hope you take my word for it when I say that you are."

Then, he grabbed an iced coffee and strode out of the kitchen, leaving her alone with his words.

After standing in stunned silence, Hyphen regained her senses and scurried back to her desk. As she struggled to control her breath, she found herself nearly tearing up. The luxury surrounding her felt unreal, almost overwhelming.

Why me? She wondered, glancing around the empty office. Surely there are more qualified people for this job. *What if I can't handle it? What if I disappoint him?*

She took a sip of coconut water, its sweetness doing little to quell the bubbling in her chest. The ease of the job so far only added to her unease.

As she attempted to focus on her laptop screen, Hyphen's thoughts drifted to the kitchen incident. Heat rose to her cheeks as she recalled Promise's easy forgiveness, his assurance that her comfort mattered. Was he being manipulative? Or was that a normal part of a healthy work environment?

She glanced at the clock, surprised to see how little time had passed. The day stretched before her, full of lingering questions. Hyphen took a deep breath, trying to ground herself.

I can do this, she told herself, straightening in her chair.

One step at a time.

With trembling fingers, she opened her email, determined to prove—to herself, if no one else—that she deserved to be here.

As the clock struck 5 PM, Hyphen's phone buzzed with a text.

Char*: TV night at Alt's. You in?*

Hyphen glanced at her unfinished work, then back at her phone. With a pang of guilt, she replied: "Sorry, still at work. Maybe next time?"

Almost immediately, her phone lit up with responses:

Tilde*: It's 5 PM! You shouldn't still be there!*

Hyphen sighed, typing back: "I know, but Promise is still in the office. It feels weird to leave before my boss…"

Alt: *That's a classic tactic to exploit workers. Don't fall for it.*

Before Hyphen could respond, another message from Char popped up. It was a picture—one from four years ago. In it, a younger Hyphen looked away from the camera, holding a pink water gun to Promise's head as he sat tied up on the floor. The caption read:

Don't forget who's really in charge ;)

Hyphen stared at the image, feeling a jolt of guilt for even perceiving it at work. Just then, Promise's voice interrupted her thoughts, and she almost dropped her phone in shock.

"You've done a great job today," he said, appearing at her desk. "You should head home."

"Oh, I just wanted to finish up this idea," said Hyphen. She gestured to her screen, which showed a graphic of a Voidpet eating a computer.

Promise pouted with concern. "Nah. I can't have you burning out on me. Go on, get out of here. The work will still be here tomorrow."

Conceding, Hyphen packed up her things and headed out. As the elevator descended, she texted her friends: "Change of plans. I'm free after all. See you soon?"

***

That evening, Hyphen entered Alt's dormitory to find her friends already deep in conversation. Tilde's voice carried above the others, her tone urgent.

"Guys, I saw something weird last night," Tilde said, leaning forward in her wheelchair. "I think Promise captured my manager."

Char's reaction was immediate—a long, exasperated sigh followed by a dramatic face-palm. "Tilde," he groaned, "the manager probably *is* his pet because he owns the restaurant."

A moment of silence, then: "Ohhhhhhhhhhh," Tilde breathed, realization dawning.

As the work conversation progressed, Hyphen felt herself caught between two worlds. Tilde launched into a passionate rant about fair labor practices, detailing the endless stream of customers at McGreedy's. Alt chimed in with cynical comments about corporate exploitation. Their words washed over Hyphen, clashing with her memories of Windfall Tower's beauty, of Promise's unexpected generosity.

Char caught her eye, raising an eyebrow. "So, how was your first day serving the enemy?" he snarked, only half-joking.

Hyphen opened her mouth, then closed it again. How could she explain her day at Windfall Tower without sounding like a traitor? Before she could answer, Char began speaking with an agenda of his own.

"Listen, Hyphen," Char said darkly, "I got an inside scoop about your fancy new job."

Hyphen felt her stomach knot but nodded for him to continue.

"Apparently, the Windfalls weren't just looking for a task monkey. They needed someone to like... babysit Promise's *emotions*."

Hyphen's brow furrowed in confusion. This didn't align with her experience at all, and if anything, seeded further doubts in her competence. "But... why did they care so much about GPA then?" she protested.

Char pressed on, undeterred. "Apparently, Pecunia told my sister Dyna—you know how they gossip—that Promise is a total *mess*. An emotional *wreck*. So torn up with mommy issues he can't think straight."

Hyphen wanted to protest but held her tongue as Char continued.

"The whole family was *desperate* for someone to keep him in check, so he didn't blow up the whole company with his mood swings. Like, apparently, he pushed Pandora out the window."

Hyphen swallowed hard, her mind racing with doubts.

"Just... be careful, okay?" Char finished, his voice softening slightly. "Sounds like you're walking into a minefield. Don't let them take advantage of you."

Hyphen looked to Tilde and Alt for their opinions, but all they could do was grimace with shared worry. It was no surprise that they sided with Char on this one.

Alt pulled out his laptop, putting on an old episode of *SLoTS* to break the tension, but Hyphen's dread remained.

As the others laughed at the show, Hyphen sat in silence.

Chapter 54: Y

Promise's eyes flung open, and he grasped for his phone like a lifeline.

3:31 AM. He squinted into the harsh glow of his screen, allowing the cute wallpaper of Greed and Lonely to bring him back to the waking world.

He hated sleeping.

His dreams were laced with too many bizarre dimensions to count, full of haunting images that lingered in his mind. He checked his hands to make sure that they had not, in fact, been chopped off and turned into sandwiches—and tasted his mouth to confirm that he did not, in fact, just eat them.

He scrolled his phone to anchor himself in the pettiness of real life and felt joy return.

An activist influencer had posted a viral hit piece on him. Followers debated whether he was misogynistic for exploiting Pandora. Business gurus were jumping to analyze how he spent his time, citing his posts as evidence of incompetence.

As he scrolled, a mischievous response formed in his mind, deftly tailored to fuel the flames.

With a practiced face, he lifted his phone to record another video.

"I'm just a girl~" the cheery sound played. He conjured an iced latte and sipped into the camera with practiced satire.

His fingers typed a haphazard caption:

pov: when working hard is hard so u just don't

—and posted it.

Promise put down his phone, the screen's harsh glow fading to black. He didn't bother checking the flood of comments that undoubtedly ensued. His eyes drifted to his real-life Greed and Lonely, sound asleep at the foot of his bed. His only job now was to finish his coffee and recover from his dream.

Promise propped himself up on a stack of pillows, silk cool against his skin. The twilight view stretched before him, the few city lights twinkling like earthbound stars. From the comfort of his California king, the world seemed small.

He was happy. Reality was too good. He'd wanted everything, and effectively attained it.

He closed his eyes, savoring the solace of the night, before opening them to a jarring sight:

A Nightmare. No, it was a *person*.

An uncanny silhouette appeared before the foot of his bed. At first glance, it resembled a paranormal apparition, but closer inspection revealed details that disagreed.

Promise's heart rate elevated slightly, like someone who'd just spotted a cockroach. He'd seen enough Nightmares to be rather desensitized to such intrusions, but what gave him pause was the humanness of this individual.

Black hair cascaded from her head, spilling onto the floor in a pool of shadows. Unlike any Nightmare he had ever seen, she was clothed in a white T-shirt, the oversized garment hanging down to her knees.

He bit back the instinct to dispatch the unwelcome guest, noting the Pain on the floor beside her. If she had a Voidpet, she was almost certainly human.

"A knock would have been nice," he ventured, sarcasm masking his rising alarm. If there was one thing he inherited from his father, it was the ability to calm himself down with the sound of his own voice.

As the girl looked up to face Promise, he felt chills. Her eyes were impossibly large, like twin black holes begging to pull him in. On her forehead, an upside-down Y was etched, the marking raw on her nearly translucent skin.

Y—as he decided to call her—gave no response, and instead bent down to lift Pain into her arms. She plopped the creature onto the foot of Promise's bed, where it landed beside his own sleeping Voidpets with a quack.

As the blunt sound echoed off his bedroom walls, Promise's eyes darted to process the full scene. Pain, Promise thought, was what a geoduck would look like if it looked anything like a duck.

Meanwhile, Y's hands were bound by oversized shackles, the moonlight revealing circular markings etched into the metal. The chains led nowhere, as if she were a prisoner of something intangible.

"Can I help you?" Promise asked, his words unhurried despite the urgency in his thoughts. He sipped his coffee from his stack of pillows, underscoring the silence with the sound of jostling ice.

Y stared wordlessly, before climbing up onto the foot of his bed herself. Promise recoiled, his eyes widening at the sight of her feet.

"*Woah* there," he snapped, "you can't do that in *shoes.*"

Y froze apologetically and obliged, peeling off her sandals before seating herself on the mattress, scooping Pain into her arms.

So, she could understand him.

Before he could further contemplate the audacity of her behavior, he froze at the markings on her shackles:

A circle with a line through the middle.

Carved haphazardly, as if by hand. They matched the carving he'd seen in the mirror, nine years ago. A sight he could never forget.

As his pulse began to pick up, he contemplated his approach.

"You wanna tell me why you're here, or am I supposed to guess?" His face twisted into an automatic smile, and he moved his straw to his mouth for another casual sip. Controlling his own reaction was the key to controlling any situation.

Y looked distraught, as if unable to speak. After frowning at him, she lifted her index finger like a writing utensil. With a flustered expression, she moved a dirty fingernail to trace letters on her arm.

"Ew, *no*. Not like *that*," Promise interrupted. He summoned a fountain pen and leather notepad. "Here."

Y accepted the offering with a gratuitous bow. Gripping the pen in her fist, she scrawled three words on the paper: *I AM LOST.*

Promise raised an eyebrow. How a lost person could find their way into his penthouse, he was uncertain but intrigued.

"Where's home for you?" he asked, and Y turned the page, writing a single, enormous character: *5.*

Promise set down his cup, its cool condensation lingering on his fingertips as he narrowed his eyes. "Is that... *Layer* Five?"

Y stared blanky as if she didn't understand.

"Well then. Wherever that is, I'm sorry, I don't know how to help you." Promise gave a sympathetic shrug expecting the girl to disappear, but instead, she moved closer. He winced as she crawled toward his pillows, nestling among them as if yearning for safety. There, she sat solemn, rocking slowly as she wrapped her arms around her legs.

Promise sat still in thought. Y had no concept of personal space, but she was rich with mysterious clues. If she really was from Layer Five— if those markings on her shackles were connected in any way to his parents' disappearance—he had to know.

As he scrutinized her face, he saw that her translucent skin was pockmarked with scars, ashy as if it'd never been cared for. Clearly, she was in a state of distress, so he'd need to be tactful about extracting information. With a flick of dark matter, Promise conjured a collagen face mask between his fingers, filling the air with the scent of rosewater.

"Here. Put this on your face." He handed it to Y with an outstretched arm, unable to bear the sight of her poor skin any longer.

The girl looked bewildered but seemed to unwind at the smell of roses. Gingerly taking the mask into her hands, she sniffed it, licked it with the tip of her tongue, and dabbed it on her cheek. Then, she looked back at him, as if waiting further instruction.

Promise sighed, before conjuring another one for himself. "Like this," he placed it onto his own face.

Y followed his example, her bottomless eyes now button-like as they peered out of the hydrating sheet mask. She stared out the window with her shackled hands folded across her belly, relaxing at the cool texture on her skin.

"Good job," said Promise. The sight of this tormented, otherworldly visitor finding solace in spa-day aesthetics was amusing.

"You want?" he asked, conjuring a tin of mints. He fished one out for himself, demonstrating that they were edible, before passing the box her way.

Y grabbed the tin hungrily, cherishing the mints as if they were a blessed gift. Her chains clinked as she ventured one into her mouth, nibbling the candy as her gaze returned to the window.

"You like them?" He asked with a grin, and Y nodded. Promise allowed himself to join the reprieve, sinking further into his pillows to take in the view. They sat on opposite sides of the mattress, gazing forward out of the window in the comfort of his spacious bed. He could hear her breathing deepen, as if she was enjoying her first moment of peace in a long time.

"So," Promise asked, deciding he'd disarmed her enough to pose his most pressing question, "How'd you get *these*?" he turned to face her, gesturing to his wrists.

But Y was gone. As quickly as she had come, the mysterious visitor had vanished along with her Voidpet, leaving nothing but an imprint of wrinkles in his sheets. He blinked though his face mask, watching the sky slowly lighten outside his window.

Certainly, it had only been another strange dream.

Chapter 55: Lulu the Lonely

Hyphen's next day at work was rife with trepidation. Her morning classes went by in a blur of worry, and now, she was back at her desk at Windfall Tower, reading Promise's emails.

Could it be that the catch was Promise's temper?

Should she be worried about her safety?

She looked out the window and gulped.

What if he decided to push her out of the 100th floor?

Her friends had insisted she pack a parachute just in case, and her backpack was bursting at the seams with a bundle of fabric that Alt had sewn out of sheets. As she worked, it sat beside her, a symbol of moral support than anything else.

"Hey Hyphen!" He approached her desk with a little wave and a smile that lit up the room. His hands were tucked in the pockets of his hoodie, his sky-colored eyes sparkling in the direct light.

Relief washed over her once again as she took in his benevolent aura. Perhaps Char was stretching the truth a bit, or her friends had blown the situation out of proportion. He looked so calm, so happy in the sunshine, the thought of him launching anyone out the window suddenly seemed preposterous.

Suddenly, one of her Anxious knocked her bag off her desk, sending the parachute fabric spilling out.

Promise looked surprised. His eyes narrowed, before arriving at what sounded like a logical conclusion for him. "Oh, did you want to go skydiving?"

"Oh no no, I just..." Hyphen felt blood rush to her face.

"I mean I can take you if you want, I'm not sure if it's safe to use... *that.*" He waved over the pile of what appeared to be bedsheets.

He followed up with a curious head tilt. "Is that what you wanted?"

Hyphen did not want to go skydiving. But she also feared saying no to a bonding activity would be some sort of corporate faux pas. And she couldn't clarify that the parachute was for if he tried to push her out the window.

"Oh! Ah... yes!" she answered, instantly regretting her words.

"Sweet. Can you fly or anything?" Promise asked immediately.

"No," Hyphen answered, as if she were guilty of a grave sin.

"Ah." Promise looked conflicted. He looked at his hands, and then at her, then at the little Anxi jittering.

He put his hands into his hoodie pockets. "Maybe another time then." He replied with a measured smile, before turning away and heading off.

Hyphen sighed a big breath of quiet relief. She was glad that her accidental suggestion of skydiving had been thwarted—and grateful that her manager was cognizant of her boundaries.

Once again, Hyphen allowed the tranquility of the office to soothe her. The pink coconut water stood as a reminder to prioritize her comfort. Small clinks could be heard from the Anxi playing, and the room smelled like mint and eucalyptus.

As Hyphen settled into her routine, she returned her attention to sorting through Promise's emails. Most were standard fare, but one anonymous message caught her eye, making her squirm a bit in the professional setting.

Heyy Prommy. Can't wait to see you up close.

XOXO, your biggest fan.

Hyphen grimaced. That one wasn't exactly hate... but it didn't seem appropriate for work either. She pressed delete, a knot of unease forming in her stomach as she continued to archive Promise's inbox full of solicitations. Her earlier tranquility began to slip, permeated with moments of doubt.

Hyphen barely noticed the gentle movement at her feet. Promise had disappeared somewhere, but his Lonely was back at her desk. It wiggled up to her feet, purring, before floating straight up towards her face.

"Oh hey there!" Hyphen cooed as the bean shaped Voidpet floated up and licked her cheek. She giggled, surprised by its affection. Had it remembered her from long ago?

"Are you hungry?" she asked, offering a granola bar, but Lonely wasn't interested. Instead, it closed her laptop with its snout and perched atop. It blinked its round googly eyes, wagging its little tail as if demanding attention.

"Well look at you!" Hyphen exclaimed, charmed by the Voidpet's playful behavior.

But her amusement faded as minutes ticked by. "I really should get back to work," she said gently, trying to nudge Lonely aside.

It didn't budge.

"Come on now, I need my laptop." She coaxed, but Lonely simply rolled, still firmly planted on the device. Its googly eyes blinked, uncomprehending or perhaps deliberately obtuse.

Hyphen's hands hovered over the Voidpet. Would it be inappropriate to physically grab Promise's pet? She didn't want to upset the creature, but she needed to do her job.

Finally, deciding she had no choice, Hyphen attempted to lift Lonely from the laptop. To her shock, the small Voidpet was impossibly heavy. Though it sat lightly on the laptop, trying to budge it from its position was like trying to lift a squishy boulder.

"Please," Hyphen whispered, her voice cracking slightly. "I don't want to get in trouble on my second day of work." Lonely just wagged its tail, seemingly oblivious to her distress.

Hyphen's palms began to sweat. What if Promise came back and saw her trying to manhandle his pet? What if she couldn't get any work done? Would she be fired? Hyphen felt trapped, unable to move this inexplicably heavy Voidpet.

As the room grew colder and darker, a thought struck Hyphen. Why did Lonely still look like a Stage 1 Voidpet? Its small bean shape belied the overwhelming power emanating from it.

Something wasn't adding up.

All her friends' pets evolved as they got stronger, and Promise's Greed had clearly grown to Stage 5.

Why hadn't Lonely changed in four years?

Lonely's cartoon eyes locked with hers.

Hyphen felt herself being pulled in, unable to look away as Lonely's pupils consumed her like black holes. The air grew thick, almost syrupy, like water. She began to see shadows dancing across the windows, darkening the entire office with chilling whispers.

As her vision blurred, her consciousness snapped to a series of visions.

In the first she was scrambling for safety as the ground before her collapsed. Next, her hands were stained with ash, alone in a city on fire. Then, she was stranded in a blizzard, shivering as she lost her way in a whiteout. Finally, she was digging through a desert, slowly sinking under the endless dunes.

Hyphen gasped, her eyes flying open as she snapped back to reality. Her pulse was racing, and she could feel a thin sheen of cold sweat on her forehead. The visions of isolation lingered like a bad dream, leaving her disoriented.

She blinked rapidly, trying to ground herself in the present moment. The office came back into focus—the soft light, the gentle hum of the air conditioning, the faint scent of mint and eucalyptus. Lonely was curled up in her lap, purring contentedly as if nothing had happened.

Hyphen's hands trembled slightly as she instinctively stroked Lonely's back, the action helping to calm her frayed nerves. She took a deep, shaky breath, willing her heartbeat to slow down.

"Aww, Lulu likes you!" Promise's voice signaled his return, making her jump slightly. He was now dressed in his imposing outfit, complete with the gold belt, tailed coat, an iced latte in hand. Hyphen forced a smile, hoping it didn't look as strained as it felt. "Oh, yes!" she managed, her voice only slightly unsteady, "She's very friendly!"

She straightened in her chair, trying to maintain professional composure. Her mind raced, wondering if Promise could tell something was off. Should she mention the visions? *No, that would be inappropriate.* What if it was just a daydream? A manifestation of her own anxiety?

"Lulu's so cute, isn't she?" Promise cooed. He walked over to scoop up his Lonely and buried his face in her side with a big nuzzle.

"She sure is!" Hyphen squeaked, aiming for an airy tone. Her eyes bugged out as she noticed that her computer was still closed. "I was just about to get back to work, actually!"

As she reached for her laptop, Hyphen's hand was shaking. She took another deep breath, determined to push through and act normal. Whatever had just happened, she couldn't let it interfere with her career. She had to focus and bring her A-game.

Yet even as she opened her computer and pulled up her work, she felt herself gripped with the inexplicable urge to cry.

Chapter 56: Bottled Happiness

The smells of paint and cheap pizza filled the air as Alt made his way through the crowded student art showcase. His stomach growled, a painful reminder of his near-empty wallet. To celebrate Hyphen and Tilde's new jobs, he dreamed of treating them to a celebratory dinner at Mr. J's—the new hotspot everyone was talking about. But with its 1000 VM per person price tag and month-long waitlist, it might as well have been on another planet.

Alt's fingers brushed against the 35 VM in his pocket—barely enough for a decent lunch, let alone a fancy group dinner. He sighed, the weight of his financial limitations settling on him like a dark cloud. At least the showcase offered free food. He grabbed a lukewarm slice of pizza from a cardboard box.

As he chewed the rubbery cheese, Alt made his way back to his station. The buzz of conversation and occasional burst of laughter faded into background noise as he stood before his latest creation. Gold splashes danced across a black canvas, bold and chaotic. It was a stark departure from his soft and detailed realism.

Alt studied the piece with doubt. The gold paint caught the harsh fluorescent lighting, creating an almost gaudy, amateur effect. He couldn't shake the feeling that this wasn't really *his* work. The speed at which he'd completed it, simply upending buckets of paint onto the canvas, felt sacrilegious compared to his usual painstaking process.

The memory of his recent in-class critique made him wince. The confused looks, the awkward silences, the artistic weaknesses his peers brought up all came flooding back. Alt's excitement about the showcase began to curdle into anxiety. He took another bite of pizza, barely tasting it as he braced himself for the reactions to come.

As other students and faculty began to mill around the displays, Alt found himself holding his breath. Would people think this piece was a joke? Would anyone understand the vision? Did he even understand it himself? Next to him, Sad perched on a wooden stool, looking around the room with dread.

As Alt stood lost in thought, a familiar voice slipped through the ambient chatter of the showcase. "These are lovely," Pecunia said, her platinum blonde hair spilling over her shoulders as she leaned in to examine Alt's more traditional pieces. Her manicured nails traced the air above the intricate sketches, a gesture of appreciation without touching. She nodded politely at each one, murmuring compliments that didn't quite reach Alt's ears.

Then she stopped. Her whole body seemed to freeze as her gaze landed on Alt's latest creation. The chaotic shapes of gold on black captured her completely, her green eyes widening, pupils dilating as if trying to absorb every detail.

"Now this..." Pecunia said, her voice filled with awe, "This is like... what I'd call *stunning*."

"It's like you were able to capture happiness in a bottle..." her eyes looked misty as her voice trailed off.

Alt shifted uncomfortably, unsure how to respond to such intensity. Now that Pecunia was standing right next to him, he noticed her perfume. His nostrils flared as they sensed notes of pink pepper and jasmine, underscored with a sweet chamomile.

"The texture and composition..." she breathed softly, "it's like a fusion of... Pollock and Kandinsky," her nails waved as she remained transfixed.

Alt's eyes narrowed. He didn't like being compared to other artists, and wasn't sure if that was an underhanded jab at his lack of originality. At least, he figured, it sounded like she was actually familiar with some art history.

"I'd love to buy it," Pecunia declared suddenly, turning to face him with her eyes agleam. "How does 100k VM sound?"

The words hit Alt like a truck. He blinked rapidly, certain he had misheard. "I... what?"

"100,000 void matter," Pecunia repeated, her tone earnest.

"Is that enough?"

Alt's mind reeled. Was this even allowed? The sum she casually offered was more than he had ever seen in his life. He tried to picture it—a pure crystal of void matter the size of a refrigerator. The image was absurd.

"I... I don't think I could even carry that much," he stammered.

"Oh don't worry about that," Pecunia giggled with a wave of her hand, "We'll have it shipped to you!"

A thread of suspicion wormed its way into Alt's thoughts. This was Pecunia Windfall, after all. Apparently the most unethical person in the most unethical family in the Void—the one Windfall who was rumored to be a straight up scam artist. Was this some sort of trick? Would she take his art and disappear?

"I'm sorry," Alt heard himself say, his voice steadier than he felt. "It's not for sale."

Pecunia's expression flickered with a confused pout, before settling back into a polite smile. "I get it," she said with a small shrug. "It really is amazing, though! You've earned yourself another fan."

"I'm Pecunia by the way," she said with a coy smile, extending an elegant hand decked in diamonds.

Alt knew that already—in fact, he had known for years. But he wasn't surprised she never knew his name. He felt his hands getting clammy beneath his sleeves.

"I'm Alt," he said, hesitating to accept the handshake. Not wanting to reveal the condition of his hands, he deflected with a wave, keeping his fingers tucked beneath his sleeve. Pecunia seemed to understand, as she withdrew her hand and smiled.

"Nice to meet you, Alt!" she sung with a little wave, "I'll see you around!" And with that, she turned and drifted towards the next display, her interest apparently genuine as she engaged with other student artists.

Alt sank into his chair, his legs suddenly weak. His heart raced, adrenaline coursing through him as if he'd narrowly escaped danger.

But had he?

Or had he just made the biggest mistake of his life?

He watched Pecunia move through the crowd, her presence unsettling, yet somehow still alluring. He had never seen her on campus without the other Windfalls or her sorority sisters, so why was she here alone? Could it be true that she was a passionate art connoisseur? Was it possible that they had something in common?

As Alt watched Pecunia move further away, a wave of regret washed over him. His heart pounded, thoughts somersaulting over each other. *What was he doing?* This could be his big break. A chance for him to have a serious art career.

Before he could second-guess himself, Alt was on his feet. He weaved through the crowd, mumbling hurried apologies as he brushed past other students and faculty.

"Pecunia!" he called out, his voice cracking slightly. She turned, surprise flickering across her face.

Alt skidded to a stop in front of her, slightly out of breath. "I'm sorry," he blurted out. "About before, I mean. I just... I got overwhelmed. I didn't know what to say."

Pecunia's eyebrows raised slightly, a slight smirk returning to her face.

"The truth is," Alt continued, his words tumbling out, "I'd be honored if you wanted my piece. It's just... it's a lot to process, you know?"

He took a deep breath, steadying himself. "If you're still interested, I'd like to accept your offer."

Pecunia's face broke into a radiant smile. "Oh, good!" she said, her eyes sparkling. "I'm glad you changed your mind!"

She extended her hand, and Alt grasped it, suddenly forgetting to be ashamed of his missing fingers.

"Let's discuss the details," Pecunia grinned, leading him to a quieter corner of the gallery.

As they spoke, Alt's mind drifted to ancient artists. He thought of one who'd similarly poured hours into his intricate sketches but got famous for painting a bunch of rectangles instead. Was it fair that his simplest piece was the most successful one to date?

Perhaps it was—for it'd captured a moment of spontaneity with the help of all his preceding years of dedication.

Alt began to daydream of his new future ahead. It dawned on him that he might be able to make dinner at Mr. J's happen after all.

Chapter 57: Mr. J's.

"Dinner?" Promise asked.

Hyphen froze, her mind racing. Was this appropriate? A dinner with her boss? She must have looked as conflicted as she felt because Promise quickly added, "It's just downstairs on the 99th floor. It's basically our food court. On me."

"Or you can sit here and eat trail mix if you prefer," he quipped, tongue between teeth.

The offer of free food made Hyphen's stomach growl traitorously. She hadn't realized how hungry she was. "Ah, yes, sure," she found herself saying. "That sounds great!"

They took the elevator down to the 99th floor, Promise humming tunelessly as they descended. When the doors opened, Hyphen's jaw dropped. It wasn't a food court—it was a high-end restaurant with a sleek, art deco design, bustling with Voidpets and humans alike. The aroma of exotic food wafted through the air, making her mouth water.

Promise led her past the main dining bar to a special back entrance, where they entered a private room paneled in dark wood. Inside was a large conference table overlooking the twinkling city below, and they took two seats by the window.

"Is there a menu?" Hyphen asked, not seeing one anywhere.

"Nah, you don't have to bother with ordering," Promise said, "The chef sends whatever he wants. But don't worry, it's like, always good."

He pulled out his phone, leaning his chair back. "I'm just gonna..." he trailed off, already absorbed in his device.

Hyphen sat stiff, unsure what to do with herself. But soon, a Merry server appeared and greeted them.

"Do you have any allergies or dietary restrictions that the kitchen should be aware of, Miss Hyphen?" The Voidpet asked, and Hyphen shook her head no.

Shortly after, the Merry returned with the first of many small plates. As each dish arrived—delicate nigiris, colorful crudos, artistic arrangements of food she'd never seen before—Hyphen gasped with delight.

The parade of exquisite dishes continued, but Promise's disengagement was obvious. He ate without really looking at what he put in his mouth, scrolling through his phone as if he were eating fast food.

Without warning, a figure entered the room, sporting four elegant wings and a long, feathered tail. Hyphen's eyes widened as she realized it was a Stage 5 Judgement. The Voidpet's pterodactyl form was clothed in an immaculate chef's uniform, complete with a towering white hat.

"How do you like today's courses?" the chef asked politely, a deep voice resonating from his beak.

"Good stuff, bro," Promise fist bumped the Voidpet's iron talon with a metallic clink, and he nodded with respect.

"It's incredible, sir!" Hyphen gushed, unable to contain her enthusiasm. "I've never tasted anything like this before."

As the chef bowed his head in appreciation, suppressing a flattered purr, Hyphen noticed a small pin on its lapel: 'Executive Chef Mr. J.' Her heart skipped a beat as realization dawned. This was *the* Mr. J's— the exclusive restaurant she'd heard so much about.

Panic set in as she remembered the rumors about the price—1000 VM per person. She felt a cold sweat break out on her forehead. As the chef excused himself, Hyphen turned to Promise, her voice tight with concern.

"Um, Promise? Is this... is this very expensive? I really don't want to take advantage of the company or anything."

Promise looked up from his phone, seeming surprised by the question. "The food itself? Nah, it's pretty cheap, no big deal." He popped a nigiri into his mouth like a chicken nugget.

"Are you sure?" Hyphen's brow furrowed in confusion. "It's just that I heard…"

"Oh, we've got some *thick* margins alright," Promise set his phone down with a self-satisfied smirk. "It's exclusive and we hype it up, so people pay for that. But the actual ingredients? They're just made of VM."

He leaned back in his chair, and flashed an evil grin. "All these yuppies are *dying* to cough up 1000 VM just to say they ate here. That's kind of the whole point of this place."

Hyphen nodded slowly, trying to process this information.

"But also," Promise continued, "Mr. J really does have the best taste. So it's not like it's not worth it. His skill is top tier. You can't get this anywhere else in the Void."

Promise reached across the table for a slice of toast bejeweled in seafood. "And apparently he's a good looking Voidpet," he shrugged and took a bite. "That sells."

Hyphen nodded again, trying her to best to act like she understood as she took a delicate nibble of her own toast.

Promise paused his next bite as he caught her confusion. "I mean I wouldn't really know myself, but Peach said so," he added, before returning to his phone.

"Oh yes, I know Peach," Hyphen assured politely, realizing he was referring to the pink manager from Pandora's Bread.

As they finished their meal, Promise's demeanor shifted slightly. He set his phone aside, fixing Hyphen with a more serious look.

"Listen, Hyphen," he began, his tone careful. "I need to ask you something. It's about the Seven Layers of the Void."

Hyphen felt her heart rate pick up. She nodded, encouraging him to continue.

"Was your friend telling the truth about Layer Two?"

The question hung in the air between them, and Hyphen found herself at a crossroads, unsure how to respond.

Chapter 58: Cluck-ee's

The bell above the door chimed as Char entered Cluck-ee's gas station. The fluorescent lights flickered, casting an ugly glow over dusty shelves stocked with snacks no one ever seemed to buy.

A Voidpet resembling a giant chicken peeked out from behind a grimy office door.

"Char?" he bawked.

Char squeezed out a begrudging smile and followed the creature into what he assumed was the manager's office. The room smelled of stale corn chips and resignation. He was the only one in his friend group still broke and unemployed, reduced to interviewing for jobs he'd never imagined stooping to. Cluck-ee's was probably at the bottom of his wish list, but beggars couldn't be choosers.

"The name's Pete," the manager introduced himself with a twang, extending a feathered hand.

"Pleasure to meet you sir, I'm Char."

"So. 3.9 GPA huh," Pete clucked, scanning Char's resume as he stepped in.

"Yes sir," Char smiled as best he could, trying to suppress a scowl. He didn't need a reminder that the job was beneath his qualifications.

"So, tell me son. Why are you passionate about customer service?"

Char nearly winced. He hated customer service more than anything. Fortunately, he was also a gifted liar.

"I spent my entire childhood working at my parents' dumpling shop," Char replied, feigning nostalgia. "I love working with Voidpets, making sure every customer feels cared for." He looked Pete in two of his big round eyes, making sure the message landed.

"Service is a language of love," Char continued, the words leaving a bitter taste in his mouth. "There's nothing more heartwarming than seeing someone's face light up because you made their day a little more delightful."

Pete nodded, the two feathers on his head bouncing like antennae. Char finished with a flourish, "It's a privilege to be considered for this opportunity."

In reality, it was an absolute disgrace.

After a moment of contemplation that involved more head-tilting and eye-blinking than Char thought necessary, Pete simply said, "Ok. You're hired."

Char blinked. Was that it?

Of course it was. This was a gas station.

Pete produced an apron and hat from beneath his cluttered desk, handing them to Char with instructions to man the cash register. "Your job is to check people out and watch out for shoplifters," he added before promptly falling asleep in his chair and snoring.

Char changed in the grimy bathroom, grimacing at his reflection in the spotted mirror. The uniform hung loosely on his frame, as if even the clothes knew this wasn't where he belonged.

For nearly an hour, Char stood at his post in the empty mart. Not a single customer walked in—which was utterly unsurprising. No one drove cars in the Void, so why would anyone need a gas station? As he observed the sleeping manager and the layer of dust on everything, Char realized this was typical of Voidpet-run businesses. No wonder Windfall Inc. had managed to monopolize nearly every sector. The rest of the economy was in absolute disarray, run by creatures who were just going through the motions, role-playing out of boredom.

These ethereal beings seemed to have jobs just for fun. As the Void's idyllic middle class, they got by on their magical powers and hardly worked out of necessity. The few thriving businesses in existence were all human-run, driven by the actual need for VM to survive.

Char's gaze drifted to the refrigerated section, where rows of coffee drinks lined up behind foggy glass doors. The green Gluttony logo of StarGluts stared back at him, the smug eyes of the laughing hydra seeming to mock his predicament. Another Windfall business.

What a surprise.

He clenched his jaw, bitterness rising in his throat. Stupid Windfalls. The thought simmered. If only they weren't just a few years older than him. If only they didn't exist.

The Void could have been a world full of opportunity. A blank canvas for anyone with a dream to make their mark. But no—he had to be born at just the wrong time. Just late enough for the first monopolistic empire to be started by someone else. Just late enough for them to snap up every promising venture, every innovative idea, before he even had a chance to finish school.

The unfairness of it all made his chest tight as Envy seethed, contained in his heart. He was smart. He was ambitious. He had plans. But the Windfalls had swooped in and bought out everything, leaving him in the dust. Now, instead of changing the world, he was stuck at Cluck-ee's gas station, selling slushes to customers who didn't exist.

As the hours dragged on in the empty store, Char's frustration gave way to physical discomfort. He noticed the taste of his own parched tongue, and his eyes drifted to the slush machine in the corner. A pop of color in a mess of drab, it taunted him with the gentle whir of its motor.

It was then that Char decided to get himself a slush. If there was anything redeeming about this dead-end job, at least his boss was careless, and he could sneak a free snack. He glanced at the sleeping Pete, then back at the machine.

With a furtive look around, Char crept towards the slush dispenser. He grabbed the largest cup available and filled it to the brim with the pink Hibiscus Tea flavor. The cup's gaudy lettering caught his eye: "FIRE UP YOUR FOCUS," it proclaimed.

As he took his first sip, Char was surprised to find that it was delicious. The tangy flavor burst on his tongue, a small surprise amidst the monotony of his day. But it was more than just refreshing—it was energizing. Like a shot of liquid power. Looking down, he noticed his hand pulse with a faint glow.

That was the one nice thing he'd enjoyed all day.

Unfortunately, the moment didn't fix his misery. As his shift wore on, the glow faded, leaving him once again with nothing but his bitter thoughts.

Five years at the Institute had done nothing to change his fate. What was the point of studying lucidity theory if he had no VM to his name? All the school did was teach rich kids how to get richer, funneling everyone else into dead-end jobs working for them. To scrape by, he was doomed to cater to the whims of wild Voidpets. Just like his parents.

It was hardly any solace what little the job paid at the end of the night. Wild Voidpets shed VM just by existing, so his salary was paid with feathers Pete dropped in his sleep. At the end of Char's shift, the Panic woke up long enough to scoop them into a crystal of 50 VM for him. Then, he promptly resumed his slumber.

On his way out, Char decided to sneak another slush—because, well, why not?

Chapter 59: Chess and Tea

The sun was setting over the Institute, pulling lazy shadows across campus. Char trudged back to his dorm room, the weight of his disappointing day at Cluck-ee's still heavy on his shoulders. As he approached his door, he saw a familiar figure leaning against the wall.

"About time you showed up, bozo," Dyna said, crossing her arms with a smirk.

"Sup, loser?" Char teased affectionately.

Despite his exhaustion, Char felt a small smile tugging at the corners of his mouth. He and Dyna had grown surprisingly close since starting college. Without the daily friction of living under the same roof, they'd found common ground in their shared history and love for gossip.

"Rough day?" Dyna asked, noting the slump in Char's posture.

"You have no idea," Char sighed, unlocking his door. "Chess and tea?"

Dyna nodded, following him inside. His small dorm room was cluttered but cozy, with posters covering the walls and a chessboard permanently set up on the carpet. As Char busied himself with the electric kettle, Dyna settled into her usual spot, Jealous curling up with a pillow on the floor. Envy emerged to play beside Jealous, though eyeing her warily.

"Oolong?" Char asked, already knowing the answer.

"Oolong," Dyna replied, with an affirmative nod.

The familiar ritual of setting up the chess pieces and pouring the tea helped ease Char's irritation. As the herbal steam rose from their cups, Char felt himself relaxing for the first time all day.

"Alright," he said, flipping a coin to determine who would play white. "Ready to lose?"

Dyna caught the coin mid-air, revealing white. "In your dreams, punk."

As they settled into their game, the air filled with the quiet clink of chess pieces.

Dyna moved her pawn, then leaned back with a dramatic sigh. "I'm so done with Verve right now. Like, can you believe she called me a gold digger?"

"Oh no she did *not*," Char's eyebrows shot up as he contemplated his next move. "Isn't Verve, like, the *definition* of gold digger?"

"I know right!" Dyna huffed, her Jealous mimicking her indignant expression. "She stopped speaking to Promise because he dropped out, and now she's talking to him again because he's like, a billionaire. How fake is that?"

She moved another piece forcefully. "I've always been chill with Volo without knowing *anything* about his background," she added with pride.

Char suppressed an eye roll, focusing on the board. Volo was the worst, but he had grown out of nagging his sister about it.

"Verve thinks I'm playing some sort of long game," Dyna groaned, "But Volo's just like, my best friend, you know?"

Char scoffed but moved his knight instead of responding.

"Meanwhile, Verve is like, off the rails. And totally projecting." Dyna's voice rose with frustration. "Promise doesn't even respond to her unless it's in the group chat with both of us in it."

"You guys have a group chat?" Char interrupted, his curiosity piqued.

"Yeah, for memes and clothes," Dyna said without missing a beat. "And now she's like, losing her mind over the new freshman intern." She paused, a mischievous glint in her eye. "Wait, she's your friend, right?"

"Hyphen?" Char asked, suddenly a little more interested in the conversation than the game.

"Yeahhh, that girl," Dyna confirmed. "The anxious one. Are you two close?" Her tone turned playful.

Char felt his cheeks warm slightly. "Yeah, she's a good friend."

"So like, *close* close?" Dyna prodded, leaning forward.

"Noooooo, not like that," Char said, incredulous. "She's not my type."

Dyna's grin widened with a wiggle of her brows. "What about your other friends? Tilde? Alt? You into any of them?"

Char shook his head vigorously. "Noooooo, we're all just friends." He paused, then added hesitantly, "But... I think Pecunia's kinda cute."

Dyna's eyes narrowed, her playful demeanor shifting. "Pecunia? Wait, but she's *so* basic. Like... She literally has no personality. She's an NPC."

"Isn't she your best friend...?" Char asked, confused by her sudden change in tone.

"Ok but like, you can't like Pecunia if I'm with Volo. That's weird," Dyna said firmly.

Char saw an opening and couldn't resist. "Wait, but you guys are just friends, aren't you?" he asked, echoing her earlier words.

Dyna's expression flickered, and she quickly changed the subject. "Ok, like, we're in college now. Have you met anyone *new*?"

Char shrugged, moving his bishop. "I mean, it's a pretty small school. There aren't many people in the Void. This isn't like ancient times where universities were huge."

"What about off campus?" Dyna encouraged, not letting it go. "Like at work?"

Char couldn't hold back on unleashing full sarcasm. "Oh gosh, I forgot about PETE the PANIC from work!" He rolled his eyes. "My new manager is literally a sleeping chicken. And no one showed up to the store for my entire shift."

Dyna giggled.

Char took a sip of his cooling oolong, the scent erasing the drab of the gas station. "How's work for you?" he asked, trying to shift the conversation.

She moved her rook, her Jealous eyeing the piece's movement with a little flutter. "It's whatever. Just the usual."

Char noticed her terse response. Dyna was good at her job but never liked discussing it. All he knew was that she was a Level 4 Nightmare hunter and could therefore live comfortably from her combat expeditions. He watched as she absently stroked Jealous, who preened under the attention.

"Hey, but I heard Pandora's been getting *coffee* with Professor Cogito lately," she said, immediately pivoting back to gossip. Her eyes sparkled with mischief as she leaned forward, nearly knocking over her teacup.

Char raised an eyebrow, intrigued despite himself. He moved his knight, capturing one of Dyna's pawns. "Oh really?"

"Also," Dyna continued, lowering her voice to a fake hush, "I think Pecunia's secretly into Luden, but don't leak that I said that."

"Luden??" Char nearly choked on his tea.

"I don't think she'll ever admit it, but that's my theory." Dyna added, moving her bishop into a threatening position, "He's tall, cute, *and* sweet. And like, her bestie. Which is a lot."

"Oh," Char muttered, somewhat crestfallen.

She paused, glancing around as if checking for eavesdroppers in the empty room. "Also, you can't tell *anyone* I said this, especially Verve and Pecunia—but Promise and Volo *both* started texting me a bunch recently." Her grin was pure mischief now.

"What?" Char was shook, his hand freezing over his next chess piece. "What are they messaging you about?"

"Just like, memes and whatever," Dyna laughed, "and like, asking to hang out."

Char suddenly felt his stomach churn, the tea sitting uneasily. What Dyna thought was friendly attention was likely a coordinated attack to get information out of her—or worse. Envy seemed to sense his discomfort, curling closer to him. He didn't want to rain on her sister's parade, but he felt responsible for saying something.

"Okay, wait, Dyna, I need to tell you something," Char confessed with a big breath, his voice low and serious. "I kind of started beef with Promise and Volo on the street…"

"You *what?*" Dyna's hand jerked, nearly knocking over her queen.

"Like, I just said some stuff I maybe shouldn't have," Char avoided her gaze.

"About *what?*" Dyna asked, all thoughts of the chess game forgotten.

"About their dad," Char mumbled.

Dyna's eyes narrowed, Jealous mirroring her suspicious expression. "Well, what did you *say?*"

"I kind of implied that I had information about how their dad might have disappeared…"

Dyna looked angry, her fingers tightening around her teacup. "*Char*, why would you *do* that?"

"Because I kinda do," Char said, matter-of-factly.

"What is it?" Dyna snapped, leaning across the chessboard.

"I can't just *tell* you right now," Char said, knowing he couldn't trust her not to snitch.

"Why not?" Dyna demanded, her Jealous now fully alert and staring at Char.

"Cuz I kind of cooked up a plan to extort them," Char admitted, bracing for her reaction.

"Oh," Dyna's face turned thoughtful, and there was a pause. The only sound was the soft clinking of Envy sniffing Char's teacup.

"Well, are you going to cut me in on it, or what?" Dyna finally said, a poisonous smile spreading across her face.

Char blinked, realizing his sister could be part of his plan. Before he could respond, Dyna's hand darted out, plopping her queen across the board.

"Oh, and checkmate," she smiled.

Two titans of ancient architecture faced off across the broad avenue:

On one side, the Atlas statue bent under his metallic globe, the remnants of an old skyscraper behind him. On the other, the most magnificent cathedral in the city reached for the heavens with spires of gleaming white stone. The black metal and white stone faced each other in silent conversation, unclear if rivals or reverent neighbors.

It was Sunday, and Promise was in a church.

He wasn't raised under any sort of faith, but the ancient religions fascinated him. Amidst the hustle of Void domination, Sunday mornings were a good time to step back and reflect.

The interior was a masterpiece of light and shadow. Sunbeams filtered through stained glass, painting the stone floor with kaleidoscopic patterns. Mystical figures gazed down from intricate windows, their eyes following him as he moved through the nave. Despite being empty, the grandeur of the cathedral alone commanded reverence, invoking thoughts of a higher power. He closed his eyes, letting the atmosphere wash over him. Whispers seemed to echo from the very walls, which had housed centuries of mystery.

Promise was enraptured with the idea of devotion. Why had these ancient people—who had built a city without the help of void matter—constructed these beautiful cathedrals everywhere?

What drove them to devote themselves so completely to labor that offered no immediate reward? Was it hope? The promise of prosperity? Or something more intangible—the indomitable human spirit, perhaps? Had their faith aided them in the creation of the city?

Promise's gaze fell to his metal hands, speckled with colors in the filtered light. He looked back up at the serene faces in the stained glass, pondering their judgment. Would they spurn him as a sinner? Offer forgiveness? Or deem his condition somehow part of their grand design?

His thoughts felt heavy, like the metal globe on the statue's shoulders. Humans didn't live forever, but humanity endured. To devote oneself to an effort, to a world beyond one's own existence—perhaps those were the commands of both the statue and the cathedral.

His hands itched for his phone—or to sip a caffeinated drink—but even Promise knew that this was not the place for that. He took a deep breath and awkwardly took a seat, attempting to meditate, or perhaps pay respects to this place in what ways he knew how.

His contemplation was interrupted by a creak of the heavy doors. Promise's eyes snapped open, squinting against the flood of bright light from outside, and a familiar shadow cast against the wall.

Of course it was Pandora. She had his location on her phone.

"To what do I owe the privilege of this interruption?" Promise asked, his voice echoing more than he'd intended. He remained seated, a small act of defiance against the intrusion.

Pandora walked forth, each click of her heels echoing in the cavernous space.

"I need to talk to you about the Seven Layers of the Void," she said, her voice hushed but urgent.

"Does it really have to be right now?" His voice was cold.

"There's a lot more to the Void than the city we live in," Pandora continued. "And I've recently gained some eye-opening intelligence. Don't you want to hear everything?"

"Not really, no," Promise said flatly.

"Why not?" Pandora asked, not seeming to understand.

"Because I'm busy right now, isn't that obvious?" Promise replied, his voice dripping with annoyance. For once, he was trying to do something wholesome, and the world wasn't letting him do it in peace.

Pandora, looking slightly abashed, lowered her voice further. "Can we go out and get brunch? I feel... disrespectful talking in here."

"No."

The nerve.

"I'll get you a salmon bagel," Pandora offered, a hint of desperation in her voice. "With the little ikura toppings."

Promise breathed out a sharp sniff. He wasn't one to be lured with food, but he was the type to lose track of mealtimes, and suddenly realized he was indeed quite hungry.

"Fine," he conceded. "But go outside and wait 20 minutes."

As Pandora retreated respectfully, Promise cast another look at the stained-glass figures above. They seemed to watch him with amusement as he struggled to regain his focus.

Unfortunately, the distraction had snapped him out of his earlier trance. Since Pandora's arrival, he found himself derailed by every little sound and feeling—distant cries from Voidpets outside, the discomfort in his legs, his own breathing. His mind began to race over the Seven Layers. What news could have warranted such an intrusion?

As the sunlight shifted, casting new patterns across the floor, Promise realized his time was nearly up. He stood, stretching slightly, and took one last look around the cathedral.

He resisted the urge to swear, since that would be disrespectful.

At this point, he might as well just go to brunch.

With one last glance at the painted figures and a pithy nod of acknowledgement, he stood up and made his way to the door. The heavy wood creaked as he pushed it open, and he squinted in the sudden flood of sunlight.

Pandora was waiting on the steps, scrolling through her phone. She looked up with a smile as Promise emerged.

"Finished with your spiritual awakening?" she teased lightly.

Promise rolled his eyes. "Let's just get brunch."

As they walked down the bustling street, Pandora snuck a remark. "You know, you don't exactly strike me as the church-going type."

"Well, that's exactly why I wanted to go," Promise retorted with a scoff. "So, where are we eating?"

"Soul Station," Pandora responded with a wry smile. "This new little place a Sonder Voidpet started. Trying to compete with us, I think." She tucked her hands in the pockets of her peacoat they walked down the street. "It's a bit further down. Quieter too."

They made their way to Soul Station, a cozy establishment nestled between two larger buildings. The outdoor patio was full of rustic charm, decorated with weathered wood and twinkling string lights. A Sonder Voidpet, its multiple eyes blinking slowly, led them to a table in a quiet corner.

"No wonder it's quiet, this place is completely hidden," Promise remarked under his breath, and Pandora nodded.

As they settled in, Greed bloomed out from Promise's coat, stretching languorously before curling up on the wooden bench. Promise absently stroked his pet as he perused the menu.

"Isn't he supposed to be at work?" Pandora teased, noticing that the donut shop manager appeared to be off duty.

"McGreedy's is closed on Sundays," Promise replied, to which Pandora returned a bemused nod.

They ordered a colorful assortment of farm-to-table brunch dishes alongside cured salmon bagels topped with ikura, and were soon left alone to converse in quiet.

Pandora leaned in, her voice lowered. "Remember the library I told you about back in high school? With the books full of cryptic symbols?"

"Like not really, but yes," Promise replied.

"Well, I've recently made some breakthroughs on that research," Pandora gushed. "I... I've been able to sneak glances of Professor Cogito's notes at my café, and I think I have some answers."

"Oh, yeah?" Promise raised an eyebrow, sunlight glinting off his hands as he reached for water. Ice clinked against the glass as he took a sip, waiting for her to continue.

"Apparently there are gateways between layers," Pandora continued, glancing around before continuing. "And conditions that need to be met for you to open them."

Promise nodded slowly, taking another sip. "Such as?"

"The gateways are hidden in liminal spaces. Places of transition for the ancient people."

"Okay..." Promise mused, tapping his fingers on the table. "So like... hallways and train stations?"

Pandora shook her head, pushing her plate aside. "No, it has to be more significant than that."

"Like what?" Promise pressed.

Pandora sighed, running a hand through her hair. "I don't know exactly yet. Clearly, the Institute leaders have knowledge they purposely aren't sharing. There's a reason they didn't teach this stuff in class."

"Okay," Promise's eyes narrowed. "So then, what are the conditions?"

Pandora lowered her voice further, causing Promise to lean in. "I can't say for certain, but my hypothesis is that it must be something incredibly costly. Something unachievable for most people. Something that involves a physical disruption."

She paused, meeting Promise's gaze. "My loose hypothesis is that it requires a force strong enough to tear the fabric of space."

Promise leaned back. "You want me to blast a wormhole to another dimension?"

"Essentially, yes," Pandora confirmed, nodding.

Promise played with his fork. "So why wouldn't the professors just tell us his? Why would they care if we just went off and blasted a portal somewhere?"

Pandora leaned in even closer. "Because I think the only known sweet spot right now is the Institute."

Promise's eyes widened slightly, the implications of her words sinking in as the ambient chatter of the café faded into the background. As the Sonder server emerged with a tray full of food, they both froze, their faces held in sober expressions.

Promise picked up his salmon bagel, a layer of cream cheese peeking out beneath a glossy pile of pink fish and capers. When the server disappeared back into the restaurant, he started cracking up.

"*Pandora,*" He slapped his hand on the table, nearly dropping an ikura, "You really pulled me out of church to tell me to blow up the school?"

"Pandora. You're foul for that." He was laughing manically as he shook his head, almost wheezing with sarcasm as he gestured with the bagel. "You're serious? That's your plan?"

Pandora rolled her eyes, spearing a cherry tomato from her farm-fresh salad. "Well, the *full* plan is that we need to find a sweet spot *elsewhere*. Somewhere the Institute doesn't know about, or is unwilling to share."

She tightened her fist around her fork and added, "And once we do that, we hit it with the force of everything we've got."

Promise looked at her, a spark of excitement leaping in his eyes. He realized he was easily baited into doing things he wasn't supposed to. "So how do you suppose we go around finding the next liminal space?" he asked, taking a thoughtful bite of his bagel.

Her face fell as she pushed a slice of avocado around her plate. "I've been doing research on ancient train stations and bus terminals, but I'm not sure. I think we might have to go and test each site one by one."

Promise laughed again, nearly choking on a mouthful of bagel. "So you want me to blast each station in the Void until a gateway appears? We really do take turns executing each other's bad ideas, don't we?" He grinned, reaching for his water.

Pandora looked sheepish, crunching on a forkful of mixed greens.

"Well, we might be in luck," Promise said, setting down his half-eaten bagel. "I have a lead for that."

"Why didn't you say so earlier?" Pandora asked, her eyebrows shooting up.

"Because it's a silly one," Promise replied immediately, brushing crumbs off his fingers. "And I don't expect much of it."

He propped his elbow on the table to lean in. "But there's a kid who said he knew something about getting between layers. And I know he grew up far out east in uncharted territory."

"Char?" said Pandora.

"Yeah, how'd you know his name?" Promise asked.

"I only went to school with him for seven years," she rolled her eyes, "I remember details."

Promise shrugged a nod before continuing, "Well if there's anything he could possibly know, it'd be the whereabouts of some obscure location."

"And I *think*," he shot Pandora with a look of mischief, "We could buy him pretty easily," he finished, popping an ikura into his mouth.

Promise and Pandora exchanged satisfied looks, both activated by the start of their budding plan.

"By the way, this place was pretty good, don't you think?" Promise said to Pandora, moving his bagel through the air in a gesture of circles. "We should buy it."

Pandora nodded, finishing her last bite of salad. "Not a bad idea. The location's a little far out, but their dishes are solid. Imagine what it could look like with some better marketing."

As they finished their brunch, Pandora went up to the owner and placed an offer.

Chapter 61: Skydiving

Luden's stomach lurched as he peered out the open window of the Sloth-copter. Ten thousand feet above Something Park, the world below was a patchwork of miniature buildings and square blocks. The four Windfall siblings crowded around the opening, their excitement audible even over the deafening roar of the wind. Apparently, this was their idea of a nice Sunday afternoon.

Meanwhile, Luden had retreated to a corner, his sweaty palms clutching the floor for dear life. Cringe, his faithful Voidpet, was wrapped tightly around him, trembling in sync with its keeper. The relentless pounding of the wind made it impossible to hear anything but the thunder of his own heartbeat.

He had volunteered for this as a personal growth mission, inspired by his school lessons on exposure therapy. The goal was to overcome his harrowing fear of heights. Now, as the icy wind slapped his face and the vast emptiness yawned beneath him, Luden felt more terrified than ever before.

The Windfalls, by contrast, were practically jumping for joy, jostling each other to be the first out of the window. Not one of them wore a shred of protective equipment, their casual clothes fluttering wildly in the gale-force winds.

Volo leapt out the window first, silently launching himself into the sky to free fall. Luden's jaw dropped involuntarily as he pressed his face against the cold glass, watching his friend plummet.

Volo's descent was a masterclass in aerial acrobatics. He began with a series of elegant flips, his body a blur against the blue sky. Then, as if by magic, Lust's four appendages erupted from his back, flattening into wing-like structures. Luden knew Volo could alter his own density, and he watched in awe as his friend's fall slowed dramatically. Soon, Volo disappeared beneath a blanket of fluffy clouds, leaving Luden to marvel at the fact that he'd land as gently as an insect after a 10,000-foot drop.

Pecunia was next, her singsong giggle dancing over the wind's roar as she leapt. Luden held his breath, unsure how she'd survive. Then, in a burst of void matter, a pair of wings unfurled from her back—taking Luden by surprise her hidden ability. Pecunia caught an updraft, her descent transforming into a graceful glide before she too vanished into the cloud layer.

Promise followed with characteristic swagger, falling backwards over the edge with a casual wave. Luden knew he'd teleport to safety at the last second, or manipulate the air to slow his fall.

Finally, only Pandora remained. She turned to Luden, her hair whipping wildly around her face, and shouted over the wind, "It was really brave of you to come up here!" Her smile was warm and encouraging.

Luden managed a weak, sheepish grin in response.

"You sure you don't want to try?" Pandora yelled, gesturing to the open sky. "Pride can fly you down!"

Despite the kindness of her offer and the reassuring weight of the parachute strapped to his back, Luden shook his head vigorously. The mere thought of jumping out the window his knees weak.

"Alrighty then, I'll see you soon for dinner!" Pandora's cheerful voice barely registered before she cannonballed out of the copter, joining her siblings in free fall. Luden knew she'd either be scooped up by Pride or simply hit the ground with the protection of her invincibility.

Two more passengers followed, which Luden had nearly forgotten about. Promise's Greed leapt out after her, three flowing hydra tails sailing through the air as the ethereal fox pranced out of the window. Finally, his Lonely followed, rolling off the edge like a stray bowling ball.

Luden almost gasped in horror before remembering that all
Voidpets could float through the air. Clearly, they could survive any
sort of fall—regardless of how clumsy they looked. He peered out the
window to see Lulu tumbling out of control, disappearing through the
clouds as if someone had dropped a potato.

Luden heaved a major sigh, knowing that the skydiving session was
ending. As the Sloth-copter began its descent, he finally allowed
himself to relax. His muscles ached from the prolonged tension, and a
thin layer of cold goo covered his skin. The roof of Windfall Tower
came into view, a welcome sight after what he'd just experienced.

Stepping onto solid ground—or, rather, the roof of the 104th floor,
Luden's legs felt like jelly. The Sloth-copter turned back into Pecunia's
Voidpet, pressing its head into him with a nuzzle of congratulations.
He took a moment to steady himself, breathing deeply and letting the
reality of being safe sink in. With shaky steps, he made his way inside
for dinner, head still spinning from the extreme adventure he'd just
survived. The view out from the roof didn't look so bad in
comparison.

***

Dinner that night was prepared by Mr. J's kitchen. Food waited on
the table.

"YAY, FRIED CHICKEN!" Pecunia squealed, skipping into the
living room with her delicate hands raised in applause.

Their hair still wet from post-skydiving showers, the Windfalls
emerged in T-shirts and sweatpants, ready to dig into the fried feast
that awaited. It was *Mr. J's* fried chicken of course, which meant
dainty karaage bites, crispy wings marinated in rich spice blends, and
colorful servings of exotic pickles on the side.

Volo immediately stacked his plate with spicy drumsticks, gripping
one in his hand and chowing down on the crunchy exterior.

"*McGreedy*, much?" Pandora teased, noticing he had claimed all the meatiest servings for himself.

"Runs in the family," Promise retorted, snatching a drumstick from Volo's plate. There was plenty of chicken on the table, he was making a point.

"There's a whole plate of soy for you over there," he added, gesturing across the table—to which Pandora harrumphed, and co-plundered Volo's plate in defiance.

As Luden reached for a regular soy garlic wing, he noted the absurdity between the lines of their humor. It wasn't lost on him that founding a successful franchise overnight was now their idea of an inside joke.

With one hand on a piece of chicken, Promise leaned back in his chair and scrolled at his phone with the other. Suddenly, his face lit up with glee. "Hey, check this out," he flashed his phone to the table, and everyone leaned in to watch as the video played.

"...Pandora's Bread puts on a front that they're ethical and Dopamine-free... HOWEVER, they're exploiting Voidpet labor at lower wages, taking jobs away from the community..." A blue haired influencer was calling out the unethical practices of both McGreedy's *and* Pandora's Bread. Behind large round spectacles that framed her almond eyes, BevBobaT spoke animatedly, and Luden couldn't help but notice, behind the vitriol of her words, that she was rather cute.

Pandora scowled, jumping to defend herself. "How am I... how am I *taking away* jobs with a restaurant I *created*...?" she sputtered, before suddenly grabbing Promise's phone. "Wait let me see that..."

"Layer Two: Daydream Fields, Dragon City Beach," Pandora murmured, "That's what the location tag says..."

Pandora blinked. "Promise, have you ever thought to *ask* BevBobaT about Layer Two?"

"No, why would I?" he scoffed and loaded his plate with pickles, "That location's gotta be fake."

"If someone wears a shirt saying 'Eat the Rich' while posting from a mansion," he shot a flat glance at the incredulous stares of his siblings— "then they're clearly fake."

"Besides, we're not like... *friends*," he took another bite of chicken as he rolled his eyes.

"Well since you two are posting videos of each other all the time, maybe you could DM Bev and ask." Pandora suggested.

"Ew, *no.*"

Suddenly, Pecunia whipped out her phone, showing a handsome man smiling with a surfboard and a prominent six pack. "Hey did you know BevBobaT's brother is a *swimsuit model*?" Her eyebrows arched as she showed the whole table the curated, beachy profile of Culverdragon42.

Promise squinted. "Well no, I didn't know that."

"How is he surfing if there aren't any beaches here?" Pandora's eyes narrowed in suspicion as she held a drumstick midair, her mind scrambling to piece together clues.

"It's *fake*," Promise drawled as he facepalmed. "*Everything* on social media is *fake.*"

"Besides," he shrugged, digging back into his dinner, "we already have our own plan to find Layer Two. So it doesn't matter."

A lull set over the table as Pandora conceded. The collective munching of chicken filled the silence.

"Wait check this," Pecunia leaned forward on the table, showing a video of Bev and Culver doing a silly trend. Two other influencers sat beside them, as the captions explained who was a cinnamon roll and who wasn't. "I feel like we could do this one..."

The siblings broke out in looks of amusement.

"Looks like a cinnamon roll, could kill you..." Pandora studied the clip, before turning to face her family. "Who would that be?"

"That's you!" said Pecunia, and everyone laughed in agreement.

"Looks like a cinnamon roll, *is* a cinnamon roll..." Promise murmured, his eyes transfixed on the video. "Are any of us cinnamon rolls?

"Luden." Volo's reply was immediate.

Promise then concluded that he was a cinnamon roll too, which launched the table into a lively debate about whether that was indeed the case.

As the topics shifted from cinnamon rolls to other threads of drama, Luden began to lose track of the conversation. His focus drifted to the evening's ambience, which he ironically thought to describe as 'normal'. The sun set outside, painting the sky in hues of pink, and it occurred to him that this was the happiest he'd ever seen the Windfalls. While their endeavors continued to escalate in magnitude, they were now more child-like in spirit than ever before.

That evening, they were a happy family enjoying a simple dinner.

In many ways, despite everything, all was well.

Chapter 62: Slush Heist

Char glared at the chicken clock, willing the hands to move faster. Another mind-numbing shift at Cluck-ee's stretched before him. He'd been here for weeks now, and each day felt longer than the last. The bell chimed as a Voidpet customer lumbered in—the first in weeks. Char straightened, plastering on a fake smile. "Welcome to Cluck-ee's," he droned.

The customer was a Grumpy, who seemed to have no intention of buying anything. "Bathroom?" it grumbled, and Char wordlessly directed him to the grimy stall in the back.

The day crawled by in a haze of monotony.

He thought of his friends, all comfortably rolling in dough. Hyphen, with her 100th floor office and custom-made fidget toys. Alt, suddenly flush with cash from his art sale. Even Tilde, working at that ridiculous donut shop, seemed to be thriving. And here he was, in a dead-end gas station, selling slushes and candy to nobody.

As the afternoon lull set in, Char's fingers twitched with restless energy. He didn't even need to check if Pete was sleeping before summoning a small orb of void matter out of boredom. He began to swipe it through the air, practicing battle techniques he never got a chance to use. It wasn't much, but it was something to do.

The slush machine hummed in the corner, a siren song of sugar and artificial flavors. Char hesitated, then filled a cup. He knew stealing was wrong, but what did it matter at this point?

This soulless job was practically robbing him of his life force, so this was only a fair trade. Plus, this business was a joke anyway, and one more cup of sugar water wouldn't hurt anyone.

As the sweetness hit his tongue, Char felt a familiar surge of energy. The void matter in his hand pulsed brighter.

The roar of an engine snapped Char from his reverie. A cherry-red sports car pulled up to the pump. Char's throat clenched as he recognized the driver.

Promise stepped out, all confidence and designer clothes. Char caught a glimpse of Dyna in the passenger seat, applying a layer of mascara in the front mirror. Another girl—one of Dyna's friends—was leaning forward from the back, her eyes following Promise into the store. The convertible was filled with shopping bags, souvenirs from a day of carefree consumerism.

Promise opened the door of the mart, and his face immediately faltered in a look of disgust. He stopped and blinked, as if noticing some sort of foul odor emanating from the establishment. Then, he turned on a dime, heading straight back into his car.

Back in the vehicle, he watched Promise say something, and his sister threw her head back in laughter like the traitor she was. The two girls both seemed to glance at the gas station, before exchanging silly faces of apparent repugnance.

Char's cheeks felt hot. He couldn't tell if they were laughing at him or something else entirely, but either way, it hurt.

While Dyna had agreed to help Char extort the Windfalls, she didn't seem to be making any progress with her mission. Her assignment was to gaslight Promise and Volo into desperation—to hype up the potency of Char's secret until they were begging on their knees—but nothing had appeared to come of it other than Dyna simply growing friendlier with them.

As the sports car peeled away, Char felt something inside him crack. He'd been working his butt off, and for what? Just to be looked down on? Treated as a joke? Betrayed by his own sister?

He grabbed another slush, downing it in angry gulps. The rush of energy was immediate, stronger this time. The void matter in his hand crackled dangerously.

Char stared at his reflection in the grimy window. This job, this life—this couldn't possibly be his future. He deserved more. And if the world wouldn't give it to him, maybe it was time he took it for himself.

Bitterness coursed through him, a familiar poison that had been brewing for years. The Windfalls had everything—money, power, influence—while he was left scraping by.

But they didn't know everything.

There was still one card he could play.

If there was one good thing that came from growing up on outskirts of town, it was that he knew of a secret location that they'd never find on their own. It was a place of transit—a major liminal space that reeked of ancient power—that for some reason, couldn't be found on any known map of the Void.

He knew he had one bargaining chip against the Windfalls, but he'd have to play his cards right to leverage it. To ensure that they couldn't force the secret out of him, he'd have to come in from a position of strength. He'd have to take them by surprise, and catch one of them alone, so that they didn't have their strength in numbers.

Strength. *Power.*

That's what he needed. A lightbulb went off in his head as he recounted his earlier moment. That little surge of energy, every time he drank a slush. His eyes darted to the machine humming in the corner.

Char suddenly had the bright idea to start gorging slush.

Chapter 63: Celebration Dinner

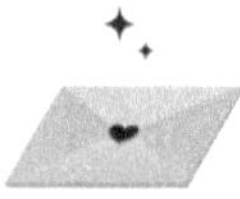

Hyphen tried to contain her excitement as the crew ascended Windfall Tower's glass elevator. Tilde danced in her wheelchair, while Char pressed his face against the glass. Alt stood quietly, tapping his foot.

Alt had surprised the whole friend group with a celebratory dinner at Mr. J's, and the day of their reservation had finally come.

"Alt... I can't believe you paid 4000 VM upfront for this," Hyphen said, her expression full of gratitude but also concern. "At the very least, you should let us chip in to cover some of it."

"No, really, it's my treat," Alt insisted, shaking his head, "I just somehow lucked into a boatload out of the blue. And I really want nothing more than to spend it celebrating with my friends."

"Well," Hyphen replied, "what if I want to celebrate too?"

"Then you can book another place and surprise me back," Alt replied with a sheepish grin. "This one's on me, okay?"

"I sold my soul to the enemy," he added with a self-deprecating shrug, "so at least let me do something nice with the proceeds."

Hyphen gently acquiesced. "Alright then, fine. Then at least let me give you another hug."

On the 99th floor, Mr. J's restaurant buzzed with energy. A Merry server guided them to the bar, where Mr. J himself stood waiting, flanked by his team of Voidpet chefs. They started with steaming cups of herbal tea, toasting to their new career milestones.

"A toast to adulting," Alt chimed from the middle of the group, "to getting our first jobs and gigs! And... surviving!"

They laughed and clinked their cups together.

As the meal progressed, Hyphen found herself enjoying the experience far more than her previous visit with Promise. Mr. J introduced each dish with flair, eliciting gasps and wide-eyed wonder from her friends. It dawned on her then, that the magic of the meal simply wasn't complete without their reactions.

The raven-feathered Judgement approached their table, his chef's hat towering straight up on his head. "Hello, Miss Hyphen," Mr. J said, his eyes blinking in a subtle smile. "Lovely to see you again. I've prepared your favorite."

With a flourish of his wing, he set before her a small plate adorned with delicate morsels of seared scallop, each topped with a glistening dollop of caviar. The aroma of butter and sea salt wafted up, making Hyphen's mouth water.

Alt's face fell, his earlier excitement dimming. "You've... been here before?" he asked, his voice barely audible over the ambient chatter of the restaurant.

Hyphen felt a pang of guilt. "I have, but..."

"Oh," Alt tried to force a smile, but Hyphen could tell he was clearly deflated.

"No, no, you don't understand," Hyphen said quickly, placing a hand on Alt's. "It wasn't anything like this."

Tilde leaned forward, curiosity in her eyes. "What do you mean?"

Hyphen took a deep breath, her mind drifting to her previous visit. She pictured Promise staring blankly at his phone, popping food into his mouth without really tasting it, all without the company of close friends or family. A drop of melancholy colored her mood, but she quickly pushed it aside.

"I came here for a work thing. It was just... eating."

Hyphen shook her head, dispelling the image. "Just... grateful to be here with all of you."

She gestured around the table, her eyes bright with sincerity. "This is so much more. It's not just about the food or the place. It's about celebrating us, our achievements, our *friendship*." Hyphen's voice grew warmer as she continued, "Watching Mr. J work his magic, seeing the wonder in your eyes, sharing each new taste together—that's the *real* experience." She smiled at Alt, her earlier guilt replaced by genuine appreciation. "You didn't just treat us to dinner, Alt. You gave us a moment to pause and really see how far we've come. It's special because we earned it! Because we're here supporting each other's dreams."

Hyphen looked at her friends fondly. "That's what makes this night unforgettable. I'm just... so grateful to be here with all of you."

A chorus of 'aww' rippled around the group, accompanied by warm smiles and nods of agreement. Alt's earlier disappointment had faded, replaced by contentment.

Tilde reached out and squeezed Hyphen's hand. "We're grateful for you too, Hyphen! Now, let's CHOW DOWN!"

As the lineup of delicious bites continued, the conversation shifted to upcoming events.

Tilde's eyes lit up as she mentioned Halloween. "I can't wait to see everyone's costumes, she grinned, her wheelchair adorned with a new pumpkin-shaped sticker. "Any ideas yet?"

Char leaned back, a mischievous glint in his eye. "Maybe I'll go as Volo. Pop in some red contacts, wear a tuxedo to school for no reason."

The table erupted in laughter, tension from earlier melting away.

"Speaking of Volo," Hyphen said, fishing an embossed envelope from her bag. "Alt and I got invites to his charity gala! We'd love for you two to be our plus-ones!"

Tilde clapped her hands in excitement. "Ooh, fancy! I've always wanted to wear a ball gown."

"Oh sweet!" Char beamed, taking the invite into his hands, "Dyna didn't invite me, but I'd much rather go with you guys."

He breathed a sharp laugh. "I heard there are a *lot* of people coming."

As they discussed potential outfits, Hyphen gazed at the ink paintings on the walls of the restaurant and began to daydream about faraway lands.

"You know what I'd love to see?" Hyphen mused, "The other layers of the Void. If they even exist."

"Oh?" Alt raised an eyebrow, intrigued.

Hyphen nodded enthusiastically. "Especially Layer Three, the Lucid Woods!"

"They call it the Ordinal Realm," she added with a tone of spooky delight, "Can you imagine a place where numbers and letters come to life as people?"

"Sounds trippy," Char mumbled around a mouthful of food.

"Apparently their politics are really intense down there," Hyphen murmured with a little giggle, "they've got all these intense prophecies, and there's a rigid social order between the numbers."

Tilde chimed in, "But what about our own layer? There's got to be more than just the city, right?"

She described her attempt to fly west, the vast emptiness she encountered. "I went for hours, saw nothing but sky. Got tired and came home."

"Maybe that's why they call it the Void," Alt said slowly, as if making a profound realization.

Hyphen and Tilde both giggled.

As the conversation about travel continued, Hyphen noticed Char's demeanor change. His shoulders tensed, and he pushed food around his plate, taking small, reluctant bites. His usual spark was missing from the discussion.

Alt picked up on it too, his sensitive eye attuned to subtle shifts. He cleared his throat, steering the conversation in a new direction.

"You know, we don't have to go far to find adventure," Alt said, leaning forward. "There's a whole world right here in the city we haven't explored. The ghost train tunnels are like a labyrinth beneath our feet."

Tilde nodded enthusiastically. "And all those neighborhoods we avoid because of Nightmares—who knows what we'd find there?"

"Exactly," Alt continued. "We've got our Voidpets and we've got each other, we don't need money to see amazing things!"

Char saw through their attempt at pity. "That's nice and all, but I'd rather dream big than settle. Don't talk to me like I can't afford to travel with you guys."

The table fell silent, the others exchanging glances.

"I'm not gonna let myself get complacent," Char's words were harsh as he gestured at the food before them. "I know there are people who eat like this *every day*. I'm not going to give up until I crawl my way to the top, so don't count me out."

Hyphen opened her mouth to speak, then closed it, unsure how to respond without seeming insensitive. It always pained her to see Char like this. They had bonded over being underdogs together, over their shared obstacles and ambitions, but nowadays, it seemed like those bonds were turning into seeds of resentment.

Thankfully, Mr. J broke the tension with an unveiling of dessert—a creative interpretation of milk and cereal, featuring condensed milk, chocolate marbling, and a delicate meringue.

As everyone's eyes grew starry once again, the four friends finished their meal in shared delight. They walked back to campus with full bellies and big dreams.

Chapter 64: Something Park Gala

Luden settled in his chair, surveying the gala with a sense of dread. As usual, he wasn't responsible for anything—but the scale of the event had him on edge.

"Thanks to your generosity," a tuxedoed Volo announced, his voice amplified to hundreds of guests as he stood on stage, "The Windfall Foundation has raised millions to protect local wildlife, including at-risk species like Greed."

Luden recognized many faces in the crowd—friends, classmates, and acquaintances mingling under the soft glow of string lights, all underscored by the gentle clinking of glasses and the murmur of conversation. Outside the white tent, Volo's Lust patrolled the perimeter with a team of burly security. The event had become the talk of the town, with humans and Voidpets alike vying for the few spots inside.

Luden glanced around his table, where everyone looked splendid, as expected. Pandora had draped her signature peacoat over a black evening dress, her wide-brimmed hat completing the ensemble. Promise looked nearly the same, though his usual coat was now on top of a fully black tuxedo set. He sat slouched in his chair, tapping his leg restlessly.

Luden adjusted his suit, carefully arranged over his bandages. His gaze drifted to the freshman table, where he caught Tilde's eye and offered a wave. He was impressed by how well they cleaned up in their formal attire; even their Voidpets sported adorable little neckties and flower crowns.

As Volo continued to make his opening remarks, Voidpets wove through the crowd, serving hors d'oeuvres. An Apathy lumbered by with a charcuterie board on its back. Merry in uniforms skittered between guests, wielding platters of small bites.

Luden held a moment of appreciation for whoever orchestrated the thoughtful seating arrangement. Humans and smaller Voidpets occupied the front tables, while an enormous buffet table stretched in the back for larger monsters and dragons. Familiar Voidpets dotted the central tables—Mr. J, Peach, and Ed among them, and the Institute professors held a place of honor at the forefront.

Volo concluded his speech, passing the microphone to Pecunia before making his way back to the table. As he settled into his seat, Pecunia took the stage in a floor-length ballgown, filling the tent with her crystalline voice.

"The sisters of Sigma Psi Alpha are *thrilled* to introduce our new art initiative," she beamed, her platinum hair glinting in the spotlight. "We are proud to partner with The Windfall Foundation in our mission to support emerging student artists."

As Pecunia detailed the program, an oddity caught Luden's eye: a young man in a white hoodie approached the professors' table, greeting them with surprising familiarity. As he walked through the room, Luden noticed that the Voidpets gave him a wide berth, their usual curiosity replaced by wary silence. The man exchanged a fist bump with Professor Bool and leaned in for a double-cheek kiss with Professor Esse. As he embraced Cogito like an old friend, Luden swore he heard the nickname '*Coggers.*'

The man then stole another guest's chair from nearby to wedge himself between Professor Invidere and Professor String. He draped his arms casually over their seats, pulling in the skeleton and hooded android as if they were best friends.

Luden felt a twinge of discomfort at the display. The man's behavior seemed too informal for a former student—almost bordering on inappropriate. The way he touched the professors felt wrong, like someone booping a nest of venomous snakes. Luden found himself holding his breath, half-expecting something terrible to happen.

Pandora's voice cut through his thoughts, her attention clearly drawn to the same scene. "Who's that guy?" she asked Volo, nodding towards the professors' table. Her brow was furrowed.

Volo's eyes narrowed slightly as he sipped his sparkling beverage. "I don't know. I didn't invite him. Probably a guest of someone in the sorority."

Pandora nodded, but Luden could see she was unsettled. The stranger's casual attire was difficult to ignore amidst the formal wear of the other guests. It seemed like a deliberate act of disrespect.

Suddenly, Pecunia unveiled a curtain on stage, revealing a gallery of student artworks. As she wrapped up her speech, Luden's attention was drawn back to the stage.

"And now, I'll hand it off to our esteemed art appraiser, Mr. J!"

A silver Judgement stepped up to the microphone, and Luden did a double take. Wasn't Mr. J a chef? But this pterodactyl looked different... Maybe it was Mr. J's brother? Son? Husband?

This new Mr. J began appraising the artwork on display, his expert eye scanning each piece. When he reached a large abstract painting of gold paint splatters, his expression changed.

"This piece," he declared, his voice ringing out across the tent, "is worth 10 million void matter."

A ripple of excitement surged through the crowd, their gasps and murmurs swelling into applause. Pecunia's smile, carefully cultivated for such moments, widened with practiced precision. "The Foundation would be honored to accept this donation from Windfall Inc."

A spotlight swung to illuminate Alt, who sat frozen in his chair, still seated at the freshman table. The sudden brightness of the spotlight made him squint, his designer suit throwing off dazzling reflections of intricate silver. On the large screen behind the stage, images of Alt's previous works flashed by, showcasing a montage of his artistic journey.

Luden's gaze darted between the stage and the freshman table. He could see Alt's mouth hanging open as his friends chattered around him. Tilde was bouncing in her seat, her blue ballgown bobbing with her excitement. Hyphen, in a stunning gown the color of sea glass, clutched Alt's arm with pride.

"So, Pecunia really did scam you after all," Char snickered in a navy polo, his remark sharp enough to reach Luden's ears.

Luden's hand moved automatically to his neck, dabbing at a bead of goo with his napkin. He recognized the look of confusion on Alt's face, feeling a pang of kinship for the young artist. Alt's breakthrough was a side effect of Pecunia and Volo's elaborate tax scheme—and despite the life-changing opportunity, Luden understood the feeling of being a pawn in someone else's game.

As the formal presentations concluded, the atmosphere shifted. Guests rose from their seats, mingling to chat about the evening's events. Luden saw his chance. With purposeful steps, he made his way through the crowd towards the freshman table.

"Congratulations, Alt!" Luden beamed, clapping the artist on the shoulder. "You're a legend!"

Alt managed a shaky smile. "Thanks, Luden. It's... a lot to take in."

"I imagine this all must be pretty overwhelming," Luden said, attempting to reassure his classmate. "I know how it feels when your world gets turned upside down. But your talent is real, Alt. Your work is going to be seen and appreciated by so many people."

Alt looked down and cracked a nervous smile. "I appreciate it, Luden," he said, reaching for a sip of water to hide his face. Despite their similarities, it was clear that the freshmen saw Luden as a Windfall, and their senior.

Luden shifted his weight, wanting to say more to relate. "You know... I remember when I first started living with them," he said, gesturing over to the Windfall's table with a small chuckle. "It was... honestly like stepping onto another planet."

He paused, searching for the right words. "It's okay if it takes time to process all this."

Alt nodded slowly, looking back up from his cup to meet Luden's gaze. "Did you ever feel like... I don't know, like you were just... along for the ride?"

"Yeah," Luden nodded, recognizing the feeling all too well. "Sometimes, yeah. But like, you learn to buckle up and go places. Even if..." he glanced around, then leaned in with a little shrug, "Even if you're not the one driving."

From his shoulder, Cringe managed a little nod in a rare display of support.

"Thanks, Luden," Alt said, mustering a small smile. "That... actually helps."

Luden smiled back with a little bow of his head, and then realized he had run out of things to say.

Panicking slightly, he blurted out the first thing that came to mind. "So, uh... nice weather tonight, right?"

Tilde, who was the picture of a princess in her periwinkle ball gown, was listening nearby and jumped in. "Oh yeah, it's PERFECT! Clear skies, starry night. Volo got lucky for this birthday!"

"Wait what? It's Volo's birthday? How did you know that?" Luden's eyes bugged out, and he nearly tripped over air.

"It's in the system at McGreedy's, heh," her eyebrows wiggled with mischief, "he got a free donut today."

"Oh!" Luden felt his cheeks grow warm, embarrassed for not knowing such an important detail. "I, uh... I should probably..."

He gestured vaguely towards nothing, desperate for an escape. "...go wish him happy birthday or something."

With an awkward wave, Luden backed away, nearly tripping over his own feet in his haste to retreat from the conversation. As he hurried off, he could hear Tilde's giggle behind him, making his ears burn more.

He made his way back to the Windfall table, intending to congratulate Volo on his birthday. Luden hesitated, realizing that mentioning the birthday might expose Tilde's snooping. And if Volo hadn't brought it up himself...

Before he could decide, Pecunia appeared, depositing a plate piled high with hors d'oeuvres onto their table. "Luden, you *have* to try these!" her voice sparkled as she popped a tiny fruit tart into Luden's mouth, and then made her way back up to the stage.

As he savored the treat, his eyes drifted to Promise's empty chair.

Suddenly, Pecunia's voice cut through the chatter, amplified by her microphone. "Distinguished guests, ladies, and gentlemen, I'm thrilled to announce that Alt's masterpiece has been sold to a generous buyer—Yandai T.—with all proceeds going to charity!"

The room erupted in applause and excited murmurs. Amidst the commotion, Luden's eyes scanned the crowd. He caught a glimpse of Promise slipping out of the tent. Moments later, Char followed discreetly.

A drop of goo oozed from his brow.

Something was about to go down.

Chapter 65: Something Park Gala II

Hyphen tiptoed through the gala, trying not to trip in her heels. Her eyes swept the crowd, searching for familiar faces amidst the sea of fancy clothes and sparkling jewelry. A flash of midnight blue caught her attention, and she made her way towards her best friend's older sister.

"Dyna!" Hyphen called out, admiring the flattering cut of her halter dress. "You—you look amazing! Have you seen your brother anywhere?"

"Um, Char?" Dyna shook her head, her earrings catching the light. "No, sorry, I haven't. I didn't even know he was here," she laughed. "Is everything okay?"

Hyphen smiled shyly. "Oh, it's fine. I'm sure he's around somewhere."

As Dyna turned to chat with another guest, Hyphen felt a familiar strain in her chest. She made her way to the bathroom, pausing at the door to address her fleet of Anxious.

"You guys, wait here, okay?" she said softly. The creatures nodded in unison, their tiny bowties bobbing with the movement.

Inside, Hyphen faced the mirror, critically eyeing her reflection. Her emerald hair, pinned up in an elegant updo, seemed to mock her with its perfection. For the fourth time that evening, she meticulously adjusted the pins, searching for a flaw that wasn't there.

The bathroom door swung open, and Verve sauntered in, her sleek red gown hugging every curve. She paused at the mirror, touching up her lipstick.

"You look *fabulous*, babe," Verve said, her eyes meeting Hyphen's in the mirror. There was an edge to her voice, a hint of something Hyphen couldn't quite place.

Hyphen smiled nervously. "Thank you," she replied, feeling a blush creep up her cheeks. She admired Verve's confidence, her poise. "You look absolutely amazing yourself."

Verve's gaze lingered, and Hyphen began to overthink about whether her compliment sounded weird. "That's kind of you to say," Verve replied, her lips curved into a small, almost private smile.

"Um, Verve, do you know if Promise is around?" Hyphen asked, remembering that she'd been one of his few friends from school.

Verve's eyes flickered with amusement. "Hm. I wouldn't know," the hint of a sneer danced on her lips, before she put away her lipstick and strode out.

As Verve's clicking heels faded down the pavement, Hyphen's moment of admiration evaporated. The silence of the bathroom pressed in around her, amplifying her nervous thoughts. She turned back to the mirror, trying to tuck a stray lock of hair back into place.

Where were Promise and Char? She'd wanted to thank her boss for the invitation, but he seemed to have vanished. And Char, her plus one, was nowhere to be found either.

Taking a deep breath, Hyphen smoothed her dress and stepped out of the bathroom. She blinked, letting her eyes readjust to the sparkling void matter lamps. The air was thick with expensive perfumes and the aroma of desserts being served. A Voidpet quartet filled the space with music, nearly drowned out by the cheerful din of conversation.

As she made her way back to the main tent, a new panic set in. Her team of Anxious had disappeared from where she'd left them and were running amok in the gala.

Oh, fiddlesticks! What a disaster.

She bunched her skirt as she sidestepped her way through the crowd. One Anxious had gotten into the trash can, and another was nipping at the tail of someone's giant Gluttony.

Oh dear, no no, she thought, scrambling to fetch her Voidpets before they caused a scene.

She quickened her pace, weaving between guests who barely seemed to notice the tiny chaos unfolding around their feet. Unfortunately, her gala attire was not made for a Voidpet roundup, and the tip of her heel snagged on her dress. Hyphen felt herself pitching forward, her arms flailing as she tried to regain her balance. Just as she was certain she'd lose her battle with gravity and fall face-first onto the polished floor, a cold hand met her arm, steadying her.

"Why the hurry, gorgeous?" a chilling voice purred, as a boy in a white hoodie caught her fall.

At his touch, Hyphen felt her whole body go cold. The void matter in her leg flickered, sputtering from a bright turquoise aura to nothing. In that moment, she felt hollow—her eyes dulling as if her anxiety had disappeared along with everything else.

"Hyphen, right?" he breathed, studying her with eerily green eyes.

Hyphen nodded, her clarity of thought giving way to a lightheaded stupor. Thoughts of her friends, her pets, and her job all seemed distant, like fictional characters in a story that had just ended.

Her vision blurred.

"Mind if I get a pic?" he asked, gently holding Hyphen upright as her legs began to wobble. "I'm something of a fan."

"Oh," Hyphen mumbled, her lips fighting to form words, "Um... are you sure?"

"Just a quick selfie for our mutual friend," the boy pulled out his phone, though Hyphen didn't know what he meant.

Just as Hyphen was about to betray her own discomfort with a reluctant 'sure', the sound of wheels broke through her spiraling conscience.

"HEY."

Tilde rolled up with a frown, her ball gown pooling around her chair as she sized up the strange boy.

"Hyphen? You okay?" Tilde asked, concern evident in her voice.

As the boy let go of Hyphen, she felt the full force of her cognition return. She stood firmly on her feet and straightened her dress.

"Tilde! Yes! I'm good," she said, her voice filled with strength at the sight of her best friend.

The stranger seemed disappointed at Tilde's arrival, and looked around to make a quick escape. "I'll catch you later, bestie," he whispered to Hyphen, before retreating into the crowd.

"HEY YOU!" Tilde shouted after him, but unfortunately, she was unable to slip through the crowd in pursuit.

As the boy disappeared, Hyphen felt as if a heavy fog was lifting from her mind. She blinked rapidly, her senses slowly returning to normal. The void matter in her leg sputtered back to life, its familiar turquoise glow a comforting sight. She took a deep, shaky breath, grounding herself in the present moment.

"I'm glad you found me," Hyphen beamed with relief as color flooded back into her face. Her shoulders relaxed as she looked at her friend. "I can't find my boss, I lost Char, I lost track of my Voidpets and then nearly tripped into that stranger," she giggled, the laughter helping to dispel the last of the unnerving encounter, "I'm such a mess!"

Tilde reached out, holding Hyphen's hand. "Hey, stop. It's not your fault."

"That dude had creep vibes," Tilde muttered, narrowing her eyes as if still hoping to track him down.

"But *you*? You look like a total princess, and tonight is still OUR night. Promise probably had to take a call or something. And Char?" She shrugged, a goofy glint in her eye. "Maybe he's got the runs."

A silly laugh escaped Hyphen's mouth.

"Come on," Tilde said, wheeling back towards the dining area. "Let's go have fun!"

Hyphen followed. As they navigated through the crowd, the familiar chatter of the gala washed over her, no longer as overwhelming as before. Tilde's presence was like a torch in the dark, making the sea of unfamiliar faces less daunting.

Amidst the attendees, she spotted a welcome sight: Pandora and Pecunia at the freshman table, deep in conversation with Alt. Despite any qualms her group had with the Windfalls, in this setting, they were familiar faces.

As they approached, they caught the tail end of Pecunia's invitation, "...we're hosting an afterparty at my apartment later. You should all come," she explained to Alt.

Hyphen felt herself relax a bit more. The night wasn't over yet, and perhaps the best was yet to come.

"Hyphen!" Pandora's greeting was effervescent.

"I wanted to congratulate you on your excellent work," Pandora said, her tone warm. "Your attention to detail is flawless. Things have been moving much faster since you took over Promise's email."

Hyphen beamed at the praise but couldn't shake her concern. "Thank you, Pandora. That means a lot! Have you seen Promise, by any chance? I wanted to thank him for the invitation."

Pandora shrugged, unconcerned. "Oh, you know Promise. He's not great with parties. I imagine he just stepped out for some air. Don't worry about it," she said, reassuring Hyphen with a rosy smile, "I'll make sure to pass along your thanks to him."

Hyphen nodded, realizing that the situation was now out of her hands. "Right, of course! Thank you."

As Pandora turned away to engage with another guest, Hyphen stood still, taking in the glittering scene around her.

Having resigned to let her Anxi roam free, she wasn't exactly anxious anymore. Though her heart continued to race at the sounds and sights, her train of thought had moved elsewhere—to a place of contentment, and of admiration for her friends.

With a deep breath, she plastered on a smile and reached for a drink, determined to make the most of the evening.

Chapter 66: Boss Fight

A storm thundered to life as Char left the park, following Promise back to Windfall Tower. As he cruised through the air on Envy's back, rain began to lash against his face. Lightning illuminated the imposing structure, towering in the sky like a supervillain's lair. As Promise entered through the lobby, Char circled the building on Envy, ascending rapidly to the penthouse level.

With a deep breath, Char steeled himself, charging up a bubble of void matter around himself and Envy. Then, summoning all his strength, he crashed through the window in a shower of glass and rain.

Aw yeah. Wrecking ball was a move that never got old.

Char landed in a crouch, water dripping from his hair. His eyes locked on Promise, who was standing before him, amused.

"Well, hello there," Promise chided, his voice carrying effortlessly over the howling wind as he looked down over Char and his puddle. "Looks like someone's been practicing their dramatic entrances."

Char straightened up, his chest heaving slightly from the exertion, a stream of blood trailing from his forehead from a stray shard of glass. "Cut the trash talk, Promise. You know why I'm here."

Promise looked amused. "Do I? What could possibly be so important that you'd stalk me home and break into my house? In the middle of my brother's party, no less?"

The wind whipped around them, causing ripples in the sheets of rain. Char took a step forward, his stance widening as if bracing against the gale.

"I know things, Promise. Things you want to know." Char's gritty voice was followed by the boom of thunder. "About the layers. About where your parents might be."

Promise's face remained impassive. "Is that so?" he asked, his tone filled with playful curiosity. "So you came here to demand something in exchange, then?"

Char's lips curled into a grin, as lightning flashed behind him. His fingers twitched at his sides, a nervous energy building beneath his skin. He'd rehearsed this moment countless times, but now that he was here, doubt began to creep in. This was it. The moment he'd been planning for weeks. He took a deep breath, steeling himself.

"Give me full ownership of Windfall Inc.," Char demanded, his voice warring over the howling wind, "and I'll lead you to Layer Two."

The words hung in the air between them, and Char grit his teeth.

This had to be checkmate.

His ultimate card had been played.

Promise stared at Char with amusement, as if trying not to laugh.

"Dude," Promise began to crack up as his face broke out in an incredulous smile. "You really think I care about my parents *that* much?" His laugh began to sound unhinged, filled with mockery, as he doubled over and wiped a tear from his eye. "Oh, that's *good*."

He repaired the window with a wave of his hand, and then headed to his refrigerator, the rain suddenly muffled behind the now intact glass. The clink of ice in a glass cut through the silence as Promise poured himself a drink. He settled onto the plush couch, sipping his beverage.

Char stood, water pooling at his feet. Once again, he was being brushed off. Treated like a joke. His jaw clenched, teeth grinding together as he fought to maintain composure. But the fact that Promise hadn't attacked or asked him to leave meant that the negotiation was still on.

"Well then," Char snapped, "what's your offer?"

Promise paused to consider. "How about a coupon for a free meal at McGreedy's?" He sipped his drink.

Char's chest surged with defiance, his fists clenching at his sides. He was being toyed with, and he knew it. Frustration overtook Char, and heat rose in his cheeks. Was this all he was worth? *A fast-food coupon?* His hands curled into fists, nails digging into his palms.

"Don't pretend you don't *care*," he spat. "I know this means everything to you. If you won't give up the whole company, then give me one chain. Hand over the donut shop, and I'll take you."

Promise's laughter echoed through the room, as lightning flashed from the storm outside. "Why would I do *that*?"

"Pandora's practically figured it out already." He leaned forward on the couch, his eyes glinting. "You don't have the leverage for what you're asking for."

Raindrops continued to patter on the seamless window, accentuating the awkward silence of the confrontation as the muted storm rumbled behind the glass.

Char's thunder had literally been stolen.

He stood there, drenched and deflated, his grand plan crumbling before his eyes. The realization that the Windfalls might figure out the gateway themselves left him feeling hollow, just another reminder of how the world seemed stacked against him.

His plan was a joke.

He had schemed for days, played all of his cards, only to get clowned on again—just like he always did.

Char's breath came in short, sharp bursts. The walls of the quiet penthouse seemed to close in around him. A frenzied energy began to build within him, threatening to lash out.

"Well then," Char growled, his voice growing desperate, "If you won't accept my trade, I guess... I'll have to fight you for what I want." The words felt dystopian in his mouth, a last-ditch effort from a kid who's had to compete for everything.

His thoughts spiraled. This was supposed to be his moment, his one shot at changing everything. Without it, what was left? More years of struggling? Watching rich kids run circles around him while he worked minimum wage at Cluck-ee's for the rest of his life?

Char's vision blurred, tears of frustration welling up. Years of pent-up disappointment clawed at his insides, demanding release. His voice, when he spoke, was thick with anguish.

"You don't understand," Char yelled, his voice quivering. "This was my *only* chance. My *one* opportunity to hustle something big." His fists clenched at his sides, trembling as sudden tears began to rush out of his eyes. "Without this, I've got nothing left. No future. No way out."

His breathing became erratic. "Do you know what it's like? To work so hard, to sacrifice everything, and still be left with *nothing*?" His last words left a haunting echo through the spacious apartment.

Char's voice dropped to a pained whisper. "And if I can't get what I came for, then I've got nothing left to lose."

The despair that had been building for years threatened to overwhelm him. He looked at Promise, his eyes burning wild. "I'm going *all out*. I'm here to fight you to the *death*."

His next words came out in a heart wrenching snarl:

"So do your worst. Kill me if you can."

The darkness around him intensified, his Voidpets feeding off his spiraling emotions. In that moment, Char felt untethered. He was a cornered animal, ready to lash out with no regard for consequences. A surge of energy coursed through his veins, Cluck-ee's slushes supercharging his focus. It was the fuel of his misery—the cheap energy that kept him going through long hours of dead-end work. Darkness swirled around him as Envy and Rejection responded. Shadowy wings erupted from his back, and liquid matter elongated his fingers into wicked claws. They oozed through the air, as if made of both metal and water.

Promise remained seated, his expression blank. He extended a hand, attempting to neutralize Char's frenzy with his matter manipulation—

but Char's will was too strong to be subdued. His bottled anguish, his thwarted ambition, all fought back as he screamed out with a guttural roar. He pushed against Promise's hold, his body trembling with the effort.

Realizing he couldn't strike Promise directly, Char unleashed his fury on the penthouse instead. With glowing claws of royal blue, he lashed out at the expensive furniture, tearing through leather and wood alike. A chair splintered under his assault, and a glass table shattered, sending shards skittering across the floor. He smashed each piece like it was a symbol of something he'd never have. With each item Char destroyed, a little more of him cracked. The shatters continued, blue sparks of his matter fading into darkness.

"How come I'll *never* be enough?" Char shouted to no one in particular, his voice cracking. "I've gone above and beyond for my whole *pathetic* life!" He overturned a bookshelf, sending volumes cascading to the floor.

"*I* should be the greatest of all time," he screamed, kicking a pillow in Promise's direction. "And as long as you exist, how am I supposed to have a chance?" He began to tear up. The admission was a wound that had long been lodged in his chest—the ever-present reality that the world wasn't fair.

Throughout Char's rampage, Promise was still, watching with an increasingly somber look. As Char's tirade continued, Promise looked on with a pity that only stung more.

The storm outside brewed, lightning and thunder underscoring the destruction in flashes. Rain continued to pelt at the window. Char stood amid the chaos he'd created, his chest heaving, transformation receding. The destruction around him felt hollow, a pointless tantrum against a system too big to care. A childish outburst at a universe who wasn't listening.

Finally, Promise stood up.

Char's heart raced, his breath catching in his throat. This was it. The moment he'd pushed too far. He watched, frozen, as Promise

advanced towards him, metallic hands glinting between flashes of
lightning.

Time seemed to slow. Char's mind, clouded by exhaustion,
conjured images of his demise. One swipe of those razor-sharp claws
across his throat. A spear through his chest. Or maybe it was going to
be something slow and painful. Char's legs trembled, threatening to
give out. He was spent, completely drained of energy and will. There
was no fight left in him. No clever escape plan.

This was it.

An embarrassing death. On the carpet.

Of the guy's house he'd broken into.

He closed his eyes, bracing for the fatal blow. The calm of defeat
settled over him. At least it'd be over. At least he wouldn't have to
wake up tomorrow and live with this humiliation.

But the fatal strike never came.

Instead, Promise's voice cut through the silence, surprisingly gentle.
"You need a hug, man?"

Char's eyes snapped open, disbelief etched across his face. Promise
stood before him, hands at his sides, no trace of aggression in his
posture. The destroyed furniture remained untouched, as if Promise
was allowing the manifestation of Char's pain to air out.

If Char were not in his current state, he'd have snapped at Promise
to fudge off.

But he was too spent for that. His body moved before he could
think, and he found his arms wrapped around the person he despised
most. He broke down in uncontrollable sobs.

After a moment, a flicker of self-awareness cut through. Char
abruptly pulled away, his face burning with shame.

Promise's face twitched, barely concealing a look of disgust as he
levitated a droplet of Char's snot from his coat. He blinked, before
turning to address Char.

"You know," Promise began, "Everyone has their own timeline."

Char blinked, confusion replacing his shame. What did that mean? Was that an insult?

Promise continued, his gaze steady. "I'm not going to be around forever. And I won't be surprised if you surpass me someday."

Char's brow furrowed. Was this the setup to some kind of cruel joke?

"You're a worthy opponent," Promise said. "You've got the drive, the heart, and the brains." He gestured at the destruction around them. "I don't need to watch you wreck my house to understand how you feel."

Char fell silent with guilt.

"You're clearly a genius," Promise said, and Char felt pride despite himself. "You deserve a lot more than what you were dealt—and you have a whole life ahead of you to achieve it." He paused, letting the words sink in.

Char's mouth opened, then closed. He sniffled loudly. "Why are you being nice to me—" he croaked, his eyes bloodshot.

"I'm not being *nice*," Promise interrupted with an eye roll, his sentence tapering in an edge as if the word itself displeased him.

"I just know potential when I see it," he said flatly. "Even if it's a little..." Promise's eyes scanned Char up and down, as if searching for the correct insult, "...*hidden*."

For some reason, the hint of snobbery returning to Promise's face felt somewhat respectful. As if he understood that that earnestness didn't sound genuine on him—and that Char wouldn't accept a false compliment out of pity.

"Here's my final offer," Promise said, a playful glint returning to his eyes. "A *lifetime* pass for free meals at McGreedy's. The world is yours to enjoy—whenever you're ready to start forgiving it."

Char stood still, digesting the offer. He had come in hoping to walk out a billionaire, and instead, was being offered fast food coupons.

But there were worse things in life than an infinite supply of free meals. He looked around at the destruction he'd caused, at his enemy's grace. If anything, he was lucky to be alive.

"Hey, you came in shooting for the moon," Promise said, a nod of acknowledgement hidden behind his sarcasm, "but you still landed among the stars, right?"

Char let out a small, bitter laugh, and wiped his face.

He thought for another minute.

"Alright, deal."

Promise extended his hand, and Char, after a moment's hesitation, grasped it. "Now," Promise said, smiling as the furniture repaired itself around them, "you have a gateway to show me, right?"

Chapter 67: Number One

The young man in the white hoodie settled beside Pandora at the dinner table, his presence immediately unsettling. He leaned in, close enough for her to catch a whiff of his noticeable cologne and gestured towards Volo across the room.

"Where virtue is without genius, genius is without honor," the man mused, reclining his head to whisper in Pandora's ear. "Which one do you think he is?"

Pandora shifted away slightly, taken aback by the stranger's audacity. Was he aware he was insulting her brother?

"I'm sorry, I didn't catch your name," Pandora said, her lips pressed into a polite smile as she evaded his question. "I'm Pandora. Have we met before?"

"Zero," he replied, taking her hand in an icy grip that lingered a moment too long. His jaw hung with a casual arrogance, as if the mere act of closing his mouth required more effort than he thought was worth.

Up close, Pandora noticed the peculiarities of his style. A white headband with circular markings sat atop jet-black hair that cascaded backwards. Strange earrings dangled from his ears, catching the light, and his scent carried woodland notes of cypress and pine. His eyes appeared to be lit from within, glowing an alien jade, and beneath each of them was a circular marking with a line down the middle.

Pandora froze, suddenly realizing that she had seen the marking before. In her house, on her mirror, nine years ago.

The day her parents disappeared.

"Where's your other brother?" Zero's drawl interrupted her revelation, his fingers idly tracing circles on the tablecloth as he rolled his head closer to her. "I wanted to tell him I'm a fan."

Pandora stiffened, her discomfort growing. "Oh, I'm sure he's around," she deflected, growing increasingly uncomfortable under Zero's gaze.

"You know, I've been watching over your family for a *long* time," Zero spoke softly, his minty breath cold against her cheek. "Such fascinating people you all are."

Pandora felt her stomach knot, unsure how to respond to such a comment.

Out of nowhere, he pulled out his phone to reveal his wallpaper: a hot tub selfie with a young woman, who looked strikingly familiar.

"She's kind of a baddie, isn't she?"

Pandora blinked. At first, she could have sworn it was Promise in a bikini—but then she realized it had to be her *mother*. The grimacing girl was none other than Madison Windfall in her youth.

Meanwhile, Zero looked exactly the same, which could have meant anything in the Void. Pandora's heart skipped a beat as time seemed to slow with questions, but the man's provocations pressed on.

"And you?" Zero's eyes roamed over her face, drinking in every detail. "You're even more captivating up close."

Pandora swallowed.

"So, Pandora," He leaned in closer, his voice almost sing-song, "Can I get you a drink?"

"No, thank you," Pandora responded with a measured smile. She adjusted her peacoat, seeking an escape. Whether that selfie was fake or the real deal, this man didn't deserve another minute of her time.

Before she could voice her excuse, Zero stood up. He bent down, his lips nearly touching her cheek as he whispered, "I'll be waiting for you, Number One."

His cool fingers brushed a strand of hair behind her ear, and he straightened up. Pandora's blood ran cold, but before she could react, he melted into the crowd.

As he disappeared, Pandora's fists flared with light, her defenses surging as if they'd suddenly come back online. Her mind exploded with questions. Rage. Indignance.

But she was in public.

Pandora heaved a huge breath and unclenched her fingers, letting the matter dissolve. She didn't like this Zero character one bit.

Chapter 68: The Terminal

The elevator doors slid open with a soft ding, revealing a vast underground garage. The air was thick with the scent of rubber and motor oil, unlike the penthouse they'd left behind. Their footsteps echoed in the cavernous space as they made their way past countless parking spots, none of them occupied.

Promise paused to summon Lonely in one of the spots, where the creature inflated to a tremendous size, before collapsing down into a sleek, cherry-red convertible. The car's surface seemed to absorb the dim garage lighting, giving it an almost liquid appearance.

The persistent patter of rain could be heard even down here. As they approached, the car's roof automatically raised, Lonely thoughtfully anticipating their need for shelter. Char ran his hand along the car's smooth surface, marveling at its seamless transformation.

"Can I drive?" he asked, his voice now giddy with childlike wonder.

Promise scoffed, holding the tip of his tongue between his teeth. "Don't push your luck." He slid into the driver's seat with practiced ease.

As they pulled out of the garage, the full force of the storm hit them. Rain lashed against the windshield, and wind howled around the car. Yet inside, it was quiet.

Char gave directions, guiding them east, away from the city center. Promise's curiosity finally got the better of him. "So, how do you know about this place?"

"It's next to where I grew up," Char explained, his voice tinged with nostalgia. "Dyna and I used to explore it as kids. We'd watch the wild Voidpets that made their home there." As they drove further east, the cityscape changed. Abandoned buildings loomed on either side, their windows dark and empty. The road became rougher, the car occasionally jolting over potholes.

Finally, the roads curved and split towards a vast structure at a scale unlike anything they'd seen in the city center. The faded sign of an airport terminal loomed before them, barely visible through the sheets of rain. They pulled up at the departures level, where a large panel of glass shielded them from the rain.

There, they stepped out of the car and entered the terminal, their footsteps echoing in the vast, dark space. Lonely transformed back into a Voidpet to follow them.

As they stepped inside, the musty air hit them like a wall, thick with the scent of decay. Promise raised his hand, summoning a stream of matter. The glowing red danced between his fingers, casting eerie shadows across the derelict terminal. Not to be outdone, Char conjured his own light source—a swirling ribbon of royal blue that pulsed gently in the darkness. The tails of red and blue lent an otherworldly quality to the air.

Their footsteps echoed through the cavernous space, each sound seeming to awaken long-dormant spirits. Behind them, their Voidpets followed like a little squad. Envy and Rejection flanked Char like wary sentinels, while Promise's two companions strutted to their own tunes—Greed slinking along with predatory grace while Lonely bounced like a bubble.

As they approached the security checkpoint, the glow from their void matter caught something ahead: an oddly modern sign, its message cryptic and foreboding:

Operating cost: 10 million VM.

Promise made a face. "What does that mean?"

Char shrugged. "It's always said that, but I've never understood what it means." He gestured towards one of the rusted security scanners. "All I know is when you try to get past one of these—" Char stepped into one of the scanners, pressing forward into an invisible barrier. It was as if the air itself had solidified, forming an impenetrable wall.

"This happens," he explained, banging against the force field.

"I've combed every inch of this place," he continued, "and this is the only thing that stands out. So, whatever you're looking for, I'd bet it's right here."

Promise nodded, his expression somewhat smug. "Alright. Let's see what happens with me."

He stepped into the adjacent scanner, his void matter light flickering slightly as he crossed the threshold. For a moment, nothing happened. Then, with a sound like a thousand whispers, the scanner whirred to life. Blue energy—pure, concentrated void matter—began to pour from Promise's form, drawn into the machine-like water down a drain.

Char winced in sympathy.

That's gotta hurt, he thought, watching Promise's face contort. Getting 10 million VM ripped out of your system had to feel horrible. The extraction seemed to last an eternity, the blue glow intensifying until it was almost blinding.

As the last wisps of energy were torn from Promise's body, an ominous hum began to fill the air. It started low, almost subliminal, but grew steadily in volume. The very walls seemed to vibrate with it. The abandoned airport didn't feel abandoned anymore.

"Good thing I got plenty more," Promise ribbed, though clearly weakened.

Suddenly, the airport erupted in a sea of blue light. Every surface pulsed with a supernatural radiance, from the cracked tile floors to the cobweb-covered ceilings. A haunting chant filled the air. Its ancient words were incomprehensible, speaking of something primal.

From the center of the terminal, the ground began to twist and warp. A colossal form spiraled into existence, defying laws of physics and sanity. It towered over them, unlike any Nightmare they had ever seen. Hundreds of eyes, each a different size and color, blinked in unsettling asynchrony across its form. Its lower body writhed like a gargantuan centipede, each segment adorned with squirming appendages. Above this horror rose a mockery of a human torso, topped with a head of flowing hair that moved as if underwater. Its face was a blank slate, devoid of features yet somehow expressing an eternity of knowledge.

"I am the God of the First Gateway," the being intoned, its voice a chorus of whispers and screams. The very air vibrated with its words. "Offer your gift to me, and I shall grant you passage."

Char felt his body go rigid, terror freezing him in place. He looked to Promise, expecting to see the same fear reflected in his eyes. Instead, he saw grim acceptance, as if he'd been expecting this moment for a long time.

Before them, a white altar materialized, bathed in a spotlight that seemed to originate from nowhere and everywhere. Atop it sat a pair of white gauntlets, their surface lucent.

As the creature's countless mouths continued their primordial chant, Char's gaze darted between Promise's hands and the gauntlets. It was clear what the 'gift' had to be. He opened his mouth to protest, to argue, but no words came out.

Promise turned to him, his face a mask of calm resolve. He pressed a McGreedy's lifetime pass into Char's hand, offering a smile.

"Thank you, Char" he spoke over the cosmic chanting. "You can drive Lonely home now."

Char nodded, feeling the gravity of the moment settle. He took the cartoonish Voidpet into his arms, his hands trembling as his feet remained glued to the ground.

"Go home." Promise clarified. "That's an order."

The command broke Char's trance. As his feet began to move, he cast one last look at Promise. He felt wrong leaving him alone, but his survival instincts prevailed.

With Lonely clutched to his chest, Char bolted towards the exit. His footsteps echoed through the cavernous space, each amplified by the silence that had fallen in the wake of the Nightmare God's appearance.

As he burst through the terminal doors, the full force of the storm hit him. The rain was coming down in sheets now, so thick it was almost like running through a waterfall. Despite the glass shelter above, Char was drenched to the bone, his clothes clinging to his skin.

Lightning split the sky, illuminating the vast, empty roads in stark flashes. Thunder followed almost immediately, so loud it seemed to shake the very ground beneath him. Char set Lonely down. The Voidpet ballooned once again, reshaping itself into a sports car. As the transformation completed, a door swung up into the air.

Char dove into the driver's seat, begging Lonely to shut the winged door behind him. The calm was unnerving after the cacophony outside. He sat panting, water dripping from his hair and clothes.

Unfortunately, his first time behind the wheel of a sports car was not as satisfying as he'd hoped. His hands were shaking too hard to hold the steering wheel. He tried to figure out how to start the vehicle, but there was no key or button. Suddenly, the engine purred to life of its own accord, as Lonely activated its self-driving mode. The wheel turned automatically, and they were off in a smooth departure.

As they pulled onto the main road, Char slumped in his seat, releasing a shaky breath. Through the rain-lashed windshield, he could see the airport in the rearview mirror, its silhouette receding between flashes of lightning.

The fact that it was raining this hard in the Void meant that something big was brewing. Char thought about texting his parents. He suddenly wanted nothing more than to be back at the party with his friends.

Chapter 69: Afterparty

Hyphen's eyes lit up as Char stumbled back into the gala. "Woah, you're drenched! What happened?" she asked, rushing over to him.

Char shrugged, water dripping from his sleeves. "Oh, I guess it was raining where I was."

Hyphen glanced out the window, puzzled. The sky over Something Park was clear, stars twinkling above. Before she could question it further, Tilde and Alt ran up, enveloping Char in a group hug.

"I missed you guys," said Char.

"We were worried," said Alt. "We saw you and Promise both vanish."

"Yeah, we just went to talk some stuff out," Char explained with a shrug. "I ended up helping him with his dad thing."

Hyphen beamed at him, proud of her friend for his compassionate decision. Char and Promise were both important people in her life. She rejoiced at the news that they'd tried to get along.

"That was really kind... and brave of you," her voice cracked as she wrapped him in another hug, her eyes nearly brimming with tears of relief.

Suddenly, Luden appeared, greeting the freshmen with a wave. "Hey! Looks like things are winding down here. You coming to the afterparty at our place?"

"Aw, yeah!" Char grinned, shaking water from his hair as he nodded to his friends. "Let's get out of here!"

The group made their way outside the tent, where the night air buzzed with excitement.

Pandora's Pride stood in the grass, boarding passengers onto its back. Alt clambered aboard, offering a hand to Hyphen, while Char summoned Envy, his own steed. As the Voidpets took to the air, Tilde manifested her ghost tail to follow them—Pride taking care to transport her wheelchair in its paws.

They soared higher, wind whipping Hyphen's face as her flock of Anxious trailed behind. Below, lights twinkled. The Institute loomed ahead, then fell away as they climbed higher. At the top of the tower, Volo's penthouse came into view. Music pulsed from within. They touched down on the sprawling balcony, where the party was already in full swing.

Outside, Voidpets of all kinds were busting moves. A Judgement twirled with a Merry. An Anxious had overcome enough anxiety to breakdance. University students danced among them, bobbing to explicit music with the Voidpets.

Inside the house, everyone's shoes were off. Volo stood atop his kitchen island, orchestrating a bizarre game of Twister. Luden and Cringe contorted themselves into increasingly ridiculous positions, giggling as they slipped on goo.

"Left hand blue!" Volo called out, and Pandora nearly toppled over trying to reach a far-off spot.

Meanwhile, Pecunia and her sorority sisters were gathered around the same kitchen island, playing an intense cup game. Balls of void matter flew across the table as the sisters fought to score, with Volo occasionally intercepting shots as some sort of penalty.

Char, Hyphen and Alt settled on the living room couch, sipping punch as they watched the festivities unfold.

"This party is BONKERS," Tilde laughed from beside them, watching a Gluttony chug a bottle of soda upside down.

"I can't believe we're actually here," Alt said, his wide eyes swimming with the colorful lights in the penthouse.

Char leaned back, propping his legs on a malformed coffee table. "Pretty funny how things turned out, huh?"

"By the way, check this out," Char dropped his gold McGreedy's pass onto the coffee table with a decadent clatter, and the group's eyes widened.

"A lifetime of FREE meals? What tier prize was that?" Tilde gasped, her hands flying to her face in surprise.

Char smirked. "I got *real* lucky with that one."

Hyphen's eyes scanned the party, hoping to catch Promise now that she was in his apartment. But he was still nowhere to be seen.

"Hey, I think I'm just going to do a quick circle and look for my boss if that's okay. I feel a little weird being in his house without saying hi," she prepared to stand up, but Char stopped her.

"He's not here," Char said, his eyes betraying a subtle guilt.

"Oh?" Hyphen faltered.

"He had some business to figure out," Char explained, his voice somber as his eyes looked down. "And he won't be back for a while."

Hyphen glanced at the McGreedy's pass, scrambling to connect the dots. "Char, do you know if... he's okay?" She asked. She wasn't just anxious. It was concern for her colleague's wellbeing.

Char looked around, unsure what to say.

"Wait, so what happened between you two?" asked Tilde, sensing something was amiss.

Char's face was paling, as if he'd run out of jabs make about the Windfalls.

"Hey look," Alt jumped in, his words directed at Tilde more so than anyone else, "we're at a party. We don't have to talk about that tonight. Let's just get out onto the dance floor and have a good time, okay?"

With that, Alt and Sad stood up, making their way to the balcony to join the dance crowd. Nodding along, Tilde gleefully followed suit with Anger, rapping along to the music with aggressive jubilance. Envy and the Anxi decided to join as well, floating to the dance floor with the others.

Char heaved a sigh from his planted position.

"Should we go dance with them?" Hyphen offered.

"Nah, you go ahead if you want, I could use a rest," Char leaned back to take in the view.

"Well... I could use a rest too," said Hyphen.

Instinctively, her hand began to fidget with her charm necklace, her legs curled pensively on the couch. The Void looked picturesque in the dark, the city sprawling for miles under the moonlight. Char smiled at her, his eyes gracing her necklace. They sat together in silence.

In the end, it didn't matter where Promise was. He was an adult. Her coworker. Not someone she was responsible for.

She was well. Char was safe. Tilde and Alt were having fun.

And that's what mattered.

All was well in the Void.

Chapter 70: Offering

Promise stood alone in the airport.

Its abandoned halls were alight with blue runes, and the air was thick with an electric charge, sending ripples through his hair. Floating stones materialized in the air, defying gravity. Ancient chants echoed off the walls, their melody filling the air as if heralding some forbidden ceremony.

The entity loomed before him, its hundred eyes fixed on his every move. Its centipede-like lower body writhed into an endless pit, while its human torso remained unnaturally still.

Promise looked at the Gateway God, pondering a future without his hands. The Hands of Greed. No doubt they were the offering in question.

Promise's heart raced with the weight of the decision. His hands were an extension of himself—their energy thrumming along with the very blood in his veins. They were his power as much as they were its price; every nightmare, ache, and thought of death a multiplier on his lucidity. Whether or not they'd doom him to a fractional lifespan, it didn't matter. Time was a construct of the mind, and life was only as long as you were alive for it anyway.

But he *could* live without them.

Power, too, was a construct of the mind, and he'd achieved enough to feel proud. He'd still be powerful, and he didn't have to in fear of scarcity. He could live in peace anywhere he wanted—maybe somewhere with a yard and a pool. Adopt a bunch of Voidpets. Work on his mental health. Maybe start a family.

He watched as the beast eyed him, wiggling its meaty fingers at the thought of claiming the hands for itself.

Promise looked ahead at the gauntlets, studying their cleansing glow. "Perhaps letting go is the ultimate act of strength, isn't that right?" he spoke to the beast, "Allowing a successor to take the reins."

The centipede's legs clattered.

He opened his eyes to look at the creature, serenity settling into his features. "So, this is my destiny, then, isn't it? The end of my era. You're here to rescue me from myself. Your deal—your offering—it's the remedy of virtue, of normalcy, of peace."

"Have you made your decision?" The creature's voice boomed.

Promise nodded, swallowing hard. "I have."

Each step forward felt heavier than the last, the cold stone leeching warmth from beneath his feet. As he reached the altar, he held out his hands—their inky sheen surreal in the blue light.

"I've done a lot with my gift," Promise's voice echoed. He flexed his fingers, feeling the familiar crackling of energy.

The creature's hollow eyes gleamed, a wide smile revealing rows of triangular teeth. As Promise spoke, his voice grew stronger, reverberating off the walls of the terminal.

"So, to sacrifice them for the next leg of my journey would be poetic," he continued, his eyes locking with the creature's gaze. "A cleansing of vice to earn passage to ascend."

The creature watched him, its smile widening impossibly further. It rumbled in agreement, the sound sending vibrations through the floor.

"But the next layer is *below* us, isn't it?" A sneer curled Promise's lip. "This journey has nothing to do with ascending upward. It's about going deeper down."

The atmosphere in the terminal shifted. The blue light intensified, pulsing in rhythm with Promise's quickening heartbeat. The chanting grew louder, a discordant chorus that seemed to expand the space around them.

He taunted the beast. "You're no deity. You're a Nightmare," Promise declared, his words cutting through the cacophony.

The creature's reaction was immediate. It screamed in rage, the sound so piercing Promise had to resist the urge to cover his ears. The creature rattled with fury, sending tremors through the ground.

"A hybrid between a Limit and a Spiral," Promise followed, forcing himself to stand his ground as the creature's human torso snaked up to his face. He could feel its hot, metallic breath on his skin. "You're a limiting belief. A decay of abstraction."

Promise held up his hands, mere inches from the creature's face. "The notion that I'm nothing without my power. That I'm doomed without some sudden, dramatic... *self-effacing* sacrifice." He jabbed a clawed fingertip into the Nightmare's chest, feeling its unnatural solidity. "That's what you represent."

"You FOOLISH mortal," the creature roared. Its hand lashed out, striking Promise across the face with shocking speed. The blow sent him reeling, pain blossoming across his cheek. He tasted blood.

Steadying himself, Promise took a deep breath. He could feel his body trembling, but he refused to back down.

"Well," he said, steeling his shaky voice with cold resolve. "I trust myself more than I trust your word."

An orb of void matter materialized in his hand, convulsing with barely contained energy. Greed emerged, its three heads snaking around his arm. Promise locked eyes with the creature one last time. "And I don't worship false gods."

He produced a pair of noise cancelling pods from his pocket and placed them in his ears. He tapped his phone screen, scrolling through his playlist with a practiced indifference.

The creature's eyes bulged, its writhing body momentarily stilling. Its mouth opened, perhaps to shriek, but Promise was listening to something else now.

Around him, the wind began to pick up as he summoned his void matter. The force in his hands grew. Its power crackled, small arcs of cosmic energy dancing between his fingers. The Nightmare's hundreds of eyes locked on him as it coiled itself to strike.

When the beat of his song dropped, and Promise hit it with everything he had. *Just like Pandora said.*

The blast erupted in a beam of red, scorching the air itself. The creature lunged in shock, but it was too late. The beam struck it full force, the heat so intense Promise could feel it searing his own skin.

The red gave way to white, vaporizing the Nightmare entirely. The music drowned out all sound as its countless legs were erased in the brilliance of energy. As the last of the creature dissipated, the beam suddenly shifted to blue. Promise sensed a change in the air, as if some ancient mechanism had been set in motion.

He redirected the now-blue beam towards the ground, drilling with catastrophic force. The impact looked like a supernova, evaporating with the earth with the force of a hundred million units of void matter multiplied by ten. The runes of the airport flashed to life, creating a protective field that contained the destruction. A column of sparkling debris shot towards the sky, forming a beacon of light.

As the dust settled, Promise found himself standing at the edge of a yawning chasm with nothing but the sound of music in his ears. Where solid ground had been, there was now a wormhole—the gateway to Layer Two.

Finding it was almost too easy.

It only took 21 years.

End of Book I

Author's Note

Hello, I'm Linda, and thank you for reading my book!

I wouldn't be here today without all of you who supported Voidpet and gave my work a chance. If you have time to leave a review on Amazon or Goodreads, that would mean the world to me as a first-time author.

This book is a continuation of the Voidpet game world. To learn more and collect Voidpets of your own, you can check out *voidpet.com* to play our latest apps!

References

While the Void is a fictional place, here are some of the real-life references you might find interesting—or have noticed already.

Since the book is a work of fantasy, these notes are simply suggestions to inspire your own research. I've only loosely summarized a few notable references—and will leave it up to you to dig deeper and connect the dots.

Cogito's Lecture

This class is based on Philosophy I and II at Boston College—two of my favorite university courses. The opening quotation is paraphrased from Alexis Tocqueville, and the titles he assigns are all real texts.

The Atlas Statue

There is an Atlas statue in Rockefeller Center—also in the same area of NYC as the other landmarks. I visited it often, and even snuck out of my house to talk to it in the middle of the night. For some reason, I found it comforting, like a friend who could intimately understand feelings of stress.

212 Something Park South

The Windfalls' house is based on several different residential buildings in Manhattan where I gave tours one summer as a real estate intern. Most notably: 432 Park Avenue, Central Park Tower, One57, and 53W53.

Something Park, Neon Square, Angel Station.

These are direct references to Central Park, Times, Square, and Grand Central Station respectively; three landmarks which form a triangle around the neighborhood I grew up in. Grand Central Station is adorned with a winged sculpture—which I passed every morning on my subway commute to school.

<u>The rectangle artist</u>

The artist Alt vaguely alludes to is Piet Mondrian. As a casual enjoyer of art history, I found his story to be particularly resonant—especially in an age where what the public remembers you for can look very different from the painstaking craft of your behind-the-scenes.

<u>Mr. J's</u>

Mr. J's is based on a restaurant called Mr. K's in Midtown East. It was one of the few upscale yet authentic Chinese places in Manhattan, and gave me a newfound appreciation for my culture—back when Chinese food didn't feel like something cool. Unfortunately, it closed.

<u>Food</u>

All foods mentioned are real ones—based on authentic Chinese recipes, delicious meals from various cultures, or creative dishes prepared by modern chefs. I thought it'd be fun to highlight unique foods that readers could enjoy in real life, and recommend you try them if you haven't already!

<u>The Cathedral</u>

St. Patrick's Cathedral is across the street from the Atlas Statue and Rockefeller Center. As a child, I always marveled at the beauty of the church, but given how crowded it was and my unfamiliarity with religion, was terrified to step inside. Ironically, it was more comfortable to confess my woes to the oil titan instead.

<u>Virtue without genius, genius without honor</u>

Also paraphrased from Tocqueville.

My adventure, in brief.

2005

- My favorite childhood book was Titan—the biography of John D. Rockefeller, by Ron Chernow. I loved it because John's parents reminded me of my own. My dream was to start my own business and be like him someday.

2008

- My very first business idea was selling collectible character art. I made my first website and sold drawings to my 4th grade classmates. For 10 cents, I'd draw them a random character with a different rarity. (The most popular character was Ice Cube, which was just a cube.)

2015

- My second business idea was starting a tutoring company in Asia. I helped students prepare for the SSATs/SATs, and worked as a ghost writer. I invested my savings into Ethereum and hoped for the best.
- I aimed to get full scores on all my standardized tests, but got one question wrong. Feeling like I was cursed to fail, I beat myself up relentlessly, spurring random public meltdowns that went on for months. It became clear that my mental health had been deteriorating for years.

2016

- I started college, majoring in computer science. To save money and graduate early, I fit as many classes and jobs as I could into my schedule. It was then that I built my first iOS app, Mac Daddy, and won my first app award on campus.
- As I struggled with depression, I began to rely heavily on my imaginary characters from childhood. They said they came from a fictional franchise I created in the future. They wanted to help me with my mental health so that I'd eventually get around to creating them.

2017

- I worked briefly as a real estate intern in my hometown of Manhattan, where I had the fortunate opportunity to give tours on Billionaire's Row. It was there I began to develop robust imagery of where my fictional characters wanted to live.
- In many ways, that job felt like a dream, but I couldn't deal with the daily reminder that I was not, in fact, a billionaire myself. Given the state of my ego and self-worth, working in those beautiful buildings made me feel like an impostor.

2018

- I did my first corporate internship at WePay. There, I fell in love with Silicon Valley, and wanted to start my own business ASAP.
- The Forbes conference in Boston convinced me to drop out of college. I moved to Chicago to work on an app with my friend, and sublet a room for $400 a month. I had my heart set on raising venture capital, building a successful app, and making it onto Forbes Under 30 myself someday.

2019

- Depression got worse as failure and loneliness set in. I went back to school, squeezing 7 classes and two jobs into my last four months.
- I managed a 4.0 that semester, and graduated early. Then, I moved to California to work on a new app with another friend. COVID hit, and I started experimenting with TikToks.

2020

- I worked on three different ideas with my friend in Berkeley. We built a hotel app, a delivery service, and a video-conferencing shopping game — all of which were a lot of fun, but never took off.

2021

- After a whole year of trying things, I was running out of ideas. While taking anti-depressants, I drew doodles of anxiety and sadness as little dragons. That month, I had my first ever viral TikTok with 500k views. 1000 people joined the Discord to follow the project—which was the most support I ever had.
- With $200 a month on Patreon, it was good progress, but I still couldn't afford to live in California. Exhausted and running out of cash, I scrambled to grow my channel while building out the game designs.
- Beacons found me on TikTok, and offered me my first full time job. I joined when the team was only 5 people, and learned a ton about working at a startup.
- That summer, I met my cofounder, Ben Awad, who was another creator on TikTok. He loved the monster drawings, and believed that they could make a great game someday.
- After a good run at Beacons, I was itching to start my own company again. I moved to a small town in Tennessee where I could afford to work at my own pace, and resolved to keep going until something took off.
- Ben came up with the name Voidpet, and helped me build a website to collect signups. He told me to keep posting my game art until I went viral, and everything would work out.
- 7 days later, one of our TikToks went viral with 10 million views, leading to 150k people joining our Discord. 2 million people tried to sign up for the game, even though it was just an idea at the time.
- Ben and I quickly built a scrappy concept of the game, where you could pick a Voidpet, check in on it, and explore a few screens in the Void.

2022

- We added trading, an auction house, random events, and multiplayer features inspired by childhood nostalgia. It was a fun experiment full of good times, but still didn't look like a sustainable business. Thanks to our fans and angel investors, we were able to keep chugging along for the rest of the year.

2023

- We launched Voidpet Garden, which was a new take on Voidpet as a journaling app. I could finally afford therapy, and built the app based on my own wellness practices.
- By the end of 2023, it became clear that Voidpet had a future as a business. We were featured in Forbes 30 Under 30, won an App of the Year award from Google, and finally raised a venture capital round (after trying for 5 years)!
- We worked with a team of 40 artists to launch a battle expansion in Voidpet Garden. We also sold out our first plush drop. It felt surreal to hold plushies of my own characters and see professional artists take them to the next level.

2024

- After a year of therapy (and using Voidpet Garden), I slowly cut out sugar, alcohol, caffeine, medication, and social media. I started going to church, and tried to make new friends. To do great work, I resolved to be mentally fit—not just mentally well.
- There's a world of adventures to share with Voidpet. Players had so much fun with battle and plushies, we realized how crucial it was to build experiences that were available beyond the wellness app. While we love Voidpet Garden and are continuing to grow it, it's only the beginning of what we set out to do.
- As I write this, it is nearing the end of 2024. Stay tuned for more Voidpet content coming soon, and visit *voidpet.com* to see the latest!